Seduction

Center Point
Large Print

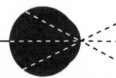

**This Large Print Book carries the
Seal of Approval of N.A.V.H.**

Seduction

M. J. ROSE

LP

CENTER POINT LARGE PRINT
THORNDIKE, MAINE

The text of this Large Print edition is unabridged.
In other aspects, this book may vary
from the original edition.
Printed in the United States of America
on permanent paper.
Set in 16-point Times New Roman type.

ISBN: 978-1-61173-750-9

Library of Congress Cataloging-in-Publication Data

Rose, M. J., 1953–
Seduction / M.J. Rose. — Center Point Large Print edition.
pages cm
ISBN 978-1-61173-750-9 (Library binding : alk. paper)
1. Large type books. I. Title.
PS3568.O76386S43 2013
813'.54—dc23

2013006589

brassiO

To Christopher Gortner,
who helped me find this novel's soul.

And to Liz Berry,
who helped me find its heart.

There are thoughts which are prayers. There are moments when, whatever the posture of the body, the soul is on its knees.

—VICTOR HUGO

One

Every story begins with a tremble of anticipation. At the start we may have an idea of our point of arrival, but what lies before us and makes us shudder is the journey, for that is all discovery. This strange and curious story begins for me at the sea. Its sound and scent are my punctuation. Its movements are my verbs. As I write this, angry waves break upon the rocks, and when the water recedes, the rocks seem to be weeping. As if nature is expressing what is in my soul. Expressing what I cannot speak of out loud but can only write, here, in secret, for you, Fantine.

This is the story of a lost man. An exile not just from his beloved country but also from his sanity. I believe it to be a true and honest account. Whether or not you will, I know not. But I owe you this effort—to try to explain my actions and myself and how what transpired came to be.

This story begins in the south of France in early September of 1843. The first scene, as fate would have it, set against the sea.

I had been on a monthlong holiday with my mistress, whom you know of course as Juliette D.

We had been traveling for three weeks when we reached the Island of Oléron. The weather was oppressively hot without breeze or relief.

"So this is what living in hell must be like," I said as we rode to our hotel. Ah, but I had no idea how portentous those words were.

Everywhere we went the talk was about the monstrous weather and the mystifying plague that had stolen the lives of dozens of children. Even my beloved bay offered nothing pleasant for once. There were no invigorating sea breezes, no birdsong. As I walked the salt marshes, forced to step in seaweed to avoid the mud, only the distant voices of the convicts, one after another, as they were counted in for the evening kept me company.

For the first time in my life I was unhappy by the sea. It seemed death was in my soul. As if the island was a coffin laid in the sea with the moon as torch.

Concerned about the mysterious fevers and wanting to escape the melancholy atmosphere, we decided not to stay as long as planned and made immediate arrangements to depart the following morning.

On the boat the next day, the talk among the sailors continued to be morbid as they focused on several recent drowning incidents that had occurred in the vicinity.

"As if death is following us," I told Juliette.

By the time we arrived at Rochefort on the

mainland we were depressed, tired and thirsty. Since we had a few hours to wait for the evening coach to La Rochelle, we proceeded to the main square to find refreshments. Café de l'Europe was open and not crowded. We found seats and ordered beers.

There were newspapers available. Juliette picked up a copy of *Le Charivari* and I, a copy of *Le Siècle*.

Just then a square-bodied woman passed in front of the window, distracting me from the front page. She had a child with her, a little girl of eight or nine. As they walked by, the woman tripped and went sprawling. The child stood frozen for a moment, as if astonished her mother was capable of falling. Then, her face etched with grave concern, the little girl knelt down and gently offered her mama her hand.

I drew the moment in my mind. A scene to pull up when I was writing, an image to file away for future use. I wanted to remember the worry on the child's face and the love on the mother's as she let her girl help her up.

Then, with my usual foreboding, I readdressed the news. Politicians are fools and the games they play are fools' games. There are lives at stake and yet these men solve nothing with their endless posturing except to fatten their own wallets. Power corrupts morals and turns men to monsters all. Not surprisingly, the newspaper was filled with worrisome articles about all this and more. Spain was in crisis . . . there were rumblings of yet more conflict in Paris . . . and then my own name swam before my eyes.

I was not unused to seeing items about my politics or my poetry in the papers, but this was different. Terrible words leapt out and assaulted me. Suddenly I could not breathe. Sweat poured down my face. This was not possible. I could not be reading the words correctly.

"What is it, Victor?"

I looked up but could not focus on Juliette's face.

"Something horrible," I said, and pushed the paper toward her. The words I'd just read ran through my mind, repeating as they would for hours, days, months and years to come . . .

"A yacht has capsized . . . on board was M. Ch. Vaquerie's wife, Leopoldine, the daughter of Victor Hugo . . . The corpse of M. Pierre Vaquerie was recovered. It was first assumed that M. Ch. Vaquerie, who is an experienced swimmer, had been washed downstream in the attempt to save his wife and relatives . . . the net dredged up the lifeless body of the unfortunate young woman . . ."

In the newspaper, I discovered what my wife, Adele, who was at home in Le Havre, had known for days what my sons and other daughter already knew: my eldest daughter, my dearest Didine, had drowned along with her husband of only eight months in the Seine in Villequier.

For the next few hours Juliette and I wandered through the town, waiting for the coach to be readied that would take us back to Paris. Juliette told me later how the sun beat down on us, and how we walked around the square and into the countryside to try to escape the heat and the prying eyes of townspeople who had heard the news and, recognizing me, followed the progress of our sad stroll.

But I don't remember any of that. I could only see images of the terrible accident. I pictured the boat sailing down the river. Wind whipping the waves into a frothy frenzy. The boat keeling. Dipping. Rocking. Then capsizing. The ferocious current swirling around the bodies. My darling's face surprised by the watery chaos. Struggling to swim in the churning current. Her dress billowing out around her. Her arms reaching for help. Desperate for air, she must have swallowed mouthfuls of that muddy river. I imagined her face underwater. Her skin losing color, her graceful hands flailing. Fish swimming into and becoming tangled in her beautiful hair. Her eyes wide, searching the murky darkness for a ray of light to climb toward.

It was not possible that this report was true, I kept telling Juliette, even as I knew it was, even as the grief began to form around me in a pool, then a stream, then a river, then an ocean. Until I too was going to drown.

Ah, if only I could join Didine, that at least would be relief.

With every step we took, I absorbed more of the horror of what had occurred. Soon guilt was pounding at me, like waves in a storm.

I had been with my mistress on holiday while my child died. My wife, Adele, was alone dealing with this tragedy.

And worse—would Didine even have been on the boat if I had been in residence in Le Havre? Adele and I might have been invited on the boat. And if I'd been there, maybe I could have saved her.

But I had not been there and the daughter of my heart, the child of my soul, was gone.

There is no greater unrelenting sadness that a man can bear than to lose his child. But that is what happened to me and what ultimately brought me to the state of mind I was still in, two years ago, when I first arrived in Jersey, in a self-imposed political exile from my beloved France. A decade of grieving had deposited me on a slim shore of hope. Though I do not believe in formal religions or the clergy, I have strong convictions. I have faith that we live again and I anticipate another life for me and for those I love. How could I not? If there were no continuation, what would be the point of all this suffering we are forced to endure? What kept me breathing one day to the next was the idea that Didine was not gone for all time.

My love for my daughter is at the heart of this story. My delightful daughter. My sunshine. I know every father says this, but she truly was special. Even in this world she was visibly living a higher life. I had seen her soul. It had touched me. In this world of misery, suffering and horrible injustice, Didine was my own wonder, my own happiness. And in Jersey, she became my own madness.

After someone you love so dearly dies, you are absent from the world for a time, living only loss. The pain of existing without the other is too hard to bear. Only slowly do you return to life. To being hungry, not just eating for sustenance. To pouring a glass of good wine, not just drinking to quench a thirst. To hearing the words of those around you and answering. To being stirred into having indignation at the statesmen, at the clergy, at the government. One returns slowly. And then one dawn as you watch the sun rise, you realize your daughter is dead but you are still alive.

What I didn't know then was that an ache, as steadfast as my love, would remain. My grief for Didine is a living thing. My longing to see her again has never abated, never lessened. I never stopped yearning to hear her speak, to watch her eyes fill with laughter, to feel her lean over my

15

shoulder to read what I am writing. Oh, if only I could just once more engage in conversation with my daughter about my ideas—my ideas that were hers also.

For all these years I have ached to dream about her just once. To have her visit me even behind my closed eyes. I prayed to the terrible God who had taken her to allow me to see my daughter again. Even if only to say good-bye. To apologize to her for not being there when she was buried. To tell her I grieved even more because of that. I prayed to him who is not kind or just to let me glimpse where she was so I might know she had passed through his gate and was safe in heaven's arms. Not even in sleep was I allowed a visitation with my dead.

So it was that shortly after our own arrival in Jersey, on the anniversary of Didine's death, my childhood friend, the playwright Delphine de Girardin, arrived from Paris for a weeklong visit. Along with all sorts of delicacies and delights she brought with her a devilish sort of alchemy. And nothing has been the same since.

My daily rituals in Jersey are not that different from what they were in Paris. We dine *en famille* most nights. Usually a simple meal of fish, vegetables, fresh bread, wine and then a pastry. Our cook here is every bit as good as the woman we employed in France but younger and more comely. Caroline's *tarte framboise* is as delicious as her lips, which she has occasionally allowed me to taste.

For Delphine's first dinner, Caroline had made a feast that began with a fine lobster soup and ended with a perfect chocolate mousse. All as superior as you would find at Grand Véfour in Paris.

No one referred to Didine's death anniversary as we ate. My wife and I lived with our loss daily; we did not need to honor this one day above any other. And there was no reason to spoil anyone else's evening with morbid talk. Instead, Delphine filled us in on the gossip from Paris. How our friends were. Who had moved to the country. Which plays had succeeded, which had failed. The affairs of the heart and the scandals. Which new restaurants had opened. Which had closed.

And then she told us about a craze that was sweeping the city: a parlor game called *talking tables* that allowed you to speak to the dead.

The single word echoed in the dining room. Did Delphine notice how my wife stole a glance at me? How I looked away after seeing the pain in Adele's eyes? How my son Charles drank too quickly from his goblet. How his brother, François-Victor, cleared his throat. And how my youngest, also Adele, named after her mother, looked down in her lap, tears immediately flowing from her lowered eyes.

If Delphine was aware of our reactions, it wasn't obvious to me. Breathlessly, she continued on, describing the séances she'd attended and the spirits who had actually visited the assembled guests.

I had always been curious about the mind's ability to reach beyond its bony confines into the beyond. One of my experiments had led me to form the French Hashish Club with fellow authors Balzac and Dumas. The sweet cannabis did in fact produce dreams beyond anything I'd imagined. But I'd felt I was traveling further inside my own mind instead of venturing outside it. And that was what I yearned for, to leave the narrow boundaries of my own reality.

I also experimented with Friedrich Anton Mesmer's provocative theories. The scientist believed our bodily fluids link us to each other and the universe and that their balance affects our mental and physical health. Firsthand, I'd witnessed magnets recalibrating my son François-Victor's fluids and restoring him when he was ill. I'd even allowed an expert in mesmerism to attempt to put me into a trance, hoping I would emerge more perceptive to the point of being able to divine the future. Alas, I never reached the state for which I yearned.

Now Delphine's *le spiritisme* sounded promising. The father of this new movement, Hippolyte-Léon Dénizart-Rival, who now called himself Allan Kardec, believed we can communicate with the dead. He claimed we live plural lives. That we have been here before and will return again. In his talks, he explained that he'd learned about reincarnation during his lifetime as a Celtic Druid and then in another lifetime in ancient Greece when he knew Pythagoras.

The man's heritage struck me as a curious coincidence and I told Delphine about the hundreds of Celtic ruins here in Jersey. "It's common while taking a stroll in the woods or on the beach to stumble upon remains of their temples and graves."

She asked if I would escort her the next afternoon on a tour, and after I agreed she continued telling us about the séances she'd attended in Paris.

"But how do you contact the spirits through *les tables tournantes*?" my wife asked.

"We choose a medium, who places his or her hands on a small three-legged stool you put atop the table. When the stool is ready, the spirits speak by tapping the stool's legs in code. Speaking to the dead," she said, "is in vogue."

We all bombarded her with questions, which she answered patiently. "There's really no way to explain it," she finally said. "It would be better to let me show you. We can attempt a séance ourselves." She looked around the table. "Yes?"

Everyone but my wife was enthusiastic.

"*Bien*," Delphine said, "there are six of us; at least one of us will have the ability to make a connection."

The idea seemed harmless enough. I was intrigued but doubtful. It sounded too playful, too frivolous a way to communicate with the spirit world. And so it began.

That first night, I did not sit at the table myself but watched as each member of our group attempted to bring forth a spirit from the four-legged stool. No one succeeded, but all were gripped with the desire. Now that they had tasted the possibility, determination had set in. So the following day, after our tour of some of the island's strange monuments, Delphine asked if I'd take her shopping so she could purchase a smaller séance stool. Perhaps, she told me, our square one was the impediment.

But when we tried again, the new, smaller, three-legged version didn't solve the problem.

After four days, bored with the game, I encouraged everyone to give it up for the folly it was.

"Just one more try," my eldest son pleaded. "This time, Papa, you come sit at the table too, and I'll put my hands on the stool. That's the only combination we haven't tried."

Against my better judgment, I agreed. I was always too critical of Charles and since coming to Jersey had been trying to be more supportive.

We made what I anticipated to be our last attempt on the afternoon of September 11.

At dinner that night we hosted Delphine, August

Vaquerie, General Le Flo and Pierre de Revenue. All dined on roasted chicken, herbed potatoes, tender asparagus and an apple tart. A good red wine was served, but I drank little of it. Since I was going to sit at the table, if anything did happen, I wanted to be aware and receptive to it, and wine muddles the brain and causes bouts of sleepiness. Instead, after dinner while Delphine set up the séance, I indulged in some postprandial hashish to stir the brain, encourage my awareness and aid in my receptiveness.

Our house at Marine Terrace in Jersey overlooks the Channel and the window opens on the sea. That evening she was eloquent. Her ceaseless waves crashed on the shore, filling the silence with angry music as we arranged ourselves at the table. It was a restless song, I thought, as if the sea too were anxious with impatience, waiting for something to occur.

And it did. The fourth séance was terrifying and joyous. Frightening and beautiful. Powerful in a way that no man, no beast, no God can protect against. Another world opened up that night, one beyond the sea, the sky, even beyond the stars.

We discovered a crack in the wall that separates the present from the past. When the wind blew through our parlor windows on the evening of September 11, 1853, it blew in the unthinkable. A portal opened. The sea howled in rebellion. And a humble man was tempted with a gift that might have proved his ruin, and yours.

"Put your fingertips on the stool's top," Delphine instructed.

Charles did as she suggested.

"Keep your fingers there no matter what occurs. François-Victor, when the stool's leg begins to tap, take careful notes. One tap for yes, two for no. Remember what I told you, words will be spelled out one letter at a time, the number of taps corresponding to that letter in the alphabet. We can decipher the conversation later."

We sat in a circle around this twenty-five-centimeter-high centerpiece on our card table. Adults playing a parlor game. All curious, but one with a desire so strong it must have extended out into the ether, to the spirits. It gave off sparks. And shone.

As I watched, I allowed how profoundly I wanted this trick to be real. I desperately wanted to speak to the dead. On the last day of the week of the anniversary of Leopoldine's death, I longed to speak to my daughter.

"Open your minds," Delphine instructed us all. "Let the spirits in. Make them welcome and allow them to speak."

Nothing happened. With each passing second, I felt my hope ebbing. Then after almost a full minute, the little stool began to move. One of its legs tapped. And then again. And again.

"Is someone here with us?" Delphine asked, the excitement in her voice rising like bubbles in a champagne glass. "Are you here?"

Tap, tap.

I will never forget the reverberation of that wood against the table. It was no different from the sound of a tree branch snapping. Of a door shutting. Of a box lid closing. An innocent sound, I thought then. But how wrong I was, because with each rap, another seed of madness took root in the fertile soil of my mind. The tapping was wicked, degenerate; it was depraved.

"Is someone there?" my wife cried out, clearly unnerved.

The taps continued at a slow pace. François-Victor diligently made notes, but I was certain they would prove to be random and inconclusive knocks. From the expression on Delphine's face, I could see she thought the same.

Another effort, another failure, I thought.

And then the rhythm changed. The tapping sounded more determined.

As François-Victor laboriously recorded the number of taps, I somehow anticipated the word being spelled out as if I were having a conversation with a ghost; I was able to understand these whispers of air. Ah, this is difficult to explain, even for me. So much of this adventure is. But believe me, during that séance and those that followed, our spirit guests spoke to me. Not out loud so others could hear, but not in my imagination either.

I am here. I am with you.

Then the tapping stopped. The stool ceased to move. This time it remained still for two full minutes. I was ready to push my chair away when it finally started up again. The stool appeared agitated. Jittering. Sliding a bit, then pushing back. Was Charles doing this himself?

"Are you the spirit who was tapping before?" Delphine asked.

Two taps.

No.

"Who are you?" she asked.

The stool tapped four times. Then stopped.

D.

Then one tap.

A.

Then a long flow of even taps. Charles counted twenty-one. Then a stop.

U.

Then seven taps.

G.

It had taken me one second to hear what it took the stool several minutes to spell out. One word, *Daughter.*

Then it stopped for a slight pause before starting up again. Immediately the stool tapped out four more taps.

D.

Then five.

E.

Then one.

A.

I knew this word too, long before its last letter tapped out. I put the two words together.

Daughter. Dead.

"Who are you?" Delphine asked once more.

The spirit identified herself this time by tapping out her name. Letter by letter.

L.E.O.P.O.L.D.I.N.E.

"Is it truly you, Didine?" I asked. "Is it you?"

I did not have to wait for the tedious taps. I knew. Nevertheless a single tap confirmed it.

Tap.

Yes.

"Are you happy?"

Yes.

"Where are you?"

Light.

"How can we be with you, my dearest?"

Love.

"Do you watch over us and see our unhappiness?"

Yes.

As a student of human nature, I have trained myself to read faces and see what is in someone's heart regardless of the words they use. As that stool tapped out its answers to the questions we were asking, I watched those present for chicanery and guile. Was Charles exerting some kind of pressure upon the stool? Could he have been so desperate as to make it move out of grief? Or so cruel as to make a joke of such a somber occasion as this?

I asked him outright and he assured me he wasn't manipulating the stool. Were my other children in on it somehow? Or my wife? She claimed to suffer because of my dalliances, but she didn't hate me enough to punish me like this. No, Adele was not capable of such a hoax. In fact she was sobbing and our daughter, her mother's namesake, was crying with her.

No, this was no prank. Sybil's tripod had come to life.

Outside the wind picked up, sending plaintive pleas to the sea, who answered with roars and splashes. Nature communicates all its attitudes better than any man's words.

I asked Didine one last question.

"Will you come back to talk to us more?"

One glorious tap. The *yes* I had yearned to hear.

And so, in a matter of moments, a life changes.

I who had never been haunted, who had been skeptical of visitations, suddenly accepted all possibilities. Or as a priest would say, in that moment, I allowed the devil into my life.

But the priest would be wrong. I did more than allow him in. I gave the devil a warm hearth and a hospitable place to rest for as long as he wanted one. I gave him access to my very soul.

Two

AUGUST 14, THE PRESENT
UPSTATE CONNECTICUT, USA

Since she'd left Paris six weeks ago, every day when she woke up, Jac L'Etoile vowed she was going to heed her brother Robbie's parting advice and be *present*. When they'd said good-bye, he'd kissed her on the forehead, brushed her curls back off her face and said, "If you can do that one thing, Jac, you will begin to heal."

Now, as she trekked through the woods with Malachai Samuels, she tried to pay attention, as Robbie would say, to this moment, right now, and not allow her mind to drift and sink into grief.

Be present.

There was much to be present for. The air was fresh with the smell of grass and apples. She was with a trusted mentor, who had something important to show her.

Be present.

She noticed a fence of No Trespassing signs up ahead. As they approached, the lovely summer day clouded over. The electric scent of a coming storm blew in and Jac felt a chill. A foreboding that they should turn back. Then chided herself for her childish reaction. This was no Grimm's fairy tale. She wasn't Gretel. And Malachai certainly wasn't Hansel. The Oxford-educated psychoanalyst was the codirector of the prestigious Phoenix Foundation in New York City, a one-hundred-and-fifty-year-old institution dedicated to the scientific study of reincarnation. He owned this land. These woods had been in his family for nearly two centuries. There was nothing bad that could happen to her here.

Earlier, after finishing lunch, Malachai had suggested she get ready, that they were going to take a walk.

"Where?" she'd asked.

"To see my secret garden," was all he'd offered.

Malachai was unapologetically secretive in a way that was both old-fashioned and refreshingly avant-garde. He performed sleight of hand without revealing his tricks. Cured children of their nightmares while refusing to explain what spells he used. He was a magician. Perhaps the only true one Jac had ever known. Hadn't he made her own mental illness—hallucinations that had plagued her as a child—disappear and vanish into the Swiss Alps' crisp mountain air when she was fourteen?

Dressed for their hike, she and Malachai exited the turreted and gargoyled manor house through the great room's French doors. Stone terrace steps led down to a well-tended formal garden nearing the end of its summer glory. They followed a pebbled path that bordered organized-chaos beds of blue hydrangea, late-blooming sedum, pink roses and lavender Russian sage.

The floral bouquet scented the air and stayed with them as they passed through ornate iron gates. By the time they reached the Victorian gazebo the smell of fresh-mown grass joined the mix.

From there it was a few dozen yards to an apple orchard. The trees were old and gnarled but the branches were laden with hard green fruit, still weeks away from ripening.

Coming out the other side, they climbed a small hill and arrived at the wood's apron.

Here the cultivated grounds gave way to unbridled nature. Gone were all signs of civilization save the handmade notices that hung at odd angles off naked tree-trunk poles tamped into the ground at six-foot intervals. The warnings were written out in uneven letters painted in black on rough wooden planks.

Private Property.
Intruders will be prosecuted to the fullest extent.
Pilgrims and tourists alike.

Pilgrims?
Jac wanted to ask Malachai to explain, but he was already yards ahead, waiting for her on the other side of the implied border.

She met him at the edge of a grove of hemlocks and pines and they stepped inside the forest.

The blue-green darkness and its scent assaulted her. Usually she loved the smell of tree resins, but its intensity here was overwhelming. It stung. As if the sharp tips of the evergreen needles were pricking her olfactory sensors.

"Beautiful, isn't it?" Malachai asked as he opened his arms, embracing the woods.

"Yes," she said, but she was thinking that there was violence here as well as beauty. The primeval forest that rose up around her seemed threatening. She felt slight beside the trees. These pines had outlived her mother. Many were older than her grandmother. They inhabited this land. She was the interloper.

Jac and Malachai were completely inside shadows now. Submerged in them. The canopy of trees so thick it filtered out whatever sunlight broke through the clouds. Jac felt enveloped in a pervasive gloom.

As someone who produced and wrote a cable TV show exploring the origins of myths, Jac knew all too well the deep significance shadows held in ancient Greek and Egyptian mythology.

Of all the classics she'd read, the most frightening—the one that she often visited in nightmares—was the tale of Agave, Pentheus' mother. Under Dionysus' spell, Agave lost her shadow and with it her identity as a mother and a woman. Assuming masculine attributes, she became dark, brutal and less emotional. As her rational impulses yielded to irrational ones, her passions trumped her intellect. Wild rage consumed her. More and more often her unconscious overwhelmed her conscious mind. Until in one final furious frenzy, she did the unthinkable. Agave murdered her own son.

It was then, after the filicide, that she suffered the fate that haunted Jac. The fate said to be the most difficult to bear of all. Agave buried her own child and lived long past him, evermore mourning her loss.

Jac had read what Jung wrote about our shadow selves being the negative, unresolved aspects of personality. The part of the psyche we must confront and come to terms with if we ever hope to become whole. Jac knew she hadn't yet confronted all her shadows. And that one day she'd need to.

Malachai knew it too. He'd been the Jungian therapist assigned to her case at the Blixer Rath clinic in Switzerland seventeen years ago. They'd been talking about her shadows for a long time.

"Are you all right?" Malachai called from up ahead.

"Fine," was all she trusted herself to say. How to explain her inexplicable overreaction to this place without making him nervous? He watched her too carefully since her trip to Paris in May when she'd gone home for the first time in years to help her brother look for a lost book of fragrances that was part of a family legend. She'd wound up helping save Robbie's life, but the danger they'd been in and the memories that had been stirred up had taken a toll on her equilibrium. And so now Malachai took her emotional temperature too often. Seemed almost constantly checking to make sure she was all right. He hadn't been this concerned about her well-being since she was fourteen years old.

No, Jac didn't want to ruin this excursion by worrying him. Malachai had made it clear it mattered to him that she see this special place. For all he had done for her, the least she could do was to soldier on. But before she took the next step, she did turn and look back. The path they'd taken to get here was no longer visible. Even if she wanted to escape, the way out was lost. They'd left no trace of their route.

Escape?

They were not venturing into danger but taking a walk on the grounds of his estate. Her imagination was spiraling.

Be present.

Following Malachai's footsteps, she trod the next stretch of forest as the route wove through monstrous pines. A thick carpet of needles and leaves camouflaged aboveground roots and fallen twigs and made the trail treacherous. She tripped, but Malachai was ahead of her and didn't notice. Only the birds bore witness to her clumsiness. Righting herself, she continued on.

Suddenly, from somewhere in the distance, she heard a new sound and smelled a new combination of scents. Both were hard to identify until she and Malachai rounded a bend and came upon a waterfall cascading over boulders. The spray on her face smelled of iron. The air, of petrichor, the oil produced by plants when they're wet. The aroma intensified as the path followed the resulting rushing stream down a slight incline.

"Do we have a destination?" she asked, when they'd been hiking for more than thirty-five minutes. "Or are you just showing me the woods?"

A dead pine, a victim of a storm, or rot, blocked their way.

"Time is too precious to squander. I always have a destination. You should know that by now. The one I'm taking you to today might be just what you're searching for."

"What do you mean?" Even as she asked, she knew he wouldn't answer. Malachai loved to be provocative. As she watched him navigate the felled tree, climbing awkwardly because of his injured hip, she worried for his health. She wasn't sure how old he was, but guessed he was in his mid-sixties, perhaps older. He was the most determined man she'd ever known. Sometimes his emotional immunity in light of his resolve to accomplish something made him seem inhuman. But he wasn't. He wouldn't always be there for her.

She was doing it again. Spiraling into the negative. Since coming home from Paris she'd been more anxious than usual. Existential dilemmas that used to pique her curiosity now disturbed her profoundly.

We are all fragile.

Tragedy can strike in an instant.

Almost nothing is within our control.

On the other side of the tree, Malachai brushed off his hands.

"We're almost there," he said as he returned to the path.

After another three or four minutes, the trail stopped twisting and became as straight and sure as a cathedral's central aisle. At its end, Jac glimpsed a clearing.

Malachai threw open his arms expansively. "Welcome to my secret garden." He smiled enigmatically and led her into the grove of oaks in full leaf. The air was cooler inside this copse. The sensual, earthy odor of oakmoss scented the darkness.

When dried, oakmoss smells of bark, of wet foliage, even of the sea. But since ancient Greek and Roman times its importance had never been its individual odor. Instead, its greatest value was

34

as a bonding agent; oakmoss brought ingredients together, imbuing the end result with a velvety, creamy oneness. Adding an unrivaled richness and longevity to a perfume.

"These are amazing trees," Jac said.

"Majestic."

The oak was important in mythology too and so had a special relevance to Jac. "The name *Druid* means 'knowing the oak,'" she said. "The priests carried out their religious rituals in oak forests."

"Interesting you chose to mention Celtic mythology."

"Why is that?" she asked.

Malachai didn't answer, just motioned for her to follow.

The path through the trees was hidden by layers of last year's dead leaves, twigs and acorns. For a second time, Jac tripped. The moment slowed. She began to fall.

Before she hit the ground, Malachai's hand gripped her arm and he helped her find her balance.

"Are you all right?" he asked in the concerned tone she'd heard so often that summer.

"Fine. Thanks."

"The roots and sinkholes are impossible to see under all that foliage. You need to be careful."

Jac nodded. She'd been paying more attention to everything but the uneven terrain. By now she was almost drunk on the aroma of the moss, decaying leaves and moisture. The fragrance teased her. Tricked her into thinking she was smelling the passage of time. This was the scent of earth turning over year after year, of flora and fauna regenerating and becoming nourishment for the next season's growth.

It could have been a scent of rebirth. But instead Jac smelled the encroaching fall. She smelled death.

They'd reached an outcropping of quarried stones carefully arranged in a double circle. Like other ancient calendars she'd seen here in New England and in Europe, there was little question as to its function. No wonder Malachai had commented on her Celtic reference.

Her host walked around the impressive ruin with her as she examined it.

"I'm sure you've had these dated?" Jac asked.

"They predate two thousand BCE."

"Fantastic." She felt a real kick of excitement.

Approaching a slab set just outside the circle at twelve o'clock, she began her inspection. For a few minutes, she examined both its sides and scarred surface. "Based on these burn marks, this looks like it was a ritual site."

"I concur," he said. "But we haven't been able to verify it."

"No, it's hard to find detailed answers in scarring. There's so much we don't know about the past," she whispered as she ran her hand over the weathered stone, trying to imagine what—or who—might have once lain on its smooth surface.

Malachai chortled. "And so much we could know were we not afraid of exploring outside realms of traditional science."

She felt chastised but didn't respond. Malachai was one of the leading reincarnationists in the world. They'd argued enough in the last two months about her refusal to accept reincarnation as a fact. Yes, she'd had a half-dozen unexplained hallucinations this summer in Paris. But they weren't necessarily past-life regressions. Yes, they had appeared to be a response to an olfactory trigger. But that in itself was not unusual. There were many substances in nature that functioned as hallucinogens when ingested, imbibed or inhaled. Shamans and monks, mystics and Sufis had been using them for years to enter meditative states and receive visions.

Malachai was certain the wild rides she'd taken in her mind were reincarnation memories, but Jac wasn't ready to completely accept them as such. Finally she'd asked Malachai to stop pestering her and told him she needed time to work out what had happened. He'd reluctantly agreed. But jibes like this one sometimes still slipped out.

"Who do you think built this circle? Native Americans?" She nudged the conversation back to the ruin.

"Well, we've found arrowheads, pottery fragments

suggesting Paleo-Indians, but we believe there were others here before them."

"So you *do* think it's Celtic?"

"Let's keep going, there's more to see."

The stone circle alone would have been well worth the hike. "More? Really? This is exciting, Malachai. How many more sites are there?"

"Several. This parcel is two hundred and forty-five acres and we've identified at least five ruins dating back that far."

"How long has this land been in your family?"

"The group of transcendentalists who found it believed the site was sacred. But my ancestor Trevor Talmadge was the only one of them who had the money to buy it. He purchased it in the eighteen seventies with the intention of building a retreat here. The plans for it are in the library."

"What happened?"

"He was shot to death before he got around to it."

"How horrible."

"No one was ever apprehended. I suspect fratricide. After the murder Davenport Talmadge conveniently married his brother's widow, moved into the family manse, adopted his niece and nephew and took over management of the family fortune. Younger brothers can harbor great resentments."

Jac wondered if there was more to Malachai's comment. The tone he'd used in describing

Davenport was strangely sympathetic for some-one who might have been a killer.

The trees had thinned. Walking through areas of grass and thick shrubbery, they passed an earth mound with a small stone hut built into the risers—only its entrance exposed. It was another typically Celtic structure from the same period. She itched to stop and examine it and asked Malachai if they could.

"On the way back," he said.

"This place is a treasure trove. How come I've never read about it? How have you kept it a secret for so long?"

"With great effort. Especially because Trevor Talmadge's death was quite newsworthy. There's nothing like a few skeletons dangling off the family tree to keep historians nosing around. We've had to work diligently to keep this sanctuary private."

"Not to mention the noise you make investi-gating reincarnation. Being in the news for cutting-edge scientific inquiry into past-life regression therapy techniques isn't the best way to keep a low profile," Jac joked.

"Hardly." Malachai laughed. "But we've managed nonetheless. There was a bit of attention about thirty years ago when a local Native American tribe attempted to claim the land. But since there was no evidence the ruins were built by their forefathers, their fatuous claims were quickly dismissed."

"No. Even if Indians found this place and used it, they didn't build it," Jac said.

Malachai gave her an approving glance. They'd reached an incline and he led the way, climbing a staircase of rough-hewn rocks. Despite his hip's giving him a hard time, he didn't falter.

Above them the storm clouds intensified. The sky darkened. Jac looked up just as the first few droplets fell.

"You don't melt, do you?" Malachai asked, smiling.

She always had thought his smile was odd. His mouth moved the right way, but the sentiment somehow eluded his eyes.

"Not that I know." She smiled back.

"Then there's no reason to be afraid of a little rain, right?"

No, Jac wasn't afraid of rain. Or of storms. And Malachai knew it. Just as he knew she panicked at edges. The rare phobia had first cropped up when she was a child. She and Robbie had been playing hide-and-seek and she'd gone out on the roof looking for him. The many chimneys and eaves were excellent hiding places. As she crawled around, looking for him, she heard voices. Walked to the edge. Looked down. Her parents were below, standing in the street, arguing. Their altercation was especially nasty and loud. She was so absorbed in their insults and threats she didn't hear Robbie coming up behind her. He said her name, startling her. She turned too fast. Her left foot slid over the edge. She was falling. Robbie grabbed her, held on, and pulled her up across the tiles. Scratching her as he dragged her, but saving her from what would have surely been broken bones or worse.

In her therapy with Malachai, they'd explored the metaphor of her almost falling off that roof and into the violent argument. When talking about it hadn't cured her, Malachai had worked on the phobia in a series of hypnosis sessions. When that didn't work either, he'd suggested her fear was a holdover from a past-life tragedy.

As she did with every attempt he'd made since those early days at Blixer Rath, to connect her present issues to a past life, she'd rejected the idea.

"If it gets too nasty we can always take refuge in the stone shelters up ahead," Malachai reassured her. "I wanted to show them to you anyway. During the summer solstice the sun enters a pinhole in the east wall, sending a light beam onto the floor and illuminating a series of stones incised with runes. No one has yet been able to translate the symbols."

"Can I take a fast peek?"

He nodded. Jac walked closer and began to inspect the hut. Dropping to her knees she ran her finger over the carved runes.

"I recognize some of these designs," she said.

"You do?"

"Look at this one." She pointed. "To me he looks like Dagda, the chief father god in Celtic mythology. He had a harp made out of oak that he played to keep the seasons in order. Don't you think this could be a carving of that harp?"

Malachai stared. "You know, you might be right. We can come back this way again. We should go now. I want to show you the rest before the rain comes," he said.

"I can't believe the huts aren't the main attraction," she said.

He chuckled.

As they continued on, she asked who'd dated the sites. She wasn't impressed that whoever he'd brought in hadn't recognized the harp symbol.

"It's been a delicate dance—wanting information but fearful someone would become too excited by what we've found and reveal our secrets and location. Generous grants to the archaeologist's and historian's personal research funds have proved a satisfactory bribe in every case. There's not a trace of what we've found in a single book or anywhere on the internet. But at the same time there have been experts I haven't been able to bring in."

Up ahead was an allée of gracious giant oaks. Just past it, in the center of a clearing, Jac glimpsed a monolithic rock. Even in the darkened afternoon it shone silver. What was making it glow like that? Mica chips?

When they were within fifteen yards, Malachai held her back.

"Wait. Before you get any closer, tell me, how do you feel?"

"Great. Why?"

"I want you to focus for a moment. Become aware of your psychological and physiological state."

"But why?"

He shook his head. "All in time. Just do it, please?"

She nodded. Closed her eyes. Got her emotional and physical bearings. Then she nodded at him. "Okay."

Still holding her arm, he led her forward. "Several of the experts I've brought here concur these structures were built at least four thousand years ago. One highly respected member of the esoteric movement actually thinks the area was once an intergalactic portal. That people took off and landed here."

"But you don't believe that, do you? Reincarnation is one thing, but extraterrestrial activity?"

"Extraterrestrial activity . . . a Celtic monument . . . whatever it might be, given your search for a new myth to base a season on, I thought this might tempt you."

Malachai was referring to *Mythfinders*, Jac's

television show and also the title of the book she wrote on the same subject. "That's amazingly generous," she said. "Especially because I thought you wanted to keep this place secret."

"I do, but surely you can film here without giving the location away to the public."

Jac was thrilled by what he was saying. If there were enough ruins here, this forest might be the end of the long tunnel she'd been traveling since the early summer, looking for her next mythic mystery to feature on her show. Before she could start suggesting myths that might have some connection to a place like this, he started talking about the gigantic menhir just yards way.

Jac had never seen one this large outside Western Europe.

"I believe this stone"—Malachai gestured—"this monument, is the heart of the entire ancient complex. We can examine it more closely if you like."

There was something curious in his voice. Had they been anywhere else, had she not been so intrigued by the ruin, she might have questioned him about what he wasn't saying. But what she was looking at was too enticing.

In a clearing was a giant boulder. Standing over eleven feet tall, the rock was at least sixteen feet around. She took a few steps closer. Weathered by the centuries, its surface was smooth and incised with runes. Craning her neck, she thought she

44

recognized Dagda's harp again. And perhaps his bottomless cauldron of bounty.

On the ground, a two-foot-wide moat of pebbles encircled the plinth, cutting it off from the grassy mound.

It started to drizzle steadily. Jac looked away from the rock, at Malachai. "Can we wait a few minutes before we head back? Can I just go up to it, touch it?"

He nodded.

Jac crossed the gravel stream, walked up to the monument and reached out.

Its surface was warmer than the air. She sniffed and searched the encyclopedia of scents in her memory. This was how she had always imagined the moon to smell. Gunpowder, earth and salt mixed with a harsh but beautiful metallic note.

She turned to ask Malachai, who'd stayed on the other side of the moat, what else his experts had said about the stone, when she was overcome by a profound and sudden wave of sadness. More than anything, Jac wanted to weep.

Rooted to the spot, as the rain fell on her, she waited for the feeling to pass. But it only intensified.

"Jac?" Malachai's voice was low and caring. "Are you all right?"

She couldn't find her voice, but she nodded.

"Jac? Are you really all right?"

"No, not really." Her voice sounded shaky in her own ears.

"What is it?"

She didn't know what to say. All her efforts at being present had failed at once. How to explain how alone she suddenly felt? As if her mother, who had been dead for seventeen years, had just died. As if she had this moment learned of her father's Alzheimer's. Of her grandparents' passing. As if today, not eight weeks ago, she'd said good-bye to Griffin North in Paris.

All the grief was pressing down, forcing her to feel the magnitude of all the deaths, all the defeats, and of the fresh loss of the lover she'd so desperately wanted to hold on to. Jac felt as if she'd walked into a giant silken web woven of sadness and was now trapped in its threads.

"What's happening to me, Malachai?" she whispered. "This has nothing to do with any myth I've ever heard of."

"Scientists have gotten extreme electromagnetic readings here that they believe have an effect on the emotional center in the brain. I prefer what those who are more evolved suggest: we're in a sacred vortex. The earth's energy is being channeled and collected here for a purpose we've long since lost the ability to recognize. You are being affected by that energy."

Jac wanted to escape. Cross the gully of gravel and step back over to the mossy bank where

Malachai was, clearly, safely out of the range of the electromagnetic field. But she couldn't and stood rooted to the spot as if she were, like the magnificent trees surrounding her, part of this landscape now.

"Do you feel it too?" she asked Malachai.

He shook his head. A look of frustration mixed with misery crossed his face. She'd seen the same expression when she'd asked him if he had past-life memories and he'd admitted that he never had. No matter what he tried, from meditation to hypnosis to experimenting with drugs, the man who spent his life studying regressions had never been able to access one of his own precognitive memories.

Suddenly a clap of thunder cracked. A downpour followed immediately. It happened so quickly, neither Jac nor Malachai was able to run for cover. Almost instantly, they were soaked.

This wasn't a kind rain but an angry outburst. A fury unleashed. In less than a minute the moat around the rock filled and Jac was encircled. Logically she knew the gully couldn't be deep at all and that she could jump across it without any problem. Even step in it if she had to. But the pervasive sadness restrained her. Pinned her to the stone and prevented her from moving.

One after another, three flashes of lightning lit up the dark sky. Each was followed by a burst of thunder. Each outburst louder than the last. This was the sound ancients ascribed to Tarnis, the Celtic god of thunder.

Malachai was shouting too, but she couldn't make out his words over the storm's fury. From his gestures, she knew he was telling her to move, to come to him.

She wanted to, desperately, but she just couldn't.

The next round of thunder was deafening. And then a wild bolt of lightning illuminated the scene in its electric radiance. For a moment Malachai seemed to glow. A tree limb fell nearby. Jac smelled the bitter, burned wood.

Malachai was gesticulating wildly and yelling. She made out the words—*take cover*—but she still couldn't move. Wasn't even sure she wanted to. All the tears she had held back for so long were somehow being released by the sky. She needed to honor them. To let them pour down and wash her clean so she could finally be present.

"Jac!" Malachai yelled just as thunder and lightning hit almost simultaneously.

Time slowed. The rock's scent, even stronger in the rain, overpowered her. Jac felt suspended between now and the next instant. Sensed it might never come. Thought everything might end in the brilliant burst of illumination. She was aware of exactly what was happening and was surprised at just how acute her senses were. Astonished by the number of separate thoughts she could cram into so few seconds.

Research she'd once done on Zeus flashed in her mind like lightning. She remembered excruciating details. At any given moment 1,800 thunderstorms are playing havoc somewhere on the planet. Lightning strikes 80 to 100 times a second; 40 million strikes a year.

The amount of electricity discharged, like so many other things in nature, was a mystery still to scientists. But not to shamans. Not to mystics and wizards. Not in myths. In those last crazy seconds, Jac was aware that a woman standing in a clearing in a storm was an ideal target for the massive electrical discharges filling the sky, searching for places to touch down. A woman standing out in a clearing was the perfect vessel for the lightning's ire. For its one fiery kiss.

Three

Jac was unsure of where she was, only sure that she was in pain. A cramp tightened her stomach. Then was gone. And with its exit she fully awoke and realized she was in Malachai's guest room.

As her eyes adjusted to the dark, she saw him, sitting about ten feet away from her. Sprawled in a large armchair by the bed, he was asleep, his book splayed across his chest where it must have fallen.

She remembered Malachai saying he was going to stay with her and make sure she fell asleep. But why? What was wrong? She tried to remember what came before he'd said that.

They'd been walking through the woods, she'd seen the giant stone—

Another cramp gripped her. Uncomfortable, she shifted, tried to find a better position and felt the warm stickiness between her legs.

Carefully, she stood. Grabbing her dopp kit from the dresser, she hurried to the bathroom.

Jac had never been regular. Stress and air travel affected her menses. Since she'd recently flown quite a bit, she hadn't paid much attention to missing her period in June. Or in July. Besides, she hadn't felt different. And people said you did. That you knew. But she hadn't known.

That's why, a few days ago, she'd finally bought the test. At home, she unwrapped it and then sat on the edge of her bed and stared at the plastic stick as if it were a priceless object discovered on one of her expeditions in Greece or Turkey or Japan.

She'd just looked at it and wondered what she'd do if indeed she was pregnant. Jac didn't have a husband or a boyfriend. All she'd had was a moment out of time—a passion resurrected for a few brief nights in Paris in late May—with a man she'd been in love with it seemed, for better or worse, for most of her life. But Griffin was married. Had a family. Was entrenched in problems with his wife and trying to salvage their relationship. Jac couldn't interfere. If she was pregnant, how would she handle it?

Jac wasn't like most of her friends. She never imagined herself with children. Never allowed herself to yearn for a baby. She was just too worried she'd be the same kind of mother hers had been to her and Robbie. A childhood fraught with that much trauma causes damage, and Jac couldn't conceive of damaging another human soul. Would never want to inflict anything like what she'd been through on someone else.

But could she give a child up if she was pregnant? Especially Griffin's child? Hadn't she given up much too much already?

So she hadn't taken the test. Jac had put the plastic stick in her medicine cabinet and decided to deal with it after her weekend with Malachai. Now that wouldn't be necessary. Now she knew. She just didn't know how she was going to cope with what she knew.

As she cleaned herself she tried to reconstruct what had happened to her in the woods that had made this happen.

The lightning hadn't struck her, but it had hit right next to her. For a moment, the flash had blinded her. The resounding crack had deafened her. The earth had trembled. The shock came up through the soil. The power and intensity of it rattled her bones and hurt her teeth. The acrid scent of burning leaves filled her nostrils. She'd jumped back and smacked into the rock's hard, unyielding surface. Around her leaves fell and branches broke and all the while the rain, the interminable rain, never lessened, never yielded.

Finally Malachai rushed out, dragged her across the moat and pulled her into one of the stone huts, where they waited out the rest of the storm. She remembered he'd helped her take off her sneakers. The rubber soles were burnt and her socks were singed. But her skin was untouched. He'd said he didn't think any electricity had been conducted up into her.

But wasn't the proof of its power slowly seeping out of her? And didn't it mean there was now one more loss to mourn?

As Jac zipped up the dopp kit, she remembered the terrible sadness she'd felt just before the storm struck. And the beautiful but bitter scent. A primordial scent like the forest. Like the stars. She'd recognized it but didn't know it. If such a thing was possible, it seemed the scent was in her DNA. That she knew it on a very subliminal, primitive level.

Malachai said he hadn't smelled anything. Hadn't even really seen what had happened to her because the lightning had blinded him too.

Jac scooped water in her mouth and used it to swallow two painkillers. Then washed her face.

Brushed her hair. Put her robe back on and belted it tightly.

Even if the cramps abated, she wasn't going to be able to sleep again so she didn't go back to the bedroom. Instead she ventured downstairs. She'd do what Robbie always did, make a cup of tea. Just thinking about her brother helped. She'd call him. Tea and then phoning Robbie. A plan. And right now, she needed one.

The mansion was designed in the gothic revival style of the mid-1800s, so though it was glorious during the day, at night it was ominous. Walking along the dimly lit hallway, she listened to floorboards creak under the carpet and watched her shadow's progress on the walls.

The grand staircase was two stories high, and she felt dwarfed walking down the steps. Dark oak gothic arches framed the melancholy family portraits that hung at even intervals. The dead relatives' eyes all seemed to follow her as she made her way to the ground floor.

In the kitchen, Jac turned on the kettle. While she waited for the water to boil she stared out the window over the sink. Weak moonglow illuminated towering trees bending in the wind. Leaves were flying, even though it was weeks until fall. Jac watched a ten-foot limb break off and sail though the sky, toppling a stone angel off her perch, before crashing into the reflecting pool.

The library was slightly more welcoming. Here

at least heavy damask drapes covered the windows and offered a buffer from the relentless sound of the storm.

Jac's hands were shaking. On the bar, next to the fixings for the martinis Malachai had made the night before, was a bottle of Armagnac. She poured some into her tea and took a sip. The smell was pungent and bracing. The liquid, warm and reassuring.

In this room, like the rest of the house, there was no sense of the present. Modern accoutrements were designed to maintain the conceit that you'd stepped back in time, into another century. Upon first arrival, Jac had found it odd, slightly disconcerting. But now it was an appreciated escape from her reality. As was the scent of leather. The aroma was warm, masculine and dark. Creating a leather—a *cuir de Russie* scent— was a rite of passage for every great perfumer. The leather in this library reminded her of her grandfather's *Russie*. The House of L'Etoile still produced it, and even though it was marketed as a men's cologne, Jac often wore it.

As she sipped her tea, she examined the bookshelves, reading the gilt lettering on the spines, imagining the people, through the decades, who had amassed this collection and read these volumes.

A glow emanated from behind a pile of books on the partners desk and she walked around to see what was causing it. It was Malachai's state-of-the-art laptop. A stark exception in the perfectly preserved nineteenth-century room.

The screen showed a search engine page. Jac sat in the comfortable leather desk chair, put down her tea, typed *lightning strikes* and hit the return key. Within seconds the first of hundreds of thousands of results appeared. Scanning, she clicked on the tenth item, titled "The Body Electric" and read the harrowing story of a woman named Anne Downy who'd been part of a group of kayakers all hit by lightning.

Not everyone in the party had survived. Those that had had been severely injured.

"As millions of volts of electricity pass through the body, brain cells are burned, 'insulted' or bruised, which can result in cerebral edema, hemorrhage and epileptic seizures. Passing down through the body, the electricity hits the soft-tissue organs—heart, lungs and kidneys . . ."

A word leapt out at her. She jumped ahead.

"And when pregnant women are hit, either spontaneous abortion occurs, or else they carry the baby to full term but after delivery the infant dies."

Jac closed the laptop. Then her eyes. The idea of the miscarriage was too large and complicated to grab hold of. She didn't know how to absorb it yet.

She stood quickly, wanting, needing to get away

from the computer. In her haste she didn't see Malachai's briefcase on the floor and tripped over it. It fell open and spilled its contents on the rug.

Bending down, Jac picked up the papers, stuffing them back inside the case. Outside the wind continued to howl and the rain to fall. Each time more thunder broke, she involuntarily shuddered. She tried to tell herself that the worst was over now. Or the best. That it didn't matter that she might have been pregnant. Dwelling on it wouldn't resolve anything. *This too shall pass,* she intoned silently, repeating her mother's oft-used phrase.

This too shall pass.

Jac wasn't paying attention to the documents she put back in the briefcase until her own name jumped out at her from an envelope she was holding.

Jac L'Etoile
c/o Malachai Samuels
The Phoenix Foundation
19 West 83rd Street
New York, NY

The script was heavily slanted, indicating someone left-handed. In mythology being left-handed was associated with Lucifer and black magic.

Turning the envelope over, she saw it had

already been slit open. An almost surgically clean cut made with a letter opener. Like the lapis lazuli one Malachai kept on his desk at the Phoenix Foundation, she thought. But why would Malachai open a letter addressed to her?

Jac glanced at the return address.

Wells in Wood House, Isle of Jersey, England

The words were engraved on the expensive, heavy stock. A memory teased her but remained elusive.

Who was it from?

Pulling out the single sheet of paper, she scanned the writing—not yet reading—just searching for a signature.

Theo

Without a last name. She hadn't known his last name back then either. None of the patients at the Blixer Rath clinic knew each other's surnames. The institute's policy was to protect their patients' privacy.

Jac hadn't thought about him in years, but now she recalled the strange and wonderful boy she'd met seventeen years ago. How amazing that after all this time, Theo had found her.

It had been summer. The first time she'd seen him, Jac had been walking on one of the mountain paths when she'd turned a corner and found him sitting on the promontory that was her secret place. He was looking out over the countryside and didn't know she was there until she stepped on a twig.

Theo wasn't handsome as much as striking. Tall and skinny. His sun-streaked hair was pulled back off his face in a ponytail that exaggerated his already prominent cheekbones and broad forehead. The eyes that were unabashedly examining her were a pale blue, watered down as if tears had drained them of most of their color. He had a haunted expression on his face.

Jac had felt as if he were a magnet and she were a heap of helpless slivers of iron. She'd never before met someone she was drawn to so swiftly, and her response surprised her.

She was fourteen, with raging hormones and an overactive imagination. Primed for a boy to come along and stir her up. Especially one who aesthetically fit her image of the young Greek heroes she read about in mythology classes.

Jac, like so many girls her age, was not quite sure of herself. Meeting a boy, she became self-conscious and more aware than ever that she wasn't really pretty, not in a traditional sense. Like her mother's, her auburn hair fell around her face in Medusa-like waves. Her neck was too long. Her nose too strong. Her eyes were green, an underwater jade, not sparkling but brooding. Jac looked old-fashioned, unlike the girls she saw on television or in the pages of magazines. Jac only recognized herself in Pre-Raphaelite paintings in the museums she visited with her mother. Found resemblances in the heavy-lidded women in nineteenth-century compositions of medieval subjects done in abundant detail and intense colors.

But Theo hadn't looked at her as if she was out of fashion. He'd stared with curiosity. And as he did, Jac saw heat flush his cheeks that was matched on her own. Unused to feeling desire, caught off guard by it, she turned. And ran.

Jac and Theo had spent the next two weeks dancing around each other—flirting with looks but not ever really talking. They were like any two high school kids, attracted to each other but too shy to do anything about it. Except they weren't in high school but at a psychiatric clinic in the Swiss Alps that dealt with cases of borderline personalities, schizophrenia and mood disorders.

Patients at Blixer Rath were not locked up. No one was under guard. Only young adults who were highly functional and not deemed dangerous were admitted. The patients were encouraged to make friends with each other and engage in social activities. If they were doing well and had permission during daylight hours, they were allowed to check out to take hikes, go swimming or play tennis with each other during free periods.

Romantic liaisons, however, were not allowed. Alcohol, cigarettes and recreational drugs were prohibited. Packages were inspected and contraband was removed.

Breaking one rule merited a stern talking-to. Breaking more than one meant privileges were curtailed. Theo broke all the rules. But for a long time no one but Jac knew.

He said rules made him feel like a prisoner. So instead of checking out, he'd sign into the library then leave via an open window in the back of the stacks where no one ever went. He had smuggled drugs in with him when he arrived, somehow managing to escape detection. Mostly marijuana but some more potent illegal substances. He bribed the kitchen help with exorbitant sums of money even they couldn't resist, and had a steady supply of cigarettes and wine.

Until Theo arrived, Jac had been a model patient. She'd never even thought about breaking the rules. Once she met him, that changed. Because she'd been at Blixer Rath for several months and was trusted, her initial infractions, staying out later than curfew, didn't alarm anyone.

Not at first.

Dear Jac,

It's been a long time since that summer we first met. And what a strange summer it was. My biggest regret about my time at

Blixer Rath has always been that I left without getting my friend's surname or any other information about you. For years, I wanted to find you but didn't know how. In some of my bleakest moments, I even wondered if you were real or a figment of that very confusing time.

To bring you up to date, quickly. I live on the Isle of Jersey, in my ancestral home, with two great-aunts. I own and run a local art gallery I inherited from my mother. I was happily married until six months ago. Sadly, tragically, my wife died in an accident. We were childless.

It's been a period of unspeakable grief for me. In my search for solace, or at least a way to cope with and try to understand my unrelenting state of mourning, I turned to reading. I've been spending my time in the overflowing library here at Wells in Wood and at the local bookstore.

Which leads me to this letter.

It was in that store that I stumbled upon the book you'd written and learned of your work with mythology. It was a wonderful book and brought back so many memories about our summer at Blixer Rath. It also provided me with that missing clue—your last name. But even with that, I wasn't able to find out where you live or an address.

So I'm writing to you care of Malachai. I don't know why I didn't think of that sooner. Perhaps because my need to find you wasn't as important then as it is now.

Two weeks ago I found a letter in a nineteenth-century book in our family library. The letter, written in 1855 by a well-educated gentleman of note, suggests there is proof here of the Druid myths you mentioned in your book.

And I have reason to believe that the drawings we did at Blixer Rath are connected to this mystery. Do you remember? The circle of rocks? Impossibly, this gentleman drew a very similar circle in his letter.

And so . . . this invitation. Would you like to come to Jersey and help me search for the proof? It would—

"Are you all right?"

Jac looked up, jarred out of the letter.

Malachai stood in the doorway. In his trousers, silk dressing gown and velvet house slippers, he looked elegant. Not at all like he'd been sleeping in an armchair.

"I woke up," he said, "and you were gone."

Jac nodded. "I . . . I couldn't sleep."

There was no reason to mention the cramps. If he were a medical doctor maybe . . . but even then probably not. She hadn't been far enough along to require immediate medical attention unless she was bleeding excessively. And she wasn't. Forcing herself, she put it out of her mind. There was time enough to deal with it when she was alone again. Now she had to find out about the letter from Theo.

Looking at her mug, then at the decanter of brandy pulled out of line on the bar, he asked, "Do you mind if I join you?"

"Of course not."

Malachai always spoke in an oddly formal manner, and while it was unusual, it was also reassuring. His old-fashioned ways comforted her. Reminded her of her grandfather, who was responsible for both her name and her love of books. When she was born, he'd brought Jac's mother a large bouquet of freshly picked hyacinth. Audrey had been so taken with the flower's scent—one of the few that couldn't be extracted for perfume—she'd borrowed its name for her daughter. *Jacinthe*, French for "hyacinth."

Malachai poured an inch of the amber liquid into a crystal glass and sat down on the other side of his desk, facing her.

"Now I think the house was built for nights like this, but when I stayed here as a child, storms at

63

night scared me. There are tombs beneath the foundation and I was obsessed with the image of the rain loosening the dirt and letting the dead escape," Malachai said.

Jac had been ready to confront him about the letter but was too curious not to ask whose tombs.

"Family crypts going all the way to Trevor Talmage and his brother Davenport."

"Directly under the house?"

"In a subcellar, yes. I'll show you tomorrow if you like. It's a beautiful underground stone garden complete with marble benches and a working fountain. It's actually a lovely place to sit and meditate."

"Why under the house?"

"My ancestor didn't want to be buried in a public place where grave robbers could disturb his resting place. He didn't believe it was final, you see."

"Because he believed in reincarnation?"

"Quite. Convinced reincarnation was real and that his death was only a respite between lives, he made elaborate plans so that when he returned in his next life he'd be able to find and access his home, his treasures and his fortune without having to start over again from scratch."

"Has anyone ever come back claiming to be him?"

"Not that I've heard of but . . ." He paused. Malachai had noticed the envelope in front of her. Looked from it to the letter she was still holding.

64

"What is that you're reading?" he asked.

She pushed it toward him.

"How did you find this, if I may inquire?" he asked.

"It's addressed to me and you opened it. I think I get to ask the first question," Jac countered.

"Except to find it you would have had to go looking through my briefcase. I'm not sure which of us has the right to be more outraged."

"I do. I knocked over your briefcase by accident, and when I was putting everything back inside, I found the letter."

The corner of his mouth lifted in an ironic smile. "There are no accidents, just as there are no coincidences."

"Which gives you one less excuse. So if you didn't open it by accident, why did you open it?"

"In order to protect you."

"Oh, Malachai. We're not in a nineteenth-century gothic novel. That sounds ridiculous. You read what Theo wrote," Jac said. "He thinks there's proof in Jersey validating a specific Celtic myth. Why would I need to be protected from doing my job?"

"You can explore Celtic myths without visiting Jersey," Malachai answered without addressing her question.

"Why does where I do my job matter to you? Jersey is renowned for having hundreds of important Neolithic and Celtic ruins. If he's really on the trail of something proving Druid—"

"Isn't what I showed you today important enough?" Malachai interrupted.

"Malachai, you're obfuscating. What's wrong with my going to Jersey? Is that why you brought me here? To offer me your ruins in exchange for the ones you were hiding from me?"

"Not at all. I just think—" He broke off, then began again. "Can't you accept that I have reasons to believe the best course of action would be for you to ignore his offer?"

"No."

"Don't you trust me?"

"Malachai, you opened a letter that wasn't addressed to you and then held on to it without telling me about it. That's a fairly serious invasion of privacy. I'm not sure I should trust you."

The cramps, which had been dormant for the last half hour, kicked up. Jac took a long sip of the now lukewarm brandy-laced tea.

Malachai stood, walked over to the fireplace and set to making a fire. Even though it was mid-August, it was a chilly night and she knew the fire would be welcome, but she also knew he was buying time. Thinking through his best possible course of action. As she watched him, this man who knew the inside of her soul, she thought about how little she really knew about him. It had always been a fairly one-sided relationship.

"Malachai, what's going on?"

He lit a match. The scent of sulfur stung Jac's nose. With a practiced flick of his wrist, Malachai threw the light into the nest of kindling. A first spark caught. Sputtered. Then the sticks burst into flames. Now Jac could smell the bright fresh edge of sandalwood and cedar . . . She smelled sweet smoke and then the odor of bitter tar.

"Why won't you answer me?" she asked.

Slowly he turned away from the fire and back toward her. The firelight was behind him, his features cast in shade. His shadow loomed large on the ceiling. He was about to say something. Then he changed his mind and instead walked over to the bookshelves, where he plucked something nestled between two books.

"Malachai, what is going on? There has never been any actual proof that Druids existed," Jac said. "If Theo has access to that proof, I want to see it. Why are you being so cryptic?"

He caressed the thing in his hand for a moment and then brought it over to the desk and placed it in front of Jac. The perfectly carved amber-bejeweled owl was no more than three inches tall. In the low light from the Tiffany lamp, the bird's diamond eyes glinted almost magically.

Fabergé. Malachai's voice massaged the single word, giving it weight and importance. "It's very rare and extremely valuable." He picked it up and handed it to her.

She was aware of his watching as she inspected it. He'd been one of the most important people in her life. But what was she to him? Another curio in his collection? *Objets d'art* and patients—by now he had amassed a great number of both.

When she was young, Malachai had been the first therapist out of half a dozen who'd actually helped her. She'd arrived at Blixer Rath suffering borderline personality symptoms exacerbated by the recent death of her mother. The suicide had devastated both Jac and her younger brother, but she'd been upended by it. Jac had been the one to find Audrey and read the note that made no mention of either of her children, only vitriol for her most recent lover.

It was Malachai who, over twelve months at Blixer Rath and more than a thousand hours of therapy, had given Jac the tools she needed to save herself. In the intervening years, he'd remained in her life, touching base every few months, making sure she was all right. Always offering encouragement. Checking to see if she was still on track or needed a tune-up.

Then this past May, when her brother had gotten into trouble and she'd flown to Paris to be with Robbie, Malachai had followed. He'd looked out for her and helped in a way she hadn't expected and wasn't used to.

"The owl," he was saying, "is one of the most curious creatures. A bird that stays awake when the rest of the world sleeps. He can see in the dark. I find that so interesting, to be mired in reality when the rest of the world is dreaming. What does he see and what does he know that the rest of the world is missing?" He paused. "You know, I had an owl once."

Malachai so rarely talked about himself, Jac was surprised by the admission.

"He let me pet him," he said wistfully.

"Did he live in your house?"

"No. We were residing outside London on an estate that had a bird sanctuary on the grounds, and the owl befriended me. He must have felt sorry for the lonely little boy who was always by himself. I learned a lot about animals and birds from those who inhabited those woods. Creatures have an authenticity about them, a purity people don't possess. Our complexity overwhelms us."

Jac handed the amulet back to Malachai, and he reverently returned it to the shelf and picked up another object. It was an amber sphere with a complicated design carved into its surface.

"No less amazing," he said as he handed it to her. "This is an Asian seal. A very rare one. No matter what part of it you press down, you get the exact same configuration."

Jac expected him to pull out a stick of sealing wax and demonstrate. She had no doubt that he used it on his personal letters. Like the woods, this mansion, its antiques and collectibles, Malachai was oddly out of time. And she was an explorer of other times, of the ancient stories we've turned into holy grails. That was their tie, she thought. What had kept them bound to each other, long after her stint in therapy was past.

"Or so you think upon first glance." He was expounding on what he'd already said about the seal. "But there are minute markings, only visible with a magnifying glass, making each configuration unique." He took it back and rolled it between his palms. "Nothing is what it seems."

"When are you going to answer my question?"

"Theo was a troubled boy."

"Yes, he was, and I was troubled then too."

"The two of you were a terrible influence on each other."

"I don't remember that at all. We were good friends. He was my only real friend there."

Malachai sighed. "You're going to have to trust me on this, Jac, but due to patient-doctor confidentiality, I can't reveal what I know or explain why Theo's a dangerous personality for you to interact with. But he is, Jac."

She looked at him. Trying to read his unreadable visage.

"Druids believed in reincarnation," she said, eyeing the translucent amber egg he was still holding. The soft light made it look as if there were living fire trapped in its heart, burning forever.

"Yes, they did," Malachai said.

"If I went, I would share what I found with you. I could look for proof of your myth while I'm looking for mine."

"Reincarnation is not a myth. You know, I had this very same conversation with Griffin North not two months ago."

Jac held herself steady. Bit the inside of her cheek. She felt tears threatening. She couldn't allow herself to think about Griffin now. She'd just lost even more of him. He wasn't part of her life. They couldn't be together. He was with his wife and little girl where he belonged. She took a breath.

Focus.

"I'll look for proof of your theory then, is that better?" she asked, fighting to stay in the moment. "Maybe there are memory tools in Jersey."

Jac knew how much Malachai yearned to find one of the legendary sacred objects presumed to be memory aids to facilitate past-life regressions. It was believed that four to six thousand years ago, in the Indus Valley, mystics created these meditation tools to help people enter into deep states of relaxation, during which they would have access to past-life memories.

There were supposed to be twelve memory tools, Malachai had told her, twelve being a mystical number repeated all through various religions and in nature. Twelve objects to help pull

71

memories through the membrane of time, he'd said.

Malachai believed two of these tools had been found in the past few years. The first was a cache of precious stones and the second was an ancient flute made of human bone. Both had subsequently been lost. A third tool, a fragrance that acted as an olfactory trigger, had also surfaced for a short time, but that too had disappeared. But the legends about these tools had grown. There were rumors that men had killed for them and that fortunes had been lost trying to find them. Treasure hunters never gave up looking for the fabled devices, and hustlers tried to defraud innocent collectors with objects they tried to pass off as authentic. Adventure movies had been made and thriller novels had been written about spectacular searches for the memory tools, or fantasies about how they were exploited for evil.

They were Malachai's holy grail. Jac knew he lusted after finding one the way some men lust after money and power.

"Bribery will not change my mind. Your well-being is more important," he said.

"I'm surprised to hear you say that. I didn't think there was anything you wanted more than finding a memory tool."

"You wound me, Jac. Do you really think I'd sacrifice your safety for some object?"

She studied his face in the firelight. Until that

moment, if she'd been asked that question she might have said she wasn't sure. Malachai didn't just study reincarnation. He believed in it deeply. It was the reason he'd been at Blixer Rath in the 1990s.

Like Jung, Malachai theorized that many people suffering from what traditional therapists think are personality disorders are in fact suffering from past-life issues. Memories of other incarnations that are bubbling to the surface and causing fears, phobias, anxiety, even alternate personalities. They believed many issues could be tracked back to unresolved past-life conflicts demanding attention in this life.

Malachai had been at the clinic because regression therapy was part of their protocol. Using hypnosis, he explored patients' recent and more buried pasts. Jac hadn't been a good subject, though. Under hypnosis, she hadn't been able to regress any further back than her own recent childhood.

Reincarnation was not Malachai's passion, it was his lifeblood. Jac admired him for his zeal and for believing in something so profoundly. Envied his certainty. She questioned everything and yearned for a code, a creed. Jac had always wanted to be one of those people who know exactly who they are and operate from a position of unquestionable loyalty to their core.

Instead she was fascinated by all beliefs, myths

and legends but had faith in none. If pressed, the only thing in the world she was sure of was that no matter how deeply you care about someone—friend, family or lover—sooner or later, one way or another, you will be hurt or disappointed. She had come to believe in the instability of the known. Time and experience had made her a cynic.

Mythfinders, both the book and TV show, was a cynic's look at mythology. The stories had value as metaphor, of course. But she thought it was important to expose the fragile ground fables stood on. Jac hoped by tracing a myth back to the actual person or event whence it had sprung, and showing how that small moment had been exaggerated and romanticized into a fantasy, she'd help people manage expectations. Trying to live up to grandiose ideals made life more difficult. Yearning to be who we cannot be, for what we cannot accomplish, engenders discontent.

Hadn't she seen it firsthand? Her father had exhausted himself trying to live up to the family legends and lost most of what he'd cared about in the process. Her mother's ambition to achieve literary goals beyond her talent had so destroyed her self-esteem she'd turned to ruinous affairs.

But the opposite of what Jac had imagined had happened with *Mythfinders*. People found it inspiring. The kernel of proof she tried to show was so small backfired. To know the legends had sprung from reality—even a kernel of reality—

was empowering and encouraging. Her followers had found hope in her deconstructions.

"Well, if that's your best shot, you've failed," Jac said, folding up Theo's letter and putting it back in the envelope Malachai had left on the desk. "You haven't given me a good enough reason to refuse the invitation."

"Your safety isn't a good enough reason?" he asked.

"It would be if I believed my safety were actually at stake. But what you're saying is vague. All you can tell me is that when we were both teenagers, Theo and I were potentially—what? Partners in crime? I know that. I remember the rules we broke that summer."

"You didn't just break rules. You fell under his spell. You were attracted to his need to seek out and put himself in danger. You hiked on unexplored trails that were off-limits. Stayed out past curfew. He offered you wine and you drank it. Marijuana and you smoked it—"

"I was a fourteen-year-old and had a crush on him."

"It was more serious than that. You were susceptible to him in a profound way."

"Maybe I was but I was just a kid."

"What if I told you that you still could be susceptible to him? We had to send him home, Jac. We couldn't treat him. He still might be untreated."

"It was seventeen years ago. He was a sixteen-year-old kid in some kind of distress. Do you realize, even for you, how illogical and far-fetched this all sounds?"

"No matter what I say, you're determined to go, aren't you?"

"Stop talking in riddles. What else could you say?"

"He could seduce you, Jac. And I don't just mean sexually. I mean emotionally. At your core. He could use you to achieve his goals."

"Malachai, you're talking about it as if you think he's some kind of evil sorcerer."

"As far as you are concerned, I think he is."

Five

SEPTEMBER 8, 1855
JERSEY, CHANNEL ISLANDS, GREAT BRITAIN

For the last two years, it had become the habit of our household and closest friends to hold séances often, if not every night. We turned off the gas lamps and lit candles, two on the mantel and two on the sideboard. We sat around our card table, with one of us placing his or her fingers on the small stool in its center, and took turns asking questions while my son François-Victor kept track of the responses. Often the spirits who visited spoke so much, the sessions lasted long past midnight, but no one seemed to mind.

Whether we returned time and again to the table out of boredom or fascination, I cannot speak for anyone but myself. For me it became an obsession to talk to my Didine again. I wanted her to reassure me of her place in the light and of her peace. She rarely visited us. Only twice since the initial stop had she returned, and then only briefly.

I was bereft. Her teasing appearances had increased my sense of loss. She'd left us once in the flesh, and now as a spirit again. Instead of my mourning lessening, it had become sharper. My grief seemed rawer for the fleeting glimpses of her soul.

Apart from my desire to communicate with Didine, the séances were a huge success. More than that, they were shocking. Our little group had become the conduit for attracting the most amazing minds of all civilization, who all arrived in order to speak to me and impart their wisdom: Shakespeare, Dante, Mozart, Hannibal, Walter Scott, Joan of Arc, Moses, Judas, Galileo, Napoleon, and yes, as blasphemous as it sounds, even Jesus Christ visited with us. Over one hundred and fifteen different souls, some not even figures but abstract concepts with names like India, Metempsychosis, and Ocean.

But this journal is not about the talks we had

with those great sages; I've done other writings regarding them. The purpose of this journal is to write of the one who snaked his way into my soul and almost destroyed me. And, my dearest friend, Fantine, almost destroyed you too.

On the night of the eighth, we were seated around our table trying to raise a spirit when I heard a barking dog. This wasn't the sound of a typical country hound howling at a chicken. This was a ferocious and yet forlorn noise. After a few moments, other dogs joined in. An unholy cacophony befitting mythology's hellhounds. You have heard of these creatures, have you not? They are described as supernaturally fast dogs with malevolent glowing red or yellow eyes. Their duties are said to include guarding the entrance to the world of the dead, hunting lost souls and protecting supernatural treasures. It is written that if you look into their eyes three times you most surely will die. To hear them howl is an omen of death or even worse.

We were all distracted and discussed the jarring howling, conjecturing what might have happened to set the dogs off. In the midst of our conversation, my wife rose from her chair. "This situation with the dogs has unnerved me," she said, and told us she was retiring for the evening.

I was not eager to abandon the séance and asked the rest of our party if they would like to remain and see if we could indeed summon a spirit. They agreed, and Charles returned his fingers to the stool.

"I have the sense someone is waiting to speak with us," he said. "Spirit, are you there?"

I hoped it was Didine. I always hoped it was Didine. In those moments before the spirit announced himself, I yearned for it to be my lovely daughter. But that night, it was not she who answered our pleas. Instead came a spirit very much unwanted.

The first sign was that the air in the room became colder. My daughter Adele left the table and added a log to the fire. But it did nothing to chase away the damp chill that had invaded the room. Outside the wind picked up and blew in through the open windows, extinguishing the candles on the mantel and sideboard. The only light left to illuminate our sad group came from the blazing fireplace. The black spaniel Ponto, who did not belong to us but had adopted us, began to growl, low and deep in her throat. Our cat Grise hissed and scampered up the stairs.

"Who is there?" Charles asked.

Finally the tapping began, and with it so did the voice I heard inside my head during the séances, the otherworldly voice whose words corresponded perfectly to the translations François-Victor would later provide.

A friend who can help.

"Help with what?" I asked.

Find Leopoldine.

The chill in the room entered into me. My blood's temperature lowered. I felt as if I were being frozen from inside and my heart were turning to ice.

"You mean bring her to us here in these sessions?"

If that is all you wish.

"What else could I wish for?"

No answer.

"Is there another way you can bring her to me?"

Perhaps.

"What do I have to do?"

Prove you are worthy.

"Is it a quest? Are you giving me a test?"

Yes.

"Who are you to demand such a thing?"

We have met before. I'm insulted you do not recognize me.

"You play games with me, sir. Reveal yourself."

You want your daughter. I can return her to you.

"In spirit?"

Your daughter again by your side.

"What does that mean?"

You will understand in time.

"Why not explain more?"

I cannot reveal more until you have proven.

"Who are you?"

You haven't guessed?

"No, damn it. Who are you?"

Do you believe in evil?

"Yes."

You have seen proof?

"Yes, of course. I have seen evil. I have seen men hanged at the gallows. I have seen innocent children beaten. I have seen women starve to death."

And you believe in independence and intellectual freedom?

"Of course. For all men. For all time."

Of all the archangels, who represents those?

I was almost afraid to say his name. In awe of the idea that was forming in my mind.

Who?

"Lucifer."

Yes, he who is feared and revered. Like you, Hugo. Your intellect and insights both revered and feared, yet you are no devil, are you?

"No."

For a man of letters you are quite monosyllabic.

I could not help myself, I laughed. The tapping did not abate, the voice in my mind did not pause.

Here is your test. I request a great poem, bard. To resurrect me and show me for what I am. To the spirit that is mine and that is yours. The spirit of man soaring, achieving, creating, not being beaten down by the hypocrisy of small-minded, power-hungry men. The title is up to you—but I think The End of Lucifer. Or perhaps you might use my other name. The one I prefer.

I did not have to ask. I knew the name he preferred and whispered it.

"The Shadow of the Sepulcher?"

He didn't answer. He didn't have to. In fact he chose that moment to leave. I knew because the room was no longer cold. My blood warmed too. I didn't realize I had been shivering until I stopped.

Making my excuses, I went upstairs posthaste. I had developed the habit of transcribing the evening's conversations immediately afterward, while they were still fresh in my mind.

Our house, as you know, Fantine, faces the ocean. Upstairs in my room, it is as if I am perched on the very tip of a precipice with the great foaming waves beneath my window. I wrote in a letter to Franz Stephens that "I inhabit this immense dream of the ocean; slowly I become a sleepwalker of the sea. Faced with these prodigious sights and that enormous living thought in which I lose myself, there is soon nothing left of me but a sort of witness to God."

That night, as I usually do in these *après-séance* writing sessions, I flung open the windows and took in great gulps of the sea-washed air. I had smoked a bit of hashish before the event. Now I relit my pipe, stood at my desk and transcribed the words the Shadow had spoken to me.

With nothing to distract me but the ink flowing onto the paper, the walls of my resistance crumbled in these sessions. The rules of logic relaxed. I opened my mind to the possibilities of the night, to the magic of the dark, to unfathomable ideas that had been presented to me.

I am blind to everything but the scrawls of black moving across the paper when I write. I didn't hear the house hum around me, or my own heart beat, or the waves pound on the rocks. I only hear the words that I set down. Though not my words, no. During those *après-séance* writing sessions I was no different from a scribe recording the words spoken by another. The spirits revisited me in my aerie, elaborating and elucidating to me as if the séances were but rehearsals and these communions the true ones.

After I transcribed the exchange above from the spirit who identified himself as the Shadow of the Sepulcher, I was bathed in sweat. My large room, even with the windows open, was suffocating. I needed to escape. To breathe the night air and find some comfort in the corporeal world. I would go to Juliette's, I decided. The walk to my mistress's home would revive me, and then I could climb into her bed and she would soothe me.

Even though the sky was strewn with storm clouds, I decided to walk on the beach instead of taking the main road. Always I am drawn to the unrelenting waves, the salty, briny air and the feel of the sand shifting beneath my feet.

Reaching the shore, I stood for some time just

looking out on the rough sea and thought about the offer the spirit had made. I was filled with both wonder and dread, curiosity and chagrin. How could I believe such a thing? It was not possible to bring back my daughter. And the price? A piece of poetry? The whole exchange was ludicrous.

As I pondered these thoughts, I became aware of a presence nearby and turned. No one was there.

I looked up at the sky and wondered if Didine was one of the stars peeking through the clouds. Could she be looking down and watching over me at that moment?

I had always believed that if we cannot chart the geography of the heavens, if we cannot ride over heaven's hills or sail over its seas, then we cannot know for sure who dwells there and how they interact.

But in the last two years, in over a hundred séances, I had been given glimpses of that geography. Hadn't I?

That was the question on my mind as I walked the beach. After a time, I noticed someone up ahead. At first I couldn't tell if it was a man or a woman from that distance. But when I came closer, in the light of the moon I recognized you, the comely servant girl whom my mistress had recently employed. Fantine, you were walking along the shore, staring out at the vast ocean. The sky had cleared and the moon glow shone on your white chemise, making it stand out like a beacon.

When I'd noticed you at her house, Juliette had told me you were another exile from Paris. I'd only seen you two or three times but had been acutely aware of your sadness. You wore it like a frock. It clouded your eyes, turning the blue sky to gray. Even the scent that lingered in a room after you'd left it reminded me of grief. It was the fragrance of flowers past bloom in their death throes.

As I approached, you became aware of me, and when you turned, I thought I saw the silvery track of tears on your cheek.

I was sorry I'd intruded, but it was too late for me to turn back without being rude. "Good evening, Fantine."

"Monsieur Hugo, good evening."

In Juliette's abode, you were demure. Here you seemed less so. In her home you would have lowered your eyes and been slightly embarrassed in my presence. But you were none of these things on the beach. You were forthright, almost defiant. As if I had interrupted you. As if this were your beach and I were trespassing.

I fell into step beside you and must admit was still so absorbed by what had happened in my house that for the first few minutes of our stroll, I paid you little heed.

Lost in thoughts as dark as the sea, I tried to make sense of the evening's revelations, tumbling the thoughts in my own head. Getting nowhere, I finally felt the need to discuss what had occurred with someone who hadn't been in my house and exposed to the table tapping.

"Do you believe in spirits?" I asked.

"Do you mean ghosts?"

"Well yes, I suppose so. The spirits of those no longer alive. Do you think they are capable of communicating with us?"

You nodded, and your dark curls dancing on their own endowed the grave question with a certain ironic frivolity. "Oh yes. I've often felt my mother's presence and smelled her perfume in the air when there's no one nearby. It's always very comforting."

"Is she really communicating with you or are you just remembering her vividly? Do you actually believe some shade of her is here, watching over you, visiting you?"

The beach was rocky where we were walking, and as you started to answer, you tripped. I reached out to steady you. Closer, I marveled at your fragrance. The same I'd sniffed in Juliette's house, but so near now I could smell other subtle scents mixed in with the roses. Night-blooming jasmine, lemon . . . I shut my eyes for a moment, to fix the curious smell. In Juliette's house you wore your hair up, covered it with a cap, and donned a uniform that hid the ample bosom and small waist now apparent. Now your thick dark hair fell in waves around your face and down your back. In my mistress's house you were an ordinary maid. Here you were a wanton, suffering woman.

"I believe she has truly communicated with me."

"Tonight is the anniversary of my daughter's death," I said.

The words hung on the wind for a moment and reverberated like church bells until the sound of crashing waves overwhelmed them.

"I lost a child too," you whispered. "She was stillborn."

"But you are so young."

"I'm twenty-five," you said, as if it were very old indeed.

"What of your husband?"

Your gaze returned to the sea.

"Lost?" I asked. The sea claimed so many lives, as I knew all too well.

"He was not my husband. But yes, lost."

"Did you lose them both together?"

You shook your head no. "But I can't stop mourning either of them."

"Would you, if you could, talk to your mother now? If she is in the netherworld, would you want to know how she was, what it is like? Find out if she is looking after your baby for you?"

"Of course."

"What would you pay for such a privilege?"

"Anything asked of me." And then you looked at me as if I were half mad. "You aren't suggesting there's a way, are you?"

"I might be," I said, and then told you about the séances. I remember how at first you had to hold back from laughing at me. From the questions you asked, it seemed you found me foolish and absurd. But as we continued our walk and I told you more about the sessions and spirits, your initial skepticism turned to curiosity.

I fell in love with you a little then. I admire nothing so much as the willingness to suspend disbelief and open one's mind to new ideas.

"What was your daughter's name?"

"Leopoldine," I said. "But I called her Didine."

"So have you talked to your Didine?"

"I haven't heard her voice, but I believe she is speaking to me."

You turned your gaze upon me now. No longer as if I were daft but as if I might not be entirely human.

We continued walking for a few steps in silence. I was thinking about you now. Wondering about you. Clearly you were well educated. Out of place, being a lady's maid in the Channel Islands.

"How long have you been in Jersey?" I asked.

"Two and a half years. I worked for another lady before Madame Drouet."

"What happened?"

"She was elderly and passed away this summer."

"And were you a lady's maid in Paris too?" I asked.

"No, I worked with my father in his shop."

"What kind of shop?"

"My father was a well-known perfumer."

"He is no longer with us?"

You nodded.

The sound of the water crashing on the rocks was an ominous symphony to all this talk of death. I knew I was prying. Your short, compact answers suggested you weren't comfortable talking about your past. And I did worry about offending you. But I am a storyteller; I wanted to know your story. I tried to go gently.

"And what happened to your father's shop?"

"My uncle who worked there also took it over."

"Have I heard of this shop?"

"Probably, it has been in business for a very long time."

She named the family concern. I recognized it, in fact, knew it well. Often I'd bought gifts of fragrance for my wife, my daughters, even for Juliette at the establishment. I was lost for a few moments, thinking of Paris. It had been so long since I'd been home and I was nostalgic for my city.

We'd walked a long way, far past Juliette's house. We were on a stretch of beach I didn't know well, because except at low tide, like now, there was no beach to tread upon. This rocky section of shore was all cliffs. And where there were cliffs there were usually caves. Indeed, in the moonlight, I noticed many openings and was intrigued. The locals talked of cave walls covered with ancient drawings, rooms deep in the rocks that were used in older times as retreats, temples and burial grounds. I'd explored several caves, mostly on the other side of the island at Plemont Bay. They were majestic and mysterious, but I had yet to stumble upon a cavern I could be sure had any mystical significance.

"Have you been inside any of these caves?" you asked, as if reading my mind.

"Not here."

"Oh, you must. Some of them are astonishing."

"You've gone in? You weren't afraid of being trapped? They say the tide in this section of beach can sneak up on you and suddenly your only exit is the sea itself."

"I wouldn't have minded."

Such a simple way of declaring your suffering. You said it without pathos, not inviting my sympathy but simply stating the sad truth of your existence. You gave me this confidence, not knowing it would be like a seed that grew inside me. And what misery it would lead to.

I nodded then, bowed my head to your grief. Sorrow was something I understood. The temptation to seek relief from never-ending sadness was one I knew well.

"I too have . . ." I hesitated. I could not go on and speak of my own disconsolate heartache.

To utter the words was to become lost in them. In your way that I have come to know and appreciate, you did not say anything. You didn't push me to say more. You waited. Your patience is a gift. You trusted our silence. Ah, Fantine. Thank you for that.

"What happened to you in Paris," I asked after a time, "that made you flee?"

When you hesitated, I realized I had done exactly what you had not. So before you could answer I apologized. "I'm sorry. My wife says I am rude and Juliette agrees. She laughs at me and says I am too desperate for people's stories. That I am too greedy to hear about the comedies and tragedies of their lives. She claims I listen so I can file away the twists and turns of their journeys and romances. That I collect people's particulars, add spices to them, stir in other ingredients, cook them up and then present a book to the world. But I am only trying to offer up my interpretation of life as a mirror by which men may see themselves in another light."

You remained staring out at the infinite black sea when I finished speaking. I noticed your shoulders were trembling slightly.

"Are you cold?" I asked. "Would you like my coat?"

"No. No, thank you."

"Then what is it?"

You gestured to the churning water. "Sometimes

I think I hear it calling to me. I wish I were brave enough to listen."

"If you were, what would you do?"

I was afraid of your answer, but something in me demanded I listen to it.

"I would heed its call. I'd give myself to it."

"You want to die that much?"

"No. It's not that I want to die, it's that I can't bear to live. I can't bear to miss someone so much. To long for him like this."

And then you turned to me, and I could see you were shocked by what you'd said.

"You didn't know that about yourself?" I asked.

You shook your head. "Please forgive me. I have no right to speak to you like this. To inflict my thoughts on you and lay my burdens at your feet."

Indeed you looked mortified.

"Do not insult me, Fantine. All this time we have been talking and walking as equals. A man and a woman who share a common sadness that comes from loss. A man and a woman exchanging confidences under the night sky. If I had not wanted to hear what you had to say, you would have known it a long way back."

You bowed your head. I took your chin in my hand and lifted up your face. Your skin was fine to my touch, and despite all our morose talk I felt the stirrings of pleasure. Such is my blessing and my curse. My passions run deep but are always close to the surface. Sexual enjoyment is my true escape in a way that none of my stories, my plays, my poems or my political writings are.

Those take me deeper inside myself. Only by indulging in my cravings, my lust, do I find the oblivion I seek.

I leaned forward slowly to signal what I was about to do—I am not an ogre or a letch and do not like taking kisses by force. You didn't step back, didn't hesitate. And so I kissed you gently. There was no response from you. Your expression in the moonlight did not change.

Ah, Fantine, you were already almost dead and you didn't yet know it.

"Do you need any money?" I asked. "Does Madame Drouet pay you enough?"

"Yes, she does." Now it was your turn to hesitate.

"What is it, Fantine?"

"I have heard about you, Monsieur Hugo."

"Yes?"

"From some of the other servants . . ."

You left off. I smiled. "So tell me, do they say terrible things about me?"

"No, quite to the contrary. They say you are kind and generous, and if a girl needs money you are tender with her and ask for very little."

"Would you like me to be generous with you?"

"If it would help you, monsieur. If you need me, I would be happy to give you what you'd like, but I wouldn't want any money."

"And why would you want to do that?"

"Because of the sadness."

"In you?" I asked.

"No, monsieur, in you."

I didn't know what to say. It had been so long since anyone had had such insight into me. So I kissed you once more. And then we turned back, following our own footsteps now.

"I would like to pay you, though," I repeated my offer.

"No, that won't be necessary."

"But if I don't pay you . . ." I stopped myself. Why was I becoming angered at your stubborn refusal to take the coins in exchange for what I would ask of you? Why did I want to pay you so badly?

For the second time that night, you anticipated my thoughts. "I know what you were going to say. If you don't pay me then you will have to care for me, and you don't want to."

You were like a night nymph standing before me. A wisp of a girl with wild hair and sparkling blue-gray eyes reflecting the phosphorescent waves and the moonlight.

"But you want me to?"

"No one has cared about me for a very, very long time," you said. "I would like to know how it feels again. Even just a bit of caring. I would like to test it and see if it is enough to keep me alive."

"What an astonishing creature you are. You are offering me a bargain."

You smiled. "I suppose I am."

I reached out and touched your beautiful hair, lifting one of the curls. As I did I breathed in your scent again. What a fine perfume. One more suited to a woman seated in front of a silver tea set under a crystal chandelier than to a servant girl walking on the beach in Jersey.

From my pocket I pulled out a handful of coins and opened my hand to you.

"You are sure you won't take these?"

"There are others on the island who would gladly take your centimes, monsieur. But not I. If you want something from me, I will give it freely in exchange for what you might come to feel for me."

Boldly you curled my fingers over the coins, closing up my hand. Rejecting the offer as completely as you could. And then, then you leaned forward and both gave a kiss and took one. My breath caught in my throat.

When you pulled back, you said two words, "Thank you."

I was astonished. "What on earth for?"

"For making me wonder for the first time in a long time. Now I must go back."

"Let me walk with you."

"No, you have important things to think about— more important than me."

But I didn't want you to wander off into the inky black sky. I was afraid that you might venture into the sea instead of walking back to the house. I couldn't bear to think of you in the water, with your dress soaking up the sea, pulling you down, swirling around you, sand and seaweed in your beautiful hair. I wanted to save you, Fantine. Save *you,* to make up for the other young woman whom I had not been able to save.

I saw you to the passageway where the road came down to the beach and then partway to Juliette's house. I wouldn't be going there after all. I craved solitude. So I returned to the beach and took the long way home, by the sea.

On my way back to Marine Terrace, I sensed someone walking behind me and thought I smelled a particular scent of smoke and incense, but when I turned to look all I saw were the rocks' dark shadows and all I could smell was the sea's salty, briny fragrance.

With only the roar of the waves there was little to distract me from my thoughts, until somewhere in the distance a dog began ferociously barking. Not alerting his master to a stranger approaching but quite the opposite. This dog was warning everyone who heard him that he was to be feared. Within moments other dogs were howling and the air was filled with their noise, just as had happened earlier that evening.

I was not usually worried about being accosted

or assaulted by man or beast, but it had been such a strange night, I bent down and picked up a good-size rock. It was large enough to throw at a man. Or a dog if one approached. As I continued home, I held the stone in my grip, finding comfort in its craggy surface and heft.

Only when I was inside my own house with the door locked firmly behind me did I relax enough to gaze at the rock. In the candlelight I saw that it was almost a perfect oval of clear white quartz with a slightly fleshy pink tone to it. Actually very much shaped like a head. In fact the crevices and grooves, bumps and depressions even gave the appearance of a woman's face. But not just any woman's face. With wonder, I stared at the rock that could have been an unfinished portrait of my own daughter, my own Didine. It was as if Rodin himself were working the stone and had just begun to rough out her appearance, had chiseled just the essence of her.

I placed the rock on my mantel, continuing to appraise it, wondering if in the morning Didine's sister or brothers or her mother would notice and see the resemblance.

Upstairs, I opened my windows and looked out at the sea as I stripped down and stepped out of my damp clothes. I poured myself some brandy and sipped it as I returned my gaze to the infinite blackness.

I remembered the feel of your soft cheek on my

fingers, your yielding lips on my mouth, your scent of roses and lemons. I could hear your melancholy words ringing in my ears.

It had been a relief to talk to you without pretense, the way I must all too often with my wife, even with Juliette. I could allow you to see how my grief still consumes me without worrying the knowledge would affect you.

I walked to my writing table. Pen in hand, while the wind washed over me and the household slept on the floors below, I began to write the story of this strange night that began with a séance and ended with two ghosts meeting—yours, Fantine, and mine.

Six

AUGUST 22, THE PRESENT
NEW YORK CITY

The ring felt icy on Jac's forefinger. As the cold shot up her arm, she shivered despite the comfortable temperature in the basement room in the Metropolitan Museum of Art. The ancient jewelry was made out of a copper alloy that had a deep plum cast to it. Typical of the period, it was a knot without any loose strands. The carved Celtic design was intricate. In its center was a strange ghostlike face with hollow gaping eyes staring back at her. Jac was fascinated. Everything about her research was making her more and more excited about the upcoming trip to Jersey.

Who had last worn the twenty-six-hundred-year-old piece of jewelry? Was it a man or a woman? Was this a ritual piece? Jac knew the Celts were divided up into tribes, each ruled by a king. The population comprised Druids or holy priests or priestesses, warriors, nobles and commoners. Jac had read that chiefs gave rings to warriors to use as a badge of office and symbol of their power. Priests also wore them to denote their station.

"How long has this piece been in the museum's collection?" Jac asked Christine Bullock, the curator of the medieval department.

"It was a gift from Josef and Brigitte Hatzenbuehler in 2009. They gave us a very generous portion of their collection. Almost all of it is now in our department."

Jac turned her hand to the right and the left to catch the light. The jewelry ignited her imagination. This beautifully wrought metal object was bringing the Celtic culture to life. Making her anxious to leave for Jersey and begin her quest.

Despite Malachai's pleading, or maybe perversely because of it, she'd decided she couldn't pass up Theo's fascinating invitation. There were over a hundred known Celtic ruins on the island. Because of how the landmasses shifted, occasionally new sites were uncovered. If Theo Gaspard had discovered one, she wanted to see it.

Jac's ritual when investigating a new topic was to read as much as she could as well as search out facsimiles of art and artifacts related to the subject that she could look at and touch and hold. In the weeks since finding Theo's letter she'd gathered hundreds of photos of ruins, archaeological finds, paintings depicting Celtic myths and legends.

This trip to the Met was proving to be the highlight of her research to date.

Bullock had met her in the museum's great hall and via elevator taken her to a sub-basement. They'd walked for over fifteen minutes through labyrinthine tunnels to reach this windowless, quiet room that appeared to be some kind of storage space. Floor-to-ceiling racks of shelves were filled with hundreds of tantalizing tagged artifacts that all seemed to be from the medieval period. Jac itched to explore them, but her focus was on the dozen Celtic pieces Bullock had displayed on the table in the center of the room.

In addition to the ring, Bullock had chosen two bracelets, a sword, three coins, two brooches, a belt clasp and an assortment of items related to saddling a horse. All utilitarian objects, they were exceptionally made and beautifully designed. Simple but elegant.

Very little was known about these people whose

civilization could be traced back to the Bronze Age in 1200 BCE. Most of what had been written about them came from biased and bigoted accounts from the Romans who considered the pastoral, pagan Celts barbarians. Pull away the veil of prejudice and what emerged for Jac was a complex, deeply spiritual and evolved society.

"Are you working on any particular myth?" Bullock asked.

"Not yet. I'm going to wait until I get there and see what we find." As she spoke, the ring distracted her. She was conscious of its heft and how the metal felt against her skin. Jac usually wore earrings but not rings. They somehow looked wrong on her, and she always worried she was going to lose them. But this one looked as if it had been designed for her. It was different—she felt as if it had just been found, not lost.

"Where was this ring discovered?" she asked the curator.

Bullock looked at the card from the ring's tray. "At a burial site in the British Isles." She raised her eyebrows. "Nice coincidence."

Malachai's favorite refrain repeated in Jac's head. *There are no coincidences.*

Bullock was still speaking. Jac concentrated on what the curator was saying.

"Like the Egyptians, the Celts, especially the noble class, were buried with their personal and household goods, including weapons and chariots.

It's one of the reasons we have so many antiquities from that time."

"When you believe the soul is immortal and the living and the dead exchange places all the time, burials take on a different meaning," Jac said, as she started to pull off the ring and felt a pang of—what was it? Melancholy? For a moment the emotion threatened to overshadow the thrill of examining the rest of the items. Bullock hadn't noticed—she was reaching for one of the other items—so Jac left the ring on and took the sword that the curator was handing her.

"This is a treasure," Bullock said. "The artistry is highly evolved for the period."

The hilt had been stylized into the form of a human warrior. His carefully carved face featured almond eyes and articulated hair.

"It's beautiful," Jac said.

"Probably the best one of its kind that's been unearthed."

"Do you know where this was discovered?"

"In Switzerland. Proof of the Celts' expansion as well as their sophistication. We received it in 1999."

Jac held on to the sword. Mesmerized by the verdigris, she examined the way the copper's oxidation had created green crust circles and swirls that were as artistic as the weapon maker's design.

Then Jac heard a sound. Was the rough clanging a bell ringing? She raised her head and listened. It was so far off. Too distant to hear clearly. Slowly she became aware there was a scent in the air now that hadn't been there a moment before. She was sure of it. Sniffing, she smelled burning wood, smoke, incense and something sweet. What was it? She sniffed again.

"Do you smell something?" Bullock asked.

From the way she'd asked the question, Jac knew the curator hadn't. It wasn't that unusual for Jac to sense a scent others couldn't. Her nose was better trained and so more attuned. Before this past summer, it wouldn't have bothered Jac. But in Paris whenever she'd smelled an aroma no one else could, it had led to a hallucination. The return of the condition that hadn't plagued her since the summer she spent at Blixer Rath perplexed and depressed her.

Since returning to New York in June, though, she hadn't had a single episode and had stopped worrying about them. But if they were back . . . Jac hadn't been able to control the incidents in Paris; would she be able to now?

Suddenly the telltale shivers that presaged an episode ran up and down her arms. Painful, cold pinpricks warned her a flare-up was beginning. The smells around her intensified. The light dimmed. She tried to fight back against the attack, but the shadows continued to descend.

Jac's thoughts began to waver as if she were leaving her own mind and traveling into someone else's. She looked around. The white walls were now dripping thick rivers of red. Seeping onto the floor, the blood was pooling. It smelled so sweet. Pitiful keening filled the air. A woman's grief-stricken cries, so piercing they hurt Jac's ears.

Summoning all her conscious strength, she tried to realign herself with reality. It was imperative to break through the nightmare vision. She feared disappearing into one, never to return with her faculties intact.

At the clinic, Malachai had taught Jac exercises to help her find her way back to her own mind. Her sanity commandments, she called the string of instructions.

Silently, she intoned them now.

Open a window. Get fresh air.

There wasn't one in the room. Move on to the next step.

Take long, concentrated breaths. Count . . . two . . . three . . . four.

Jac inhaled. Counted . . . two . . . three . . . four. Did it again. And again. She smelled something manufactured. Something real. Of the present. A too-sweet gourmand perfume. Bullock's cologne. Good. She was returning to the moment. Now she had to stay there and keep her mind from spiraling out.

Give yourself a task.

She'd try to identify the notes in the curator's scent.

Jac inhaled again. Found them, then named them: musk, benzoin and caramel.

She was feeling better. Now to control her shaking. Jac carefully put down the sword she'd been gripping, inhaled again and counted . . . two . . . three . . . four. And again. Much better now.

How long had the episode lasted? It had seemed like five minutes or more, but Jac knew from recent experience it was probably only seconds. Glancing over at Bullock, Jac didn't think the curator had noticed. She was still talking as if nothing eventful had occurred.

"There are still a fair number of Celtic tombs being found. Since so many were covered with funeral mounds, land configurations give them away. Over the years, they can be disguised and then come to light when the landscape changes for one reason or another. There was a recent find in Scotland discovered when part of a forest was cleared."

Bullock got up and for a moment cast a shadow on the ring. When she moved and it left, the copper seemed to glow brighter. It was surely her imagination, but it felt to Jac as if the metal was warmer than it had been. And after a few more seconds it seemed almost hot. By the time Jac took the ring off there was a faint mark on her finger where it had been. Like a reverse sunburn. The rest of her hand was paler and the band under the metal was tan. Her skin stung a bit but she refrained from rubbing it. It must be that she was having an allergic reaction to some special solvent the museum used to clean or protect the metal.

But for the rest of the afternoon and all of that night, the band of burned skin on the forefinger of her left hand stung. Two days later at the airport on her way to England, when she handed the flight attendant her boarding pass, Jac noticed the discoloration was less pronounced, but it was still there.

Seven

SEPTEMBER 5, THE PRESENT
THE ENGLISH CHANNEL

With the tourist season over, there were but a dozen passengers on the ferry. The boat rocked in the choppy sea and the wind blew wildly, but Jac was enjoying the crossing. She'd spent a few days in London, first sleeping off her jet lag, then doing more research. This morning she'd taken a pleasant four-hour train ride to Poole and then a short taxi to the ferry station. The three-hour-and-forty-five-minute trip to the island was half over. Jac had been alone on the upper deck the whole time until a few minutes ago when a woman joined her. She appeared to be in her mid- to late sixties. A silk scarf, tied under her chin, kept her auburn hair from flying in the wind. Under her rust-colored cashmere jacket, she was wearing a matching sweater. Black slacks and low-heeled black boots completed the outfit. Very well dressed for a boat ride, Jac thought.

As the woman walked toward a seat, the boat pitched and she stumbled.

Jac was out of her seat quickly. Reaching the woman before she fell, grabbing her arm, offering support.

"Are you all right?" Jac asked.

"I'm fine, dear. Thank you." Then she looked down and noticed her bag's contents had spilled and were rolling about. The boat was still pitching.

"Let me help," Jac said, and knelt down.

There was nothing unusual about the wallet Jac handed back to her. Or the silver comb and mirror. All expensive, but ordinary.

"I was thinking of getting some tea," Jac said as she handed back a tube of lipstick. "Would you like some? Or coffee?"

"That would be delightful. Tea, please, with lemon, no sugar."

When she returned, the woman was seated and looking out at the passing seascape. She exuded both strength and stature. Like a woman who knew her own mind and ran her own life. The kind of woman you'd expect to have a high-level job in a cosmetic or publishing company. Who had fresh flowers on her desk. Whose pearls were real. Who didn't suffer fools.

"Thank you for jumping out of your seat," the woman said, after she had taken a sip of her tea. "That could have been a nasty fall." She shook her head. "I've just returned from seeing my daughter and am afraid I've let it get to me."

Jac wasn't sure what to say, so she drank her tea.

"It's her husband who has me so rattled," the woman continued. "We've always been oil and water. My daughter rebelled against her iconoclastic mum and married a minister. Righteous and full of his faith to the point of lunacy, if you ask me. Olivia doesn't seem to notice how narrow-minded he is. Of course, he thinks I'm a terrible influence."

"Why?"

"Fear of the unknown can be a powerful force." The woman took a long sip of tea.

The fog had thickened. Jac couldn't see in front of them or behind them anymore. It was as if all the clouds in the sky had lowered and surrounded the boat. Her skin was damp with it, her curls already tightening. The smell of sea and salt was as primordial in its way as the forest had been in Connecticut the afternoon she and Malachai had been caught in the thunderstorm.

"Have you ever noticed how you can spot a stranger as soon as you see one?" the woman asked. "I don't mean a stranger as in someone you haven't yet met—like us—but someone who will forever remain a stranger to you? Someone you know you'll never be able to understand or communicate with. It's actually the very same ability that helps you quickly identify kindred spirits."

"Yes, I have noticed." Jac nodded.

"So it's happened to you?"

When Jac had first met Theo Gaspard seventeen years before, she'd felt that instant bond. And years later when she'd met Griffin North she'd felt it again. They'd connected to each other in some deep, unfathomable way almost instantly. It was a connection she was still struggling to break. They couldn't be together. They didn't belong with each other. She had to find a way to stop mourning what was not meant to be.

"When it does happen, you need to trust your instincts," the woman said.

"Why did you say that?" Jac was startled. It was almost as if the woman had been reading her mind.

"No magic, I'm afraid. I'm a therapist. I know how to read people. I was watching your expression," she said. "If I said something that disturbed you, I'm sorry."

In Jac's bag was a bright-green leather notebook from Hermès. Her mother had bought it for her on her thirteenth birthday. "To write down your dreams and your nightmares," she'd said. "Because if you write them down you make them real, and then you can control them instead of the other way around."

The trick hadn't worked for Audrey. Not even her own poetry had saved her. Nonetheless, Jac continued doing what her mother had suggested. And when she got to Blixer Rath, Malachai had encouraged her to continue keeping the dream journal. He'd even added a suggestion: to also keep a running list of the coincidences she encountered. So she'd turned the notebook around and going back to front, started to list them.

"One day," Malachai had told her, "you'll be able to read over your lists and see your life's path. At each important juncture you can look back and understand what brought you to the next point. But understanding your journeys isn't the only goal; you need to be in the moment and live them. When you are well enough to do that, my job will be done."

Every year, Jac bought a refill for the Hermès journal from their store on Madison Avenue. She had eighteen of them in a steel filing cabinet at home. These days, in the front of the books, she kept ideas and notes about myths for her work. In the back she still listed coincidences. Even if she never went back and looked through them, it had become a habit.

Somewhere far off, a foghorn sounded and

resonated across the water. A cry of warning. More human-sounding than machine.

"What kind of therapy do you practice?" Jac asked.

"Jungian."

She wasn't surprised. Things the woman spoke of had suggested it. "I thought you might. Jungian therapy is something that's been part of my life for a long time," Jac said, just as the foghorn sounded its warning again.

Despite her years of traveling, she was still a nervous traveler. Not so much because she was afraid of planes crashing, trains derailing or boats sinking, but because the idea that she was on an unknown path, filled with endless potential wins, wonders and disasters, overwhelmed her.

"Are you visiting Jersey on vacation?"

"No, for work," Jac said, brightening.

The woman's bracelet had worked its way out from under her sweater.

It was three braided ropes of blackened twisted gold. It looked very old and reminded Jac of the Celtic artifacts Bullock had shown her.

"Let me guess," the woman said, appraising Jac. "Most people who come to the island for business are in finance . . ."

From her research, Jac knew Jersey was one of the few offshore banking capitals of the world. Although there were fewer than 90,000 inhabitants, the island had forty-five banks and 32,000 registered businesses. There was in excess of 189 billion pounds deposited on the island at any one time.

"But no . . . finance is too soulless for you. I should know, my family owns a bank. My father ran it. His father before him. My nephew runs it now. Cold, cold business. You try to be stoic like that, but you don't manage it well, do you?"

Jac noted the shift from the business to personal and laughed. It was the best description of herself she'd heard in a long time. Exactly the kind of thing her brother would have said about her.

"Ah, I know what you're doing here," the woman said, still trying to figure it out. "You're chasing your fate."

"What do you mean?" It was such a curious comment, Jac thought.

The older lady smiled. Her green eyes twinkled. She was enjoying herself immensely now.

"Well, you aren't wearing a wedding ring or any jewelry. So it appears you're unattached. Not much luggage. You haven't pulled out your cell phone the whole time we've been on the boat. No checking for texts or emails means no urgent, pressing matters, business or personal. No strings tethering you to people or places. That's the obvious part. The not so obvious part is that you have all the hallmarks of a seeker. I've known a few in my time. I've even been flattered to have been called one. You chase special knowledge.

112

You find threads of connections and then share them with the people who need them. I can read it in the way you've been looking out past the boat's railing, how you looked at me, the questions you ask, but more importantly, the ones you don't."

Jac was slightly uncomfortable that a stranger was analyzing her but she was also intrigued by how perceptive the woman was.

"Don't mind me. It's an occupational hazard." Opening her pocketbook, the woman reached inside and then handed Jac a small card. It was heavy stock, engraved with a heraldic design of a large bird that could have been a phoenix or an eagle. Under that was her name—Minerva Eastmond—with a phone number and an address in St. Helier's Parish, Jersey, Great Britain.

"This is my office number and address," she said. "If you need anything while you are here. A cup of tea, books on historic folklore, or just a friendly face. I have a lot of maps too. Old ones especially. The family has a large collection."

"Thank you, I may take you up on that. I'm here to do a bit of exploring."

"It's one thing to be shown the path. Traveling it is something you can only do on your own."

This whole conversation was surreal, Jac thought. "What made you say that?"

"We all share a consciousness. We breathe in each other's air. Sometimes two souls can see each other's shadows even when the sun isn't

113

out." Minerva looked up at the fogged-out heavens. "It's sunnier in Jersey than any of the other isles. But we're having a bleak spell just now. A fog like this can linger for days. And if it turns cold, the damp can get in your bones. It's almost as if after the summer rush of tourists, the island wants to rest, so she pulls closed the shutters and locks the door. It shouldn't stop you, though. Sometimes I think secrets prefer the mist. We have a lot of hiding places here, not just our banks but the caves. They are our real treasure. That's where the island myths are most alive."

The deep sonorous foghorn blasted once more.

"We're coming into port now," Minerva said. "It's good to come home."

Jac searched the morass for any sign of land or buildings or boats, but all she saw was a thick gray wall of shadows.

Eight

SEPTEMBER 14, 1855
JERSEY, CHANNEL ISLANDS, GREAT BRITAIN

Being haunted is frightening. That, I might have guessed. But I never could have imagined how debilitating and exhausting it would be. I feel as if I am being consumed, suffocated and overwhelmed. Oh, how much attention all the spirits crave. And how clever they are to tempt me, promising to imbue me with powers. I have become addicted to their adoration. Terrified by their intensity. What a sacred horror I feel in their presence.

Some of the spirits no longer constrain themselves to visit during the séances but now come to me afterward. By disturbing my sleep night after night they play havoc with my temperament. I cannot shut my window or my door on them. Walls are not barriers for these bloodless creatures. I cannot keep them at bay.

For the last four nights, one has been bolder than any of the others.

It begins with odd noises once the house has gone to sleep and all the lamps are extinguished. Floorboards groan, windows creak. My belongings stir even though the shutters are closed tight. Papers fly. And slowly a light fills the room, a brightness not of this world. In its center is the woman the islanders call La Dame Blanche.

She visited the table once last year and then not again till the day after I saw you on the beach. Since then she has returned each day. And not just to the séances. This prehistoric coquette calls on me in my room, teasing me while I dream, causing me to awaken. Standing before me, this ancient temptress, who is as beautiful and skilled as any Parisian whore, offers me her favors. In exchange she wants what the Shadow wants—for me to write poetry in her honor.

I know I can never satisfy my longing for a ghost. The thought alone is madness! But I crave her. I want to experience her in the way that only mortals can experience each other—with taste and touch and smell. But she has none of these. She is shadow and smoke. Knowing that makes no difference. My passion won't listen to logic. And so my poetry fills with her. My sleep has begun to suffer. Day after day, I find myself desiring to commune with the dead more than with the living.

And I am no longer alone in being aware of her. La Dame's spirit is so strong she is seeping through the membrane between the corporeal world and the fantasy world. My barber claims he saw her skulking around our house late one night as he made his way home. The grocer's boy claimed to have seen her while making a delivery early one morning when it was not quite light out. Terrified, he ran away and hasn't been willing to make any more deliveries to us.

Have you heard the local legend of this Woman in White? She's one of the Druid myths that the islanders are so fond of retelling.

About one and a half kilometers from my house at Marine Terrace an imposing menhir rises from the ground. This is one of the great standing stones of Jersey, dating back to Druid times. Of that there is no question. What is less certain is the legend connected to the stone. It is said to be the vessel for the lady's spirit, her prison during the day, where she pays penance for her crime. Only at night is she allowed to roam the island; at the first rays of sun, she is sucked back into her jail.

La Dame murdered her child. In our séances she had admitted as much and claims she is the first woman on Jersey to have killed her own infant. Her punishment has lasted for the last three thousand years, and she imagines that her soul will be forever imprisoned in the great standing stone.

Yesterday afternoon she visited our séance once again, talking of eternity, infinity and the sentence she was serving for her crime. Afterward I retired to my room and spent several hours transcribing her conversation, hearing her voice in my mind and writing down all the details she shared. As I worked I became more and more heated and uncomfortable. I opened the windows to let in the breeze, but no sooner had I done so than that infernal barking started up. The noise was a terrible distraction. But when I shut the window, I found myself almost unable to draw breath.

Throwing down the pen, leaving the paper on my desk without putting it away, I fled down the stairs and out the front door. Gulping fresh air, I raced to the beach. I needed to be by the sea, far away from the Lady's smothering soul and the sound of the hellhound.

I had walked for only fifteen minutes when I heard a man call out to me.

"Monsieur Hugo?"

I turned to find the head man of the honorary police force, the *connétable* Jessie Trent. His silver-tipped baton caught the moonlight and gleamed.

"Good evening, Connétable."

Trent was a tall, fit man with deep lines around his eyes and perennial frown lines crossing his forehead. I ran into him often during my nocturnal rambles, and over the last two years we'd talked about everything from the political problems on the island to the difference between sons and daughters. His first wife had died in childbirth three years before, after delivering their fifth son. He had remarried; his new wife had recently given him his first daughter. He always struck me as an unusually responsive father: there was always a child's plaything sticking out of one of his pockets to bring home to his brood, and that night was no exception. I noticed a bit of red cloth tied in such a way that it resembled a dog.

"Have you been out walking long, sir?" Trent asked.

"Not more than a quarter of an hour. Is there a problem?"

"Did you hear that infernal racket?"

"The hounds? Yes. Why?"

"There's a child that has gone missing. Her

118

mother said there was a dog barking near the house. It has everyone nervous. You know islands like ours are full of fool legends. We're out looking for the little girl."

I'd heard a lot of the folklore about the dogs on Jersey. The most often repeated involved a black dog that roamed the cliffs of Bouley Bay in the parish of Trinity. Walkers who have encountered the hound claim he circles them at great speed and then simply disappears.

"Whose child is missing?" I asked.

"Tom Meecham's. Do you know him?"

"The fishmonger?"

Trent nodded. "Lilly is a pretty thing. Just ten years old last week."

He spoke about her as if he knew her and he probably did too. If I was correct his oldest was about that age.

"How long has she been missing?"

"We can't be sure. Lilly went to bed along with her two sisters around seven o'clock when Mrs. Meecham settled down to do mending. About an hour later she heard a dog barking outside the cottage. It didn't sound regular to her. Or to her dog, she said. He started pacing by the windows and growling. It was disturbing enough for her to get up and go around closing up. When she reached the room where her children sleep, their window was open and Lilly's bed was empty. First she searched the cottage. Then the garden and the lane.

Lilly's a good girl, and very attached to her mum. If she had heard her calling, Lilly would have come out. When she didn't, Mrs. Meecham sent one of the boys to the tavern to tell his father. Meecham came straightaway to me. Children don't go missing often in St. Helier. Of course we have our runaways who stow away on boats, but never as young as ten, and boats don't leave port at night."

"Is it possible that Lilly just went out to find the barking dog? She might be especially sensitive to how distressed that hound sounded. I know I was."

"I do think exactly that. But the question is, was the hound distressed or vicious? And while looking for him did she venture too close to a cliff? Or the sea? Did she fall? Is she hurt?"

"If there's a search party under way, Trent, I would like to volunteer my efforts and those of my sons if need be."

"And I'll gladly accept," he said. "If my men don't find her tonight we'll knock on your door at sunrise."

"No, please at least let me help tonight. I wouldn't be able to sleep now anyway, knowing what you've told me."

Trent found me a stick that would work like a baton and said he was glad to have me. "If that dog's rabid, it's better if I'm not alone. I've split all the men up in teams, but we were an odd number."

We set off down the beach.

"I know there's crime on the island," I said. "Fights, drunken brawls, thievery, but are there many unexplained crimes here? Have there been many murders?"

"She's a missing child, Monsieur Hugo, not a dead one."

But I had a feeling—one I wished I didn't have—that she was dead. Or was soon going to be dead if we didn't get to her.

"Don't be letting your imagination get ahead of you," Trent continued. "A man such as yourself who writes fine books and plays might think of the most dramatic scenario, but this is probably just a little girl gone missing while searching for a dog she heard barking."

The island's honorary police force of one hundred and fifty-seven men was divided into twelve parishes. St. Helier, having a robust population of over twenty thousand people, had almost thirty police. All of them and others, men like myself who'd heard about Lilly's disappearance, were walking the roads, searching fields and forests, climbing the rocks, exploring the caves on the beach, all calling out the little girl's name.

Lilly . . . Lilly . . . Lilly . . . The chant filled the air and became a solemn refrain. Sometimes sounding like a hymn to hope. Other times a funeral dirge.

The night grew chilly around us. We walked for

a long time, making a huge circle, and then returned to St. Aubin's bay. Elizabeth Castle was in sight. The castle can only be accessed by foot at low tide and we'd missed that. We looked out and wondered aloud if the little girl might have gotten across the sandbar earlier. The ruin is impressive during the day and foreboding at night. Especially that night. The fog was rolling in, diffusing the moonlight. But within ten minutes we lost sight of the castle as a dense mist descended. Trent insisted we curtail our search and resume in the morning. There was really little choice. We could no longer see one foot in front of the other. If we took a step too far we could go off a cliff or fall into a crevice.

The fog was so heavy that within minutes we had lost all sense of direction. "There's no use trying to find our way back," Trent said in exasperation. "We're too close to the rocks. In this soup we could come to great harm."

"What do you propose?" My face was dripping with condensation. My hair was soaked through as if it were raining.

"We need to try to get away from the sea and inland just a bit." Trent stood still and breathed in deeply. "To the right up here, there's a field of some kind, I think. I can smell the cow dung. We should be safe enough."

I could smell it too, the scent of land as opposed to the salty treacherous sea.

We followed our noses toward the earthy odor until we found the field. Trent looked like a blind man with his hands out in front of him, taking baby steps, being careful. I must have looked the same.

"There's a wall over here, Monsieur Hugo," he called out. "It will provide some shelter. Come, follow my voice."

Once we had settled down and were safely tucked into a turn of the stone wall, protected a bit from the wind, I asked him to tell me what he knew about the castle. I'd seen it often enough but hadn't explored it yet. Was it a place a child might hide? Would she be safe there overnight?

"Elizabeth Castle was named after the queen and built in 1590. It sits on the site of the hermitage where our patron, Saint Helier, lived in the sixth century. Our history books say it was first inhabited by Sir Walter Raleigh when he was governor of Jersey and then later by the future Charles the Second himself, who was seeking refuge during the English Civil War. There have been quite a few accidents since I've been a policeman. Tourists who aren't fit enough get brave and try to climb the turrets or battlements. But if she's there she should be safe enough."

"As long as there aren't any ghosts?"

"Monsieur Hugo, this isn't a night for talk of that kind of thing."

"Actually it's a perfect night for it."

"A well-educated man like yourself," he said, "you don't believe in ghosts, do you?"

I almost answered with the truth and told him that a few weeks ago I would have said no, of course not. But not anymore. "There are many things, Connétable, about which we cannot be certain."

"In any case, I should think you'd be the one telling me the stories."

"But I know all my own stories."

He laughed. It was a pleasant enough sound for the moment, but then an odd thing happened. It seemed to ricochet off the wall and echo back. But now it was hollow and pensive and full of worry. I'm sure he heard it as well as I did. But neither of us said anything. Instead he apologized for not being able to entertain me.

"I'm sorry, sir. I don't know any ghost stories to tell."

I'm not sure why I didn't believe him. Was there a hesitance in his voice? But I was certain gothic tales were hiding in the castle's stones, waiting to be exposed. Convinced you'd find one behind each granite rock you pulled out of the façade.

With both of us silent, the night's noises, almost inaudible minutes ago, became raucous. Waves crashed on the rocks, owls hooted, far-off dogs howled, crickets screamed and a lonely wind did battle with every structure in its path. While the symphony of sound assaulted me, Trent fell asleep.

Men who work as hard as he does sometimes develop the knack of dropping off swiftly regardless of where they are and how uncomfortable their surroundings. I was not as blessed, so I sat back against the damp stones, listening to noises of the night, straining to hear a young girl's cries and imagining her parents' terror.

To be a decent writer you must have both empathy and imagination. While these attributes aid your art, they can plague your soul. You don't simply suffer your own sadness, experience your own longing and worry about your own wife and children, you are burdened with experiencing the emotional states of multitudes of others you don't know.

I have only to learn about someone else's misfortune and I run, stumbling into their mind, buffeted by their pain, assaulted by their ills. Their turmoil becomes mine to bear. Their worry becomes my burden.

For me, escape is hard-won and most often found only in a woman's arms. In that very different kind of fog, I can give up, let go, become lost in the pleasure that wipes out all else.

Oh, for the distraction of a woman's smell or touch, I thought as I sat in the dark, suffering a melancholy spell that I feared would keep me in its grip till morning. It was difficult for me to remain sitting against the rocks while the night picked at my sleeve and tempted me the way a vixen might. I shut my eyes, trying to force myself to relax, to put myself to sleep. But with my eyes shut, my hearing became even more attuned. The barking dog seemed suddenly closer. His yowling more urgent. More specific. As if there was a precise communiqué in his baying. Was this the same dog I'd been hearing for days? What was he trying to say?

And then suddenly I felt a presence nearby, and I smelled smoke and incense and something else that reminded me of ancient objects that had not been disturbed for a long time. It was an odd aroma to smell outdoors so near the sea.

Thoughts of you, Fantine, came to me then. I meandered through the story about your family's perfume business as if it were a warren of streets. I peeked into windows and saw scenes you had only hinted at. Meeting your lover for the first time. You working in the perfumerie. Your father dying. Your uncle casting you out. What it had been like, to be a woman suddenly adrift, alone after a lifetime of security.

A sudden urge to see you seized me. Why at that moment? What about your story was so compelling to me? I didn't know then. But I think I do now. It was your emptiness that attracted me and made me so curious. I had never met a woman who was as empty emotionally and accepting of it as you were. Who was as dead inside and so at peace with it.

When I only know one part of someone's story, the missing pieces can plague me. I yearn to fill in the gaps. And so it was for me with you. Who was your lover? Why had he abandoned you? Had he known you were with child?

I wanted more. I wanted all the details, wanted the entire tale. It seemed more than idle curiosity. My need was urgent. But why?

You want to possess her soul so you can heal your own.

It was not my thought, but I heard it in my mind. An idea planted there by someone or something else. It surfaced the same way the words of the spirits do when they speak to me.

"No," I argued back, but silently in my mind. "I have no desire to possess anyone's soul. I am no monster."

Ah, but you are. All men are. Accepting that is the first step.

"To what?" His response had been so real, I'd answered aloud this time.

Trent was sleeping lightly, and hearing me, woke quickly.

"Has something happened?" he asked.

I shook my head. "No, I dozed off too," I lied, "and fear I was talking in my sleep."

I was afraid, but of something much more serious and alarming. Had one of the spirits from the séance followed me out of the house? Had some entity called up by our parlor games not returned to the netherworld but remained with me? Had he just engaged me in a conversation so real I had responded?

Nine

THE PRESENT
JERSEY, CHANNEL ISLANDS, GREAT BRITAIN

Most people would have found the room in the Webber Inn welcoming. The walls were covered with cabbage rose and ivy vine paper, slightly faded but in the most charming way. The wicker furniture's cushions were covered in a matching fabric that gave the room a cozy feeling. The Victorian bed offered thick down pillows and a comforter, and the floor was covered with a plush forest-green carpet.

But Jac preferred sleek and modern over antique and charming. White towels, not pink ones with lace edging. Her work was all about history. The dust of the centuries was always in her hair. She craved clean and simple when she was above-ground.

As Jac unpacked she thought about the ferry ride. Traveling through fog, without being able to see in any direction had been peculiar. The feel of the mist on her face was like moving through spiderwebs. And the odd woman who had guessed too much about her was curious.

It was as if the ferry had done more than cross the channel but had crossed some invisible barrier and deposited her somewhere out of time. She couldn't even get a sense of what Jersey looked like because the island too was shrouded in fog. There hadn't been anything exotic about the few glimpses of streets and buildings, cars or people she passed during the twenty-minute taxi ride here.

She knew from studying maps how remote this island was. How cut off they were. She couldn't just leave if she wanted to. She'd need to wait for a boat to get away—one way to England, the other to France.

Jac put the last of her clothes in the closet, stowed the suitcase and sat down at the desk, where a jug overflowed with old-fashioned damask roses. These were perfumers' favorites, grown since ancient times for their fragrance. Lowering her head, burying her nose in their velvet petals, Jac inhaled their sweet perfume.

Few modern scents captured the true intoxicating beauty of the flower the way her family's *Rouge* did. It was the only rose-based perfume Jac ever wore. But even *Rouge* didn't compare to the flower itself.

When she lifted her head, she noticed that

outside the window it appeared the fog was lifting. It was only six o'clock and would be light out for another two hours at least, and she wasn't expected at Wells in Wood till seven thirty. Theo Gaspard had emailed earlier that week inviting her to dinner her first night in Jersey.

As long as you're not too tired, he'd written. And asked her to please feel free to call and cancel if she was. *Don't feel pressured,* he'd added. *We have to dine with you or without you. So other than picking up one place setting, Claire won't be too put out.*

Who was Claire? Housekeeper? Sister?

The only thing Jac knew for sure was that she wasn't Theo's wife, since he'd written he was a widower.

Jac wasn't tired. After the last few days in London, her jet lag was gone. But even if she had been feeling any effects from the journey, she was too anxious to meet Theo again to wait. She was also intrigued to see the house he'd described as an ancient monastery built on what were believed to be Celtic ruins. Other than saying there was a funeral mound on the grounds as well as several other ancient ruins, he had kept his description vague.

I don't want to spoil it for you, Theo had written. *You'll have plenty of time to explore. I'd rather be vague and let you be surprised.*

Even though the scent of the roses was lovely,

130

Jac reached for the travel candle she'd brought with her and lit it. This was her ritual whenever she arrived at a new place. Infusing hotel rooms with the scent of *Noir* settled her. As the fragrance filled the corners and seeped into the fabrics, it transformed a strange room into a familiar one. With so few constants in her life, and so much of her family gone, scent was how she remembered and kept herself sane.

Jac showered and changed. She'd learned the art of dressing from her grandmother who was French to the core. As much as Grand-mère loved her daughter-in-law, she never appreciated the insouciance of Audrey's blue jeans and boots, worn leather jackets, T-shirts and Indian beads, and neither did Jac. She admired her grandmother's style and adopted it as her own. The principle was simple. You buy the best there is, even if it means only one good piece a year.

Jac stepped into a pair of black gabardine slacks. Then pulled a round-necked, cream-colored cashmere sweater over her head. She didn't like wearing colors. Her mother had been wearing a bright green blouse when Jac had found her. Like an abstract canvas, it had been spattered with perfume oils that stained the fabric.

Jac slipped her feet into ankle-high black suede boots and zipped them up. She shrugged on a black and cream tweed jacket. Vintage Chanel that had belonged to her grandmother. The last touch was a matching cream cardigan sweater, tied around her neck like a scarf.

In her ears, Jac wore the small but brilliant diamond studs her grandparents had given her on her twentieth birthday. Her only other accessory was her mother's Cartier watch. White gold, it hung loose around Jac's wrist like a bracelet. The tiny diamonds on the 12, 3, 6 and 9 were so small you only knew they were there if you looked for them. There was more jewelry in the vault in Paris, but Jac had never claimed it. Generations of pieces that had passed down from mother to daughter, daughter to son stayed locked away. Jac felt encumbered by those jewels. As if the stories and dreams attached to them weighed too heavily on her when she wore any of them.

But her mother's watch was different. Sometimes she imagined the ticking was her mother's heart, still going, still beating. Even more than Jac mourned and missed her, she hurt for her. Audrey hadn't been able to fight her demons.

It was a failure that had profound effects on the twelve-year-old son and fourteen-year-old daughter she left behind, the full scope of which Jac would never really know. Who would she have been if not for the tragedy that sculpted so much of her personality?

Jac grabbed her bag, another vintage piece that had belonged to her grandmother, and left her room.

"Forty-five minutes, as long as the fog doesn't creep back again," Noreen O'Neil said as she unfolded a map to show Jac the way to Wells in Wood on foot. "And you can't be sure it won't." The proprietress had stylish auburn hair cut to frame an oval face. In her sixties, her skin was creamy and she carried her age well. Wearing navy slacks with a white sweater and simple strand of pearls, she was dressed to impart graciousness but not outshine any of her guests.

"You start here and follow this path, which will give you a lovely view of the sea. But then it's uphill for quite a ways," Mrs. O'Neil said as she pointed to a pathway with a gnawed wooden pencil. "And here you'll have to go through some woods. I don't recommend it this late in the day. It's not lit for nighttime strolls and some of the paths border the cliffs. If you dawdle and it gets dark, you could seriously hurt yourself."

But Jac had hiked and trekked all over the world. She'd gone underground in Egypt and above the clouds in Peru and had never gotten lost. She had a compass on her cell phone, the phone itself and the hotel's number as well as the number of the Gaspard house.

"Thank you. I won't dawdle, so I should be all right." She reached out and took the map.

"But mind you, you can't come back that way. Not at night. Not under any circumstances. The house is up there on the rocks. It's a lonely place.

The old man made sure of that. Nothing could be built on it that wasn't already there. He wanted it left rough the way he'd found it."

"Made sure?"

"One of the grandsons wanted to develop some of the estate. But Alexander Gaspard had protected it in a trust. No one can build a stick of a structure on it for the next hundred years. No matter how good his intentions, he's controlling that family from the grave." She shook her head. "It's wonderful the land is protected, but wills that cause strife among the living aren't good things."

Jac wanted to find out more about the Gaspards, but being too nosy her first day there wasn't smart. Jersey was obviously a small island. A few too many questions before Jac knew all the players and where they stood could backfire. She was, after all, a guest of the Gaspards.

"We can come and get you after your dinner," Mrs. O'Neil said as she handed Jac a card. "We have a service, my son is the driver. And a very good one," she added, and smiled.

Jac thanked her and pocketed the card.

Outside, the breeze ruffled the map as Jac consulted it. Four routes were marked in different colors. In her room she had a more complicated topographical map downloaded to her tablet, but for the walk she was glad to have a simple printed foldout.

The path Mrs. O'Neil had pointed out was easily marked and led her around the back of the hotel and along a cliff walk with an unobstructed view. Patches of fog still clung to rocks and hovered over the water, but there was more than enough visibility to see the shoreline, and the distant lighthouse. The horizon was out of focus, and the sky seemed to just melt into the sea. In the mist the vista looked like an impressionist painting, both atmospheric and suggestive.

As she stood and stared, Jac breathed in and sniffed. The salty air reminded her of summers with her brother and her grandmother in the south of France. No matter how often she talked to Robbie on the phone, it wasn't the same as spending time with him. When this excursion was over, she planned to go to Paris for a few days to be with him before returning to New York. Robbie was her staunchest protector and champion. And the only other person in their family who loved the water as much as she did.

Malachai had once joked that Jac must have been a mermaid in another life. She wasn't sure which point to argue—that there were no mermaids or that there was no such thing as reincarnation. She'd done neither. Issues and conflicts, strong likes and dislikes could be manifestations of a myriad of things. Not necessarily ever, as Malachai suggested, residual leftovers of previous life traumas.

"If you could just grasp one thread of who you've been—of what you've lived—you'd be able to reel that past in and learn from all your different souls," he'd said to her. "Your career is all about learning from the past. Why are you so resistant to this?"

Stubborn, her mother had called her. Robbie often teased her about that aspect of her personality too and told her that objects that were too rigid had a greater propensity to break than those that could bend. He was an artist with scent and a practicing Buddhist who brought his Zen sensibilities to the family perfume business.

The path curved around a clump of trees and then brought Jac back to a different view of the island's coast. She could see a wide stretch of beach where the shore met the rock. In the shadows of the cliffs were openings to caves. There were over two hundred of them, she'd read. More than had ever been counted or could be, since fallen rocks and land shifts over the years obscured openings.

While most of the caves had already been explored, Theo had written there were still some undiscovered. But what were the chances that the one he'd alluded to hadn't already been found and stripped? What clues did he have? He hadn't really revealed anything.

Jac climbed as the path rose up an incline, and then after hugging the edge of the cliff for a few

136

hundred feet, she followed its turn, heading inland.

The woods here were thick with ash, oak and silver birch trees. Now Jac smelled resins and earth with only a whisper of the salty sea. The combination reminded her of a fragrance she had created when she was younger. She sniffed again. It was almost exact. How curious. As she walked deeper into the forest, she thought about how long ago she'd mixed that particular juice and how proud she had been of it.

When Jac was ten and Robbie eight, their father had built them a child-size perfumer's organ modeled after the giant multitiered desk where every generation of L'Etoiles had practiced their art.

The full-size organ housed over five hundred bottles of precious essences and absolutes—the perfumer's tools. The miniature contained almost a hundred. A treasure to the children. Enchanted with their gift, they'd invented a game: building scents evocative of emotions and actions. *The Fragrance of Loyalty. The Perfume of Shame. The Perfume of Liars.*

Jac had used the same scents she smelled now— forest and sea smells—to create what she'd named the *Scent of Memory.* At the time she hadn't been able to tell her father why she thought those smells went together and why she thought they related to memory. But now, walking through this ancient forest that her research had suggested might be eight thousand years old, she realized how right she'd been to choose just those essences.

The ground beneath her feet was packed down with the detritus of the ages. Twigs, leaves, seeds, nuts all crushed and trampled on, turning to compost, becoming soil, nurturing more trees and plants that fell and started the process all over again. The water in the sea evaporated and rained back down into the sea. An endless process that Jac had always believed moved ahead in one direction. Just like time.

But in the last few months she'd been presented with the possibility that time was not a straight-forward stream. Robbie and Malachai believed it was a continuum that the soul traveled in no one direction, but in all directions, returning to where it began and then jumping across ponds of centuries to find other selves living other lives.

Entering a grove of hazels, Jac walked down a narrow center aisle, noting how the ancient trees' arthritic branches twisted and turned. Nature was a fine sculptress as well as perfumer. A leafy canopy shaded the allée and the air smelled sweet. Hazels were rich with symbolism, and the air around them was said to be laced with magically charged energy that helped those who breathed it to gain wisdom and poetic inspiration. Witches practicing white magic used wands made of hazel.

Forked sticks of hazel wood were used like divining rods to find buried treasure.

At the far end of the passageway was a large stone slab sitting on six stone pillars. In Jac's research she'd seen pictures of Jersey's dolmens, but she hadn't expected to stumble on one her first day here. Something about how the monument fit the site made it look as if, like the hazel trees, the dolmen had grown in this spot from stone seeds.

Jac approached the small pagan temple and stood before it. Felt the wonder of the history that shrouded it. In awe of fragments of ancient times, she marveled at it. The men who built this were long gone. And with them the meaning of the stone arrangement. But proof of them remained. It wasn't enough, but it was something. It was a lot.

She'd been right to come. To get away. To throw herself back into work again. Yes, the monuments on Malachai's property were intriguing. But there was so much more potential here. It was like comparing a tiny department store perfume sample to a full bottle of juice.

Jac didn't know how long she stood there before she became aware of the humming. Then the wind blew through the trees and she lost it. When the wind died down she heard other sounds. Crunching leaves. Breaking branches.

Then a pair of dark eyes glittered at her from out of the shadows and a dog barked a sharp warning.

Startled, Jac stepped toward the stones as if they could protect her.

The dog ran out into the clearing. She was a beautiful sleek creature with wavy and silky fur in a mixture of browns, blacks and creams. Sniffing and inspecting Jac, she seemed to be assessing her to see if she was a threat.

"Tasha, come back, girl. Tasha!" a male voice rang out.

The dog turned, looked back, but didn't take off.

Through the trees, Jac saw a man approaching.

"Tasha!" he called again. The dog didn't move. "Tasha, come!"

The man was close enough now for Jac to see that he was tall and lean with sandy-colored hair. His jeans were tucked into boots and he was wearing a worn brown hacking jacket.

He reached the clearing, looked at the dog, then followed Tasha's gaze toward Jac. His face was in shadow.

"I'm sorry. I hope she didn't frighten you. She's really very friendly." His accent was British. His voice was deep and seemed to pour out of him.

"No, she didn't."

"Or at least not too much?" he joked.

"No, not too much. She's beautiful. I've seen paintings with dogs like her in them—but never seen one in person. What breed is she?"

"A Russian borzoi. And yes, very popular with artists in the 1920s. Their profile fit the times.

Borzois are excellent athletes. She's my great-aunt's—but I offered to take her for a run so I could send her out looking for you. Asked her to find the prettiest girl in the forest."

Jac was taken aback.

He noticed and frowned. "You are Jac L'Etoile, aren't you?"

She nodded.

He stepped forward out of the shade. "I was pretty sure but then was worried I'd made a mistake. It's me, Jac. Theo."

"Theo?" She tried to match this grown-up man to the teenager she'd known. The dirty blond hair that fell into his face was darker than she recalled. He had laugh lines around his eyes now. His two- or three-day stubble made him look even older than he was. The deep hollows in his face aged him too. His eyes showed a raw unrelenting pain that unsettled her. Once, when they had been close, it had been all right for her to see those emotions. But now she felt as if she were intruding.

There was an awkward moment while she waited and wondered if she should shake his hand or if he was going to reach out for her. They'd lain in each other's arms in the sun on the side of the mountains. Touched. Kissed. She knew the smell of his skin, of his hair. But so little about this man standing in front of her was familiar. When he was at Blixer Rath he'd been a young boy with so

141

much before him. Troubled, yes. But there had still been the aura of possibility around him. Now he was thirty-three and seemed almost ruined. So much of their time at Blixer had been spent together, holding hands, breathing in each other's breath. She'd forgotten all that physicality till now, and suddenly was shaken by the memory of it. So she didn't move closer, didn't respond, just waited awkwardly as if she were fourteen again and meeting him for the first time.

"I didn't know it was you," she said.

She half hoped he'd come forward and put his arms around her and fuse their long-ago bond, but he stayed where he was. Only his eyes embraced her.

"I could tell that." He pushed his hair back off his forehead in a well-remembered gesture and offered a self-deprecating smile, and she could see the boy she'd known.

Finally she smiled back and felt as if she had arrived at her destination. The island suddenly seemed like a welcoming place. She took the step forward, not him, stood on her toes and kissed him on the cheek. His arms moved around her back. It was familiar and at the same time slightly awkward. They had lived complicated lives since Blixer Rath. So many years had passed. And then there were the recent tragedies. He'd lost his wife. She'd lost her way.

They separated and he started walking, leading

her in a different direction from the one she'd thought led to his house.

"When I saw your picture in your book, I recognized you instantly," he said. "You're not fourteen anymore, but your face . . ." He looked at her frankly, assessing her, in a way that might have been rude if they hadn't known each other so well so long ago. "You haven't changed as much as most people do. I can still see the girl I knew."

Jac had been attracted to Theo when she was a teenager, so she knew she shouldn't be surprised to feel the stirrings of that attraction again. But she was. She knew this wasn't real and of the moment; it was a memory response. She'd have to be careful to stay aware of that. The last thing she was ready for was a romantic liaison. She'd only said good-bye to Griffin two months ago. And from his letter she knew Theo was still deeply mourning his wife.

"How did you find me? How did you know I'd be here?" she asked, suddenly wanting or needing to fill the silence with banter that didn't have any subtext.

"I went to the hotel to fetch you, and Mrs. O'Neil told me you'd taken off on foot. She said she'd warned you it can get dangerous out here in the dark; why didn't you listen to her?"

"It's not dark yet."

"But it will be soon. Evening falls early and quickly here. I know these paths well, but it still can get dicey once the sun sets. Bad things can happen in these woods."

"Dicey? As in ghosts?" she asked, surprised she'd asked such a jejune question and done it with so little panache.

But he wasn't looking at her as if it were an odd juvenile query at all.

"Well, I meant dicey as in wolves," he answered. Paused. "But yes, some say ghosts too. Does that frighten you?"

"Which, that there are wolves or that there are ghosts?"

"Either? Both?"

"Well, I'm not scared of ghosts," she said. "I don't believe in them."

"That's good."

"But the wolves do give me pause."

"That's good too. One shouldn't underestimate the power of nature's creatures. They rarely attack humans unless they're rabid, but then they can be very dangerous and entirely capable of killing. There's a horrible local legend about a little girl stolen by a wolf from these woods." His voice ended in a deeper register. He was frowning again. "Be careful; there are some thick roots under this foliage. Don't trip."

With the twilight descending, the forest was taking on a more sinister aspect. After a few minutes, they reached a fork in the path. Jac realized that she might have lost her way in these woods after all. The route Mrs. O'Neil had drawn on the map didn't include this turning point.

"It's this way," Theo said. "I'm parked just on the other side of these trees."

Once they'd reached the road, Theo opened the Range Rover's back door for Tasha and then the passenger's door for Jac.

Inside the car she was aware of Theo's scent: eucalyptus, honey, cinnamon and oakmoss. The same he'd worn at Blixer. She'd asked him about it once and he'd told her the name, but she'd never heard of it.

With the memory, Jac suddenly remembered the feel of Theo's skin when they lay in the grass, exploring each other. She looked at his hands on the steering wheel. The same long lean fingers that used to touch her.

As the scenery sped past, Jac watched the green turn to black as what was left of the day gave way to night. After a quarter mile on a narrow twisting road, Theo turned into a long driveway that cut through a forest of silver birch trees. The configurations on their white and black slender trunks looked like eyes. Thousands of eyes watching out from the woods. After a few hundred yards they reached tall stone pillars. On one was a simple bronze sign.

Wells in Wood House
Private

"How long has your family lived here?" Jac asked as the road curved through more woods. There was still no structure in sight.

"My grandfather used to say Gaspards have been in Jersey as long as the stones. But if you mean this house, since the mid-eighteen hundreds. It was a monastery first, built in the twelfth century. Then rebuilt in the fifteenth. In the last hundred and fifty years, the family had it renovated and made additions, but the original structure is still intact."

At the next bend, in the sunset's last light, a sweeping vista came into view. Tall hazels bordered this road. Many of them looked as if they'd been there for centuries too. Shaped by the constant wind coming off the water, they were slightly bent over like old men.

From a distance, it looked as if there were stones placed in between the trees, but as they passed the first and then the second, Jac realized they were almost life-size sculptures of hooded figures. Simple modernized forms of men in habits, their faces hidden in their cowls. Some faced the driveway. Others turned toward the house. An army of holy men protecting their fortress.

"Are the sculptures old or new?" she asked. "I know some ancient sculpture has a simplicity that makes it seem current. These could be either."

"Old. We've done some research on them and they predate the foundation of the monastery. The stone they were carved from is prehistoric, so it's difficult to date them precisely, but the experts think they were sculpted around one hundred CE. "

"During the Iron Age, then, when the Celts lived here."

"Precisely."

"They're so evocative," she said, unable to tear her gaze away from the monks.

"And quite scary when you're a little kid." His voice was full of shadows. "Especially when you look in their faces. Each one seems as if he is seeing right through you . . ."

He'd been alternating between melancholy and rebellion at Blixer Rath, Jac remembered. Either he stayed by himself in the library reading for hours, or he was challenging every rule, as if he needed to prove he could break them all.

Now that she was seeing where he grew up, she realized how much like this place he was. The unyielding monuments. The rugged cliffs. The haunted woods.

"Did you spend your whole childhood here?" she asked. "For some reason I thought you were from London."

"We lived in London till I was eight and my dad died. Mum brought us back here. My aunts and uncles and cousins all lived on the grounds. It was a big family then, with my grandfather at its helm."

"You said your mother brought *us* back?"

"My brother and I."

His voice had shifted again. Now it was flat and without emotion. Despite not really knowing this adult Theo, Jac could hear his tension and was certain there were problems between the brothers.

"Younger? Older?"

"Younger. He's followed in the family tradition and become a banker." He said *banker* almost as if it were a dirty word. "And here we are," Theo added as they approached the house, effectively ending conversation about his sibling. Jac realized he hadn't even used his brother's name.

Ten

The dimly lit estate loomed up out of the evening mist. There was just enough light to illuminate its presence but not enough to make it a beacon. It wasn't welcoming but rather curiously inviting. Challenging almost. As if it were a puzzle daring you to try and solve it.

No stately country manor with grace and charm, this edifice was characterized by bewildering excess. The center two-story building must have been the monastery Theo had mentioned. Clearly it was the most ancient. Flanking it were two wings, three stories high, each slightly smaller

than the one beneath it—like a stack of boxes—
each topped with a round turret.

The windows on the additions didn't match the
mullioned windows on the original. In fact they
seemed an almost deliberate assortment of
different sized and shaped windows, starting with
tall arches on the first floor, squares and ovals on
the second and smaller rounds on the last.

There was a Juliet terrace on the second floor of
each wing and a curious wraparound walkway
winding around each turret.

The only things consistent across the main
building and the extensions were the shale roofing
tiles and gray stone. These must have been
indigenous to the island because they matched the
cliffs Jac had seen on her walk. In fact the more
she looked at it, the more she thought the house
looked as if it had been carved out of the rocky
landscape.

"It's astonishing," she said.

"It's a monster." He parked and then came
around to open her door, but Jac had already
gotten out. "Too big. Too costly to keep up. Too
much history to tear down. It holds too many
secrets and has seen too many sins."

As they walked to the front door, Jac could hear
the sea. "Are we on the ocean?"

"Almost everything in Jersey is. Come look."

Theo detoured to show her how the house was
indeed built on the edge of a high cliff.

Out over the Channel, the sky was washed with the purples, blues and grays of evening. The house's stones were the same hue. In this light, the building blended into its background, almost as if Wells in Wood weren't quite real.

As they reached the front door, Jac heard an owl's distinct soft hooting and, as she crossed over the threshold, thought about Malachai. He'd be taken by this moody place and its history. She wished he'd given his blessing for this trip, but they'd argued up until she left. His parting words shouldn't have disturbed her but did: "If you need me for anything, call. Make sure that you keep my phone number on your cell in case of an emergency."

"What kind of emergency are you talking about?" she'd asked.

He shook his head. "Hopefully we won't find out."

Inside harp music played. A lush and ethereal accompaniment to the colors in the night sky, the twisting trees, the dour-faced figures and this house. The scents of frankincense and vanilla suffused the air. Her senses bombarded, Jac stood inside the front hall with its high ceiling and looked around.

A gargantuan chandelier—made not of crystal but of large translucent ostrich eggs—hung down from a thick silver chain. The light it gave off was a diffused and muted yellow hue. Byzantine and medieval religious artifacts filled dozens of small niches scooped out of the smooth stone walls. A faded gilt wooden Madonna glowed in the buttery lamplight. A Celtic cross studded with cabochon jewels gleamed. There were urns tucked into the recesses. Fragments of early stained-glass windows, broken pieces of stories, studded the walls, illuminated from behind.

As Jac inspected them she saw they weren't religious allegories but mythological scenes. Icarus and Daedalus on their ill-fated sun voyage, Leda and the seductive swan, the Minotaur in his labyrinth.

"Welcome to the Gaspard shrine to antiquity," Theo said with some rancor, as if he resented his home.

"It's astonishing. This house must have so many stories."

"And my grandfather tried to collect them all. In fact he died searching for more."

"Was he an artist?"

"No, a banker, but one of the few with a soul."

"Theo?" A woman called out in a resounding voice. "It's drafty in the hall. Do come in. I'm just making drinks."

"Right there," he said. Then he put his hand on Jac's arm, holding her back for a moment. "I told them you were an old friend. I didn't say anything yet about what you do for a living or that you're going to help me search for a Druid ruin."

151

There was no time for her to ask any questions. But she wondered why he'd kept her purpose here a secret.

As Jac and Theo walked into the great room, the white-haired woman seated at the harp ceased her playing. The final notes hung in the air. The reverb lingered. Only when they dissipated did she lift her head, rise from the small delicate gilt chair and walk toward her guests.

"Hello, you must be Jac L'Etoile," she said, extending her hand. Her voice was reedy and her hand was thin and very small. The veins showed through her papery skin like a map of her life. Only about five feet tall, she walked with a slight limp. Her deep-set blue eyes matched her elfin features.

"This is my aunt Eva," Theo said, introducing her.

"Welcome," Eva said. "And this is my sister, Minerva." She gestured toward the bar in the far corner of the room. Jac was surprised to see the woman from the ferry, holding a pitcher of what appeared to be martinis.

"Well, hello!" Minerva said. "I never asked your name, did I? But I should have guessed. How many young women would be coming to the island off-season?" She nodded toward the pitcher. "Now it's my turn to offer you refreshments. Would you like a martini?"

"Yes, that sounds wonderful," Jac said.

Minerva gave her a glass with a delicate stem and then proceeded to pour.

When everyone's glass was filled, Minerva raised hers in a toast. "Welcome to Wells in Wood."

The drink was iced perfectly and just dry enough. Jac enjoyed its first bite as she took in more of her surroundings.

Three of the walls were covered with a mélange of art. Drawings and paintings crammed side by side. No one piece was given more attention than the others, but when you studied them, you realized how really good they were. A small fortune hung on the walls, Jac thought. The fourth wall was all glass and faced the sea. Jac walked over and looked out. She felt as if she were hanging over the ocean and if she opened the windows she could dive down to the water. The sensation turned from fascination to fear almost instantly, and she stepped back quickly, retreating from the temptation.

Minerva was there instantly as if she'd sensed something. She took Jac by the arm and brought her back into the center of the room. "Come sit down," Minerva said, gesturing to the seating area where two sea-green velvet couches faced each other. Jac settled into the soft cushions and realized that the room seemed to be arranged in sections.

In one corner a grand piano sat next to the harp.

In another was an easel, a drafting table and a taboret overflowing with art supplies. In the third corner a loom was set up in front of shelves filled with a rainbow of colored yarns. The weaver was spinning a beautiful sea-blue cloth that shimmered in the lamplight. And in this corner, beside the couches, end tables were piled high with books, needlepoint projects and sketch pads.

"What a wonderful room," Jac said.

"We spend most of our time here," Eva answered. "The house is so very big, and since there were just the two of us here, we shut off quite a bit of it. Even with Theo here it's still cavernous."

"Can I look at the loom?" Jac had never seen one in person and was drawn to it.

"Of course, let me show you." Eva got up and together they walked over.

"Are you the weaver?"

"Yes." Eva nodded.

Jac wasn't surprised. The harp and the loom seemed like extensions of each other.

"She's very modest," Minerva said. "My sister is well known in Jersey for her fabrics and is considered one of the island's finest artists. She's had shows in London."

"I'm not surprised," Jac said. She was mesmerized by how the threads wove in and out of each other. "This is so beautiful. Like you've turned the sea into fabric."

"Thank you." Eva beamed. "It's a privilege to be able to make beautiful things." Her eyes clouded a bit, her smile faded. "We need more of them. We can never have enough of them."

Jac was disturbed by the dainty woman's sudden melancholy. It had descended so quickly. "The house is lovely too. As are the grounds," Jac said. "I can feel the past here . . . it's very evocative." And sad, she wanted to say but left out in deference to Eva.

But it was sad, she thought. If you looked for it you could see the sadness everywhere. In the cobalt color of the weave. In the worn navy rugs and pale robin's-egg walls. The house was tinged with blue. It seeped through the stained-glass pieces and threw shadows on the floor. It was as if the house were in mourning. Without knowing it consciously, Jac had been aware of it since she walked in. Heard it in the harp music.

"Yes, there's so much past here with us," Minerva said. "These grounds have been inhabited for centuries. The monastery is so old. Many souls have passed through these rooms, and so many of their ghosts live here with us still. We can't seem to clear them out." She laughed.

Minerva had mentioned ghosts. Theo had mentioned them too.

Eva was quick to qualify her sister's comment. "She didn't mean literal ghosts, of course. Not real ghosts." Eva was talking quickly as if she were sweeping away her sister's comments. "We don't have ghosts other than the figurative historical ones. You can't take two steps or look in any corner of this house without bumping into someone's past or their passion. Their portraits. *Objects d'art.* Their books. Their furniture. Everyone in the Gaspard family has an antipathy to throwing anything away."

The dinner table was set with delicate Limoges plates decorated with a gilt, green leaf and violet pattern and heavy silverware Jac was certain was at least a hundred years old.

Eva acted as hostess and fussed over everything; the meal was served by a young woman with red hair named Claire, who wore a fresh white shirt and black slacks. This was the woman Theo had mentioned in his invitation to dinner.

The roast chicken was crispy, the potatoes buttery and the tomato, zucchini and garlic stew was piquant and sweet at the same time. The fine crystal glasses were kept filled with the robust burgundy. Chopin's nocturnes played in the background.

On the wall facing Jac a mural depicted a bacchanalian Greek scene of a feast in the fields of Elysium. She recognized Hermes, Aphrodite, Athena and Apollo. The artist had rendered them in an aesthetic Pre-Raphaelite style and they were all a bit too tall and too beautiful with slightly removed and haunted expressions. But she was drawn to them.

"The murals are beautiful," Jac said.

"We have a long history of artists in the family. My grandmother painted those," Theo said.

"Before she went mad," Eva said. "She was beautiful. And brilliant. But batty."

Minerva shot her sister a reproachful glance. Jac guessed that as a therapist she didn't appreciate the unprofessional idiom.

"Well, it's true, isn't it?" Eva defended herself.

"She had an associative personality disorder," Minerva said. "You know that."

"She was crazy," Eva countered. "And she was hardly the only one. Our family has had our share of disturbed relatives."

"I'm not arguing that point. Just the choice of the word *batty*," Minerva said.

Eva bristled. "Ever the academic."

"The interesting thing about families," Minerva said to Jac, "is how ingrained our childhood roles are. My sister and I are still really only eleven and thirteen. Do you have any brothers or sisters?"

"I do, a brother. Robbie's two years younger than me. And we do that too. Argue about the same things in the same way we did when we were kids."

Eva sighed. "It can be tiresome when you've been at it as long as we have."

"So you and Theo are old friends," Minerva

said, obviously changing the subject. "How long have you known each other?" she asked Jac.

Unsure what she should or shouldn't reveal, Jac looked over at Theo for a second, searching his face for a clue about what was okay to say and what wasn't. But she couldn't glean anything.

"We met the summer I was fourteen."

"In Switzerland?" Minerva asked.

Jac understood the woman was being cautious by only saying Switzerland. If Jac hadn't been at the clinic, Minerva wouldn't have revealed anything about her nephew's past. If she had, then she'd know what Minerva was referring to.

"Yes, at Blixer Rath."

Eva leaned forward in her chair, an expression of concern on her face.

Jac wasn't sure if it was compassion or worry that another "batty" soul was at her dinner table.

"Were you there long?" Eva asked.

"A little over a year."

"We don't need to talk about Switzerland," Theo interrupted. "It's long ago and far away." His voice was strained. "Jac, why don't you tell my aunts about what you do. I'm sure they'll find it fascinating."

Why didn't Theo want her to discuss the clinic? She'd have to ask him later. Now she told them about *Mythfinders*.

"So that's the work that's brought you here?" Minerva asked once Jac had finished.

"Yes. If there is any actual proof of the Druids, anything, it would be quite a find. There's so little we know about them that we can be sure of." Jac wondered if Theo was going to step in now and explain more.

But it was Eva who spoke: "After dinner we'll have to take you on a tour of the house. We have a lot of artwork here to interest a mythologist. We have all the great legends covered from ancient Egyptian, to Greek, Roman and Celt."

"Our grandfather believed he was reincarnated from the Celts," Minerva said.

Jac noticed Eva shrink back in her chair a bit. "Another example of our family's peculiarities."

"Reincarnation?" Jac asked.

"The family has been involved for decades. One of my ancestors was a major figure in the spiritualist movement in England," Theo said. "Pierre Gaspard, the man who built this house. Didn't you know that?"

"Why would I?"

"He was involved with what was at the time called the Phoenix Club, as was his son later on. I assumed Malachai Samuels would have told you. The Phoenix Club is the forerunner of the Phoenix Foundation."

"I know that, but not that your family was involved with it," Jac said.

"Malachai's well aware of it. We talked about it at length when I was at Blixer. In fact that's how I got there. Other families have connections to Oxford, we had connections to a mental clinic."

"And to Oxford too," Minerva said, then turned to Jac. "My ex-husband taught Malachai Samuels when he was a student there."

Jac was confused. Why hadn't Malachai mentioned anything about Theo's family connections? He often talked about the cabal of men and women who'd started the Phoenix Club in the mid-1800s. Why leave out the fact there was a Gaspard in the mix?

"In fact most of our family has remained fascinated by reincarnation," Minerva was saying. "My grandfather used to talk to me about it when I was a little girl. It's what led me to Carl Jung and the psychology of the collective unconscious."

"Not all of us are so fascinated with the past," Eva said. "I prefer dwelling in the present."

Jac was half listening while she tried to put all this information in context. While she was at Blixer, Jac hadn't known Malachai was a reincarnationist. It was only later that her grandmother had told her. In fact it was why Grand-mère had lobbied for Jac to go to Blixer. None of the conventional treatments had helped stop Jac's hallucinations. If there was any chance her granddaughter's problems were related to a life before this one, Grand-mère was willing to give it a try.

Clearly in Theo's case there had been no leap of faith in sending him to the unconventional clinic. Malachai was well known to the Gaspard family. Minerva's husband had taught Malachai at Oxford.

So why *hadn't* Malachai said something before she left? Why had he kept this family's history and interests a secret?

Eleven

SEPTEMBER 15, 1855
JERSEY, CHANNEL ISLANDS, GREAT BRITAIN

As soon as dawn broke the next morning, dozens of men joined in the hunt for Lilly, the fishmonger's missing child. There were no able-bodied men in St. Helier who didn't come out to walk the beaches and forests, search in the caves and ruins. The plentiful rock temples and burial grounds on the island were old and many had crumbled in on themselves, creating perfect hiding places for a child. Or a child's body.

The effort was made all the more difficult by a steady rain that started just as we set off and didn't abate all morning. It cast a spell of gloom that wasn't needed. We were already worried that the child had fallen off a cliff and been drowned. With so many rock shelves and such a voracious sea it was more likely than any other scenario. But no one wanted to give up hope and so we kept searching—fathers, sons and brothers—all secretly sharing a fear of dreaded discovery.

Trent and I were joined by six others who combed the shore, traipsing in and out of caves, exploring ancient rock formations and looking for somewhere she might have gotten trapped. Each time a large wave crashed we watched the beach to see what was deposited on the sand. None of us wanted to be the one to find her— hair matted with seaweed, cheeks scratched by sand.

Of all of us, I think I was most terrified by the idea of such a sight, for it would be the manifestation of the image I had been seeing in my mind for a decade of my drowned Didine.

"What would have made the child leave her bed?" one man asked another. "A barking dog should have scared her, not enticed her."

It was a logical question, but I could picture a likely scenario. I saw the child going to bed in the room she shared with her sisters. Saw her close her eyes. Dark eyelashes a shadow on rosy skin. Saw the pale blue vein in her neck. Saw her little neck loll as she relaxed into the bedding. Watched the rise and fall of her chest slow. Heard her deep breaths. And then . . .

I saw the dog at the window. A dog with liquid topaz eyes that appeared almost human. A black creature, larger than most dogs, with a coat that gleamed in the moonlight. He probably looked hungry.

Children love animals. Lilly had grown up with dogs. This one's barking could have concerned her. Why would she have been scared? There was a dog in her window with limpid eyes who looked like he was starving.

The tide was low and Trent suggested we walk out to Elizabeth Castle and search the ruin and its environs. While it was unlikely she was there, no area could be ignored. If she had been abducted, her captor could have taken her to the castle on a boat. If she was on her own and following the dog, she could have walked out across the sand bar last night when the tide was low and spent the night like us, camping out, sleeping, then waking and wandering around the castle. It was a favorite playground for island children. Exactly the kind of fairy-tale structure that excites their imagination. She might not even realize the havoc she was causing.

I'd meant to visit the cavernous ruin since I arrived in Jersey. Abandoned and unused for centuries, it was a tourist destination and nothing else. Finally seeing it, I was surprised by how truly desolate it was.

Four of us walked through the great carcass of a building that morning. To this day I've never discussed what occurred at the end of that visit, for I cannot explain it. After I escaped from the castle—and yes, I use the word knowingly—and stood gulping in the fresh sea air, I decided it would be prudent not to speak of it lest people think I had gone mad. Perhaps I should have. Perhaps I might have avoided some of what came to pass.

As soon as we walked through that first stone archway, the damp took hold of me like a vise. Gripping me and wrapping around me. In Jersey the humidity permeates everything, but this was concentrated. As if the castle's rocks had sucked up years of moisture and it were all leaking out now.

The fortifications were a meter thick and cut with long narrow slots that let in light and ventilated the rooms. Outside the sun intermittently broke through the clouds, and as we crossed the floors we cast long shadows. Some of the walls were partially covered with the tattered remnants of tapestries. Once they must have been beautiful, but they were now so threadbare they looked as if you could blow them away with one good breath. I could see ghostly bodies visible in the weavings. Faces, arms and legs, partially eaten away by the elements and moths. Like decomposing corpses, I thought, as if I needed another metaphor for what happens in the grave.

The only words we spoke as we ventured deeper into the shadows of the citadel were those we used

164

to call out to Lilly. Her name echoed as we explored the wreckage.

Some of the roof was intact, other sections had rotted out. The furniture was in a pitiful state of decay. Wood that must have once gleamed was now worm-eaten and destroyed by the damp. The giant dining table was covered in dust. Its chairs overturned, their guts hanging out, perfect nests for mice. The drawers were missing from a large breakfront, the gaping holes black and deep.

Nature had taken over in a way that I wasn't used to. In Paris or Naples or other important cities, the paucity of space can't allow for large structures to languish and rot. Needs require they be rehabilitated, or if it they are beyond help, torn down and something new put up in their place.

We climbed a still-intact stone staircase. It was in the second upstairs room I visited, that I guessed had been a nursery because of the two small-sized bed frames and wooden cradle, where I first became aware of the scent. The smell of the briny sea air that filled the castle was suddenly replaced by the aroma of smoke and sweet incense. Had someone come in? I turned around. No, I was alone.

I looked at the fireplace, half expecting to see a fire burning. But there was nothing except dust in the hearth. There was simply no explanation at all for the perfume.

In my exasperation, I called out to the *connétable.*

Trent and one of his men came running.

"Did you find something?" Trent asked.

I shook my head. "Do you smell that scent? Someone has been here recently."

The men sniffed the air. Nodded. "I smell flowers," Trent said.

The other said, "Smells like a fire," then sniffed again.

But there were no flowers and no blaze. So where was the aroma coming from? The room was an ordinary rectangle with but a single door and two long casement windows. The walls were empty save for a large tapestry that had slipped and hung at an awkward angle.

This one was as decrepit as those we'd seen downstairs.

Could something be behind it? A child hiding?

I pushed it aside. Fabric disintegrated at my touch and fell at my feet. There was in fact something behind it. Not a child but a doorway.

Holding my breath, I opened it.

It was a simple closet. And it was empty.

Carefully I ran my hands over the walls, examining them, searching for hidden panels.

"Is anything there?" Trent asked.

"Nothing," I said. As I turned to go, I happened to glance down and notice the trapdoor incised in the wooden planks. A metal ring nestled in a depression made to hold it. I tried to pull it up, but it appeared too rusted to move.

"Give me a hand," I said to Trent.

Using his knife, he was able to pry the ring up. I held my breath as he pulled the door open. Together we peered in. There was nothing but dust and the bones of some vermin inside. Rats, I thought from their size.

"We might as well move on," Trent said, after the disappointing revelation. "There's nothing here."

He and the other policeman walked out, but I remained behind. I was still confounded by that scent. *Where was it coming from?*

I walked around the perimeter of the room once more, examining the stone wall, pressing here and there and trying to find a second hiding place. I didn't find anything. When I got to the fireplace I stopped and sniffed once more.

Was it my imagination or was the scent slightly stronger here?

It must have taken huge fires to warm these rooms and chase away the damp, so it was no wonder the hearths in the castle were oversize compared to those we had at Marine Terrace or in Le Havre. I actually was able to walk inside the fireplace opening without stooping. Bending down, I touched the iron cradle positioned over the ash box. It was covered with cinders and cold.

How long ago had the last fire burned here?

Who had lit it? Had it been decades or centuries? Or was my romanticism getting the best of me? It might have been last week when boys camping out here had roasted themselves some dinner.

Looking up the long chute, I glimpsed a sliver of sky so blue and vibrant compared to the gloomy rooms, it cheered me for an instant. That's when I realized the scent of smoke and incense was in fact more pronounced here than it had been anywhere else in the room.

The stones inside the fireplace rose straight up for a meter and then stepped back. It was a curious design, and I didn't understand why it would have been built like that. As I walked around the ash box to better examine the back wall, I dislodged the dregs of that last fire. Puffs of black dust caught the draft and swam in the air. I coughed and rubbed the dust out of my eyes. Able to see again, I shone my torch on the right wall. Then the left.

What I saw wasn't visible when you stood outside and looked in. Like the back and the right wall, this one rose a meter and then stepped back. Beyond it was a riser and then another tread. It was a stone staircase leading down, presumably to the ground floor and then perhaps deep into the castle's underbelly.

I did not hesitate and descended, following the scent, ten steps, then twenty, then forty and sixty until at eighty-five I reached the bottom and found myself opposite a heavy wooden door that opened with only a modicum of difficulty.

Inside was a surprisingly uncorrupted room almost untouched by the rot and damp that had ruined so much of the furnishings in the rest of the castle. The tapestries on these walls were still intact, unharmed by moths or mice. Each of the four was a different view of the same garden with animals, including unicorns and phoenix, frolicking with a group of young children. The foregrounds were filled with plants and flowers, many of which I'd never seen before. These tapestries were fine pieces of art, as well made as any I'd seen in Paris museums.

So taken was I with the sight of them, it took me a moment to realize that I'd found the source of the smell I'd been following. The scent emanated from these fabric blossoms and blooms.

Impossible, but true.

I was inhaling smoke and incense, roses and hyacinth and jasmine and something else I couldn't catch hold of. How was this possible? The longer I stood there, the more confused I became, until I began to wonder if I was getting drunk on the aroma.

I was tired—but shouldn't I have been? I hadn't slept the night before. And I was slightly dizzy. But I hadn't eaten except for an apple Trent had given me that morning. And I'd just climbed down four flights of stairs.

A dog barked. The sound had come from the right. I turned. The tapestry featured a group of canine creatures romping near a waterfall. I heard the barking again. It seemed to be coming from a large black dog who was closer to the size of a goat. He was looking out at me with topaz eyes that seemed to glow. Not with malevolence but intelligence.

My exhaustion and desperation must be affecting my imagination, I thought. I could still feel the grit in my eyes. Maybe it was affecting my vision. I rubbed my eyes once more and then opened them and stared at the tapestry. Now there was a child with the large dog. A little girl with blond hair. She hadn't been in the scene a moment ago. Or had she?

I shut my eyes. Counted to five. Opened them.

The child wasn't playing anymore. Now she was crying in pain and reaching out to me. There was a wound on her arm that could have been a dog bite. It dripped blood. Twigs and leaves were tangled in the child's hair. She had a nasty scratch across her cheek.

I didn't stop to think. If I had I would have questioned my sanity. I simply raised my arms, reached out to the silken creature and offered her my hands.

Her fingers were not thread but flesh and felt warm in mine.

The dog barked again. Was he warning me? Saying good-bye to her?

"Hold on tight," I said to the child and then pulled her out of the tapestry and into the room. The effort and release caused me to fall backward. I went sprawling and she fell on top of me.

Her blood was wet on my hands. I had to do something to stop her bleeding. She was pale and her breathing was shallow. The child was in serious danger.

Don't interfere.

I didn't hear the voice as much as sense it, almost the same way I did at the séances.

Let her go.

I recognized the voice but couldn't stop now to question it. The child's wound had to be tended to. Taking off my jacket, I made it into a pillow and put it under the girl's head. Then I used my vest to apply pressure to her wound.

This is the chance I said I would give you. Let her go, Hugo. Let the child go.

I didn't understand what he meant. All my energy was focused on saving Lilly.

Ego misplaced is an opportunity lost. You're waging a war against the wrong angel.

I kept the pressure against the wound.

This is what I am offering you. Don't you understand? Don't you want your daughter back?

"Hugo? Are you there?" It was Trent calling from above.

"Yes, but I need help. Quickly. Down here."

"We're coming."

The dog growled and kept growling until the men arrived.

"Oh my lord, is she all right?" Trent asked as he rushed over and knelt down beside us.

"I think she will be," I said.

"Let me look." He bent over her, taking charge. I was glad to be relieved of the responsibility. Surely the head of the police force would be better equipped to deal with a medical emergency than I was.

The shouts echoed up the stairs and beyond.

"She's all right."

"Hugo's got her."

"Hugo found Lilly."

A roar went through the castle as the news reached all the men.

After a few long, long minutes, Lilly opened her eyes. She looked first at Trent and then at me. She appeared confused, unsure of where she was or what had happened to her. But not in very much pain. She was a stoic child and didn't whimper or cry but let Trent inspect her wound, take her pulse and listen to her heart.

We were interrupted by heavy footsteps clattering on the steps as the fishmonger came rushing into the room. He uttered a short exclamation of joy and then knelt down by Lilly's side. Looked at her, touched her hair gently, then gathered the little girl in his arms. He murmured to her, a string of questions that he probably didn't expect her to answer.

"Are you all right, Lilly? What happened? How did you get here? We were so afraid."

She buried her head in his chest and her little back shook as she wept, finally letting go now that she was safe in her father's arms.

Once Trent had checked again and was sure that the bleeding had stopped, he told the fishmonger he could take Lilly home.

Both of us watched them leave.

"Well done, Monsieur Hugo," Trent said. "We can go now too. I'm sure you want to be getting home."

I let Trent start up the stairs, while I lingered for a moment. What had happened? I didn't understand. I waved my torch back over the tapestries. The group of doglike creatures were back to romping near a waterfall. I inhaled, but the scent of smoke and sweet incense was gone. I took a last look around so that I would remember this place, knowing one day I was going to want to write about what had happened. Then I turned my back on the room and began the ascent up the stairs. It went slow because I was spent and dizzy again with the effort or confusion or hunger, or all of them combined. As I climbed, my footsteps echoed in the narrow stone stairwell. That was all I heard until I reached the final tread. And then I heard a distant barking.

Was it a farewell? A warning? I had no doubt which canine creature was trying to communicate with me. It was the beautiful black dog with the topaz eyes. I just didn't know what he was trying to say.

Twelve

After Jac and Theo and his aunts had finished the main course, Claire brought out an apple tarte tatin. The perfectly browned and glazed confection scented the air with the combination of caramelized sugar and butter. Slices were served along with a dollop of thick cream on the side.

"Jersey cows," Eva explained after Jac complimented the luxurious taste. "The butter and cream here are better than anywhere in the world."

"Not that we're prejudiced," Theo teased.

Claire walked around the table and poured coffee.

"Theo told me a little about this house," Jac said to the two sisters, "but I'd love to hear more of its history."

Minerva looked at her sister. "Why don't you do the honors? You don't rush through it the way I do."

Of the two sisters, Eva did seem like the mistress of the house. Other than making the drinks, Minerva had left everything to her. But she'd watched her make sure everyone had what they needed, fuss with the flowers on the table, smooth the tablecloth and reposition the silverware. And when she wasn't watching Eva, Minerva was observing her nephew. It occurred to Jac that the woman was monitoring both of them in a clinical way. Keeping tabs on them and making sure nothing was awry.

Eva began the tale. "Our ancestor, Pierre Gaspard, bought the monastery and its surrounding land in 1850. He was a jeweler, who like Tiffany in the United States, had begun working in stained glass and had aspirations to turn this place into a workshop and glass factory for lamps, windows and extravagant vases. He didn't need much of a house. He was a childless widower who never anticipated marrying again. So he set aside a few rooms to use as living quarters and turned the rest into a showroom. He built a factory on the grounds too. All became his canvas. We have letters where he calls it his version of Ali Baba's cave. He'd traveled extensively and was taken with the exotic story. There are even a series of windows upstairs that illuminate the famous tale.

"Everything changed though in 1855, when Victor Hugo, who was living in exile in Jersey at the time, introduced Pierre to a young Parisian woman named Fantine."

"I didn't realize Hugo lived in Jersey," Jac said. "I thought he lived in Guernsey."

"He lived here for the first three years of his exile," Eva explained. "In St. Helier right by the sea in a house called Marine Terrace. It's gone now, though, long ago turned into moderately priced housing."

"Fantine was a perfumer," Theo said to Jac.

Jac felt as if she had stepped into an irrational alternative universe where too many seemingly unconnected events connected back to one central starting point.

There are no coincidences, Malachai always said.

"A perfumer? What was her name?"

"Well, she married Pierre, so her name was Fantine Gaspard. I don't know her maiden name," Eva said. "Do you, Minerva?"

"No. They were married here so there might be a record of it in the town hall. Is it important?"

"My family have been perfumers in Paris since before the French Revolution. I was just curious."

"Oh, I should have made the connection. House of L'Etoile perfumes? I love *Verte*," Eva said, naming a fragrance Jac's father had created in 1987. "Of course you'd be interested in Fantine, then. The story is she came to Jersey because of problems she'd encountered in Paris. A family crisis, or some kind of scandal. Hugo might have known her in Paris first. How they met and what their relationship was has never been quite clear. But we do know he befriended her and introduced

176

her to Gaspard, who fell in love with her perfumes and then with her. At the end of 1855 they married. He built her a perfume workshop. They had a daughter within the year. Followed by four sons."

Claire came into the room. "Would you like me to make more coffee?" she asked.

When no one said they wanted any, Eva thanked Claire and then suggested they move back into the great room for after-dinner drinks.

A fire was blazing in the hearth, illuminating brilliant iridescent turquoise, sea-green and lilac tiles framing the fireplace. They were the same colors as the threads in Eva's weaving.

"Are those tiles Pierre Gaspard's work?" Jac asked.

"All the tile work and windows in the house are, yes," Minerva said. "My mother once told me that those were Fantine's favorite colors."

All the L'Etoile's signage included those three colors and had since the inception of the firm. Jac had seen the antique blue, green and lavender boxes and bills in the archives. She hadn't noted the color scheme before. But the turquoise, aqua and lavender were repeated and echoed in the heavy velvet and raw silk upholstery, rugs and chandeliers. It didn't seem possible that Fantine could have been a L'Etoile before she married. But Jac would have to call Robbie later and ask him to investigate.

Theo asked if anyone wanted any brandy and then poured glasses for himself, Jac and Minerva. Eva declined.

"What happened to Fantine and Pierre?" Jac asked.

"They prospered," Eva said. "Pierre's stained glass and jewelry were much sought after. Two of his lamps are in the decorative galleries of the Louvre," she said. "But for the women in our family, Fantine was the hero. She was quite unconventional for her time. Few women then had vocations out of the theater arts. But despite managing her duties as a wife and mother, she created and sold perfumes. She and Hugo remained friends too. He even gave her some drawings. They're all hanging here and there at the house."

"He wrote her often after he moved to Guernsey and continued to stay in touch once he returned to Paris. We have some of those letters," Theo said.

Jac noticed that at the mention of the letters, Minerva frowned and Eva started to play with a red braided thread tied around her wrist.

"Wasn't the name of the prostitute in Hugo's *Les Misérables* Fantine? The woman whose child Jean Valjean takes care of?" Jac asked.

"Yes," Minerva said. "One and the same. Named for our ancestor."

"They were very close," Theo said. "Hugo introduced Fantine to spiritualism."

Eva turned her head sharply toward her nephew. "We don't have to go into all that."

Minerva smiled at her sister reassuringly. "Relax, darling, talking about it really isn't going to do any harm. We've been through this." She turned to Jac. "Yes, Hugo was involved in spiritualism."

"I had no idea," Jac said.

"Yes, his politics overshadowed some of his more esoteric leanings, but he was extremely involved. He had more than a hundred séances at his house while he lived in Jersey. Pierre Gaspard was a frequent guest at many of them."

"Hugo kept records of all the sessions," Theo said.

"We have a book of transcripts," Minerva added and nodded toward the hallway. "It's in the library if you're interested."

Eva was playing with the red braided thread again. Turning it half a rotation to the right, then bringing it back to the center. Then turning it to the left.

"Jersey is a very spiritual place," Eva said, as if this were medicine she needed to take. "Some say even magical. Of course Hugo would be affected while he lived here. Everyone is. We have hundreds of Neolithic monuments. Wells and sacred springs every few hundred yards. There's one behind the house. Druids were said to have bathed there. I think that's why there are so many churches on the island. Paganism is in the soil here even though the church kept on building to try and tamp it down."

"I'd like to hear more about the séances," Jac said.

"Have you ever been to one, Jac?" Minerva asked.

"No."

Minerva stood up and walked over to the corner of the room where the easel rested. Behind it was an elaborately carved wooden credenza inlaid with more of the turquoise, purple and sea-green tiles that framed the fireplace.

Minerva opened one of the drawers.

"What are you doing?" Eva's voice was tight and high-pitched.

"I just thought I'd show Jac some family history. I think she'd be interested."

"I don't think you should," Eva said.

On the opposite side of the room, one of the glass doors blew open. Jac felt the cool wind brush past her.

"See!" Eva exclaimed. No longer just apprehensive, she sounded afraid.

Theo got up quickly, strode over to the door, closed it and locked it. "It's nothing, Aunt Eva."

"That never happens," Eva said. "Why would it have happened at just that second?"

"Of course it's happened," Minerva said. "It happens all the time."

"No. It's because of you. What you're doing. I

don't want you to," Eva said to her sister. "I've asked you before."

Jac was uncomfortable. Whatever was going on between the sisters wasn't any of her business. Putting down her glass, she turned to Theo.

"It's been a long day and a lovely night but I think I should go back. Do you think you could call a taxi for me? Mrs. O'Neil said there'd be no problem getting one to pick me up."

"I'll drive you back," Theo said.

"No need to go to that much trouble."

"No trouble."

But there was trouble. It had settled over the house and crouched in the corners.

Thirteen

Theo was taking the turns in the road too fast, Jac thought. Fog had settled over the island again and his headlights illuminated only a few dozen yards ahead. The ride seemed as if it might go on forever. The woods she remembered being on either side of them were now invisible. No cars passed. They could have been going anywhere. Or nowhere.

"Why didn't you tell your aunts why you'd invited me here?" she asked.

"We may not find anything, so I didn't want to get them excited."

"Good excited or bad excited?"

"Good excited," he said, but she wasn't sure he was telling her the truth.

"Really? Your aunt Eva seemed worried when you mentioned the letters."

He accelerated as he took the next bend. When he answered, his words were measured. "Eva is nervous about her own shadow. She doesn't like upheaval. Status quo is her heaven. She hates the idea of me picking up where my grandfather stopped."

"Your grandfather?"

"He was looking for the same treasure I'm looking for. That's how I found the letter. It was in a book with his belongings after he died."

"How did he die?"

"He fell out on the rocks and broke his hip, then got pneumonia."

"How long ago was that?"

"Eleven months."

"How horrible. You lost both your grandfather and your wife in the last year?"

He nodded. "I appreciate your concern, but can we move on?"

Jac sensed his pain and felt awful for him, but he clearly didn't want to dwell on his grief. She could understand that. So she returned to what was confusing her about his aunt's reactions to his quest.

"Minerva hardly seems the kind of person

who'd be nervous about anything. I'd imagine she'd relish the idea of the search as well as the potential find." She was thinking back to the ferry ride when Minerva had told Jac they were both seekers.

"Yes, she would. And you're right about her, she's not the nervous type at all."

"Well then?"

"It's me. She's concerned about me."

"Can you tell me why?"

He drove on without answering. Was he concentrating on the road? Considering her request? Composing a response?

"She thinks I've been too preoccupied with my wife's death."

"How does that have—"

He cut her off. "I haven't really been able to work through the mourning process. Minerva thinks it's premature for me to take on this project."

"I'm not sure I understand how one could have to do with the other."

"You need to read the letter. It's at the house in the safe." Theo drove on for another moment in silence. "I'll bring you back tomorrow when both of them are working. And then we can talk about how to proceed. I really don't know how to go about doing this without an expert."

"Despite your aunts' concerns?"

"I asked you here, didn't I? I think this could be

as important a find for you as it is for me. And not despite their concerns, but because of them."

"You're right. I don't understand."

"You will."

Up ahead was a glimmer of light coming from the hotel. The atmosphere in the car lifted now that there was something besides fog outside the windows.

"Do you understand how you got to this point in your life, Jac?" Theo's question was so serious it caught her off guard.

"I haven't ever thought about it."

"We get to any given point via the choices we make. Even those that seem insignificant have far-reaching implications. Do you think you've made all the right choices?"

She thought about the question. "No, of course not. I'm sure I haven't."

"Do you understand why you've made them?"

"Probably most of them. At least at the time."

"I don't understand why I've made most of the decisions I've made. Sometimes I feel as if I'm reacting, but I don't know to what."

She looked at his face in profile. He had grown into his high forehead and long nose. He'd been disturbed and confused when she'd known him before. And still was. Had there been stretches in between when he'd had periods of peace and calm? She hoped so.

Theo pulled up in front of the hotel and put his

hand out on her arm. It wasn't an embrace; he was keeping her there, stopping her from getting out yet. "You helped me a great deal when we were at Blixer."

"And so did you help me." He'd given her moments when she could move beyond her mourning and be exhilarated. Hours at a stretch when she didn't wonder if she was going crazy or not. During so much of the time they spent together they were both just two kids, exploring, rebelling and finding themselves in each other.

He looked surprised. "I don't remember that. Seems to me I got you into loads of trouble."

She smiled. "That too. But no, you helped. You'd let me talk on and on about my mom. It must have been boring but you never acted as if it was. You'd let me talk myself out and then help me climb out of that past and into the present. Maybe I can repay the favor a bit while I'm here."

He turned his head and looked away. Jac wasn't sure if he was hiding his reaction from her or had just been distracted. When he turned back, his expression was inscrutable.

"I have to go to the gallery first thing in the morning. But I can pick you up at noon if that's convenient. You can look at the letter and we can have some lunch. Does that work?"

"Yes, that's fine."

He got out of the car and came around to open her door.

"Are you all right here?" He nodded toward the hotel. "Would you like to come and stay at Wells in Wood? You're welcome to."

The house was fascinating and she was tempted, if only so she could spend more time exploring its artwork, its history and secrets. But she didn't relish the idea of giving up her privacy.

"I'm fine here," she said, and smiled.

Theo leaned in.

At first she thought he was going to kiss her on the lips. And she hadn't moved to avoid it. A fact that surprised her. But at the last moment, Theo seemed to change his mind and planted the kiss on her cheek.

Inside the hotel, Jac walked by the lounge on her way to the staircase. She wasn't tired yet and the room looked inviting with a roaring fire, an old-fashioned bar, small tables and cozy slipper chairs.

She sat at the bar, ordered a glass of port and looked around.

There were only two occupied tables. At one was a middle-aged couple writing out postcards, and at the other two men were poring over some papers.

Jac tried not to listen, but the room was small and their voices carried.

"It's a good plan," the younger one said. He was in his thirties, aristocratic-looking, with high cheekbones and a shock of blond hair. The other man was heavyset and about fifty.

"I thought so too, Ash. I'm glad you agree." He glanced at his wristwatch.

"It's been a fruitful meeting. Why don't you let me take care of the check? Don't wait for me. You have a wife at home."

The man stood. From his slightly deferential attitude and the way he said good night, Jac guessed he worked for Ash, not the other way around.

After gathering up his papers, Ash stuffed them in a worn leather portfolio and then tucked that under his arm. On his way out, he stopped at the bar.

"Thomas? Can I settle up?" he said to the barkeep.

Ash was standing close enough to her for her to be able to smell his scent and identify its notes: lemon, verbena, bergamot, tonka bean, patchouli and something else she couldn't decipher. It was always the elusive ingredients that intrigued her. Usually she could articulate every note, but sometimes the way an essence changed depending on what it was mixed with altered it beyond recognition. She sniffed again. Tried to single out that one missing element, but it was hiding. Jac was surprised at how much she liked the fragrance. She was demanding when it came to modern scents, even those her brother created.

This was the first in a very long time that had intrigued her. It was sensual, with a hint of citrus, which her father always said made a blend more inviting.

Ash sensed she was focusing on him and turned. He gave her as frank an appraisal as she was giving his cologne.

Jac was momentarily caught off guard. For a moment, thinking she knew him. But no. She was good with faces. His was strong but somehow incomplete. As if a sculptor had been carving his face but never gave it the final polish. She knew that if she'd met him before, she would have remembered. Just as she decided it was a déjà vu, he introduced himself.

"I'm Ash," he said, offering her his hand.

She shook it, and flinched. He'd given her a shock. He smiled. "Ah, static. Sorry about that."

She looked down at the floor. There was only an area rug. Static? But it had to be, because what else could have caused a shock?

He finished introducing himself. "Ash Gaspard."

Now she understood why he looked familiar. He resembled Theo, but with lighter hair and a less troubled countenance. That must have been what she thought was missing.

"Hello. Actually I know your brother," she said.

"Really?" He seemed surprised.

"Yes. He's the reason I'm here in Jersey."

"Would you mind if I got my drink?" He nodded at the table where he'd been seated.

She should go up to her room, it was getting late. But when Theo had mentioned his brother, Jac had sensed there was tension between them, and now that she'd met Ash, she was curious.

He was back in a few seconds with a balloon of brandy.

"So what exactly brought you here to see my brother? A job offer perhaps?"

She was slightly confused and told him no, and then gave him the same explanation she'd give Theo's aunts, that she was here doing research on Druids on Theo's recommendation.

"Yes, well, if that's what you're after, there are certainly enough ruins here to keep you busy for months." He took a sip of his drink. "Wait a minute, does this have something to do with that damned letter?"

Since he obviously knew about it, she nodded.

"Wild goose chase. We should sell the damn thing and bank the money."

"Sell it?"

"As a piece of ephemera with that signature it would probably fetch at least four thousand pounds."

Theo had never told Jac who'd written the letter and she didn't want to let on that she didn't know, so she just nodded. "So you don't share Theo's spirit of adventure?"

"Is that your question?"

"My question. As opposed to whose?"

"My brother's. He and I don't see eye to eye on this." Ash shrugged. "Or on many things. Complicated family dynamics."

"Not all that unusual."

"I suppose not." The sadness in his voice was palpable. He sipped his drink. Then shook his head as if he were having a conversation with himself. When he didn't add anything else, Jac filled the silence.

"Wells in Wood is a wonderful house. Do you live there too?"

"Not in the main building, I have my own place on the edge of the grounds. It's too crowded for me in that old drafty relic. My family has made holding on to memories into an art form."

"You don't like history?"

"I appreciate it, but I believe in living in the present."

"Just what your aunt said."

"Eva." He laughed. "She's a character. Minerva is too in her own way. I can't imagine how they've managed to live together for so long without killing each other." The light tone was gone and one far more serious had accented the last part of his comment.

"But you can't blame anyone for holding on to memories," Jac said. "Letting go has its own timetable."

"Now you're talking about Theo."

She was about to say yes, then changed her mind. That wasn't the truth. And for some reason she wanted to tell Ash the truth. "No, actually I was talking about myself."

Ash gave her a look that was both compassionate and questioning. "I'm sorry. I do know how hard it is to get past a loss."

"You shouldn't be so hard on your brother," Jac said.

"He's not making any effort. And my aunts aren't helping. Eva coddles him. And Minerva . . . well, busman's holiday and all that. She's too close to him. And there we are. How embarrassing that we're talking about my brother again. I apologize. Tell me more about you. What exactly is your job that it allows you to go searching for Druid ruins?"

She explained about the show.

"Mythology," he said. "Well, you fit right in with the Gaspards. Since you were at the house, I assume you saw the murals?"

"I did, they're extraordinary."

"I'm not up on my myths. It's more my aunt's and my brother's—" He stopped, paused and then interrupted his own thought. "Wait, are you the girl who was with Theo at Blixer Rath?" Before she could answer, he spoke again. "Oh, I'm sorry. That's rude of me. It's your private life."

"No, that's fine. Yes, I was."

"I know about you. Theo only talked about two things when he came home that summer. Mythology and you. He was totally smitten. He seemed to think you two had some kind of strange connection. Am I right?"

"Yes."

"What was it? Something to do with a drawing?" She nodded. "Yes."

"I was so jealous. Hated you quite a bit, in fact."

"Hated me?"

"Back then I looked up to him. I was so pleased when my father said Theo was coming home sooner than expected. Until he actually arrived, that is. If he had been troubled before he left, he was even more distant and disturbed when he came back. He wouldn't explain anything to me. Treated me with even more disdain. All he did was write you those letters and—"

"He wrote me letters?"

"Yes. Dozens. He wrote you every day for weeks."

"I never got them." Jac wondered if Malachai had prevented her from receiving them.

"That must have been why he finally stopped writing." Ash took a long sip of his drink. When he put it down, the glass clinked sharply against the bar. "He doesn't know this, but I read a few of them. Though I'm not proud of it now. It was cheeky and none of my business, but I was desperate to understand what had happened to him while he was gone to push him further into his depression."

"And did you?"

"No." He paused. "But he seemed to think you were a key to his getting better."

"Really? I don't know why."

"Neither do I. You do know my brother is very troubled, though, don't you? I say even more troubled. It's more than just his current state of endless mourning. He's been depressed for a long time. As long as I can remember. I doubt you're going to appreciate me giving you advice since you don't know me—or I you—but please, be careful."

"Of what exactly?" Jac felt instantly protective of Theo. First Malachai, now Ash.

"My brother's intensity isn't always good for those around him."

"I don't think it's necessary to warn her off me, Ash. You've already done enough damage in that arena to last me a lifetime."

Jac spun around. Theo was standing behind her, glaring at his brother. The book about Victor Hugo's years in exile was in his hand. He held it out to Jac.

"You left this in the car. I got halfway back to the house and noticed. So I thought I'd bring it round. You seemed so keen to read it."

She took the book. "Theo, thank you. I was—"

"How did the two of you wind up meeting?" Theo interrupted, quizzing her. His tone was accusatory, suspicious, and she was taken aback.

"Purely by accident. I wasn't ready to go upstairs and—"

"It was a coincidence, Theo. Drop it," Ash said, stopping Jac from explaining further. "I saw a pretty girl alone at the bar and stopped to say hello. Really, don't go rooting around and looking for sinister motives."

"I'll decide what to do," Theo said.

"Speaking of deciding—so you've taken up the search again?" Ash asked Theo.

"I never gave it up. I needed help from an expert, and now that Jac's volunteered, I have it. If there's any chance that there's a secret journal in one of these caves, I can't leave it there to rot."

Ash shrugged as if he thought the effort a folly. "There's other work waiting for you. Work that you've been leaving to rot that's more urgent."

Jac wondered what work that was. In the art gallery?

Theo turned to look at Jac dead on, blocking out his brother. "So I'll see you as planned tomorrow?"

"Yes, of course."

Theo nodded toward Ash without taking his eyes off Jac. "This is my brother's modus operandi. He tries to poison people against me. He's full of crap, though, is all."

Then he leaned forward and kissed her lightly on the lips and walked out of the bar before Jac could respond. To what he'd said. Or done.

Upstairs in her room, as Jac undressed and got ready for bed, she went over the scene in the bar and tried to order her various reactions and impressions. That the two brothers were battling each other was obvious. She could almost smell their aggression toward each other.

Jac's grandfather had trained her to sniff the air for emotions. He believed powerful feelings affected a person's body chemistry and that if you were sensitive to it, you could smell those changes. It was just one of his theories. He was always proposing new ideas about aroma or reintroducing ancient ones. Not only was he a perfumer, he was also a student of Egyptian mystery schools, Greek philosophy, alchemy and the magicians of the Middle Ages. He also studied the Egyptian Book of the Dead, the Gnostic bibles, the Kabala.

"Perfume is magic. It's mystery. We re-create the smell of a flower. Of wood. Of grass. We capture the essence of life. Liquefy it. We store memories. We make dreams," he told her once. "What we do is a wonder, an art, and we have a responsibility to do it well."

Jac had never forgotten how he tried to hide his disappointment when she told him that she wasn't going to become a perfumer. He loved mythology and he said he was proud that she'd chosen a subject that fascinated him too. But she could see through his words to read the letdown on his face. Jac knew he'd dreamed of her and Robbie together wearing the mantle that her ancestors had borne for almost three hundred years.

How fascinated he would have been with the house she'd visited tonight, Jac thought. And how curious Grand-père would have been to hear the story about Fantine, the exiled perfumer from Paris, who lived there and cooked up scents to fill her husband's jeweled flacons.

Robbie would be just as intrigued. Suddenly she was homesick for him. She tied her robe around her and walked toward her bag to get her phone. To call him. Just then, the cell began ringing. Jac was startled but not too surprised. They were close and often sensed when one was thinking of the other. But glancing at the LED readout she saw it wasn't Robbie. It was someone else who would be just as interested in the house she'd visited and the people she'd met, but for very different reasons.

"Good evening, my dear." Malachai's mellifluous voice came over the line. "I thought I'd check in."

After their repeated arguments about her making this trip, she half expected him to launch into a tirade that she come back, and when he didn't, she relaxed and told him about the house and Theo's aunts.

She was glad the tension between her and Malachai was behind them.

"I was surprised when Minerva told me she knew you. You didn't mention that."

"I didn't? I thought I had. Yes, I knew her and her brother and I studied with her husband at Oxford. He was a fine therapist and so is she. But tell me, Jac, how do you find Theo?"

Brooding and disturbed, she wanted to say but didn't. No need to bait Malachai. Instead she chose a less provocative way of describing her childhood friend. "War-torn, I think. He said he hasn't been able to really get past his wife's death."

"Did he tell you how she died?"

"No."

"I did a little research."

"Why am I not surprised?"

"Would you like to know?" Malachai asked.

"Would it matter if I said no?"

He laughed.

Sometimes, like tonight, his laughter had a tone in it that reminded her of a character named Waldo Lydecker in the 1940s black-and-white murder mystery *Laura*. Played by Clifton Webb, the acerbic Lydecker loved Laura in his own twisted way, more than he could cope with. He had an imperious laugh. As if he stepped down to laugh. She didn't like it from the character in the movie, and even less from Malachai.

"His wife drowned, Jac."

"How horrible."

"Yes. It was horrible, truly horrible."

There was silence on his end.

"Malachai? What aren't you saying?"

During the pause that held for another two or three seconds, Jac flashed on Ash talking about concerns for her in regard to his brother.

"It was ruled an accident," Malachai said, putting emphasis on the word *ruled*.

"Yes?"

"She'd recently started seeing a therapist and rented a flat in London."

"What does any of that mean? People who rent apartments or see therapists never get in accidents?"

"There was some suggestion she committed suicide."

"Even if that is true, how is that going to scare me away from looking for a cave used by Druids?"

"When the two of you were at Blixer Rath you were uncharacteristically sympathetic to Theo."

"So you've said. But I still don't understand your point."

"I think he has unresolved issues, and I don't want you to become entangled in them. Just promise me that if you have any concerns, you'll come home."

"I promise I'll call you. Is that enough?"

"At the first sign?"

"Yes. All right?"

"Yes."

"Now I have a question for you."

"What is it?"

"Why did you keep the information about Theo's family from me? I found out tonight that one of his ancestors was an original member of the Phoenix Club. The whole family seems to have believed in reincarnation and various aspects of spiritualism. In all the times we talked about me coming here you never mentioned any of that. Why?"

"Doctor-patient confidentiality."

"Which part was confidential? That his family history intersected with yours? That you knew members of his family?"

"Discussing any part of a patient's background is unacceptable, Jac. You know that. If I talked about one patient to you, you would never trust that I didn't talk to another patient about you."

"Did you also know Theo's grandfather?"

"Yes. I met him first when I was a boy living in London. They had a house in town in those years as well as in Jersey, and owing to the Phoenix

Club connection our families saw each other fairly often. Alexander was quite a bit older than me, but it turned out we had many of the same interests. There was another sister too. A very nervous sort. I can't remember her name. "

"Eva."

"Ah yes, now I remember. Their grandfather had been quite obsessed with exploring the unknown and included the children in his experiments. Alexander and Minerva took to it all but I seem to recall hearing that Eva was a bit traumatized by it, and his death affected her badly. There were allusions to an accident." He paused. "But no one ever talked about what had happened exactly."

"I can't believe you didn't tell me any of this before I left."

"It was confidential."

In the background Jac heard voices on Malachai's end.

"I have a patient, Jac. I have to hang up. But call me, please. Keep me posted, yes?"

"Yes, I will. As long as you promise to stop worrying."

"Just humor me and check in every day. This is a good time, all right?"

She started to argue but he cut her off.

"I can't keep my patient waiting. Take care, my dear." And then he hung up.

Jac poured herself a glass of water and then called Robbie, but her brother's cell phone went to voice mail. She left a message, told him she missed him and then slipped into bed. The sheets were high-quality Egyptian cotton. Cool and crisp, they smelled of fresh air. She was relieved. Some hotel laundries used terrible commercial scents. There'd been nights when lighting her candle and spraying the bedding with cologne didn't camouflage the smell, and she'd slept with the window open even when it was too cold.

She'd left the window open tonight too. But not to chase away any odors. Rather to invite in the mild breeze and the sea air.

The pillows, mattress cover and comforter were goose down and Jac didn't feel as if she was lying in the bed so much as floating on it. Even for a quality hotel, the bed was luxurious beyond expectations. She closed her eyes and in the dark, listening to the sea pound the shore, she let her mind ride the waves.

Picturing Wells in Wood, she walked into the front entryway. Saw its hundred niches filled with fragments of ancient art and medieval relics. She'd learned the memory game from her grandfather. The ancient Greek mystery schools had taught that if you put each memory in a certain room in an imaginary mansion, you could store them there and revisit them at will. Now, Jac revisited the dining room. Looked at the murals again. Then faces of the people around the table. Eva, Minerva and Theo. She thought about how

201

he'd changed since she'd first met him. And how he'd stayed the same. She remembered back in time. In Switzerland.

Although Jac had been miserable when her grandmother left her at the Blixer Rath clinic, the beauty of her surroundings hadn't been lost on her. Paris was noisy, crowded and smelly compared to the Alpine retreat. The closest neighbor was five kilometers off and the silence of the Alps reached out to her and offered soothing solitude right away.

There were seven other young adults, from twelve to seventeen, already in residence. Full capacity was twelve. The staff consisted of three doctors and two teachers: an art and music teacher who painted and played both the piano and violin, and a science, math and humanities teacher. In addition some of the therapists taught certain classes. The staff consisted of a cook, a gardener and two women who cleaned and did laundry. Almost as many people worked there as came for help.

In the mornings after breakfast the students went to classes. The doctors preferred the term *students* to *patients*. "You're not here to take medicine and get better," Malachai had explained on Jac's first day. "You're here to study your psyche, learn from it and then use those lessons to develop coping skills."

Each student had his or her own curriculum.

Sometimes there were others in your class, but just as often you were one on one with the teacher. Jac's first class of each day was mythology, followed by a drawing class, then a piano lesson and geometry.

No one explained why she was taking those particular classes as opposed to others, and when she asked, Malachai cryptically told her they were the classes she needed.

During the afternoon each student worked individually with her therapist for ninety minutes. The rest of the time was theirs to do with as they pleased.

When Jac got to Blixer, the seven students there had been together for at least three months and had all bonded. Jac didn't fit in. The problem wasn't theirs. It was hers. The others tried to include her, went out of their way to be welcoming. At night, after dinner, they rehearsed scenes from Greek plays and once a week held a performance the entire staff attended. Malachai, their drama coach, encouraged Jac to join in. Trying to connect to the other students was some of the hardest work she did at Blixer. She gave up after a few lukewarm efforts.

The problem wasn't just that Jac was in mourning and homesick for her brother. She'd never had an easy time with other kids. At school in Paris, they used to gossip that she was a snob and aloof. They thought she was odd because she didn't have any close friends. But she wasn't a snob and she did have a close friend—her brother. She and Robbie were content in each other's company. Tied to each other by their love of scent and the training they were getting from their grandfather and father in the family business, they lived in their own world.

The year she was in fifth grade, Jac resolved to make friends, but after two months of concerted effort, she admitted to Robbie that she'd failed. She tried to talk about the topics and go places that interested the other girls, she told him, but her tastes weren't simpatico with theirs. They weren't interested in perfume and paintings and gardens. Most of them liked to read but weren't as passionate a reader as she was. Perfumes were built on stories, on dreams, her grandfather had told her. He was a wonderful storyteller. So was Jac's father. Robbie was like him, in the best ways. When her experiment had failed, Robbie told her that it didn't matter about the other girls. She had him, and he'd always be her friend.

While she was at Blixer, Jac called him once a week, which was all she was allowed. They'd decided to read the same books while she was away, and Robbie was becoming almost as obsessed with mythology as she was.

Jac had been at the clinic ten weeks when Theo showed up. He was the first new patient to arrive since she'd been there. Like her, he didn't seem to have an easy time getting to know any of the others. Another loner, she thought. But that didn't make her any more curious about him. During his first two weeks there, they didn't speak to each other except for an inconsequential *excuse me* or *good night*. There was the one encounter in the woods, but if anything it made Jac stay farther away.

Then at the end of his second week, something occurred in art class that threw them together.

Blixer Rath was a Jungian-based clinic, so there was a strong emphasis on archetypes and symbolism. Every art class began with a "dream drawing warm-up."

When Jac couldn't remember her dreams, Miss Snell, her teacher, suggested she do a few moments of deep breathing before trying to recall the imagery. Once Jac was relaxed, something always came to her, but she didn't always remember dreaming it. Which was what happened that day.

Jac saw herself in a dark wood. She was taking oval-shaped white rocks, each the size of her hand or larger, from a pile and placing them in a circle. In its center sat an owl. The bird, still and silent, watched her intently. Once she was done and the ring complete, he began to speak to her in a language Jac could neither identify nor understand.

The L'Etoiles were Catholic but not religious. "Lapsed," her mother used to say with a little laugh, and then as a postscript add a "thank God!" But Jac had been to church often enough to recognize the rhythm of the owl's chanting and know it was either a blessing or a prayer. Except instead of the owl's liturgy being comforting, it was ominous.

Jac opened her eyes. The dark forest was gone. She was in the art studio with the sun shining through the long slanting skylights, casting the room in a warm golden glow. Using a combination of soft and hard charcoal, she started to draw the stones. Concentrating deeply, she wasn't aware of what the other students were doing or the passage of time.

She hadn't yet attempted the owl, when suddenly it appeared, a shadow in the middle of the rocks. Without her drawing it. It took her a second to realize that someone was behind her.

Jac spun around.

Theo was leaning over her shoulder, looking at her drawing. Somehow his shadow had for a moment taken on a shape that conformed to the owl she'd seen in her dream.

He was standing so close that she could smell him. It was easy enough to pick out the notes of eucalyptus, honey, cinnamon, oakmoss and another ingredient she couldn't identify.

"What are you sniffing at?" He had a British accent and he sounded almost insulted.

"Your cologne. I don't recognize it."

"Why should you?"

"My family is in the perfume business."

"How odd," he said.

"Why?"

"That's my question," he said tersely.

"What do you mean?"

"Why did you draw that?" He pointed to her sketch.

She shrugged. She didn't know.

At sixteen he was already over six feet tall and very thin. He was all angles and planes except for his almost heart-shaped mouth, which softened his expression. He was wearing what he always wore: jeans and a white shirt. She noticed his skin, where his collar was open, was golden.

Moving closer to her, he spoke softly, as if he didn't want anyone else to hear.

"You need to see something," he said. "Come with me."

It wasn't a request. It was a demand. And there was a hint of desperation in his voice that she couldn't ignore.

He took her hand. His touch was urgent. And Jac felt as if something important were about to happen. But all he did was lead her to his work-table, and sketchbook. She'd seen him sketching in the dining room and during other classes. Now that she thought about it, she realized he was never without that book.

Opening it, Theo flipped through some pages.

Jac noticed elaborate, detailed and complex drawings, but they went by too fast for her to decipher. Finally he stopped on a page close to the middle and shoved it at her.

"Look at this," he whispered.

Jac's sketch was nowhere as experienced or sophisticated as this one. Theo had real talent. But the composition was the same.

In Theo's drawing an owl was encircled by stones.

"I don't understand," she said.

"This was what I dreamed about last night. And look . . ." He flipped to an earlier part of the sketchbook. "I've drawn it before. I've drawn it for years, Jac. It's a place I know. From home."

She didn't know what to say.

"Have you ever looked through this book? Did I leave it somewhere?" It wasn't an accusation. He seemed to be genuinely asking.

"No. It's your private property. I don't go snooping through other people's things."

"Don't be upset. I won't mind if you had. In fact I'd be relieved."

"Why relieved?"

"It would explain what's happened."

"Well, I didn't. I've seen you carry your sketchbook around, but I've never seen inside it."

"How could this happen then?"

Jac shook her head.

"You had my dream."

"That's not possible." But she was staring at the drawing. At the details. They hadn't each just drawn similar random rocks. They were identical. The stones' shapes and contours were the same.

That afternoon, in therapy, Jac told Malachai about what had happened.

"Have you and Theo talked to each other much before today?" he asked.

"No, not at all. I saw him once on a walk . . ." She was remembering the odd way he'd looked at her the first time when she'd come upon him sitting in her favorite spot.

"Did you do any reading in your mythology books that could have suggested that image?"

"Not that I can think of, no."

"Did it seem familiar to you when you were drawing it?"

"No. In fact I was thinking that I didn't remember dreaming it at all."

They spent another few minutes searching for a clue but couldn't find any.

"You seem almost pleased that I can't find a connection," Jac finally said.

"Why would I seem pleased?"

"You've been talking about how you want me to open myself up to the collective unconscious and accept that I might be more influenced by it than I realize. You keep saying you think that the keys to my hallucinations are there. You think that's what this is."

"You're not pleased, though, are you?"

"No. I'm frustrated."

"Why?"

"I don't know. It's all silly anyway. It's just a coincidence," she said, shrugging.

"I don't want you to think of anything as 'just' a coincidence," Malachai reminded her. "Have you been noticing more of them lately?"

"No."

"Are you paying attention? Writing them down?"

She shrugged again. "Why can't it just be a coincidence? You said there are some."

"Certainly, there are chance occurrences. But few things are of random causality, especially when you're in therapy and your defenses are down. Jac, I can give you logical explanations for what happened today. Maybe Theo was in the library with his sketchbook open to the drawing of the rock circle and you might have walked by and seen it without realizing it. Your unconscious could have stored it on a subliminal level. But even so, that wouldn't mean it was coincidence that you drew it today. Jung didn't believe in accidents. He proposed that resonance happens because we are functioning on more than our conscious level. I'd like you to think about the idea that there is a force we don't see but it ties matter, energy and consciousness together. Mystics have always been aware of it, from the Egyptians to the Sufis to the Native American Indians. In the twelfth century alchemists called it magic. They could see it. Jung postulated that modern man has trained himself not to see magic and to conform. It's how traditional religion has influenced us in order to exert more control over us."

Jac appreciated that Malachai never spoke down to her. Like her grandfather, he made her feel they were intellectual equals and there was no subject she wasn't capable of grasping despite her age. And she did understand what he was talking about, she just didn't believe it. She was certain there was randomness operating in the universe. That not every accident contained meaning. It would be too exhausting to live otherwise. If all those connections between people were threaded together, they'd create an impassable web. You'd be trapped in causality, in fate.

Later that afternoon Jac was in the library studying when Theo stopped by her table and asked her to take a walk with him. She hesitated. Something about his intensity made her unsure and maybe a little afraid. But at the same time she felt pulled to him. And her excitement won out over the fear.

On the path down to the lake, he said he'd been confused about their drawings and that he'd discussed the incident with Malachai. "Did you tell him too?"

Jac hesitated. "We're not supposed to talk about details of our therapy sessions."

He looked at her incredulously. "Do you actually follow their rules?"

She nodded. "Since I've been here I've been better. They must know what they are doing. I don't want to mess that up."

"But there's no way your telling me what Malachai said about the drawings could mess up your progress. Think about it. You and I had the same damn dream, Jac. In my case, it makes sense. I was dreaming about a ruin that's near my house. But have you ever been to the Channel Islands?"

She shook her head.

"So you've never seen the archaeological sites there but you drew one of them exactly. Don't you think that's more important than the rule that we're not supposed to talk about our sessions?"

"I . . . I don't know."

For a few moments they trod on in silence up the mountain path. There was a slight breeze and Jac could smell wildflowers and Theo's unusual cologne.

"You can't think a rule is more important than what happened to us, can you?" he asked again.

"I guess not."

"So did Malachai say anything to explain what happened?"

"No, not really. He talked about the collective unconscious."

"With me too."

"What do you think it means?" she asked.

"We share something."

"What—that we're both slightly insane?"

Theo laughed. Like his voice, his laugh was deep and poured like syrup. "Neither of us are insane," he said. "But we are both too aware."

"What do you mean?"

"I think we're more attuned to certain things than most people. That we have a sort of sixth sense. I've read about a lot of people through the ages who've been singled out, branded insane or called witches or worse. During the time of the Cathars and through the Inquisition they were burned at the stake. In early America they were stoned to death or hanged. All for just having a little bit more sensitivity. For being just that much more psychically aware. For being capable of tapping into an unseen river of information that others don't even know exists. Some of us can see the future, others can remember the past."

"It sounds like science fiction."

"It's anything but. It's tragic. So many people institutionalized just for being different. Maybe none of them—none of us—are crazy at all. Maybe it's those who don't have any special ability who should be singled out. Maybe they are just scared by how much we know and can sense, and that's why they're frightened of us."

"I'm not sure I understand what you're talking about."

"I don't understand it all either, but Grandfather has always told me that throughout history, too many men have wanted to destroy what threatens them, but that mysteries abound despite these narrow-minded souls. That's how he always phrased it too. 'Mysteries abound.'"

"You think we, you and I, have some kind of psychic ability?"

"Jung believes everything happens for a reason, right?"

She nodded.

"That an action once taken lives on. Yes?"

"Yes."

"He also said there is a record in the universe and that if we're attuned to it, we can go back and see it, hear it again, use it."

They'd reached the lake. It was a clear day, without any clouds, and the watery surface reflected the mirror images of the surrounding landscape so perfectly it seemed as if there were trees growing in the pool of liquid. Jac stood at its edge and stared down at herself. This watery Jac was almost identical. Almost. The real Jac would never have broken the rule about discussing therapy with another student.

"Why are you here?" she asked him.

"At Blixer?"

She nodded.

"I'm guilty."

"Of what?"

214

"I don't know, that's just how I feel. All the time. I can't get through a day without a sense of foreboding that I am going to cause a crisis, a catastrophe, some awful event. I am fairly obsessed with the idea that everything is going to come tumbling down because of me and there's nothing I can do to stop it. That it's just bloody inevitable. It makes me unable to function and all I want—" He broke off. He'd been about to say something terrible. She was sure of it. And she was almost glad he'd stopped himself. But she wasn't sure why.

"Not one therapist has been able to help me. And I've seen dozens."

"I didn't mean to pry. I'm sorry." She'd picked up a rock before and now she threw it at her reflection. Watched herself ripple into unrecognizable shimmers of colors. She no longer saw the girl standing on the shore. Just streaks of blues and pale yellows.

"It's an odd thing to be inexplicable to the psychiatric community. Makes one feel quite out of it. I don't usually talk about it with anyone but the shrinks. But it makes sense to tell you." He'd said it as if he was surprised by what he'd just realized.

The lake's surface had flattened out, and there she was again. She nodded. Her twin did also. "No one could help me either. That's how I wound up at the Clinic of the Last Resorts."

He smiled. "Love the moniker."

She smiled back.

"What's your affliction?"

"I had episodes. Hallucinations. They tried everything on me from drugs to electric shock. Nothing worked. So my grandmother brought me here." She paused. "I haven't talked to anyone but the doctors about it till now. But they're all on the outside watching, trying to interpret, to diagnose. Malachai's more understanding than most. But telling you . . . it's different. It's better."

The sun had started its descent for the day, and orange flames licked the water's surface. The fire was consuming her other self, the one in the lake. And Theo's too.

"Are you cold?" he asked.

"No."

"You're shivering."

"I just suddenly got scared."

"Not of me, are you?" he asked.

His voice was serious, but there was levity in his eyes too, and it was contagious.

"Should I be?"

She'd never really flirted with a boy before. It was actually fun. Jac knew she was serious. Too solemn, her mother had always warned, even though Audrey was no different. Theo was even more serious. There was a cold darkness around him that Jac could almost feel. He'd told her one secret about himself, but she was certain there were more.

"No, I don't think so," he said finally, taking so long she had to remember what the question was.

"Were you really thinking about how to answer that for all that time?"

"I was," Theo said. "Of everyone here, I don't want you to be afraid of me. But I'm not easy. Everyone always tells me that. Even my mother isn't always comfortable around me. My brother used to run away from me all the time when he was little."

"People don't talk like this," Jac said suddenly.

"What do you mean?"

"I don't know. The way we're talking just seems different."

"It is. We're not playing games. We don't have the time. You and I. We need to make the most of however long we have here. We need to find out where we fit in."

And then before she knew what he was doing, he leaned down and kissed her on the lips.

It was her first kiss and her whole body shivered, but not because she was frightened. It was as if a hundred perfume bottles all spilled out at the same time. As if the fragrance notes were meeting in the air and mixing and mingling and turning into music. She was suddenly attuned to scents and tones and sounds and tastes and touch in a brand-new way. With senses that had been sleeping until this very moment.

They were inseparable after that until the night of the accident that happened four weeks later. She'd awoken in the infirmary not remembering anything. She'd asked for Theo but the nurse had told her he was gone. Gone? Without either of them having a chance to say good-bye or give each other information on how to find each other in the real world?

Or the other world, Jac had thought. Because maybe Blixer Rath with Theo there, with the two of them together, was the real world.

SEPTEMBER 15, 1855
JERSEY, CHANNEL ISLANDS, GREAT BRITAIN

After leaving the castle, I didn't return to my own house, which I knew would be noisy and full of visitors, but rather retired to Juliette's. I craved undisturbed sleep and since there were no children underfoot at her house and no current infestation of friends from Paris, I knew I'd find quiet.

I slept for most of the day and when I awoke it was nine o'clock in the evening and I was ravenous. It had been more than twenty-four hours since my last meal.

It was dark outside and in. When I'd arrived Juliette had told me she'd been invited out to a dinner but would cancel on my behalf if I wished. I'd insisted she go. I didn't need company—just rest.

I'd gotten that and now I needed food.

In the kitchen I inspected the larder and found bread, cheese, sausage and wine. I'd just made myself a plate and poured out a generous glass of burgundy when I heard footsteps.

I remembered Juliette saying she would tell her maidservant to be on alert in case I needed anything.

"*Bonsoir*, Monsieur Hugo."

I nodded. "*Bonsoir*, Fantine."

"Madame said you might be hungry. Can I make you something more substantial?"

"No, I'm fine with this." I gestured at the plate.

"Everyone in town is talking about you finding that girl. It's quite wonderful."

"We all found her."

"But they are saying it was you. Yes?"

"Well, yes, but only because I went down the stairs first."

"Finding a lost child is a very worthy day's work."

The melancholy expression in your eyes spoke more than your words. I knew what you were thinking. And as I looked, I admit I noticed more than the expression in your eyes. The sweep of your hair, your sweet scent, the swell of your breast under your chemise, I took them all in.

"Would you like some wine?" I asked.

You hesitated for a moment, then something flared in your eyes and replaced the sadness. Bravery? Rebellion?

Taking a glass from the cupboard, you sat down beside me. Poured some wine and then drank.

"The child was unharmed?"

I finished chewing the bread and swallowed. "She had a nasty cut on her arm, but that will heal."

"How did she get to the basement of the castle in the first place?"

"She said that she followed a dog who'd been playing outside her window."

"But there's more to it than that, isn't there? I hear it in your voice."

I shrugged, not ready to talk about the stranger events that I'd witnessed. Or thought I had. At that juncture, I hadn't even accepted what I'd seen. I was troubled by the possibility that my mind was touched and I'd manufactured a vision.

"What have you been doing this evening?" I asked, anxious to change the conversation.

"Sitting by the window, watching the sea. You would have thought that by now I would have stopped waiting. I know he is not coming. That he will never come."

"Why won't he?"

"His family. They didn't approve of me. I was working-class, he was aristocracy. They threatened him with his inheritance. After I'd been here for a few months I realized his having me come ahead and saying that he'd meet me was all an elaborate lie. It was just a ruse to get rid of me and the child he had no intention of legitimizing. And yet I watch the sea. I know there's no reason to hope, but sometimes when I hear a ship's horn coming into port, I still think . . ."

"Hope is the most difficult emotion to give up."

"What do you hope for, Monsieur Hugo?"

"That you will let me seduce you." I ran my thumb back and forth across your palm. The soft skin not hardened yet by housework. Juliette employed a laundress. I was glad of that. It would have been a shame to ruin that silkiness.

I waited for your reaction. When you neither resisted nor responded to my touch, I lifted your hand to my mouth and pressed my lips against your palm. I smelled a sophisticated and delicious scent. Lust surged inside me, which was a welcome distraction from the disturbing events of the last twenty-four hours.

"Is the perfume I smell one your father created?"

"No, it's one that I made. I have a small laboratory in an unused bedroom."

"Could I see it?"

"Of course."

221

"Your blush makes me desire you that much more. Your innocence is a delight," I said.

Following you upstairs, I watched your skirts move and caught sight of your ankles. I imagined putting my hand up that dress and searching out the warm wet spot between your legs. I wondered if you perfumed yourself there the way some Frenchwomen did.

At the landing, instead of turning left toward Juliette's room, we turned right. I'd never explored this end of the house as there'd been no reason to before. I smelled which way to go. Led like a dog by the nose to the far end of the hall.

As you opened the door a cacophony of scents reached out and embraced me. I'd never smelled such a rich, complicated aroma. For a second I closed my eyes and just inhaled. I was transported to a lush flower field, a spice market, a citrus grove, the forest and the sea all at once.

When I opened my eyes again I was surprised at how unadorned the room actually was. The smells were so decorative and elaborate. The furniture consisted of a long table, a single chair and a tall glass-fronted cabinet. There were two frosted glass wall sconces and a fairly simple two-tiered crystal chandelier already lit. Noticing that, I surmised you'd been working.

There was a bay window. And it faced the sea.

And there were all of your utensils and supplies. Everywhere were gleaming glass jars, canisters, small bottles and large beakers. Around me, the smell evolved. I found myself thinking I was inside a library, then a church, then a bedroom smelling a lover's body, hot with want.

The whole world of scents resided in this one single room. How was it possible?

"This is amazing. You are a true alchemist," I said.

"No, just a perfumer."

"Certainly that. Certainly that. Tell me, Fantine, why are you working as a lady's maid if you have all this talent?"

"I'm a woman, monsieur. You of all men know that. No establishment in Paris would have me except to wait on customers and fill bottles. Women are not noses. We do not create."

"Would you like to open a store in Jersey?"

Your shrug saddened me. There was so little energy in the movement of your shoulders.

"No. It's enough for me to mix up scents for Madame Juliette and her friends. I do it to please her and because I miss my father and my home. While I work, I can pretend I'm back there for a little while."

"But I might be able to help you set up a thriving concern and sell your perfumes in the village. Perhaps you'd find some joy in it that you can't anticipate. Madame Juliette is an independent woman. Can't you use her as a model?"

I knew when you didn't answer it was because

you were too well-bred to argue with me. What I'd said wasn't true any longer. Juliette had been independent when I'd met her. But she'd since given up acting to accompany me, and now she was as dependent as my wife was.

"Do you have all the materials you need? All the utensils?"

"That's very kind, but I have everything. Madame Juliette orders what I need from Paris."

"Will you at least show me how you mix a scent? Make one for me?"

Finally you gifted me with a smile.

I settled in the chair and watched your performance, fascinated with the change in you as you worked. You were animated in a way you hadn't been before. The haunted look in your eyes was replaced by a determined concentration as you picked up one vial and then another, sniffing and searching and then settling on which one to use. Every movement was assured and knowl-edgeable, and I found myself as entertained as if I were at one of Juliette's plays. Drop by drop the formula in the tube filled up. Every so often you would dip a small length of ribbon in the liquid, wave it in the air, then close your eyes and inhale its essence.

I imagined you were dreaming your own dream, oblivious that I was even there. And that increased my desire for you. Often the wanting is more satisfying than the fulfillment. I have come to prefer anticipation to satiation. Longing can make one feel alive in a more profound way. You see everything through champagne bubbles. Your senses are alert. You imagine how your lover's lips will feel, how her skin will taste. What it will be like to unbutton her chemise, slip it off her shoulders, press your mouth to her skin, cup her breasts in your palms and feel her excitement harden her nipples. You picture her leaning into you, showing you just enough of her want that it ignites yours.

That knowing is all. You forget your enemies, your fears and your nightmares.

To live in the moment of desire is to be yourself in the most pure and painful way possible, because beneath every touch is the knowledge of how fleeting the pleasure is. How elusive the passion. How impossible it is to contain it for long.

"I think you might like this." You held out a small container filled with topaz liquid.

I held it up to my nose.

"No."

I was pleased to hear your laugh as you shook your head.

"Never smell directly from the bottle. Scent needs to breathe and interact with your skin. You have to put some on."

I held the vial out. "Would you please put it on me?"

A moment's hesitation. Your uncertainty was charming and seductive. The moment was a river to cross. On one side was the past, on the other side the future. I wondered what you were thinking. Then you tipped the bottle, wet your forefinger and gently ran your fingertip down the inside of my right wrist and then my left. I shuddered at your touch.

The scent wafted up and filled the air. You'd captured the aroma of a primitive forest. Mysterious and woody. I visualized deep grottoes and mossy glens. I traveled a whole journey in just one inhalation.

"So is this how you see me?" I asked.

"My father taught me to paint portraits in perfume."

"Perfume portraits," I repeated, never having heard the expression before and enchanted by it. "Can you put on more?" I was teasing, testing, and was delighted when you obliged and touched your wet finger to small space behind my left ear.

"There are other places too," I said.

"I know." A whisper of a laugh. Was it excitement or just nervousness?

I took the perfume and put my finger over the top of the bottle. "Would you let me do the same to you?"

"If it would please you."

"What about pleasing you, Fantine?"

That shrug, again without enthusiasm. I wanted

to make you feel, push you to enjoy. I unbuttoned your top button. When you didn't resist, I worked on another button. I might as well have been buttering toast.

"What are you thinking? Why do you look so sad?" I asked.

"You are making me remember that I used to care about a man touching me."

"Do you want me to stop?"

"No, it's all right. If you want to . . . please . . ."

I finished unbuttoning your chemise and pulled it down off your shoulders. Your skin glowed in the candlelight. It was the color of the inside of a nautilus shell. Your breasts were small but perfect. I wet my finger with perfume and painted circles around each nipple. Then I leaned forward and got drunk on the scent on your skin.

My ministrations were not unpleasant to you. I knew that. I'd been with enough women. You didn't pull back in repulsion. But neither did you arch or purr. You simply didn't care what I did. My efforts to reach you were failing.

And yet you were willing to let me pleasure myself with you. That was something of a conundrum.

Then you shrugged off your chemise and stood facing me, naked to the waist. God forgive me but I thought of nothing but burying myself inside you and forgetting everything else. I smelled skin, woods, flowers and thought this must be what

227

Eden smelled like, and then I slipped into an embracing wholeness that gave me shelter and soothed my soul while at the same time exciting me.

I'd never made love to someone so dispassionate who was not a professional. I didn't understand. Why were you allowing this? Why were you willing to give yourself to me this way? What was wrong with you that I couldn't move you—not with my fingers or my words? As I put my lips to your lips, I determined to discover your mystery, never dreaming that learning about it might mean our very destruction.

Sixteen

The library at Wells in Wood was a large octagonal room without windows. Two stories high, it had a hand-carved spiral staircase leading up to a second level. There was not an inch of wall without bookshelves. Rows and rows of books. Hundreds of gold titles incised on red, brown, green, maroon spines gleamed in the soft lamplight.

Jac didn't think she'd ever seen as large a private library in someone's home. And the smell! Without having to be told, she knew there were ancient books here and she asked Theo how old the oldest volumes were. He walked to the far wall and pulled out a black leather-bound book. It was redolent with age.

She held it gingerly, just smelling.

"It's okay to open it." He smiled.

The medieval manuscript had been written with a quill dipped in ink. The illustrations were painted with brushes made of sable dipped in egg tempura. The colors were just as brilliant now as they had been five or six hundred years ago.

She handed it back to him.

When she was a child, the library at home had been her refuge. She had gravitated to it. When she was anxious, just taking a book off a shelf had calmed her. Opening the cover, feeling the paper's smoothness, smelling the sheets, the leather, even sometimes the ink, had centered her. Jac was enchanted with books as objects as well as for what they contained.

Her grandfather had been too. His library smelled like this. Jac felt a sudden wave of nostalgia for Paris and Robbie and even the perfume studio on the Rue des Saints-Pères.

For the next few minutes, Theo showed her a few of the more obscure and interesting volumes.

"These should be in museums," she said.

"I know. We really should donate these rare volumes to the British Library. But my aunts aren't ready to divest the house of any of its treasures. It's been this way since they were girls."

"I don't blame them," she said, understanding

why they would want to keep this amazing repository intact.

"So is this where you found the letter? Was it in a book?"

"Let me show you. Come upstairs."

They climbed the wrought-iron circular spiral. Its steps were narrow and turned on themselves sharply, making them hard to navigate and easy to fall down, Jac thought. The upper balcony hung over the first floor.

Theo walked her to a second bay of shelves. "This section is devoted to Victor Hugo. Books written by him and about him. Quite a few first editions. Some inscribed only to Fantine. Others to her and Pierre."

Just in front of these shelves sat a green leather chair, deeply cushioned and worn. Next to it was a wooden table with claw feet. A few books rested on its surface.

"This was my grandfather's favorite place in the whole house. He used to sit up here and read for hours. Hugo was one of his favorite authors." Theo put his hands on the back of the chair. His fingers tightened. "After he died . . ." He stopped and cleared his throat. Then continued. "After he died, I was helping my aunts deal with his belongings and came up here to see if there was anything important. There were piles of magazines and papers everywhere. Over a dozen books were sitting out, open to various pages, with paper markers in them. I found a file with more than two dozen letters in it. My grandfather, it turned out, had been communicating with Hugo scholars for the last five years. It took me two days to get through all the material and figure out what he'd been up to."

Theo turned back to the shelves, reached up and pulled out a slim volume bound in bottle-green leather with ornate gold scrollwork and handed it to Jac.

She read the title.

The Ocean's Song by Victor Hugo.

"Open it."

On the frontispiece were the words BROWN & SELDEN PRINTERS and then 1856.

"There's an inscription on the next page," Theo said.

The letters were spidery but certain and the black ink was still so dark, she doubted it had been exposed to light often.

As Jac read them in French she spoke the words out loud in English. "To my dear little friend on the celebration of the birth of your first child. Your servant, Victor."

Beneath the words was a pen-and-ink seascape of a rocky coast. A single shaft of sunlight broke the cloudy sky, turning what would have been a dismal drawing into one of hope.

Something about it looked familiar. Had she seen it before? Yes, there were drawings like these in Hugo's apartments in the Marais. She'd visited there on a school trip once. That must be it. And then she remembered something else. Theo's sketchbook, the one she'd seen at Blixer Rath, had drawings of rock formations like this in it.

Jac turned to the next page, came to the first poem and started to read it silently to herself.

"Would you mind translating it for me?" Theo asked. "I wanted to send it to a translator, but at the same time didn't want to bring any attention to it in case . . . Well, I'll explain that later . . . Would you mind?"

With a French father and an American mother, she was equally at home in either language.

We walked amongst the ruins famed in story
Of Rozel-Tower,
And saw the boundless waters stretch in glory
And heave in power . . .

She stopped and looked over at Theo. "I'm sorry, poetry is more difficult to do justice to than prose. I'm afraid I'm not making it very eloquent."

"No, your version is quite poetic."

"Was the letter in this book?"

"Yes. Let me show you." He held out his hand.

Jac gave him the book and he flipped to the back.

"These pages haven't been cut all around. Only

the top has been slit, creating an envelope." He showed her. "I wonder if Hugo asked the binder to leave it like this or if it was an accident he took advantage of. Either way, when I picked it up to put it away, the back cover felt thick to me, oddly bulky. That's when I found the letter. And a map of Jersey ruins that Grandfather had marked up. X-ing out certain sites."

Theo gave her the book back. "I'd like you to read the rest. There may be a clue in one of the poems that I'm missing because of my trouble with the language."

Jac looked in the pocket. It was empty.

"Where's the letter?"

"Back this way."

Downstairs, Theo offered Jac one of the four oversize leather chairs.

"We have a safe here."

He walked to the center bay of books and pressed inward on the edge of the third shelf from the bottom. The whole section of shelves swung out.

"Fantine's eldest son, Louis, married into a very well respected banking business in Jersey and took to the trade. The firm of Stillwell and Gaspard is a result of that union. When he inherited the house, Louis had this safe built. It's where I've been keeping the letter."

He stepped through the opening.

Jac could see a small room. Walls of steel

drawers glinted in an overhead light. Theo opened one of the compartments. She heard the sound of metal riding against metal.

Seconds later he emerged holding a plastic sheath. From inside he pulled out a sheet of thick creamy paper, approximately five inches by seven, and gingerly placed it on the table in front of her.

The letter was neither brittle nor yellowed. The pouch in the book where it had been hidden all these years had protected it. Familiar with dealing with antiquities, Jac leaned over. It was always better not to touch something if you didn't have to.

She started to read.

My Dear Fantine,

I know we agreed that what occurred between us would be best hidden away and not spoken of. The spirit we encountered, that tempter, proved to us he can only do us harm. But what I did not tell you before I sailed from Jersey, what I did not confide to you, or to anyone, is that I had written a full and true account of my encounter with the Shadow of the Sepulcher. As true and honest a telling as I could put down of what transpired, in the proper sequence in which it unfolded. The story of what happened to me and what almost happened to you, my dear little friend. The story of how we almost tampered with destiny and disturbed the natural order of the universe.

When I read over my account, what surprised and saddened me was how clearly it spoke of my obsession with the dead rather than my passion for the living. A lesson that has been, almost tragically, difficult to learn. A lesson that I want to share with you.

If you give in to one you give up the other. You cannot hold on to both. You must choose. It was a hard lesson taught in a hard way. One that when I think of the consequences makes me bow my head and thank the God of mercy that you are alive. That I am. That the Shadow of the Sepulcher sleeps.

So, my dear, I am writing to tell you that I have hidden this account along with our billets de passage where we started our journey, where we found them, in Lucifer's Lair.

Were there truly once ancient Druid priests who practiced their arts there? Who used that incense the same way I did? Were they affected as we were? Is the story the cave paintings tell true?

The answer to those questions is best left to historians.

What I do know without doubt is that we stumbled upon a sacred site. We encountered evil there, yes, but goodness too. And for that I am thankful.

My account of our journey is yours to take or to leave to rot. My fate is in your hands in this matter, as it should be. Perhaps I never should have written it down. Or perhaps I should have destroyed it myself. But I needed to understand, and for me writing is my pathway to knowledge.

The adventure, as frightening and dangerous as it was, was one of a lifetime. What we learned! What we experienced! What we have come to know! I could not bear to destroy this record of it.

I do not think I will ever come to fully understand what happened, but I will never forget, or cease to beg your forgiveness that it did occur.

Your Humble Servant and friend,

Victor Hugo
Guernsey, England

And then, there at the bottom of the letter was a drawing. A seascape with oval rocks, each the size of a woman's hand, arranged in a circle on the shore.

"You recognize it, don't you?" Theo asked.

Staring at the familiar scene she'd sketched seventeen years ago, Jac nodded. This was identical to the rock circle that had drawn her and Theo together.

But logically, was it really so strange? Theo had grown up in Jersey. Had walked the beaches, known the paths. He'd drawn all kinds of rock formations. And Jac had seen them in his notebook without realizing it. She'd explained it all away years ago. There was no reason to question it again. What was more important was the information in the letter itself. That was why she'd traveled all this way. That was why she'd rejected Malachai's advice and come to Jersey— to find evidence that the Celtic Druids of myth were real.

"Do you have any idea where Lucifer's Lair is?" Jac asked.

Theo shook his head. "There's nothing called that, no. And there are no clues in the letter. My grandfather even tried to use the letter as a code. I have his exercises in futility too."

"But I read that not all the caves on the island have been found."

"No, they haven't. But the problem is that rocks fall and land shifts. We can't even be sure that Lucifer's Lair still exists. Hugo wrote this more than a hundred and fifty years ago."

"The cave could have just been overlooked. If you don't know what you are looking for, sometimes you just don't see it even if it's staring at you," Jac said.

"Right, but where do we even start?"

"How many caves are there on the island?"

"Literally hundreds. And not all of them are accessible all the time. Some you can only get to when there is an unusually low tide. Others that might have been accessible in the eighteen fifties have completely flooded by now."

"It does sound impossible." She'd come here on a slim chance, and now suddenly she felt defeated before she even began. Jac had spent her entire adult life chasing myths. Was it a fool's errand? Robbie had once asked her if she really cared about the ancient reality she sought out or if she was just so desperate to escape her own present reality that she was willing to wander, lost in the past.

She had never answered him.

"My grandfather always used to tell me problems only seem impossible before you've figured out how to solve them. You've come a long way to help me, Jac. Don't give up now."

Seventeen

OCTOBER 6, 1855
JERSEY, CHANNEL ISLANDS, GREAT BRITAIN

The candles flickered in their glass globes, casting shadows upon the six of us seated around the table. To date we'd had one hundred and thirty séances and met more than twenty-two different personages including Dante, Shakespeare and Jesus. But I'd only had one full-length conversation with my darling.

We began our expedition that October night no differently from any other by asking who was present.

Silently I prayed my daughter would answer.

A few moments passed, and then the legs of the little stool began to tap out a response. François-Victor recorded each hollow sound. But I didn't need to wait for him to translate them into the letters of the alphabet. I could hear the voice so clearly in my mind.

I am here. The Shadow, it said as the tapping continued to spell out the name I dreaded. *The Shadow of the Sepulcher.*

My heart hurried, my breath caught. This spirit hadn't visited for weeks, since the night when the child named Lilly had gone missing.

"What have you come to tell us?" my son Charles asked.

No response. We waited, but for me the waiting was too long. "What do you want?" I blurted out.

Temptation . . . is my . . . forte.

François-Victor was busy writing, but I heard.

Education . . . is my . . . gift.

My daughter and wife looked bored, my sons only slightly more engaged. I was surprised that my own family was becoming blasé to these astonishing revelations that came from the magic blackness of infinity. Our guests that night, who had only been to one séance before, were curious and quite affected by what they were witnessing.

Being an individual in a world of conformity . . .

I closed my eyes, which made it easier to hear the voice in my head.

. . . is no easy task with the clergy destroying goodness. Destroying me and my teachings. But you want to learn, don't you?

"Yes," I whispered, certain the spirit was speaking directly to me.

And so you shall. I impart my wisdom to you.

"What wisdom?" I asked.

There was no answer.

"Are you still with us?" my son asked after thirty seconds of silence had passed without any more tapping.

The table's legs didn't move.

"Are you here?" he asked again.

A vase resting on the mantel tottered and then fell, shattering on the tiles in front of the hearth. Water spilled, flowers scattered. A strange, almost sulfurous odor infiltrated the room.

"What a putrid smell," my wife said, as she hurried out to get rags and call the maid. "That water cannot have been changed all week."

But I didn't think it was the water. I sniffed. And sniffed again. The malodorous sulfur was lifting, and beneath it I smelled smoke and incense. And beneath that the familiar sweetness of garden flowers.

"Why do these spirits come?" my daughter Adele asked as we put away the accoutrements of the game. "What do they want of us?"

She was a sensitive and sweet child, a bit more nervous than pleased me. My wife worried the séances might be worsening her already stressed constitution. But when my wife had tried to convince her not to join, Adele insisted she be allowed to witness the visitations.

Now she was demanding an answer. "Why, Papa?"

"I believe they want me to write down their wisdom."

"I think it's more than that. That there is some other purpose." Her brown eyes searched mine. "Make them tell you what it is."

Being the children of Victor Hugo had not been easy when we lived in France and in some ways was even more difficult now that we were in exile. Away from friends and relations and all that they had grown up with and were familiar with, they were now alone with each other. I had brought my family here. I felt responsible for their isolation. Seeing my daughter's distress and consternation, my guilt did not sit well on me that night. And instead of going to my room to record the session, I decided to walk and clear my head of the noxious odor. The sea air would take care of it.

The gibbous moon offered more than enough light to guide me on the short walk to the shore. I strode down the slipway and headed north. I'd been walking for about fifteen minutes when a bank of heavy clouds drifted by and shrouded my heavenly lantern, casting me in a deeper darkness.

As I passed by the rocky promontory where I often sat to look out at the sea and gaze at France, I could make out a young man sitting on my usual perch.

He saw me too, for he called down. *May I join you, Monsieur Hugo?* He spoke French in a voice that was familiar though I couldn't place him.

"Yes, of course," I answered. Even if I hadn't wanted company—which I didn't—there was little I could do to stop a stranger from walking with me on the public beach.

Moments later he emerged from the shadows just as the moon did the same and shone down on him. Not tall but slim, he was dressed in a well-cut dark suit. His hair was black and thick and wavy and curled on the back of his neck. His almond-shaped eyes were a very light brown, almost golden, unblinking and mysterious. His strong cheekbones and refined nose were perfectly proportioned. His mouth was full and red. His beauty was almost feminine and mesmerizing.

"Do we know each other?" I asked.

We do. But then instead of giving me his name, he said, *You may have what you want, you know. It's yours for the asking.*

I was put off by the cryptic comment and toyed with saying so. But that would have been rude, and I was, I admit, curious, so I played along. To this day I wish I hadn't. If I had paid attention to the kernel of suspicion in my belly . . .

"What do you mean, I may have what I want? Pertaining to what?"

You may have all that you seek. I can create the reality you crave so very much.

"But you are a stranger to me—why would you help me?"

I'm not a stranger. I am known to you.

No, I didn't know these features. Not the nose, chin, forehead and lips, all so finely sculpted. Not the long, black curls, or dark eyelashes that fringed the topaz eyes. His attitude, attire, vocabulary and the timbre of his voice suggested he'd been raised in the upper echelons of society, attended the finest schools and been taught by

243

the most learned of men. But I did not recognize him.

Don't gaze upon my visage to know me. He waved his arm in a graceful, almost royal gesture. *Just listen to my voice, Hugo. We were just together an hour ago and yet you do not recognize me?*

"Confound you! What is your name?"

I am the Shadow of the Sepulcher.

I stopped midstep. "The waves are loud," I suggested. "I believe I have misunderstood your name."

No, Monsieur Hugo, you heard me. The Shadow of the Sepulcher. The archangel Lucifer.

"A spirit cannot be made flesh." Emboldened by my anger at whichever member of my family or friends had decided to play this game with me, I reached out for the man's lapel, to pull him toward me, to insist he reveal his true identity. But he was quicker than I, and stepped back so my hand merely waved through the air. Touching nothing.

He laughed and the ghostly sound traveled out to the sea and was lost in the roar of the waves. *You cannot touch me, sir. I am not flesh but a manifestation of your desire. Even so, I can deliver that which you want more than your life itself.*

"And what is that?"

To bring your daughter back from the dead.

"That is not possible. You speak blasphemy."

I told you when first we communicated: for a price all things are possible.

"A bargain with the devil? Is this not a cliché? You expect me to believe such foolishness? Indeed this is a joke. Well played, young man." I relaxed as I realized the folly of it all. "But somewhat in poor taste, I must say. And nothing I find funny. Whoever put you up to this has a perverted sense of humor."

I turned on my heel and walked away from him in the direction from which I had come.

With some trick of speed and using the darkness to his advantage, he was now suddenly in front of me.

I beseech you, do not squander this opportunity, Hugo. The window during which we can accomplish this goal is narrow.

Up ahead on the beach, I saw a speck of someone walking my way. I took out my watch. Nine o'clock. The time your duties with my mistress were completed.

This is the hour she takes her own nightly walk with the dead. She is so lovely, the man beside me said. *But very sad. She seems not to have the strength to distract herself as most mortals do.*

"Do you know her?" I asked.

I can help her, he said, not answering my question.

"How can you do that?"

I can provide her with what she wants.

"More of this game?"

It is not a game. I implore you to believe me.

"Well, then, how can you give her what she wants?"

Until I know you have accepted my offer, I cannot share that.

"No surprise there, since this is nothing but an elaborate ruse."

I think you will come to regret your dismissal of me.

"What an impertinent position to take," I said.

I made you this offer already once, and you rejected me. Pray be careful.

We were still walking, getting closer to you, and I wanted to be done with this joker before we reached you.

"I am not aware of what offer you are referring to."

I put the child you found in the castle. You wound up a hero but still bereft. If you'd done what I suggested, you would have been a happier one.

"This is all ridiculous."

O ye of little faith.

"Clichés you give me again? Your words are less than inspired."

You wound me, monsieur.

"Then forgive me for appreciating more sophisticated writing."

Perhaps you might write me some words, he suggested.

I laughed at the preposterous idea. "You could not afford me."

Ah, but I could. His golden eyes bored deep into mine, and I was suffused with a sense of hope that was unlike anything I had known.

You're feeling something, aren't you? he asked. I didn't trust him. I didn't respond.

Do you believe what occurs during the séances you attend? he asked.

"I do not *not* believe. Absence of proof is proof of nothing."

But you have proof. He gestured to you—only a few meters away now—up the beach. You'd stopped and were watching us, waiting for us to reach you.

You will walk with Fantine now? he asked.

I was startled he knew your name but then realized whoever had asked him to play this prank would have schooled him well, and you were, after all, my mistress's maid.

"Perhaps," I said.

Be kind to her.

"How impertinent of you. What do you know of her?"

I know how torn her soul is. Even more ripped apart than yours, Hugo. Even than yours, he said and turned away from me toward an outcropping of rocks.

"There's no exit that way," I called out. "You need to go right or left." But he kept walking. In the impossible direction, as if he were walking right into the rock face. I waited and watched, but he didn't come back out.

"Who were you calling out to?"

I turned. You had walked up behind me. But I hadn't heard you approach.

"That young man. Didn't you see him?"

"A man?"

"Yes. I've been talking to him for the last half hour. I walked down this whole stretch of beach with him."

"Monsieur Hugo, I've been watching you for at least the last five minutes as you walked this way. There was no one with you."

"It must have been a trick of light that cast him in shadow," I said, and shivered at the word I'd chosen to use. "It was an unpleasant and annoying conversation, but it was a conversation."

"Look." You were pointing down at the sand in the direction from which I'd just approached. "Look," you repeated. "There is only one set of footprints. No one was with you. You were quite alone."

Eighteen

Theo was waiting for Jac outside the hotel just before noon the next day. Once she was settled in the car, he showed her a map with black hand-drawn lines that divided it into quadrants.

"I've spent the last few weeks taking it in sections, walking the cliffs up and down, looking for any opening that might lead to Lucifer's Lair. But I've come up empty-handed. I don't expect there will be an actual spot with that name. More likely it was a phrase the poet came up with himself. Still, I was hoping the shoreline's configuration or the look of a cave would offer up a clue. But there hasn't been anything."

"Have you researched any older maps dating back to the Hugo years?"

"I didn't think of that."

"Maybe there was an area called Lucifer's Lair, when Hugo lived here, that has since changed names. Is there a library on the island where we can find old maps?"

"No need for that." As Theo drove, he explained. "In the late nineteen twenties my grandfather's art collection outgrew being a hobby and turned into a side business. He bought an abandoned fire-control tower, had it renovated and set up shop. While he ran the bank with one of his brothers, he ran the gallery with his wife."

He turned down a road and headed toward the cliffs.

"I'm not sure how much of Jersey's history you are familiar with, but during World War II our island was invaded by and occupied by the Germans. It was, according to what I've been told, a dismal time for the natives. Many people quietly tried to help the Jews who lived here. Including my grandfather. He let all his clients know he'd safeguard their art and protect it from the Nazis."

"How did he do that?"

"I'm about to show you."

The road had dead-ended in dirt. In front of them was a seemingly endless vista of sea. To the right an outcropping of cliffs, and rising out of them, constructed of the same rock, was a tower. If not for the windows cut into its surface, it might have been another cliff.

On the front, to the right of the door, was a plaque—copper turned green—that read Gaspard Gallery.

Theo opened the door. There was no artwork in the entranceway, just a glass Art Deco desk and an aluminum chair, now empty. To the right was a staircase going up, to the left, one going down. Above she glimpsed large canvases painted with tantalizing colors. Below she saw gold frames and the reflection of glass. At the same time she smelled the odors typically associated with an art gallery that did some restoration and framing: oily paints, fresh-cut timber, shellac and the tang of turpentine. And the woodsy smell of aging paper.

All suggesting long-forgotten treasures waiting to be discovered.

"Paintings and sculpture are upstairs. Down here is our ephemera collection of old posters and maps. This is what he did to help the Jews."

"I don't understand."

"To hide the artwork that the Nazis might have confiscated, my grandfather took the paintings out of their frames, covered them with maps, reframed them and hung them here, and in Wells in Wood. Quite a few more were hung in the bank. No one paid any attention to old maps of Jersey."

Jac walked through the three rooms that made up the downstairs gallery, inspecting the maps on the wall. "And now? What's behind these maps?"

"Nothing. After the war was over, my grandfather extracted the paintings and put them in the bank's vault with the intention of returning every treasure to its rightful family." He stopped beside a large flat file cabinet. "What year's maps do we want to look at?"

"Based on the 1855 date of the letter, I'd say those created after 1850 and before 1860."

Theo knelt down, opened one of the drawers and began pulling out the maps. He took all six and spread them out on a long oak table. There were four original hand-colored, hand-drawn maps and two that were printed.

"Did your grandfather manage to return all the paintings?"

He shook his head. "Only about half. By the time the war was over, some of the owners had moved or died—many were killed in the Holocaust. Records had been lost. There needed to be incontrovertible proof of ownership. It's actually how I met my wife. She was an expert in art restoration and came to the island on behalf of a client, then wound up staying to take over the recovery project and . . ." He stopped speaking suddenly, bent over the maps and began to look at them intently. Jac wasn't sure if something had really caught his interest or if he were just averting his gaze so she couldn't see him.

"You've really had a hard time, haven't you?" she asked.

He nodded and then did look up at her. She could see the grief in his eyes. This was only the second time he'd mentioned his wife. And other than Malachai saying it had been an accident, Jac still didn't know how she died.

"Thank you for coming," Theo said.

Regardless of what happened with the Druid find, Jac was glad she'd come. It felt right to be here with him—with someone who was as lost in his way as she was in hers. The strange bond she'd had with this man years ago when he was a sullen teenager was still there. She didn't quite know who he'd become, but they'd once started to help each other. Maybe they could finish that job now.

"Okay, let's get a look," she said. "If we spot anything on these old maps, we can compare it to what is now on the current map." A few minutes passed. "What is this place called Devil's Hole?" Jac asked. "That sounds promising."

"It's a crater originally called the Spiral Cave. About thirty meters across and sixty meters deep. During a shipwreck in 1851 the vessel's figurehead wound up washing inside. It was recarved by a local artist to resemble a devil, hence the name. It was my first thought when I found the letter. But sadly there's no way Hugo could have hidden anything there. One of the caveats is the area had to be accessible by foot without too much arduous climbing. Hugo was in his early fifties at the time."

"What do you think of this?" Jac asked after ten minutes of studying the coastline on the oldest hand-drawn map. "Do you think this area looks like a horn?"

Theo looked where she was pointing. "It might—but a single horn doesn't suggest Lucifer, does it?"

"Not really."

After a quarter of an hour he said, "The land hasn't changed all that much from the map I've been studying, and I just don't see anything."

She heard frustration and didn't blame him. "I'm not seeing anything either, but that doesn't mean it's not here."

"There are just too many caves and so few of them are identified. If only he'd given Fantine directions."

"She knew where they'd gone together. She knew where to look." Jac stood up, stretched and walked over to the window. The sun was shining on the sea, glinting on its surface. "Do you know where Hugo lived when he was on the island?"

"The house isn't there anymore. It's a big apartment complex now."

"Can you reach the sea from there?"

"In Jersey, you can reach the sea from everywhere."

"Can we go see it? Walk from where the house would have been, down to the water? Maybe we'll notice something."

"I've done that, but of course, yes." Theo looked at his watch. "We should go at low tide. Otherwise not all the beach will be passable and not all the cave entrances will be visible. Would you like some lunch in the meantime? There are some decent restaurants near there."

Theo called up the stairs. A middle-aged blonde woman leaned over the balustrade. He introduced Jac to his assisant, Samantha Philemon, and told her where he was going. Then he and Jac got back in the car and headed to St. Helier and the Royal Yacht Club.

The restaurant was more than decent. Jac ordered grilled salmon and Theo ordered a hamburger. They both had ale. The food had just arrived when Jac saw Ash Gaspard walk in. He had a benign expression on his face till he noticed Theo, and then Ash frowned.

Theo saw his brother coming toward them when Ash was about ten feet away. Jac sensed him stiffen in his seat. She thought she could smell fear.

The *Scent of Fear* was one of the fragrances she and Robbie had worked on the longest. Except for the *Fragrance of Loyalty*, *Fear* was one of the biggest challenges. Robbie didn't think it smelled like fear at all but instead like the air up on the roof of the maison they lived in. But that was what she was trying to re-create, she told him. She'd never been more frightened in her life than when she almost fell off that roof, high above the street. Before her brother grabbed her and pulled her back, she thought she was doomed. Robbie had saved her that day, literally. Figuratively, so many times.

"Hello, Theo," Ash said.

Theo nodded. The friction between the two of them, which she'd sensed last night, was just as strong today.

Seeing both of them in the daylight instead of

the dimly lit bar, she was struck by how much they looked alike. Ash had lighter hair and skin and looked younger. Less ravaged. Less pained. His eyes were almost the same color blue but they were more vibrant. As if he hadn't once had the life drained out of him. They both had the same build and strong aesthetic features.

"To what do I owe the pleasure of this interruption?"

"I called the gallery, Samantha told me where you were. I need to talk to you. Can you step outside for a moment?"

"No, just sit down and tell me whatever it is. It's impolite to leave a lady at the table. And I don't mind Jac hearing."

The waiter came over as Ash pulled out the chair.

"I won't be eating," Ash told him, "but I'd like a cup of coffee, please. Black."

With a precise, "Yes sir," the waiter was gone.

"I need to talk to you about the gallery."

"Yes, fine."

"A woman named Elizabeth Timmonson is haranguing me. Apparently she's been in touch with you about a Renoir pastel? Is there a reason you're not dealing with her?"

"The paperwork is complicated, Ash. This was all being done through proper channels and now . . ." He left off without finishing the sentence.

"If you would hire someone to replace—"

Theo interrupted. "It's not like finding a new secretary." His voice was harsh and raspy with pain.

It occurred to Jac that the death of Theo's wife, who had run the recovery project, had probably left many loose ends. She stood. "I'm going to excuse myself." She hoped that when she got back they'd be done talking about the gallery business.

Five minutes later they were still going at it.

"But this case isn't simple at all," Theo was saying. "The Gaspard receipt indicates a sale."

"But Timmonson says the nephew claims his grandfather, who sold it to us in 1937, was acting under duress—"

"I know the laws, Ash, and I told you already, the letters I have prove there was no duress. In fact quite the opposite in this case. He sold us the Renoir and he turned around and bought a Dürer for a few thousand pounds more."

"Well then, there won't be any problem, but you have to deal with it. You can't just let all these issues sit and wait for you to get over your mourning. We all cared about Naomi—"

"Don't you dare even say her name." Theo's voice was so low that Jac wasn't even sure she heard the right words. "You? Of all people? Aren't you ashamed?"

Ash turned to Jac. "It was lovely to see you again, Jac. I'm sorry it wasn't under more pleasurable conditions. Maybe while you're here I could show you my very different version of the island than the one my brother is—"

"Will you please leave," Theo said. "How I run my business at the gallery is not your concern."

"There you are wrong. Everything with the Gaspard name on it affects us both. A scandal at the gallery will reflect badly on the bank, Theo. We can't afford to have this drag out." He pulled a piece of paper out of his pocket and handed it to his brother. "Timmonson is expecting your call. She wants to take the ferry over and sit with the files herself. Let me know when you've set it up. I'd like to be there at the meeting. We need to make sure this doesn't turn into an incident. If there's any question as to the provenance of the pastel, I just want it returned to the family regardless."

Ash looked at Jac. "Again, I'm sorry that I interrupted your lunch."

He stood up and, without saying good-bye to Theo, walked out.

Once he was out of sight, Theo turned to Jac. "I'm sorry too." He picked up his glass and drank what was left of the pale ale. For a few moments he seemed lost in thought. Then he glanced at his watch. When he looked up, whatever concerns he'd had a moment ago were invisible.

"Time and tide and all that. Would you like coffee, or are you ready to hit the beach?"

Nineteen

They walked to the area near the bay known as Grève d'Azette, where rows of uninteresting small houses lined both sides of the street. Typical of urban sprawl in any town, Jac thought. Tear down what's charming and historic and put up new housing designed with the lowest aesthetic-to-cost ratio as you can manage and still ensure high prices.

"This is where Marine Terrace was." Theo pointed to a group of modest two-story homes so tightly packed in, their side walls were touching. "The area wasn't at all built up then and there was only a walled garden between Hugo's house and the beach where he walked so often. From his bedroom on the second floor, he could see the sea."

Theo took her arm in a companionable gesture and led the way to the end of the block and then took her down a side street to Le Dicq, the beach access pathway. At the bottom of the cobblestone slipway were towering, rugged rock formations lining the shore.

Jac felt sudden recognition. It was as if she'd seen all this before. She knew this place. Was it a déjà vu? A dream?

Theo was talking, pointing to the horizon.

"We're facing France now. Which is why this was such a favorite spot of Hugo's. He liked to climb these rocks and sit up there and stare out at his homeland. He named this formation *Rocher des Proscrits*—Rock of the Exiles. He and his friends adopted it as a symbol of their exile."

"This looks so familiar."

"There's a famous photograph of Hugo taken here, looking out at the sea. His son Charles was a photographer who honed his craft while living in Jersey. Hugo seemed to have been endlessly willing to pose for him. There are dozens of shots of Hugo on this beach among these rocks. We have quite a few at Wells in Wood. I'll have to show you."

Jac noticed the sun glinting off the rock and walked over to read a plaque commemorating Hugo. Large patches of mold and iron deposits had turned the tablet into a piece of impressionist artwork.

"This being a tourist destination, I'd guess Lucifer's Lair isn't here," Theo said. "There can't be anything undiscovered in this area."

"Just because a spot is highly trafficked doesn't mean it can't still keep secrets." She was speaking to Theo but felt as if only part of her was focused on what she was saying. "But you're probably right in this case. It doesn't look like there are any openings into these rocks . . ." She paused, then turned to him. "Theo, how can this all look so familiar? I've never been here but I know this place. And not from seeing a photograph, it's much more."

He smiled, and it might have been the first time that she couldn't see any of the ever-present pain behind the expression. "I don't know. Unless . . . it has something to do with us. I want to show you something. Let's go this way."

"Us?" He had to be referring to the weeks they'd spent together at Blixer Rath. There wasn't anything else they shared but that curious time they'd spent so connected that it had both scared and exhilarated her.

He nodded but didn't explain. "Come on, it's not too far."

They were walking as close to the water's edge as they could without soaking her shoes. Sometimes a wave hit a rock and sprayed her face. Smelling the salty brine that hadn't changed in centuries, she thought about Hugo walking here and smelling the exact same scent. Her father used to talk about how scent connects us to a past we can't always see, that seems lost but can so easily be conjured up and found.

Theo had gotten a few steps ahead of her. Now she remembered he used to do that on their walks at Blixer Rath. Always in a hurry to get to the next destination. He'd been in a rush the day of the accident too. The memory rolled in like the ocean, surprising her with its vividness.

It had been mid-May. The sixteenth of May. She was surprised she could pull up the date after so long. Since the incident with the stone circle drawing, Jac and Theo had been inseparable. For two months their connection grew stronger and stronger. Several times Jac dreamed of scenery Theo had drawn. All ruins around Jersey. All places that had some special meaning to him.

Yes! That was it.

"That's why this place looks familiar now," Jac said. "I dreamt about it at Blixer!"

"Yes," Theo said. "This place and a few others. Let me show you."

As they walked through the rocky landscape, she felt as if she were walking through those long-ago dreams. The water, the outcroppings, the barren shore. She'd been here in those dreams that Theo used to joke she stole from him, that Malachai used to attribute to her openness to the collective unconscious.

On that May afternoon she'd been playing piano, and when she looked up from the keyboard, Theo was standing there, just watching her. The sun shining through the window illuminated him, and then as she watched, all the natural light disappeared and he was thrust in darkness as if the clouds had left the sky and come down to get in between them.

"Let's take a walk," he'd said.

There was nothing unusual about his suggestion. During free periods he often asked her to roam the countryside with him. They'd start off at the same pace and then Theo would see something he wanted to explore and she'd have to rush to catch up. And then once she had, he'd outdistance her again. Like he was now, he always walked as if he had an appointment in a specific spot and he didn't want to be late. Once another one of the kids had joined them and Theo's gait was different. He hadn't moved as if he'd been on a mission anymore. The walk turned into just a stroll through evergreen glades and fields of wildflowers.

Jac hadn't liked someone else being along. But on that May afternoon there was no one with them. They were alone.

They reached the field that she thought of as the border between the clinic and what was beyond. Once they crossed it, if you looked back, Blixer was invisible. As he always did, Theo stopped to pick various kinds of flora to braid into crowns. Typically he used sprigs of rosemary. It was easy to bend and shape. Lilies of the valley had popped up that week, and so he picked those too and wove them into the rosemary. He placed a crown on Jac's head and one on his own.

At first the ritual had seemed strange, but now she expected it and loved how the flowers' fragrance surrounded her. Especially that day. The scent of the small, white bells was delicate but potent. Her father had used it as the base for his well-known and popular *Blanc de Nuit* fragrance.

Crossing the field, they entered the forest and after about a hundred meters came to a clearing. Here Theo performed what he called the "second ritual." Together they hunted for rocks, but only smooth, rounded stones because Theo had told her negative energy could stay trapped in crevices and cracks. The gathering usually took the better part of fifteen minutes. They were quiet as they worked, and she never minded when they didn't talk. The silence between them seemed like its own kind of music.

Once they'd collected two dozen rocks, he made a circle of them about six feet across.

The first time she'd seen him doing it, she asked why.

"Don't you know?" he said. "Isn't this part in your dream?"

No, she'd never dreamed anything but the circle itself. Not how they used it.

So he showed her.

They sat down inside the formation, facing each other. Then with the last three rocks, Theo closed the circle. Sitting in the lotus position they'd learned in meditation class, the "third ritual" began. This was what Jac yearned for. And the only reason she put up with the tedium of all the rest of it.

They would begin by meditating, opening themselves up to their connections, as he described it. And then Theo would lean forward and begin to kiss her.

Jac had kissed people before—as a thank-you, a good-bye, a hello, or a show of comfort or support. But those first kisses between them were none of those.

Each was an invitation to a world that was dark in the light and light in the dark. Each began with their lips pressed together but moved throughout her body. Each altered her so that she became feeling, not thought. His kisses found the parts of Jac that were waiting, dormant, and ready to bloom. They set off tiny sparks through her body. Her skin became so sensitive that if he just put one fingertip on her neck she'd spasm. He was the first boy who had ever touched her. Until Theo she hadn't known the secret ways her body worked. Or the wonder of how someone else's body could affect hers.

That May day she smelled Theo's cologne of eucalyptus, honey, cinnamon and oakmoss laced with the lily of the valley and rosemary. The scents combined in a heady mix that made her feel as if she were floating, being held aloft by stem-and-leaf arms. She wasn't sure if the flowers were kissing her or Theo was. But it didn't matter. Those first kisses fed her. They began with taste. Sweet like honey, and fresh like mint. They gave her sustenance in a way that no food ever had, were delicious in the way only something you've never tasted before can be. They were both gentle and passionate. As light as the fragrance of the lilies and as deep as the color of the green rosemary. Those kisses were as much about discovery as they were about destination.

On previous days he'd brought wine or a joint. On that day he had brought neither. Instead he extracted a folded envelope, opened it and showed her what was inside. The dark and powdery irregular disk looked like dried leather and smelled of mold. He broke off a small piece and gave it to her. Then broke off an equally small piece, put it in his own mouth and chewed. She was frightened but also curious. And she wanted to be his companion on whatever journey he took.

As the mushroom invaded her bloodstream and altered her consciousness, Jac's hearing became more attuned to the sounds of the forest. She listened to a chipmunk scurrying across a log, a bird chirping and water dripping. Her sense of smell, always intense and precise, was even more exaggerated. Resins, molds, the spicy and sharp scents of the woods, assaulted her. *The Perfume of Dark*, she thought, automatically playing the game she and her brother had indulged in for years.

"Shut your eyes," Theo whispered.

He did. She didn't. She wanted to be able to

see. She watched Theo reach out, find and take her hands. As soon as he touched her and their connection was made, strange things began to happen. First she felt a warmth coming from the stones, as if heat were emanating from their cold surface.

Then the air around Theo began to waver, as if affected by another frequency.

They each had been given mantras to help them meditate and were told they were private—to hold close and keep secret and speak only inside their own minds. But Theo was chanting his, low and under his breath and just loud enough for her to hear. She listened to the foreign sounds. Felt compelled to mouth them also. She was chanting his mantra. Except the words didn't sound Indian. They didn't sound like any language she'd ever heard. These words had tastes.

Honey. Berries. Malt.

"Budh Vid Dru Budh Vid Dru Budh . . ."

Tastes of something bitter and burnt. Charred toast? Marshmallows crisped to ash?

Jac didn't think this was the mantra the teachers at Blixer had given Theo. If it was, he was breaking yet another rule by speaking it out loud. Did that even matter anymore?

Jac felt the mixed emotions that came with doing something forbidden and risking danger all at the same time. She was exhilarated and scared. Theo had told her they were exploring Carl Jung's shadow world. In search of something that would explain their strange connection to each other. That they needed to go beyond reality into the darkness where mystics and shamans quested for answers and find their own.

For several minutes, or a half hour, or even an hour—she didn't know—the two of them sat on the pine-needle carpet and chanted. The sound became the wind. The birdsong. The rustle of the leaves. The roar of a distant waterfall.

Peace descended on Jac. Energy flowed out of her and into Theo through the tips of her fingers on her right hand into the tips of his left and back into her from the tips of his fingers on his right hand into the tips of her left. Centuries of understanding moved in them. She saw moving mandalas made of brilliantly colored yarn. Elaborately woven designs like the sacred Buddhist art she'd seen in books in her grandfather's library and that Malachai used in their therapy sessions, but now come to life and given dimension.

And then she realized she wasn't just looking at them, she was inside them. She was the red thread, Theo was the blue. They were each creating patterns as they circled each other, moving closer and closer to the center, where she knew they would become the very oneness the drawings were supposed to help the viewer find.

Sitting together in the sun, in the woods, Theo

was taking her on a journey into the cosmic soup of eternity.

As these thoughts welled up in her, she felt as if she was finally understanding concepts she'd always been confused by. And being introduced to thoughts she'd never even contemplated before. Time was disappearing. In this new dimension everything that had ever happened to her and to Theo existed on the same plane. All their histories were present in the same moment. The two of them were connected through all these events, tied to each other through their over-lapping pasts. Tangled up in the threads of each other's lives.

And then he let go of her hands and broke the connection.

In a great rush all the sounds and smells and sensations left her.

Theo had left her too. He'd risen up and was running away from her, running through the woods. Fast, as if he were being chased. She ran after him, calling out his name.

She couldn't catch up, but she managed to keep her pace steady so he remained in her sight.

At first she was so intent on following him that she didn't focus on where they were going. Then she realized they were going up a staircase of rough stone carved in the mountain. Up. Up. Farther up. She hated that she couldn't see where the steps were leading. All their hikes before had been on sloping hills with gentle inclines. But this landscape was different. They were on a rising path that hung out over the forest. At every turn Jac saw a threatening edge. But she kept going, following him.

And then he stopped. He'd reached the summit. He dropped to his knees. Knelt on an outcropping of rock. His head dropped into his hands. His back shook. He was in some kind of crisis. She barely heard his choked sobs over the sound of the rushing water. No, they weren't sobs, they were two words he was saying over and over.

"I can't," he said, as he beat his fist on the dirt. "I can't. I can't."

The heartbreak of a lifetime in just two broken words.

Slowly she climbed the last half-dozen steps, trying not to look at what lay beyond. How far a drop was it? If he fell would he survive? Would she? Panic washed over her. She couldn't keep going. But she couldn't leave him there. Her breath was shallow. Jac could feel her heart racing. She forced the last few steps and finally reached Theo.

The rock where he was kneeling was hanging out over a large pool of cool blue water being fed by a waterfall. Dizziness overwhelmed her. What if she lost her balance? Tumbled headfirst into the water? She retreated two steps. Three. Four. She was starting to panic. Wanted to run away. But she knew she couldn't. She had to get him away from the edge.

Using the method Malachai had showed her, Jac took a deep breath, inhaling to the count of four. Held the breath in to the count of four. Then exhaled to the count of four. Then held to the count of four. And then repeated the exercise.

If she couldn't control her anxiety, she wasn't going to be able to help him. And he needed help. He had stood up now and was perched even closer to the edge of the rock.

Jac pushed herself back up those four last steps and approached Theo. Should she talk to him or not? Was he even aware of her? If she startled him, he might try to get away, fall over the edge, somehow take her with him. For a moment she was absolutely certain that his action was going to be her destruction no matter what she did. That by being with him she had doomed herself. But that was crazy.

Go, grab him, pull him backward, save him.

No, run the other way, down the hill and away from here. Save yourself.

It was as if she had two totally separate sets of emotions fighting a battle inside her.

Jac watched his hair wave in the breeze, his long, lithe body shake with sobs.

"Theo?" she whispered. "Theo, it's me, Jac." She inched closer. "We have to get off this ledge."

She didn't look down, just kept her eyes on him.

"Theo? We have to get off the ledge. Take my hand."

He didn't respond.

She crept closer, then reached out and very gently and slowly took his hand. He didn't resist, but his fingers were icy. For a few moments both of them stayed like that, rooted to the spot. Her hand holding his. A skin-and-bones, flesh-and-sinew connection. She clung to his hand to bridge the gap between her fear, his survival and hers.

"Theo, what is wrong?" she asked.

His only answer was to take a single step closer to the ledge, pulling her with him.

She didn't want to, didn't mean to, but she let go of his hand. She couldn't follow him. But if she didn't, what would happen to him? She should grab him again, keep talking, and try to get him to retreat. But to do that she'd have to step out farther on the rock.

The sky rapidly and unexpectedly turned gray. Even though Jac knew the clouds had moved in front of the sun, it seemed as if Theo himself were sucking up the light. She was worried that in this sudden darkness, she might lose her footing, might step off the ledge.

But she wanted to step off the ledge.

Suddenly Jac wasn't afraid of the dizzying height. Instead, she wanted to accept its invitation and jump.

What was wrong with her? Whatever drug Theo

had given her was producing hallucinations worse than any she'd suffered at home. Those were confusing but at least linear. They were fragments of made-up stories. This was just terrible chaos.

The sun was still behind the clouds. Jac was cold. Spray from the waterfall was blowing back on her. Soaking through her clothes. The rocks below her feet were slippery. Wet rocks, wet soles. Easy to fall. Wanting to fall. Fear. Longing. The push-pull of conflicting needs.

The part of Jac that was worried about the fall was not afraid of the water. She was a good swimmer, having spent endless hours at the beach in the south of France with her grandmother and brother. She loved the surf. The smooth sand. Even the waves when they were a little rough. She reminded herself of that now. Even if she did fall, it would be into water. She would swim. The drop really wasn't that far.

There was no other option.

Reaching out, Jac took Theo's hand once more. They were connected again. She felt safer. Then more terrorized. Safety. Terror. All that kept her from falling was his hand. What propelled her forward was his hand. Where their cold skin was touching felt suddenly hot, like molten metal, bonding them, soldering them. Even if she wanted to let go, she couldn't anymore. They had merged.

Maybe he would jump and decide her fate for

her. She was incapable of action. As desperate to step back as to step forward. To throw herself over the edge. To back up away from the edge.

Theo was talking to her now. Saying something, but she couldn't make out what. The waterfall was too loud. It was too beautiful. She pulled away. Finally free. His fingers were no longer clutching hers. The water was coming up to meet her, and then it was cold. So very cold.

Twenty

Jac didn't remember what had happened when she woke hours later in the infirmary at Blixer Rath. The images in her head were a mixed-up jumble. She knew she'd fallen. Had she really jumped? Why would she have done that? Yet that was what she remembered. That and the cold. The terrible cold of the lake. Of endings. Of loss.

There were no memories at all about how she got out of the water and back to Blixer. Or what had happened to Theo.

The nurse took her temperature and seemed relieved. When Jac asked why, she said the doctor had been worried about hypothermia.

Jac fell asleep again and when she next woke up, Malachai Samuels was sitting beside her bed. For fifteen minutes he asked her questions about what had happened. But she couldn't remember most of it. She was tired. Her head hurt, she told him.

Had she hit her head?

She didn't know that either.

When she woke up next it was daylight and her headache was gone. When the nurse came in to check on her, Jac asked about Theo and the nurse said he was fine. But she said it in an odd way that made Jac suspicious. When Malachai returned to visit with her that afternoon, she asked him about Theo too.

Theo had gone home, Malachai said.

"When will he be back? I need to talk to him about what happened. He'll be able to help me understand."

"He's gone home for good," Malachai said. "He's not coming back."

She'd asked Malachai if she could write to him and thank him because she'd finally remembered it had been Theo who'd jumped in after her and pulled her out and then half dragged, half carried her back to the clinic. But Malachai had said no, that it was best if she not write him just yet. He was having a hard time.

What did that mean? she'd asked.

"It's confidential, Jac. I can't talk about another patient with you."

"He's not another patient, he's my friend." She felt tears pricking her eyes but held them back. She never cried.

Since Jac arrived in Jersey, she hadn't talked to Theo about his last day at Blixer Rath seventeen years ago. But she needed to now. As they continued walking on the beach, she said, "I felt lost without you after you left Blixer."

"I'm sorry they made me go. I was terribly worried about you. I wrote."

She nodded. "They never gave me any of your letters."

He took her hand. Was it because the path was rocky and so hard to navigate without stumbling? Or was it a gesture of friendship? Or more? Surprisingly, the connection Jac had felt to Theo when they were young was still strong. It was a tensile thread that had stretched all these years. For a moment she thought of Griffin. How their connection too had lasted over so many years. And how she was never going to be happy with Griffin's shadow in the way. Low down in the pit of her stomach she felt a sudden emptiness and thought about what had happened after the lightning storm. The baby had been conceived in love. It deserved to be mourned with love. But she wasn't ready to give herself up to the grief, not yet.

They were almost at the top when one of the rocks Jac stepped on came loose. She felt as if she was about to lose her balance, but Theo's grip tightened and steadied her.

She'd regained her stability but her heart was racing. Theo was still holding her hand.

"We're almost there," he said.

The ocean was on their right. They were only four feet off the sand. Nothing to be afraid of. She looked up. The summit was only another foot.

He noticed her assessing the height. "It's not very high. And it's all sand below. Nothing to be afraid of this time. I promise."

So he remembered.

"Theo, when we were at Blixer Rath . . ." Suddenly she wasn't sure she wanted to find out what had happened.

"Yes?"

"I know there was an accident and that I slipped on the rocks and fell into the lake. But why did you leave so suddenly?"

"Prejudice."

"I don't understand."

"Even there in that bastion of alternative thinking, they feared what they didn't understand. And they didn't understand us."

"What about us didn't they understand?"

They'd reached the top. He sat down and dangled his feet off the edge. He was right, even up here it wasn't a big drop. She sat beside him. This perspective offered a different view of the shoreline as it curved in and out, creating bays and harbors. So much of it looked unspoiled and undeveloped and very much out of time.

"My brother and I were always at each other," Theo said. "Even though I'm a year older, he was always taller and stronger. He used to try to beat me up. He never managed to hurt me, but I'd go into some kind of state whenever it happened. For a few hours after be very much out of it. A dissociation, they called it. "

"They?"

"The *theys* who couldn't help me with it."

"That's where the Clinic of the Last Resorts came in." Using her old name for it, she smiled. Theo smiled too. "So did something like that happen at Blixer after my accident? Did you black out?"

He looked at her. "You really don't remember?"

"Barely anything. I know we'd made one of those rock circles that looked like your drawings. And we sat inside and did our meditation thing. And then you gave me some kind of drug. Was it a mushroom?"

He nodded. "Not really smart of me, but yes, a mushroom."

She told him what she remembered about the climb up the mountain and then the fall. "I woke up in the infirmary and found out you were gone. Why?"

"They threw me out, Jac. They claimed it was because I'd broken so many rules. The final straw being giving you that magic mushroom. But I think the real reason they threw me out rather than let me stay and continue to work with me was they thought I'd pushed you."

"But you didn't. For some crazy reason I jumped." She closed her eyes. Tried to bring back more of that long-ago day. "I don't know why, but I did. Why didn't they ask me?"

He shrugged.

"Why would they say you pushed me? I don't understand."

"Growing up I was different, difficult, moody. Didn't fit in. My brother was the opposite. The golden child with a million friends. Great at school, at sports. Well-adjusted. Never could do wrong. There was no reason for him to be jealous of me, but he was. He was always making fun of me and picking fights. You know how kids are, I didn't want to go to my parents and tattle. I just wanted to win him over. But nothing I did ever mattered. Never. When we were young and he'd try to beat me up, I usually managed to protect myself. But then we had one fight that turned really bad. I was just trying to keep him off me, to stop him from hurting me. I pushed him away. He lost his balance and fell and hit the side of his face on a table leg. It was a horrible bash and he lost most of his sight in that one eye. I went into some kind of psychotic state after that, or so I've been told. I didn't talk to anyone for over four months. Stopped eating. They said I was trying to starve myself. Saw a million doctors. Took all the pills they gave me. Even tried to take them all at once one night and do some real damage. After that I was sent to Blixer."

"And what happened to you after you got home?"

"My father was furious and shipped me off to boarding school."

Jac felt sick. Somehow this was her fault. "How was that?"

"Awful." He stood. "And boring." He held out his hand to help her up. She took it. Once they were both standing, he continued holding her hand. She felt a surge of sensation.

"Now this way," he said leading her down the rocky slope.

The sun had broken through the clouds and the light over the sea was a liquid yellow—the kind of light the impressionists tried to capture in their plein air canvases. "Monet was a master at capturing this atmosphere," Jac said, thinking of all the times her mother had taken her to see the painter's work at the Musée Marmottan or L'Orangerie. She had a flash of the last time she'd been there, over the summer, with her brother.

Maybe after this trip she'd go back to Paris for a week and spend some time with Robbie. He'd be able to help her figure things out, to separate the past from the present so she could contemplate the future.

Theo let go of her hand and jumped off the rock.

It was only a three-foot leap down to the sand. Reaching up, he held out his hands. "Jump, Jac. I'll catch you."

She looked. Not a very big jump. Nothing to be afraid of. Yet she was. It was an irrational fear. She took a breath. Focused on his eyes. And jumped.

A second of weightless falling. Utter panic. As if she'd left her body. As if she were lost. Would never find her way back. Would—

His hands grabbed her around the waist.

From this spot on the beach it was only a few minutes' walk to a huge rock formation. Slabs of indigenous rocks placed on pillars created a covered alleyway.

"This way." He pointed inside.

They walked a few meters down a stone hallway. Almost immediately she smelled a fire. A thick, acrid bitter birch or fir fire. Her nostrils were full of the ancient earthy scent. Not unpleasant but foreign.

"What is this place?" Jac asked, stopping.

"Legends say going all the way back to the seventeenth century, witches and devil worshippers used to meet here. Archaeologists who've worked the area say that much further back than that it was a pagan site. Are you worried about going in?"

"No," she said, and followed him inside.

They reached the innermost circle. His steps

crunched. It was a small sound, but one that she recognized. She looked down. The ground around the hearth was littered with shells and bones. Shivers ran up and down her arms. Cold pinpricks warned her of a flare-up.

No, don't slip back. Stay.

Jac was sliding into a netherworld of unfamiliar voices and smells and feelings that belonged to . . . to whom?

"Jac? Are you all right?"

Theo's voice pulled her back like a lifeline to the present.

"I'm fine. How much is known about this configuration?"

"Archaeologists think that these rocks have been here for over six thousand years."

"It looks like part of a Celtic ritual site," she said.

They continued on under a stone archway. On the other side was a second grouping of stones, wide slabs evenly placed every three feet. Row after row of them. Theo walked among them with a lot of authority. He obviously knew this place very well.

"It's familiar, isn't it?" he asked.

She nodded. "Just like the rocks on the beach. This is another of the places I drew at Blixer."

"Yes, you drew all these places. It's something about us. Something that scared Malachai. We had some kind of psychic bond. It's one of the things

I wrote you about. Even the accident at the end. You were doing what I wanted to do. I wanted to jump off that cliff. But you did it."

"I don't understand. How is any of that possible?"

"I don't understand either. Not what was between us, not what it meant. Not if it still exists. But maybe now that you're here we can find out."

She nodded. "Maybe we can."

They'd reached the far end of the dolmens and the remains of a pyre.

Jac leaned over to examine it. She sniffed the air. "Can you smell that?"

Theo shook his head.

"It's a mineral scent, mixed with pinewood, almost sweet."

He sniffed again. "I can't smell anything. You can?"

She nodded.

"Do you know what it is?" he asked.

She took in another whiff. "No. I've never smelled it before."

Theo pulled a book of matches out of his pocket, searched through the rubble and found some kindling. It took him two tries but he managed to ignite a small fire. Jac breathed in the smoke. She felt the scene waving around her. The old sensation that suggested a hallucination. The telltale shivers that presaged an episode ran up and down her arms.

She tried to do her breathing exercises but the air was filled with the foreign odor. She tried to fight back against the attack. The firelight illuminated the stone columns, throwing the carvings on their surface into relief. She hadn't noticed them before, but she focused and examined them now.

Birds flew up and around the pillars, wings spread, heading upward. She'd never seen any photograph of this site that she knew of, and yet it was familiar.

Theo is going to take me into the next stone chamber now, she thought. *And when he does I'm going to see the altar.*

And he did. And she did.

Twenty-one

56 BCE
ISLE OF JERSEY

"Reports are that the Romans will be here in less than twenty days," Owain said. "Can you gather some skins of mead? Some fruit?"

"You're going on a retreat?" Gwenore asked.

He nodded. "I need to consult the gods and ask for visions for new insight."

"I don't understand. Aren't we prepared for the Romans?"

"They say that this isn't a small band of outlaws. These soldiers are traveling in a large group, ravaging everywhere they go."

"But you and the warriors are prepared—"

Owain interrupted. "Not if we're outnumbered." He shook his head. "We need guidance."

Gwenore nodded. His wife knew better than to argue. If he needed to go she would prepare his food and make do without him. He was well aware she was nervous. Even though she was a strong woman and afraid of nothing else, she had an unfounded fear of these retreats. Now he reminded her not to worry.

Outside the hut, their eleven-year-old son was working on his totem. Each novitiate had to complete this ritual task before being ordained. Brice was almost done carving the animal from the hazel tree stump.

Owain had been proud of how quickly Brice had understood his instructions.

"In the never-ending and age-old search to learn the secrets of creation, a priest needs more than wisdom; he needs to connect to the mystical realm where answers hide," Owain had explained. "A totem will aid you in your quest for magical knowledge. It will be a bridge between the physical world and the metaphysical one."

"The totem is the animal I'll merge with?" Brice had asked.

"Yes, son. Each animal or bird offers different attributes. An owl gives insight. A wolf makes one more alert to dangers."

Discovering what animal you needed help from and then creating one's own meditation tool to call upon for strength and understanding during the tough life ahead was a process that in itself built strength. Brice had been working at his for over four months, and in that time Owain had seen his son becoming a man.

Owain was proud he would be the priest to initiate his son into the Druid class. He would have the privilege of taking Brice to the secret ceremony deep in the cave where light never penetrated, close to the center of the earth and the spirits of the animals. Aided by the incense made from stones, and a sacred drink made from macerated herbs, he would show Brice how to engage in a dance with his animal familiar until he found that ecstatic place of growth and under-standing. Of otherworldly knowledge.

They had already visited the holy site once. During the winter, Brice had been taken blind-folded into the inner sanctum, where he'd inhaled the incense and drunk the liquor and talked through a dream incubation. A journey designed to help the boy discover his animal familiar.

Brice had seen a cat. He'd found his spirit guide. The creature whom he would forever after be able to communicate with during magic hours: dawn, twilight and midnight in the sacred cave or in the ancient woods.

The step after that was for the novitiate to give the spirit a physical form. And so Brice had been spending a period of time every day carving his cat.

It was a fitting animal for a priest. Cats guard the secrets of the otherworld and are liaisons with mystic realms. Protectors of esoteric knowledge, cats can open the gates through which a priest can see the future and gain insight.

Like his father, Brice was dark-skinned and tall. He was a smart boy with a gentle soul, who cared for people with a rare compassion. That he had inherited from his father. From his mother he'd inherited a sense of humor and mischievous ways, which could sometimes make Owain outwardly angry but, in private with Gwenore, always made him laugh.

And like Gwenore, the boy questioned everything.

As one of the elder priests of the tribe, Owain performed ceremonies and rituals that helped his people to live and prosper. Gwenore's questions were not always welcome. They sometimes bordered on anarchy. Rules were meant to be blindly obeyed. She didn't believe that. And Owain worried that her curiosity didn't always set a good example for their son. Or for the other women who looked up to her. He couldn't change her though. She was too strong-willed. And he wasn't sure he would have wanted to. She was his heart. From the first time he beheld her, standing beside Roan, his brother, Owain wanted her. And for the first three years of that marriage, Owain had spent part of every day fighting just how much he wanted her and cursing the gods for the injustice of her having chosen his brother.

As Brice chipped away, Owain was lost in the even, measured beat of the mallet hitting the chisel. Thinking about Roan, he felt a familiar pang of longing mixed with guilt. As much as he missed his brother—and he did—every single day, if the fates hadn't intervened, and if Roan hadn't been killed in battle, Owain wouldn't have inherited Gwenore. And she would not have given him this son.

"These last few months before Brice turns twelve are precious ones," Owain said to Gwenore. "The last of his innocence."

"We have to let him grow up no matter how hard it is for us to let him go," Gwenore reminded him, and not for the first time.

"He's worked so hard to prepare for his initiation."

"And he'll do fine."

Owain nodded, but he alone knew how hard the initiation rituals were. Not every boy succeeded, and those who didn't were demoralized and sometimes even demonized. Nervous for his son,

Owain worried the ring on his forefinger. The copper alloy had a deep plum cast to it and its carved design was intricate. When he looked at it he saw only knots, but Gwenore said she saw a strange ghostlike face with hollow gaping eyes staring back at her. This was Owain's initiation ring. In a few weeks he would be giving his son one just like it upon Brice's entry into the priesthood.

"I know he will." But his voice belied his words.

"If your brother had lived and if Brice were his son instead of yours, he'd be training to become a warrior. A far more dangerous way of life," she reminded him. "You should think of that instead."

"He's just grown up so fast." Owain was still watching Brice, unable to take his eyes off him.

"Roan isn't in him, Owain."

Everyone in the tribe believed in life after death and the spirit's ability to be reborn and live again in a new body. The undying soul was unquestioned. Did not the leaves fall off the tree and become part of the soil that nourished the tree, which spouted new leaves?

Owain had wanted Roan's soul to be reborn in Brice. He'd prayed for it and watched for it after the baby was born. For years he'd looked for proof, for a sign, for just one glimmer of recognition. And every time Gwenore caught him at it she told him what he was doing was pointless. He was never going to see Roan in their son. Because Roan was in him—in Owain.

As a witch, Gwenore knew things that remained mysteries to others. And she knew Roan had merged with Owain—with his brother—after his death. She had the mark of the witch on her too. That little star birthmark, right over her heart on her left breast. He loved the star and the fact that Brice had one too in almost the same place on his small body.

One dawn, a few months after Brice was born, Gwenore found Owain swinging a piece of metal in the shape of a star that he'd made for his son and the baby was fixated on it. Brice would reach for the star and laugh when Owain would pull it away.

"Did you sleep?" she had asked.

He didn't answer, he didn't have to. She knew what was obsessing him and why he sat and stared at their son for hours on end.

"I have something to tell you," Gwenore said. She spoke hesitantly, as if she was unsure how he was going to accept the news.

"Something happened at your brother's burial ceremony."

"What do you mean?"

"It was an overcast day. Do you remember?"

Owain nodded.

"But during that sacred service, the clouds broke. Do you remember that?"

"No."

"Well, it happened. Suddenly there was bright-ness where it had been gloom. It was a warm yellow light and it concentrated on you as you conducted the ceremony. I saw it shimmering all around you like a golden robe. So bright at first, I could barely look at you. While I watched, you seemed to absorb it. Soak it in. So that by the time the ceremony was over, it was gone. It was Roan. He was there. I could even smell him in the air. He was there, Owain, in the light, and the light was entering into you."

Owain had listened. He didn't believe what she said. If Gwenore had been speaking of someone else, he might have. But Roan—inside of him? He couldn't help but wonder if she was saying all this because she wanted it to be true. If it was just her way of keeping Roan alive and not accepting that she had really lost him.

They had both been haunted by loss. Intel-lectually he could accept that if he still mourned his brother, she would too. You don't stop loving someone because he ceases to take breaths. But no matter how hard Owain fought to understand his wife's feelings, he was still jealous of what Roan had meant to her and resented it.

"You've been watching Brice for a long time," Gwenore said, as she came back into the room and stood beside him. She handed him a cup of mead. He took it and drank. "He's going to be working for quite a while more." She took her husband's hand.

Owain turned to Gwenore, trying not to think about how she'd loved Roan first. Trying not to wonder if she still wanted his brother. She had been Owain's for fourteen years now. And she was here beside him offering him an escape from his worries.

Cupping her breasts through the fabric of her robe, her soft flesh through the rough material, he breathed her in. Her skin was scented with the oils she used to keep it supple. This was her secret scent. The smell no one but he could get drunk on. The unique combination of fertile woods, of blooming flowers and of ripe earth aroused him.

Owain pulled her robe open and caressed her thighs. Felt her shudder at his touch. A priest's fingers weren't coarse and calloused like other men's. As his brother's would have been. Roan's fingertips would have rubbed her raw. He hoped at least she appreciated that about him.

Sometimes he did feel as if Roan was alive in him. In these moments, Owain felt as if he was having sex for both of them. That when he came into Gwenore like this, stiff with want, with need, with the desire to take her and have her shiver and moan beneath him, he was fulfilling more than one man's lust.

Was it she who had put that thought into his mind? Or was it true?

Priests were taught and then taught others that intercourse was holy, procreation a part of the ritual of life and death. And yet in his secret heart, Owain didn't experience the act as holy. It was craven. Overwhelming. A drug stronger than the herbs he drank or the smoke he inhaled when it was time to speak to the gods.

Whom are you thinking of? he wanted to shout out to Gwenore as he plunged into her and felt her accept him, felt her welcome him into the slick crevice between her legs. It was like the opening to the sacred cave down on the beach. The entrance was so slight you barely noticed it, but inside. Ah, inside, it was deep and its darkness enveloped him.

Who am I to you now? Myself? My brother? Which one of us are you so eager to have inside you?

These questions were his personal torture, the mantra that echoed in his mind whenever he made love to Gwenore. These words repeated over and over in a rhythm that was in sync with his hips, with her hips, with his fingers stroking her hair, with her fingers stroking his back, with her lips moving on his, with her breath hot on his neck and his breath lost her hair, with the pattern of her heart beating in tandem with the pattern of his heart beating.

Who am I to you now? Who am I to you now? The living brother? The dead one?

293

Owain's hand gripped Gwenore's buttocks and pulled her even closer to him. Impossibly closer. As she gave herself up to him, as she yielded, she began to pant. Make small moaning sounds. Her fingers dug into his flesh. Waves of sensation surged in him. His blood burned in his veins. He breathed what felt like fire.

"Gwenore . . ." he whispered. "I want you."

"You have me."

"More. So there is no space between us. No distance. No air. Just us."

The smell of a thousand flowers scented her hair, and her mouth tasted of honey from the bees. He inhaled. Tasted. Drank.

"You bewitch me," he whispered hoarsely.

"Yes." She laughed low in her throat.

And yes, yes, she had. She had bewitched him. His witch.

They had traveled to this place together, and now their blood rushed and blessings of warmth enfolded them. He thrust up. She bit the skin on his neck. Between her legs was a whole night sky. Stars burst around him.

"Owain, Owain . . ." She was chanting.

He was chasing his own explosion, not waiting for hers. She was gone from him now. Always in these last moments she was gone from him.

And then came his release. And then hers. And then the first moment of stillness.

They lay quiet. Immobile. Cooling. Now the

scent of Gwenore's skin was infused with the scent of their sex. Outside, the steady thumping of Brice's tools continued as he carved the wood, as chips flew.

"Now I have to go to the caves," Owain said.

"For how long this time?"

"You know better than to ask. For as long as it takes for me to learn what it is that I need to do."

"It's dangerous to go there tonight. The tides are rising," she warned.

"I know." He smoothed her hair off her forehead. Her skin was damp. How long until he could lie with her again?

"I've been going to the caves since before we were together. Why are you anxious?" he asked.

She shrugged.

"Why?"

"The herbs were bitter today."

He knew how she interpreted the signs: when certain herbs were brewed and turned bitter, she foresaw doom.

Gwenore started to shiver. Strong breezes were coming off the sea.

"Winds of change," she muttered.

It had been fifteen years since their tribe had faced a threat this bad. Fifteen years since the battle in which his brother died.

"At least Brice won't have to fight," he said to his wife. "At least you don't have to fear that."

As he listened to the sounds of Brice carving his

295

totem, bringing his magic to life, Owain leaned down and kissed Gwenore on her damp forehead. "It's time for me to go, to pray, to chant and receive the visions so we can prepare for the future. Will you walk down to the sea with me?"

Twenty-two

Jac didn't tell Theo about the scene that had just played out in her mind. First, she needed to understand it herself.

In Paris this past summer, she'd had several hallucinations over a week's period, all triggered by a certain scent. Had she just stumbled on another scent that would induce visions?

The Paris reveries had progressively told a story that seemed so plausible. There were so many details that fit in perfectly. But the mind could do that. It did it in dreams, didn't it? In the fantasy that had just played out, her mind had inserted the Celtic ring she'd seen in the Metropolitan Museum.

But over the summer, she'd always felt as if she were the person she was watching. That the images and the feelings were part of her. Not this time. Jac had been seeing the scene through a strange man's eyes. Been inside his mind, but she wasn't him. Wasn't any part of him.

"Jac? Are you all right?" Theo asked.

"Yes. Why?"

"You were just staring off into space. I said your name twice."

"Sorry, just lost in thought. I was trying to remember what I'd read about amber. I think that's what the bits of stone you just burnt are. It has some curious properties. Farmers actually burn it to make fruit grow faster. But I'm not sure what else it can do." She looked closely at the pyre. Rooted around in it with a stick. Pushing aside burnt twigs, lumps of coal and charred pine cones, she found more of the bits of brownish stones.

"This looks like a ritual fire. But it can't be from Celtic times. It can't be that old."

"No, Wiccans still use these sites."

"Reenacting Celtic ceremonies?"

"So my aunt Eva says. She learned to weave from one woman who practiced Wicca. She's got endless stories if you're interested."

"I'd love to hear them."

"Why don't you come back to the house with me? You can stay for dinner. She asked me to invite you when I left this morning and I forgot."

Minerva was sitting on the couch in the great room reading a book, taking occasional sips of something tawny from a glass. Eva was at her loom, weaving the marvelous blue-green cloth.

They both looked up when Jac and Theo came in.

The two sisters were alike in many ways: both had fine skin with a minimum of wrinkles and cornflower-blue eyes. But Eva was more like a delicate bouquet of lily of the valley in an antique porcelain pitcher, while Minerva was a dozen long-stem bold, black-red roses in a rock crystal vase.

"Help yourself to drinks," Minerva said.

"A martini?" Theo asked Jac.

"Vodka and tonic if you have it, please."

Theo walked over to the bar.

"Did you two have any luck today?" Minerva asked.

Theo filled his aunts in on the afternoon as he made drinks.

"This is a doomed exercise. Didn't you learn anything from your grandfather?" Eva said. "There are too many caves. Too many ruins. Too much time has passed. You need to—"

"Eva, all those things are true, but nothing is impossible," Minerva interrupted.

"You and all your possibilities."

Jac had sat down on the couch opposite Minerva and was rifling though a book she'd found on the coffee table. *The Red Book* was a facsimile of Carl Jung's famous journal containing his mandala drawings from 1914 to 1930. He'd undertaken the project to explore his own unconscious. She was studying the intricately detailed illuminations when she thought of something. If there had been one clue about the hidden journal in the library, perhaps there was another.

"Are the books in the library catalogued?" Jac asked.

"Yes." Minerva answered first. "And the catalogue goes back to the mid-nineteenth century. The bulk of the titles were amassed by our great-grandfather. He bought up everything he could on the occult, magic, witches and mythology."

"He was the one involved with the Phoenix Society?" Jac asked.

Minerva nodded. "He wrote a few monographs about the most important spiritualists of the time." She rattled off a few names, several of which were vaguely familiar to Jac. "He infused our grandfather Henri with the same interests. When Henri was a boy, he attended his father's séances, here in the house, he used to tell us how people sometimes came from as far away as London to attend. When we were children he experimented with—"

"Please, Minerva," Eva interrupted. Her voice, usually so sweet, was suddenly tense.

"What kind of experiments?" Theo asked. "I've never heard about this."

"It's ancient history," Minerva said, then looked at her sister, but Eva had turned away and was facing the window.

"Is it a secret?" he asked.

"It's not a secret so much as something . . . your Aunt Eva has always preferred we don't talk about it. But Eva . . ." She looked back at her. "Seventy years have passed."

Theo got up and went over to his aunt Eva. He pulled a chair up to the loom, close to her, and then took her hand and held it gently. "I'd like to know what happened. Especially if it's something that hurt you."

Eva took a sip of her drink and then stared into the liquid for a moment. Sighing, she lowered the glass onto the side table, picked up her spindle, held on to it with both her hands as if it were ballast and began to talk.

"Our grandfather believed that children were more sensitive to spirits than adults. That we were more closely connected to the world we'd just come from—the world of souls: some recently dead, some dead for longer—all waiting to be reborn."

"Not unlike Jung's theory of a collective unconscious," Minerva added.

"You connect everything back to Jung," Eva said, as if even bringing up the unconscious were blasphemous.

Minerva laughed. "Because everything connects back to it." She smoothed the fabric of her long red skirt over her knees. "I'm sorry, I didn't mean to interrupt."

"Our father was a banker," Eva said. "Uninterested in the world outside the bank." She looked at Theo and exchanged a look with him that Jac wasn't sure she understood but guessed had something to do with his brother. "He spent more than half his time in London. Long stretches when our grandfather was the only male in the house. Long stretches when he supervised us. Our mother was here of course, but she seemed happy to let our grandfather oversee a large part of our activities," Eva said, and then stopped. She picked up her glass again. Took a sip of her drink. Then another. "Is it really necessary to do this?" she asked Minerva. "There's nothing to come of it."

"Theo wants to know. I'll tell him, all right?"

"Would it matter if I said I'd prefer you not to?"

"Yes, I said that if you really didn't want me to—"

Eva interrupted this time. "But you're a stone turner. And this one hasn't been moved in decades. You said that yourself. I know you. You'll just hound me until I say it's all right, so just go ahead."

"It was exciting to be included in our grand-father's world," Minerva said, picking up where her sister left off. But whereas Eva's voice had been full of trepidation, Minerva's was unfaltering and almost excited. "It made us feel special. We did things none of the adults in the house knew about. Magical things. He said they were our secrets. Between him and us and no one else."

"What things?" Theo asked.

"We had midnight séances with a Ouija board while everyone else in the house was sleeping. Grandfather Henri said we were more receptive than any adults he'd ever worked with. It was heady praise. He needed us, flattered us, and we were his for the taking."

"Did the séances work?" Jac asked.

"Oh yes. We'd receive messages from . . ." Minerva waved her arms wide, encompassing the sea outside the window. "From whoever was out there who wanted to communicate with us."

"But people just push the little marker around, spelling out words," Theo said. "You don't believe spirits were really talking to you, do you?"

"Spirits like ghosts, no, of course not. But we tapped into some kind of force," Minerva said. "I know as well as anyone how the unconscious influences us in ways we are aware of and others that are still a mystery to the most brilliant brain researchers. Thought can power movement. I was six. Eva was eight. We simply weren't capable of spelling out the messages that came through on those nights. That was what was so exceptional about what happened."

"But your grandfather knew how to spell multisyllabic words and write complex sentences, right?" Theo asked, suspiciously.

"His hands never touched the board," Minerva said, as if she were that six-year-old again, full of wonder. "Only we children had our fingers on the pointer," she explained. "Grandfather was in charge of writing down the letters the pin stopped on. He saved all the transcripts from our sessions."

"Do they still exist?" Theo asked.

Minerva nodded. "They do." She turned and looked over at the ornately carved credenza in the corner. "If you want to read them—" She stopped speaking suddenly.

"What is it?" Eva said nervously.

"I can't believe I didn't remember this before." She looked at Theo. "Old age is a cruel master. Theo, what was the name of the spirit Hugo wrote about in the letter in the book of poetry?"

"The Shadow of the Sepulcher."

"That's what I thought." Minerva looked at Eva. "You don't remember either?"

"What?" Eva asked, as if she had no idea.

But Jac thought she saw the truth flicker across Eva's face. As if she had remembered something but it had exacerbated her discomfort.

"Eva, what was the name of the spirit we talked to?" Minerva asked.

She shook her head. "I don't know. It was so long ago."

Jac was sure that Eva was lying. Why couldn't Minerva see it too? Or did she and was just acting as if she didn't, drawing her sister out this way for reasons of her own?

"The spirit we talked to was named the Shadow of the Tomb, wasn't it?" Minerva asked.

"I thought he was just called the Shadow. Like the radio character."

Minerva shook her head, then turned to Theo. "I'm sure of it. The spirit we talked to when we were children had a name. He called himself the Shadow of the Tomb."

"Did my grandfather know that?" Theo asked.

"By the time our brother was born, our grandfather had died and we never played with the Ouija board again. But I can't believe I didn't make the connection when Alexander showed me the letter. Or that you didn't," she said to Eva.

"Theo, you shouldn't be getting mixed up in this, that's all there is to it."

"Eva, everything will be fine," Minerva said. "It's a good thing to release this ghost."

Eva shook her head. "It's never a good thing to release a ghost."

"You know there's a possibility," Jac said, more to Eva than Minerva, wanting to reassure the elderly woman, "that your grandfather found the Hugo letter and, knowing the name of the spirit, told you that's who you were talking to. It's even possible that the board never spelled out that name at all, but he guessed that name based on what he'd read, and you only think you wrote it out."

"Very clever of you," Eva said, shaking her head. "I think that's exactly what happened."

"Ah, so you are a skeptic," Minerva said to Jac. "I'm surprised, given your interests."

"My skepticism is why I wrote my book, and what the TV show is based on. I search for the kernels of reality that get blown up into legends and myth. I wanted to expose how truth gets exaggerated and how we fool ourselves into believing in dreams. It's ironic that the opposite happened. Knowing there is even a little truth to these stories gives people hope."

"You sound as if you wish you were like them," Theo said.

"Sometimes I wish I could be. It would be a relief to believe without so much questioning."

As if he were suffering from the same illness, Theo said, "It sounds like a simpler way to go through life."

Minerva was searching Jac's face intently. Jac had been to enough therapists to recognize the peering gaze.

"What do you hope for?" Minerva asked.

"That I'll find answers." Jac felt sadness surge through her. She was suddenly homesick for her brother—the whimsical, creative mind that embraced the unknown without being wary of it. If she could just move a few steps in his direction, just open herself up a little to the infinite possibilities he talked about, maybe she'd be more fulfilled, less restless. Around him she could sometimes forget about all she doubted. Once, he'd almost made her believe she'd find her *âme sœur*, her soul mate, hadn't he?

Except she knew there was no such thing. Or if she was being even more cynical, maybe there was such a thing, and she'd lost hers forever when she lost Griffin North.

Eva was talking to Minerva now. Jac picked up on the conversation in midsentence. "You know that's what happened. Minerva, you know how obsessive our grandfather was about the library." She was smoothing down the nap of the fabric on the chair. "It makes complete sense that he found the Hugo letter and it influenced him, doesn't it? After all, our brother found the letter. Why couldn't our grandfather have found it before him?" She stared down at the cushion and ran her hand across it again. "Then he would have known that name and suggested it to us, putting it in our head. It's possible, don't you see?"

Minerva gave a weary sigh. "Yes, it's all possible."

"He never should have involved us." She looked at Jac. "We were just children."

"Communicating with someone you believed was a spirit must have been frightening." Jac was remembering her own childhood visions. "When we're children the unknown takes on huge and terrifying proportions."

Eva nodded vigorously.

"I wasn't frightened," Minerva said somewhat wistfully. "I was in awe."

"You were frightened. You just don't remember."

Minerva stood and walked over to a section of bookcases on the wall opposite the fireplace. The lower third were fitted with drawers, not shelves. Minerva pulled one open and began to search through the contents. She withdrew several worn leather-bound journals. A box of what looked like stationery. Sticks of sealing wax. A handful of fountain pens. Several brass and silver seals. A few sheets of blotting paper. A crystal inkwell. A treasure trove of writing instruments from a bygone era.

Minerva was still extracting things from the drawer. A stack of envelopes tied with a burgundy ribbon. Bottles of ink.

"What are you doing?" Eva asked. "Everything is carefully arranged."

"Yes, and I'll put it all back. I wish you would relax."

"Yes, I'm sure you do." Eva sighed. "But I won't know where anything is if you don't put it back exactly the way it was," she continued.

"You haven't needed anything in here for at least fifty or sixty years."

"And how do you know that?"

Theo shot Jac an amused look. Living with his grandaunts, he must have heard hundreds of these conversations.

"There's nothing to come of reading through those conversations now," Eva said.

"That's not what I'm getting," Minerva said. She'd finished emptying out the drawer and now was lifting it out of the credenza.

"Then what are you doing?" Eva asked. "There's nothing left in there."

"But there is. Grandpapa showed me this hiding place. There's a compartment here, under the drawer. I always thought you knew too. This is where he used to hide the board after Papa became so adamant about our not being included in the experiments anymore. Whenever our father came home from London," Minerva said to Theo and Jac, "the board would go back in here for the duration and then come out again as soon as he left."

Minerva pulled a long box out of the hiding space and carried it over to the sitting area.

Eva let out a small moan. As if the sight of it caused her pain. "It was there all this time?" Eva was agitated. Her voice was tight and stressed again. "Get rid of it, Minerva."

Minerva looked at her older sister and frowned. "You are being ridiculous."

"I want you to get rid of that thing." Eva's voice was raised. Her hands were clenched into fists.

Theo looked surprised, as if this level of bickering was not what he was used to.

"I honestly think that what you believe you

remember about all this is an exaggerated childhood memory. Maybe if we look at it, the experience might be cathartic," Minerva said.

"Cathartic? Why are you so hell-bent on revisiting this chapter of our lives? It's a mistake. I'm warning you."

Minerva unfolded the board. Fully opened it was about two feet long and eighteen inches wide. In the upper right-hand corner the word *yes* was printed in black ink. In the upper left was the word *no*. A semicircle of all the letters in the alphabet filled the center. Underneath that, along the bottom, were the numbers 0 to 9.

Some of the black paint had flaked off, so while the letters and numbers were legible, they looked battle-scarred. The board was mostly smooth but in spots the shellac had worn off and raw wood showed through.

"Our grandfather made this," Minerva said, running her finger over a portion of the surface where the shellac was still intact.

Eva stood up and walked to the bar, poured two inches of clear liquid from a decanter into her glass, added two ice cubes, took a sip and then another, and then stood there watching her sister.

"And made quite a mess with it too. The abusive bastard," Eva muttered, surprising even Minerva.

Theo looked from one of his aunts to the other. "What happened?"

Eva answered, "He put us at the table night

after night and had us commune with ghosts. It scared us both. Terribly, even if my sister has forgotten that. She was so young . . . it was so unfair. On the nights we played with the board she used to have nightmares, and I'd have to shake her awake so she'd stop crying out in her sleep. But it didn't matter to him. Night after night he'd have us sit at that table and play his game. Sometimes nothing would happen. Other times . . . I don't know. . . ."

"I don't understand it still, but our hands moved as if by magic, spelling out streams of words we didn't even understand," Minerva said.

"Whenever I got upset and asked if we could stop, he would get angry at me. He told us we were very special, that not everyone could converse with the dead." Eva's face was pale. The skin around her mouth was drawn and pulled tight. Her fingers gripped her glass so tightly her knuckles were white. "I would lie in bed for hours after a session, unable to go to sleep, wondering if that was true. And if it was, were they going to come and get us and take us into the place on the other side of the board?"

"It was exciting to stay up late with Grandpapa," Minerva said. "He was so proud of us, don't you remember that?"

"Not at all. Proud? No."

"When did the séances finally stop?" Theo asked.

Minerva answered quickly. "When we were nine and eleven."

"They stopped because our grandfather died," Eva said very softly. She took a long sip from her glass, then got up, walked over to the fireplace, picked up a poker and shoved a log so hard sparks sputtered out.

There was something not being said. Jac knew silences like these. Had lived with them in her own family, when her mother was having an affair and her father had found out. Those silences had grown longer as the marriage broke apart piece by piece. Until her mother decided to embrace that silence forever.

"And the last time you used the board was the night before Henri died?" Theo asked.

"The night he died," Minerva said.

Without any explanation, Eva turned and walked out of the room. Jac listened to the sound of her retreating footsteps and the ice tinkling in her glass.

Minerva stood by the table, looking down at the wooden board as if it alone would resolve the tension.

Jac had thought Eva had left for the evening, but her footsteps on the parquet were returning. When she came back she was holding two glasses. In addition to her drink, she carried a small juice glass about three inches high with a floral pattern etched around its ring. It was a sweet-looking glass, the kind you'd fill with orange juice and drink in a sun-filled kitchen while fresh croissants cooked in the oven and coffee brewed.

"You've always wanted to do this," Eva said, holding the glass out to her sister.

"But you don't want to."

"No, I don't. I don't need the memories. But I need you to see that nothing will happen. You've always wanted to believe that we'd tapped into that cosmic collective unconscious you're forever talking about. You have held on to the belief that he was giving us some kind of gift. Once and for all you will know he manipulated us, Minerva. And you will forgive me."

"There is nothing to forgive you for."

"Don't lie to me. Ever. It's disingenuous and does not become you."

"What are you talking about?" Theo asked.

Neither sister seemed to have heard him.

"Why would he have manipulated us?" Minerva asked Eva. "What are you talking about?"

Now the positions were reversed. She was the less sure sister, the one who seemed nervous.

"To scare us," Eva whispered.

"Why would he want us scared?"

"You of all people should know the answer to that. You are a therapist. Are you really that blind to your own family history?"

Jac felt that she was intruding. That she shouldn't be there. She was also confused about why this conversation was happening now. Theo had told her the two sisters had lived in this house together for the last twenty years. Eva had never married, never left. Minerva had married and moved to London and had a child, but after divorcing her husband she'd moved back to Wells in Wood in the 1990s. Was it really possible these two women had avoided this conversation for so long?

"Why did he want us scared?" Minerva asked again. Jac heard a young confused girl in the old woman's voice.

"You really don't know?" Eva sounded astonished.

"No."

"He scared us so he could hold us under the pretense of comforting us. He'd been doing it to me all along. I'd become too mature for him. He was shifting his interest to you."

Minerva stared at Eva, horrified by the suggestion.

Jac could see that she didn't believe her.

For a few moments there was silence. Minerva got up and walked over to the windows. She stood, staring out into the darkness. The quiet continued for several more moments.

Eva was still holding on to the glass. "We need to do this, Minerva. I need to show you. We should have done it years ago."

Minerva didn't turn around.

Eva stood and walked to her sister. "It won't go away. We'll just be putting it off." Eva took her sister by the arm, turned her around and led her toward the card table. Minerva didn't fight her.

"Theo, come and sit down," Eva said. She looked at Jac. "You'll join us, won't you?"

Eva and Theo sat on either side of Minerva. Jac faced her. Once all four of them were seated, Minerva looked around the room as if she was searching for something.

"What is it?" Eva asked.

"If we are going to do this . . ." She got up and shut off the electric lights. Then taking a box of matches off the mantel, she lit the tapers in the candelabra. The slight smell of sulfur wafted through the air. Minerva carried the flickering flames with her toward the table. A nimbus of iridescent light haloed each candle. Suddenly the present receded into the past and Jac felt as if she'd stepped into another era. The room had been made for candlelight, she thought. For this soft glow and these shadows. For alcoves where mysteries could hide.

"This is how I remember it looking," Minerva said, as she set the candelabra down.

Eva gave a sour laugh. "Yes, like a stage set. Our grandfather was very much the dramatist. He played the role of a mystical seeker of wisdom so well. It was so very exotic. Other children had grandfathers who were farmers or storekeepers or bankers, but ours was an eccentric."

"How did he die?" Theo asked. "I don't think I know that. Is it possible you never mentioned it?"

The candlelight flickered on the walls.

Almost involuntarily, it seemed to Jac, Minerva glanced at the door to the hallway and the sweeping marble staircase.

"He tripped and fell down the stairs—" Minerva said.

Eva interrupted her sister, her voice ghostlike and far away. "And he broke his neck. He died instantly."

"How terrible," Jac said, "for both of you."

"Yes, terrible," Eva said in the same distant voice. "Grandfather's death was terrible in every way. Except one." She paused. "There were no more séances."

For a long moment there was only the sound of the surf beating against the rocks.

Then Eva put the glass on the board and gave instructions. "All right. Everyone put one finger on the glass. Like this." Her movements seemed tentative, as if she expected to be burned by its surface.

The glass was cool and smooth where Jac touched it and almost felt as if it were vibrating. Theo placed his forefinger next to hers. In his other hand was a pen poised expectantly over a pad of paper.

Minerva hesitated. "Eva, are you sure?"

"Aren't you the one who always says we should confront our ghosts?" She laughed bitterly.

Minerva put her finger on the glass and completed the fourth.

The candles flickered. A breeze floated through the room, and with it came a cacophony of scents. There was the candle's paraffin. Eva's lily of the valley perfume. Minerva's spicy Oriental. The eucalyptus, honey, cinnamon and oakmoss in Theo's scent. Mixed in with all the perfumes and cologne, Jac smelled age. Burnt wood. Ash. Mold. Years passing. She felt as if she were speeding through a tunnel of scent. Aware of each as it whooshed by her.

"Is there . . . is there anyone here with us?" Eva asked in a hesitant voice.

"That's exactly what Grandpapa would say," Minerva said softly, almost as if she were a little in awe of her older sister.

"Is there? Is there anyone here with us?" Eva repeated. Her voice was a bit bolder now.

The glass didn't move.

Eva repeated her question one more time. Now she sounded almost gleeful. As if she was proving her point.

Jac saw Theo's eyes were focused on the board. So were Minerva's.

For the fourth time, Eva repeated her question.

Now it was mocking, strident. "Is there anyone here with us?"

The glass stayed on the edge of the board. Eva's mouth turned up into a smug smile.

Theo seemed disappointed.

Minerva wasn't paying attention to any of them but staring down at their fingers on the top of the glass. "I know you are here," she whispered in a voice devoid of suspicion. "I can feel you. I remember you."

And with that the glass began to tremble.

At first Jac thought it was Eva's anger, which contorted her face, that was making the glass move. But no, her finger wasn't shaking. None of their fingers were pushing it. That was totally clear to Jac. The glass really was moving, pulling them along with it.

Racing, the juice glass slid back and forth across the board, stopping at letters so fast that Theo—who had offered to write them down with his right hand—could barely keep up.

I . . . T . . . H . . . A . . . S . . . B . . . E . . . E . . . N . . . A . . . V . . . E . . . R . . . Y . . . L . . . O . . . N . . . G . . . T . . . I . . . M . . . E . . .

Under her breath, Minerva whispered each word as she figured it out.

Jac was trying to work them out, but Minerva was faster.

"Yes," Minerva said, "it has been a very long time."

A...B...A...N...D...O...N...E...
D...M...E...A...N...D...O...U...
R...G...A...M...E...

The logs crackled in the fireplace. Heaved, then hissed. The room filled with the scent of damp earth. Of smoke. Of fire.

Minerva's face was a study in exaltation. Eva was pale and looked unwell.

"Who are you?" Minerva whispered.

Y...O...U...K...N...O...W...

"Yes, I know. But say your name. Grandpapa always made you say your name."

S...H...A...D...O...W...O...F
...T...H...E...S...E...P...U...L
...C...H...E...R...

The glass was moving too fast. Minerva had stopped saying the words. Jac leaned over to read what Theo had written down on the pad.

Shadow of the Sepulcher.

"You gave us a different name before," Minerva said. "What was that name?"

O...F...T...H...E...T...O...M...
B...

"Why did my grandfather want to reach you? What did he want from you?" Minerva asked.

H...E...W...A...N...T...E...D
...M...Y...A...N...S...W...E...R
...S...T...O...K...N...O...W...S
...E...C...R...E...T...S...

"What secrets?" Minerva asked.

318

Suddenly the glass stopped moving. Jac thought the air in the room and the flames in the fireplace had stilled too.

And then suddenly, the glass took off. Skittering across the board as if it had some kind of palsy. Theo barely kept up as he tried to catch every letter.

A log in the fireplace cracked and crashed. A window frame creaked. The glass kept racing. A door slammed. The glass zigzagged back across the board. A high keening seemed to seep from the floor, almost as if the house were moaning.

"It's the wind," Eva murmured, but she sounded as if she were trying to convince herself. "It's just the wind."

Jac watched the glass jerking from right to left and then back again. Beneath her fingers, it felt alive. With a mind of its own.

After another twenty or thirty seconds, the glass slid all the way to the left, past the edge of the board, right off it and onto the table and then off the table. They all lost touch with it. It should have fallen. But it didn't. Not yet. For a few seconds the simple floral-patterned juice glass floated in the air.

Another moan escaped from the parquet. The glass fell and crashed. Dozens of shards caught in the candlelight, sparkled.

On the other side of the room, a framed photograph fell off the wall almost at the same time. Smashing on the floor, its glass shattered too.

Eva let out a small shriek and began to whimper. Minerva leaned over and put her arms around her sister, speaking to her softly, trying to comfort her. Eva was crying now. Like a child, Jac thought.

Theo rose, hurried across the room and switched on the lights. Then he picked up the photograph and stared down at it. His brows knit. His eyes narrowed.

Jac walked over to look.

It was a very old and faded back-and-white photograph. A man wearing a formal suit stood on the rocks, looking off into the distance. Behind him was a view of the sea. Something was not right with the image, but Jac couldn't figure it out for a few seconds. Then she realized. His right foot was positioned strangely. Bent at the ankle, it was angled in an unnatural way. It couldn't have been easy to balance on the rocks to begin with— but even more difficult to do it with a foot positioned like that, pointing down.

Along the bottom of the image were four words written in script in faded ink.

Victor Hugo in Exile.

Minerva was helping her sister, who was still crying, out of the room. Once they had left and were well out of earshot, Jac asked Theo what the glass had spelled out in that last burst of frenzied activity.

Still holding the photograph, Theo went back to the table. As he figured out the words, he read them.

He scared . . . you to . . . comfort you. That was how . . . I seduced him. I have other ways to seduce other men. Some have succumbed . . . some I have lost. I will not lose you.

Twenty-three

OCTOBER 13, 1855
JERSEY, CHANNEL ISLANDS, GREAT BRITAIN

I am a rational man. I live in exile because of what I believe: that the church and the clergy are evil oppressors. That they use the fear of the unknown to control those who are uneducated. I believe in the rights of the individual and that the government is corrupt and not dedicated to its citizens.

And yet I am seeing ghosts and am talking to spirits. I believe Lucifer himself is visiting me. I am certain that I have opened a door to another realm where spirits live and somehow are able to speak through me. I write what they say with this ink on this paper, but I hear it first.

I am in dire emotional and mental trouble and do not know where to turn.

I have a responsibility to those who have followed me to this island, who have left behind all that was comfortable. In Paris, I relinquished a library of a thousand books, paintings, sculptures, furniture and money—millions of francs—because of my protest against injustice. It cannot come to pass that I have done all this to myself and others only to lose my ability to reason, to think, to make some sense of existence.

The novel that I have been working on for so long has been abandoned. I stand at my desk to transcribe the conversations I have with the dead. My critics have often said the flaw in my writing is that I use coincidence to provide emotional conflicts. I have always argued with them and asked: Why is that a flaw? Coincidences happen in life. They have always happened in mine.

But there has never been a coincidence as disturbing as the one I am about to commit to paper tonight.

Friends from Brussels have been staying with us this past week. Two nights ago we set out for an evening at the theater. A visiting troupe was performing in St. Helier and we were all looking forward to the entertainment. It was with a light heart that we left our house on Marine Terrace, but as soon as we turned off our lane and into the main thoroughfare downtown, it was obvious something was amiss.

A group of more than two dozen men were gathered in the square. Connétable Jessie Trent stood at their helm, shouting out instructions. The expressions on the men's faces were determined and concerned.

Excusing myself from my party, entreating them to go on to the theater without me and promising that I would join them anon, I approached Trent. He'd finished giving the crowd instructions and was in conversation with only one other man now. Seeing me, he broke off and gave me the news.

"Monsieur Hugo, the dog has appeared again."

"The dog is bewitched," the man with him said. "It's the hound from hell."

"But all of you, to corral one dog?" I said to Trent. "It seems extreme."

"No, not to trap the dog. We are organizing a search for Monsieur Bertan's daughter."

"Another child?" I asked, as my stomach turned sour. "How old is this one?"

"She is eleven," said a man who stepped out of the crowd. I recognized the haunted, glazed eyes, the drawn mouth and the haggard expression. "My daughter," he continued, "has not been seen since last night. Right after we heard all that barking."

"The castle?" I asked Trent.

"We searched there first." He shook his head. "Now we're splitting up. I was in the process of assigning areas. Would you care to help?"

I thought of the man on the beach I had been talking to a week before. The man who had seemingly walked into the rock formations from which there was no exit. And who had not come out again. A stranger whom you didn't see. An apparition who left no footprints. Why was he on my mind now? Then I remembered his strange words: "I put the child you found in the castle. You wound up a hero but still bereft. If you'd done what I suggested, you would have been a happier one."

"Trent, I'll take the rocky section of beach down by Marine Terrace. There are so many caves there, it's possible the child was trapped in one during the high tide this morning."

"All right, I'll go with you. Let me just give out the rest of the assignments."

I told him I would go to the theater to make my apologies to my wife and friends and then meet him back there.

Fifteen minutes later, the *connétable* and I walked down the slipway to the beach, reenacting the journey we had made all too recently.

With at least two hours of daylight left, we hurried in and out of the caverns, some filled with water up to our ankles, but saw no sign of her. And when the darkness settled in, rather than abandon the search, we used Trent's dead-flame kerosene lanterns, the same we'd used before. The fire in these portable metal and glass globes didn't blow out easily, but I found the smell foul. Wind didn't affect the flame, but if the threatening rain arrived, our lights would be extinguished and our hunt curtailed.

"Some of the men think the island is being haunted. That La Dame Blanche has come to claim her child," Trent said, as we walked the deserted beach. "The legend dates back thousands of years to the time pagans built the rock temples and burial grounds all over Jersey. According to the tale, the Woman in White had killed her own child. As punishment the Druid priests had imprisoned her inside a large stone, where she died. And where her soul remains. At night she escapes to search aimlessly for her child."

I knew the story but let him tell me again, half listening, half thinking of La Dame Blanche's visits at Marine Terrace. The last time, when my daughter had been so upset by the spirit's story, La Dame had tried to comfort her, saying she suffered but did not despair, because she knew one day she would be freed and she and her child would be reunited.

"Do the men really believe a spirit is behind these disappearances?" I asked Trent. "Are they as superstitious as all that?"

"They are. We're a beautiful island in the daylight, Monsieur Hugo, but when the sun sets, it casts dark shadows. Cut off as we are, our imaginations are left to roam as wild as La Dame's ghost."

The tide was coming in now, and angry waves crashed on the rocks not far from where we walked. We were going to run out of time. There were hundreds of caves up and down the coast, and soon many of them would flood with water and be impenetrable.

We decided to split up and each take a different cave so we could cover more ground.

I had only examined a few of these caves. Fascinated as I am with rock formations, I have drawn them, trying my hand at capturing their majesty and mystery, more than explored them. These giant hulking rocks have stood here for all time, seen all things, watched silently as men used them for shelter, religious rituals, burials, for crimes, trysts, for hiding places. I have heard some were covered with fantastic drawings, others filled with treasure troves of prehistoric utensils, jewels or bones. All I'd seen were barren. Damp and cold. Shallow and unadorned.

Those I examined that night, with Trent and then on my own, were no different. And then I noticed a small opening, so narrow I had to go sideways to get through it. I would have ignored it, but it was of a size that would be tempting to a child.

On the other side of the crack in the rock, I found myself in a stone tunnel. I followed it to what appeared to be a dead end. There a slight breeze coming from the rocks themselves beckoned me to continue. Impossible!

It was of course an optical illusion. Because of the rock's striations, crevices and coloration, it wasn't obvious that one section receded a bit and left an opening wide enough to walk through.

Once inside that deeper, cooler space, I followed the path to a more articulated entranceway that led to a large chamber and a startling surprise. The walls were completely covered with murals. The painted cave's artistry astounded me.

The ancient artwork was as sophisticated as anything I'd seen in the studios of Delacroix or Corbet. I stared at the half-human, half-animal figures, the colors as fresh as if they had just been painted. What fantastic creatures they featured: bulls with men's faces, men with hooves and tails, women with birds' bodies, cats with women's faces, necks, breasts.

I was so caught up in the paintings, I didn't even notice the sound at first. When I did hear the angry crunching under my feet, I looked down. I expected to see shells, which were everywhere in Jersey, but these were not the pretty things my wife and daughter collected on the beach. I was walking on bones. A path of fish, bird and other small animal bones was leading me down an incline and deeper and deeper into the cave.

Finally the path brought me to a cathedral-like cavern. A double row of monolithic stones, each at least three to four meters tall, created a center aisle. At the end was a wide, heavy slab resting on three upright rocks. Like an altar, I thought.

Swinging the lantern to the right and left, I was

able to make out niches carved in the walls. Upon closer inspection they appeared to be some kind of primitive seating alcoves for the participants in whatever rituals or services must have once been enacted here.

I walked the perimeter of the temple, examining each stone throne and the bits of dried leather, strings of beads and fetishes I found around them. What were these things?

My footsteps echoed in the hollow emptiness, and somewhere in the distance water dripped. And then I heard the whisper of a moan. Was it my imagination? I listened harder. It seemed to be coming from across the cavern. I looked but could see nothing but darkness until I reached the far end of the cave. There, my lantern illuminated the most lurid tableau I'd seen since those bloody days in Paris during the worst of the uprisings.

The child's clothes were ripped into shreds. Long bleeding scratches crisscrossed her exposed flesh. There was an ugly gash on her forehead, dripping blood that had seeped into her blond hair and turned it almost black. Her lower lip had swelled and was crusted with blood.

The child appeared unconscious. I put my ear to her chest and listened to her heart. Its beat was faint and her skin was cold. She was near death, whether from blood loss or the blow to her head, I did not know. But either could have the same effect. I'd witnessed death before. The signs were no different in the Paris streets or the opulent homes of loved ones.

This girl's time was near.

If she'd fought ferociously to hold on to this world, she was not putting up any such fight anymore. Her body had given up and resigned itself to the end.

I knew the moment was upon us.

And then, in that forlorn quiet, in that underground cathedral built by pagans thousands of years before, a long, low growl rose from the darkness behind me. I turned, held my lantern aloft, and searched the emptiness for glowing eyes or flashing teeth. I saw no creature. It was only my imagination now, playing with me. But I could ill afford the distraction. Time was slipping away, and with it the child. There was a slim chance I might save her still, if I could just stanch the wound and stop the bleeding. I stripped down and took off my shirt. Using my teeth, I ripped at it, then made bandages with the linen. These I tied around her little head as tightly as I could.

As I worked, I began to sense another with me in the grotto. My departed daughter's presence hovering close by. Even now I cannot explain how I knew it or how it felt to know she was there. Nor can I explain how such a thing might happen. Until that evening, in the ten years she had been gone, I had never felt her with me in that way. In any way really. Yes, her memory had been with me. Yes, she had spoken through the table tapping. But this was not a feeble ephemeral recollection. This was Didine's essence, her very soul, there with me, watching, hoping and waiting.

What was I thinking? Were there strange fumes in the cave that acted like a drug? I had heard of such things before. Perhaps the stale air was poisoned and had worked on my brain in some unknown way. My mind raced for any explanation as I continued to work on the child, but I came up with nothing.

I knew Didine was there. She was in the plinking of the water drops falling onto the stone, in the whisper of the wind whistling through the rock rooms, in the soft shallow breath of the child whose life I was trying to save.

This is the moment, Hugo.

I heard that same voice I'd always heard in my mind during the séances when one particular spirit was visiting. It was the disembodied voice of the young, beautiful man on the beach. I did not turn. I didn't need to. I knew who was speaking to me. The Shadow of the Sepulcher was here.

"What moment? What do you want?" I asked, shouting out loud like a fool into the blackness.

If you stop your ministering to her and let her go, let her die, I will bring her back to life with your daughter's soul.

"That's nonsense. It's not possible. And even if it were, I could never do such a thing." I was horrified. I should have refused from the start. That I had first said it was impossible spoke volumes and made me afraid. Was I tempted by his offer? *Sacré bleu!*

You believe the soul lives on, don't you?

"Yes, yes, I believe that, but—"

And that souls are reborn?

Was he really engaging me in a philosophical debate here and now? Concentrating on what was most important, I kept the pressure against the child's wound. It seemed to me the bleeding had stopped. If I could be sure, I could move her, take her out of here and into the fresh air. Take her to get help.

You do believe souls are reborn?

"Yes, that they are reincarnated. But no child is being born here. Leave me alone!"

This is another form of reincarnation. Upon death a soul departs, leaving the body empty. In that single moment another soul can enter. An errant soul. A lost soul. A departed soul who yearns to return. And when the body is reenergized, it awakens with that other soul inside. You have heard of people who suffer illnesses and accidents so severe that when they recover, people say it was as if they came back from the dead? And that they seem different?

"Why are you telling me this?" Even as I asked, I knew what his answer would be.

I tried to engender this exchange in the castle

but you saved the child before I could make you understand. Don't make that same mistake tonight. I have put this young girl in your path. Am offering you that which you most want. All you have to do is take away your hands. Let her blood flow. Let her die.

"No!" I shouted and pressed harder on her wound. Watched her face. Saw the first blush of color returning to her cheeks. Saw her pulse beating steady in her neck.

"Live, live!" I screamed at her.

You are making a mistake!

Suddenly he was standing in front of me, the same young man I'd seen on the beach with silken black curls and deep, penetrating topaz eyes. Lucifer was here with me in this cathedral of rock, while under my hands a young girl's soul fluttered in her body, half ready to fly away, half determined to remain. His image flashed, then faded.

"Hold on!" I shouted to her even louder this time. "You're getting stronger. You're coming back."

Now she was fighting. Now she was winning. The child was going to live.

You can have your daughter back! Why are you shunning this opportunity?

I did not respond. What he spoke of was blasphemy and impossible. And even if it weren't, the price was not one I could pay. Allow some

332

other father's daughter to die so I could have mine back?

I am ashamed to say that in that moment when I framed the thought that way, my mind leapt ahead and I imagined it.

What *would* it be like for this creature to open her eyes and say *Papa* and throw her arms around my neck and whisper that it was she, my darling, my Didine? An agony of pleasure and regret surged through me.

You are a coward. I am offering a respite from your suffering.

"I cannot . . . will not take it."

While I stood there continuing to stanch the child's wound, I suddenly wondered what I should have been curious about long before this.

"Why are you making me this offer?"

I have been maligned, and you can help me change that. Through your writings you can educate the people and redeem me. Explain that I shine the light in the darkness and explain great mysteries. That being different is not being evil, and change is not poison. You can remove the specter of evil from me. I am Lucifer. All I want is for man to have the same knowledge as God. And in exchange for your cleansing, clarifying poetry—your daughter's soul will be reborn.

I watched the bandage. There were no telltale blood spots seeping through. I had stopped its flow. Now to get her out of there.

Carefully I lifted her. She was small and weighed so little. Her bones felt as fragile as the birds' bones I'd trod over when I walked through the passageway.

I am only trying to give you what you want!

The Shadow's voice was plaintive and laced with sadness. From the sound of it, I knew he lived in his own hell. And I felt a momentary pang of guilt that I was condemning him to remain there.

Do I not even tempt you?

Of course he did, but I could never admit that to him. A spirit as strong as he was could use that against me, turn it back on me somehow.

"No, I am not tempted to allow this child to die so that my daughter might be reborn."

But even as I protested, I felt dizzy with desire at the idea of her—of Didine—of my wondrous daughter, my light, coming back to me. What would the cessation of such mourning be like to experience?

But to take one soul in exchange for another?

As I carried my burden out of the cave, stumbling over the debris underfoot, I tried to recall the steps that had opened the doorway to this strange place, the irrational world I had become involved with since arriving in Jersey and now found myself thrust into. What had I brought upon myself? What portal had I opened? And how to shut it now that it threatened me with such a heinous and tempting offer?

I thought back to the evening when I had first sat down at the table-tapping séances two years before. I recalled the questions we had asked of the spirits in the room. One by one over the last twenty-four months these beings had paraded in front of us, communicating, teasing, titillating. When had we first summoned this Shadow of the Tomb? How could we put him back where he belonged? For we had unleashed a terrible thing. Only a true monster would put these children in my path and make it seem so easy. To arrange it so I would never have to kill them, only allow them to slip away. How easy it would be for me to succumb and take his offer.

The way up and out was long. The girl, so light at first, now grew heavier with each step. The Shadow continued talking to me, keeping up his philosophical diatribe. Tempting me by plumbing my memories and reminding me of moments I'd shared with Didine.

Do you remember when you taught her to read? The time she read one of your poems out loud? The day she wrote her own first poem and showed it to you, and how her eyes grew bright with tears when you praised her? How she would challenge your ideas, do you remember? How she used to argue philosophy with you into the night? How you used to tell her she was your brightest self . . . your wonder . . . your Didine—

"Stop!" I clutched the stranger's child tighter to

my chest, in fear he might grab her now and plead his case with even more fervor.

Hurrying as best I could, I continued my climb out of the rocky passageway. I'd had to leave the lantern behind, as I needed both hands to hold the little girl. In the dark, shadows took on malevolent shapes. I was indeed in the underworld.

I know you are curious. I can hear you wondering what it would be like to speak to her again. To engage with your daughter and enjoy her company. To have your heart mended.

"Impossible. You are no more real than the witches in *Macbeth*. As the ghost who visited with Hamlet. I am a writer. I know you are a literary trope, a metaphor. Men tell stories to distract and to entertain, to teach lessons, to give people moral compasses. We scare our readers and make them afraid of the dark so we can save them from the brink of evil and be their heroes."

The Egyptians, the Greeks, the Chinese believed. Even you say you believe in the transmigration of the soul, how it travels from one body to another as it makes its trek though eternity, ever growing, ever changing. Why wouldn't that be a story to write about? Think of how it would sell! A tale of how a soul returned. Think of the wealth you would amass. The fame. Think of it!

"I have the ideas for my novels already. I have my themes. I write about injustice and freedom. Let me be."

Admit it, you have lost the ability to write your novels since coming here. We spirits are now your obsession.

I finally reached the mouth of the cave and stumbled out into the fresh night air. I could hear the ocean again and the far-off sounds of men farther up and down the beach, still searching, still calling out to each other as they covered more ground.

I turned to my invisible companion, but could sense he was gone.

Shouting for Trent, alerting him that I'd found the child, I was suddenly filled with a bone-crushing fear. Anxiety flooded my body and pushed through my veins. I had seen men who had gone mad. Was that my fate?

If it wasn't, if I wasn't going mad, then the possibility of what had been offered me would surely make me go mad. How could a man live knowing the creatures of our nightmares were real? That we could be haunted and possessed by devils and demons? What if God was not a heavenly being but only a choice between dark and light, good and evil? What if there *was* a power but it was man's own power to choose?

Trent was running toward me now, with a man by his side. The expression on his face needed no interpretation. He was the child's father, staring at the bundle I carried.

"She's hurt," I said to him as he reached for her,

"but alive. She has a wound on her head but it has stopped bleeding."

He didn't say a word. I didn't imagine he could have. He simply nodded, and when he raised his head, his eyes were shining with tears.

Twenty-four

When Jac had returned to the hotel the night before, there was a phone message for her from Ash Gaspard asking if she was free for breakfast. She'd telephoned, gotten his voice mail and accepted. She wasn't quite sure why he wanted to see her, but after the events at the Gaspard house she thought maybe he'd be able to help make sense of the visitation.

The two brothers were the light and dark halves of the same coin, and getting to know Ash might help her understand Theo, whose mysterious brooding had captured Jac's imagination. In fact the whole family had. The dowager sisters, the rambling ancient house filled with antiquities, the strange ancestors who engaged in séances and studied magic, the tragic death of Theo's wife, the hidden Hugo treasure . . . she was as caught up in it as in any myth she'd ever studied.

Three tables in the dining room were occupied. Ash Gaspard sat at one by the window. The hostess sat Jac so that she had the view of the rough waves and overcast sky.

"Good morning," he said. "I heard from my aunt Eva there was quite a scene last night at Wells in Wood."

"There certainly was."

"They can be quite a pair, those two. I hope it was at least amusing."

"It was far more disturbing than amusing."

"You don't believe in all that stuff, do you?" He was looking at her earnestly with almost the same eyes as his brother's. But Ash's had laughter in them.

"Your aunt Minerva and I had this conversation last night. No, I'm a rationalist. But I will admit there are occurrences that test my ability to reason them out. And last night was up there with the best of them."

"What are some others?" he asked.

Ash was leaning toward her and she could smell his cologne. As she had the first time they'd met, she ran through the notes, mentally listing them. Lemon, verbena, bergamot, tonka bean, patchouli and something else . . . but what was it?

"I hope you won't think I'm rude, but can you tell me the name of your cologne? My family is in the perfume business and I'm usually good at identifying scents, but I've never smelled whatever it is you're wearing."

Ash smiled. "That's because—"

The waitress arrived and he broke off.

Ash ordered the full English breakfast with tea. Jac asked for coffee and yogurt with fruit.

"Where were we?" he said once the order was taken. "Oh yes, I was going to tell you about my mysterious cologne." He smiled as if the idea of sharing his secret gave him a great deal of pleasure. "After breakfast, if you have some time, there's someplace I'd like to show you. I can explain about the cologne then, all right?"

For the rest of the meal they talked about his aunts and the séance.

"I have a favor to ask you," he said as they were finishing up.

"Yes?"

"My brother hasn't been himself since his wife died, and we're all worried about him. He's letting his work slip. The gallery is closed half the time and he hasn't hired anyone to replace Naomi. Instead of taking care of his actual responsibilities, he's become obsessed with this search he's brought you here to help him with."

She didn't feel right talking about Theo behind his back. "What is it you want me to do?"

"Can you just be aware? He won't let any of us get close to him but he seems to trust you. If he starts acting erratically, or talking about things that don't make sense—if you feel at all that he's losing touch, I want you to call me or Minerva. She's tried to get him to see a therapist but he

340

refuses. She does her best to talk to him, watch him, help him, but he doesn't believe he needs any help."

"I haven't seen him for almost twenty years. I'm not sure I'd know if he wasn't behaving like himself."

She was sure there was a subtext beneath Ash's request, maybe even a warning . . . but she couldn't be sure.

"You'd know. His wife knew."

"Of course she did. She was married to him."

"Yes, but they hadn't actually been married that long. Theo had become uncomfortably jealous of any time she spent out of his sight. He was accusing her of having affairs in London whenever her work took her back there. He was reading her email and checking her phone records. It all came to a head when he found out she was confiding in me about his behavior." Ash shook his head, pained by the memory.

"What did he do?"

"He tried to lock her up."

"Theo did?" Jac remembered how he had taken his aunt's hands the night before. How gentle he'd been.

"I know. It was hard for me to believe too. But something in him snapped. She climbed out the window and drove off. I think she was on her way to see me."

"The night she died?"

341

Ash nodded. "Theo blamed me. He thought I was the one she was having an affair with and said it was my fault. That she was distracted and upset because of me and that's why she wasn't paying proper attention on the road. The police have made it clear that she swerved to avoid another car and the accident was the other driver's fault, but Theo wants to believe what Theo wants to believe. We haven't had a civil conversation since. He won't listen to reason. We've always had a difficult relationship but it's never been like this before. And now he's obsessed with finding the Hugo papers. As if they hold some secret that is going to make things better."

Jac now understood a little better why Theo had been so angry to find her talking to Ash the other night.

"I'm not sure I feel comfortable with all this, though. It's as if you're asking me to be a psychic spy."

"I am sorry. But Minerva and I did think you should know and at least be aware. She wanted to talk to you herself. I think she would have done a better job of it too, but it was difficult for her to figure out a way to get to you without Theo around." He put down his napkin and signed the check. "Shall we go? I promise, I won't make any more uncomfortable requests for the rest of the morning, just show you something I think will fascinate you."

He drove down the same country roads she'd traveled twice with Theo. Ash didn't talk much on the ride. Some silences can be uncomfortable, especially between people who don't know each other well, but this wasn't. Their quiet was oddly companionable. Once he turned and smiled at her and she returned the gesture. It was a lovely, sunny morning and she found herself excited about the prospect of seeing something intriguing.

They'd reached the end of the long twisting road that signaled the beginning of the Gaspard land. Ash took a right, drove past the silver birch forest and then through the woods. It was darker under the canopy of trees and turned darker still as they wound their way through it. Suddenly the wind picked up, whipping the tree branches so the silvery undersides of the leaves showed and warned of rain. Right before they reached the hooded sculptures leading up to the main house, Ash made a sharp left onto an even narrower road that twisted and turned and then came to a stop.

"My home," Ash said.

For a moment all Jac saw was more woods. Then she saw a Victorian building made of red brick, peeking out through a curtain of ancient ilex, oak and hazel trees. Some were so close to the building, it seemed as if the architect had designed the structure to accommodate the trees.

Ivy climbed the brick, covering several windows.

A wisteria vine, its trunk as thick as a man's arm, wound its way around and around the porch railing, up onto the roof and down the other side. It seemed as if, long ago, nature had claimed the house for its own and no one had ever fought back. Jac thought it was enchanting.

"When was this built? Was it part of the main house?"

As he opened the door and ushered her inside, Ash explained, "One of my ancestors was a jeweler. Pierre Gaspard."

She nodded. "I've heard of him."

"Well, this was his studio. Like many artisans of the time, in addition to jewelry he became fascinated with stained glass, added it to his repertoire and became quite well known for it. I imagine you saw some of his work at the main house?"

"Yes, but this is like living inside the colors. It's amazing."

Starting at the stained glass set into the front door and moving around the room, looking from one window to the next, Jac saw that the entire spectrum of the four seasons was on display. Each depicted the same idyllic forest scene of a Japanese bridge spanning a pond surrounded by trees, but rendered in a different palette. From beds of early-spring crocus, to summer water lilies, to amber and rust leaves floating on the water's surface, and then snowcapped pines, each elaborate landscape was beautifully painted not in pigment but in jewel-toned glass.

"After he married he used the main house as a home and this became his showroom. He had a shop in town too, but that was mostly for the jewelry, lamps and other small objects. For his bigger projects, he had clients come here. It looked very much the way it does now. His idea was to make the showroom resemble the rooms in a house so customers wouldn't have to imagine what a stained-glass door would look like in their entryway, or windows in the library. Come, let me show you the rest."

Ash walked Jac deeper into the house, through the dining room with its colored glass fireplace, done in Moroccan blues that shimmered like a lake in the moonlight, and the library with its elegant daffodil-designed stained-glass standing lamps that showered soft light over each chair.

"You wanted to know about my cologne," Ash said as he led Jac down a long hallway illuminated with lovely green iridescent glass wall sconces. "First you have to know about this place. No one ever lived here until I moved in ten years ago. Pierre and then his son kept the glass business here until well after the First World War. But in the thirties styles changed and stained glass fell out of fashion. Then came the war. Our estate is very large and this structure is far from the main house. No one needed it and no one seemed to know what to do with it, so it became a sort of large storage bin. When I decided to take it on, it took months to sift though everything. Like peeling decades of wallpaper. Finally underneath all the crap, I found the original rooms with all their contents completely intact. It wasn't so much that the house needed rebuilding or restoration, it just needed to be emptied out."

He stopped in front of a dark mahogany door, quite elaborately carved with garlands of flowers bordering two panels. As Ash opened it, Jac smelled what was inside before she could see it. He flicked on the light and she stepped in.

"This was where his wife, Fantine, worked."

She knew the name from Hugo's letter. So this was her laboratory. Jac looked at the perfumer's work area, pristine and perfect. Very similar to the one at the Maison L'Etoile in Paris where she grew up. In the center of the room was a perfumer's organ. This complex, tiered work-space, surrounded by ascending rows of shelves laid out like an amphitheater, was more elaborate than the L'Etoile's. Jac imagined that Fantine's husband, a jeweler, with a heightened sense of design, had had a hand in the piece's articulated ornamentation.

Jac sniffed the air. Each organ had a unique scent, since each perfumer favored certain notes. Faded vanilla and rose, lemon and verbena hung on the air, faint but discernible.

Jac pulled out Fantine's chair and then turned to Ash.

"May I?"

"Of course."

Jac sat down and scanned the rows and rows of small brown bottles of oils and absolutes. Each had a rectangular paper label, old and yellowed, with the name of the essence written in ink in a feminine hand.

Reaching for the verbena, one of the strongest scents in the room, Jac imagined Fantine sitting here, composing the fragrance Ash was wearing.

The bottle top was stuck and she couldn't twist it off. She put it back, then tried the lemon essence. The stopper yielded and she bowed her head.

"It still smells so fresh. It's always amazing how long a scent can last. So much longer than anyone realizes. So much longer than people last." Tombs in Egypt had yielded oil residues that still offered up a bouquet of aroma. "Exactly how old is this laboratory?"

"Pierre built it for his wife in 1856 and Fantine made perfume here for almost seventy years. When she died in 1924 she was ninety-four and still mixing up concoctions. According to her ledgers my cologne was first created in 1912 and contained bergamot, verbena—"

"You have her formulas?" Jac interrupted.

"Books of them. Would you like to see them?"

She nodded, excited. "Yes. Very much."

He brought her over to a small desk tucked into the corner away from the more elaborate workstation. It was an old-fashioned piece of furniture with glass-enclosed shelves above it and drawers below. In the cabinet she could see more than a dozen black leather notebooks. Ash opened the glass door. Jac could smell the slightly sweet scent of decaying glue, of leather bindings and the woodsy odor of aging paper . . . all suggesting long-forgotten treasures waiting to be discovered.

Jac lifted one of the books off the shelf and opened it. The handwriting was the same as on the bottle labels. Each page was for a different perfume formula. The names of the perfumes were evocative and suggested that Fantine and her husband had collaborated.

Emerald Evening Shivers.

Sapphire Starbursts Lasting.

Morning Pearls Alone.

Jac read down the list of the ingredients of each scent, constructing it in her mind as she went.

"These are really lovely. Sophisticated and unusual at the same time, like their names."

"How can you tell?"

"I have scent memory, so when I read what's in a fragrance, I can create it in my mind."

"Is that unusual?"

"In my family, not so unusual. My grandfather and father had it, but my brother doesn't."

"Does that mean you can compose fragrances without sniffing as you go?"

She nodded. "But I don't."

"You don't make fragrances?"

"Not since I was a child, no."

"Can you make up the fragrances in the journal from the ingredients here?"

"Some might have lost their power, but if the room has been sealed up and kept dark for all this time, a lot of them might be as fresh as the lemon essence is."

"Would you like to mix one?"

Jac surprised herself by saying yes. She hadn't done this since before her mother died . . . since she was fourteen years old. As she pulled bottle after bottle off the shelf, following the formula written out in the journal, she thought about how for Fantine and for her too, fragrance and family were intertwined. Jac's grandfather's and father's workshop was part of their home. It was where she and her brother had played at being perfumers when they were small and where they were each taught the basics of the "eighth art," as it was called among the L'Etoiles. And now Jac was seated again at a perfumer's worktable.

Jac read the list of ingredients for *Morning Pearls Alone*. Jasmine. Orange blossom. Pepper. Gardenia. Ambergris. And something called amber.

"This is so strange. There's an ingredient listed here that doesn't exist as far as I know. I wonder if it's a mistake."

"What do you mean?"

"Fantine lists amber, but that's not an essence. I thought she might have meant ambergris, which is a very popular ingredient, but that's listed also."

"What is ambergris? The resin that insects get trapped in?"

"No, that's amber, but it's not a perfume ingredient. Amber and ambergris are totally different, and to make it all the more confusing, in perfume we use the word *amber* to denote a class of perfumes. Ambers are Orientals: warm, woody and spicy scents usually made with vanilla, tonka bean, labdanum and ambergris."

"After living with this workshop, it's fascinating to have a perfumer here," Ash said.

Jac had never referred to herself as a perfumer. She wasn't one. Not really. But she didn't correct him.

"What is ambergris then, some other kind of resin?" he asked.

"No, it's a solid gray and dull waxy substance that's secreted by sperm whales and washes up on the beach. It smells awful when it's first harvested, but eventually it gives off a pleasant, very fresh smell that reminds me of rubbing alcohol. Like oakmoss, ambergris is far more important for how it works with the other ingredients than how it smells on its own."

"Whatever made someone take something like that and even try to use it in a perfume?"

Jac laughed. "I used to ask my grandfather that same question all the time. Not just about ambergris but other ingredients, like the secretions taken from poor civets' glands."

She scanned the shelves, then found and pulled out two bottles: one marked *ambergris* and one marked *civet*, and handed them to Ash.

And then she noticed something else. "This is very odd."

"What?"

Jac reached up and picked up another bottle. She showed it to Ash. The label, very clearly, read *amber*. There was almost no liquid left, only a residue of oil on the bottom. Jac opened it and sniffed. It was familiar and for a moment she couldn't place it. Then she realized it was similar to the smell of the fire she and Theo had lit at the witches' site the day before.

She offered it to Ash. "Here, smell. It has a mineral odor but it's sweet too, almost a floral."

He bent over and sniffed.

"Now smell the ambergris."

He did.

"They're nothing alike, right?"

"Yes, right."

"Let me finish mixing the formula. I want to see how this all adds up."

Jac dipped a pipette in the bottle, sucked up the two drops called for and added them to the concoction.

She swirled the bottle so the different essences could merge and meld. Watching the mixture eddy, smelling as it began to combine, she realized she was excited. She didn't remember feeling this way since she and Robbie had created their impossible scents when they were young.

For the first time in more than seventeen years, she was making perfume.

"You have a wonderful time capsule here," Jac said to Ash. "There are perfumers who would kill to come and study these journals and get their hands on these old oils."

"Would you like to do it? Perhaps if any of the scents had merit, your company might want to bring them to market?"

Jac was caught off guard. Not so much because he'd made the offer, but because of how appealing it sounded. To spend a few months holed up here, away from Paris and New York, far from Griffin North—and how much she missed him—immersing herself in the yellowed pages of formulas with intriguing poetic names . . .

"Would you consider it? It seems a shame if there's value here not to explore it. I'd be quite interested in getting involved in a new business."

"Ever the banker," she joked. "And here I thought you might be a romantic after all."

"We are always searching out new investment opportunities. But it's more than that. This is my family's heritage as much as the jewelry and stained glass is, and it's been hidden away here. I'm serious, Jac."

"Yes, I know you are."

"If these scents wind up having merit, don't you think the story of lost fragrances being reintroduced to the world would be a great hook? The line would totally capture the imagination. I can picture the ads."

She laughed. "You make it sound as if you have it all worked out."

"Some ideas are so right that they work themselves out. You have a nose for scent and I have one for ways to make money. This has legs. Would you think about it?"

Surprising herself completely, she said yes before she reasoned it out logically. But she was feeling something in this workshop she didn't remember ever feeling around perfume. Or perhaps it was the lack of what she felt. There was no misery soaked into this wooden desk, no tears captured in these brown glass bottles, no whiff of melancholy in the air. The L'Etoile family tragedies were not part of these scents. Here she was free of her family's past, and the experience was heady.

"Would you like to smell the first of Fantine's scents to be remixed in nearly a hundred years?" she asked.

"I'd consider it a toast. We can both sniff to it."
Jac laughed.

"That first time I saw you, at the bar in the hotel, you looked so sad," Ash said. "I didn't know you, obviously, I'd never met you, but I wanted somehow to take away some of that sadness." He was looking into her face. "You don't look sad at all here, mixing up these perfumes. There's something else very much alive in your eyes."

And then, leaning down, Ash kissed her softly on the lips. After a first instant of shock, she was amazed at how easily she relaxed into the embrace and even felt herself open to him a little. Electricity surged through her, skimmed her skin, and then lodged deep inside her where she felt a sudden throb.

What was happening? This was Theo's brother!

And then the kiss ended. Ash smiled in a relaxed, easygoing way as if something delightful but not difficult had just happened. Then he opened his hand for the bottle. "I'd like to smell that now."

"We should do this the right way, the way my grandfather always did it . . ." Jac said.

She needed a tester strip. Fantine must have used something like the narrow pieces of paper perfumers used today. Searching the organ's drawers, she was delighted to find a pile of pale cream ribbons, each the length of a rose stem. Fantine would have cut them herself, since Jac knew there were no factory-made tester strips till the late 1920s.

She showed Ash. "My grandfather insisted we use ribbons at L'Etoile's also. No manufactured testers were allowed."

As she dipped the ribbon into the bottle and watched it wick up the perfume, she thought of her grandfather and his old-fashioned ways. He had loved this custom of lowering the ribbon into the bottle of scent, slowly soaking up the elixir and then presenting the ribbon to his customer like a gift. Sometimes he would surprise Jac with a ribbon soaked in a new perfume. He'd tie it around her wrist with a lovely small bow and ask her to wear it for the day and then give him her opinion. She'd saved every one of those satins. Where were they now? Somewhere in the house on Rue des Saints-Pères, probably.

Suddenly Jac felt the air wavering around her. Familiar shivers ran up and down her arms, pinpricks of cold that alerted her to what was coming. The smells around her intensified. The light dimmed. Shadows descended. Her thoughts threatened to ebb away. She was suffering the first warning signs of an encroaching hallucination.

Something she'd just used in mixing this perfume was an olfactory trigger.

Jac pushed the chair away from the open bottles of essences and absolutes. The ribbon fell to the floor, forgotten. She stepped back. Away from the organ, the sensations she was having were less pronounced than they had been in the past. And not as frightening. She almost wanted to enter into the vision that teased her. It seemed as if part of her had stepped outside her body and was hovering over this room, watching another woman making perfume here many years ago.

Jac wanted to stay, to observe the woman more closely, but she knew she couldn't allow this to happen. Not again. Not now.

She ran through her sanity commandments.

Open a window. Get fresh air. Take long, concentrated breaths. Stop your mind from spiraling by giving it a task.

Without explaining anything to Ash, she rose up, walked over to the window, pulled it open and stuck her head out. Breathing in the forest air, she focused. Hazel. Grass. Roses. Pine. The sea. Sanity.

"Are you all right?" Ash asked.

"I will be. I'm sorry. Something I inhaled had a strange effect on me."

"An ingredient?"

"Yes."

"Which one?"

"I'm not sure."

"I think it was having an effect on me too," he said.

"Yes?"

She turned to him.

Ash was looking at her strangely. As if he wasn't quite seeing her, but looking at someone else. And then before she realized what was happening, he leaned forward and kissed her again. And the sensations she had been fighting turned into something quite different, and she shuddered with a jolt of almost nothing but pleasure.

Twenty-five

It was low tide. In the strong afternoon light, the crevices and cracks in the rock formations seemed to reveal human features and expressions.

Jac and Theo had come down to the beach near Hugo's home in search of a rock configuration like the one he was standing on in the photo that had fallen off the wall. His feet were positioned at such an awkward angle, he might be pointing to something specific. It was a possible clue, and since they had no others, Theo had been willing to give it a try.

He'd run off two copies of the photo at his gallery and now gave one to Jac. Hugo, in his formal suit, stood on the rock. His gaze and his body were turned away from the photographer, looking to the left. The stones he stood on were treacherous. The photo was similar to a famous one Jac had seen in several shops and restaurants on the island. The writer apparently enjoyed being perched up high. But it was hard to imagine the fifty-year-old climbing up on the rocks in his heavy clothes.

"Which direction is he looking?" Jac asked. "Off to sea or toward the land? North or south?"

"There's no way to tell," Theo said.

"That's going to make it all the more difficult," she said.

For the next thirty-five minutes they walked down the beach, stopping often, holding the photo up against the rocks. Finally they came to a grouping that actually did resemble those in the photo.

When they'd gotten closer, Jac said, "It doesn't look like there's a cave here; there's no opening." She studied the photo again. "But it really does seem to be the same spot."

Theo climbed up a small rock. Then up another. "When we were kids, my brother and I used to spend hours exploring caves."

Jac felt a jolt of something like embarrassment. Hearing Theo refer to his brother, she thought of the two unexpected but not unwelcome kisses and what they might suggest. No time for that now. Theo was saying something else.

"All up and down the coast. We must have covered over half of them." He was on the fourth rock now. "One thing I learned is not all the cave openings are eye level." On the fifth rock. "There's a shelf back here. Hold on . . ."

He disappeared from view for a moment. Jac waited. When he came back, his voice was more animated than she was used to.

"Come see. I think we might have found something."

Jac climbed up, reached Theo and followed him through the crevice to the ledge. They were standing so close to each other that she could feel heat waving off him. She peered in. He put his hands on her shoulders, holding her protectively. The sensation was chilling and bracing. She had a sudden flash from a few hours earlier. Ash's hands had felt so different. His had been warming.

"We need to go down there," Theo said.

Below them was an enclosure, stone all around, sand in the middle. On the rock face to the right was an opening.

"Let me go first. I'm taller, it's less of a leap for me," Theo said.

He jumped and landed, splashed onto the beach.

"There's an inch of water here," he said. "Before you come down, let me just make sure this really is an opening."

She watched him walk over and then disappear. After ten or fifteen seconds he emerged and looked up at her with a solemn smile. "This might be what you're looking for, Jac."

Jac looked at the edge in panic. She couldn't stand to be this close to it. But he'd said this could be the cave. She concentrated on that, sucked in her breath and jumped.

He caught her. Put her down.

She was on the sand, enclosed by the rocks all around her, the water soaking through her shoes and socks. It was freezing.

She followed Theo up a slight incline to dry beach and toward the niche. He went in first, turning on his lantern, holding it out and back a little, to light her way.

Animal and bird bones, bleached smooth from years of water rushing over their surfaces. The smells right here were intense. Salt from the channel. Minerals from the rock.

For the second time in a few hours, she felt the rush of excitement that accompanied a new discovery. Until today the feeling was only triggered by moments such as this, finds connected to her research. But earlier she'd felt this same heady anticipation in Ash's house, when she sat down at Fantine's perfumer's organ.

As Theo took his first step inside and she followed, the light from his lantern illuminated the interior space.

"How amazing this is," she said in wonder, to herself as much as Theo.

They were in a long corridor, completely covered—walls and ceiling—with paintings done in blacks, browns and ochres. In this riot of imagery she could make out men, women, horses, cows, birds, dogs, cats . . . and then she began to notice details. None of them was all human or all animal. Each creature was an amalgam of both. A man who was half fawn, standing on hooves. A bull with a man's eyes and devil's horns standing on two human legs. A bird with a woman's face. A woman with a bird's head and wings.

"These are fantastic," she said in a voice laced with emotion. "I can't tell for sure, there have been hoaxes that have fooled scholars, but these feel authentic. Some of these creatures are Celtic gods and goddesses. Have you seen anything like them elsewhere on the island?"

"There are quite a few examples of cave paintings around, yes. I've seen them in the museum and in two caves that are occasionally open to the public. But none of them depicted these creatures."

Examining the wall closely, Jac peered at the paintings. "I'd only need the smallest sample to test these, but I don't want to disturb them myself. We should call in an expert when the time comes and—" She broke off and walked back to the opening of the cave. "I think . . ." she said, as she came down the corridor again very slowly. "There are threads of legendary myths I recognize here. But there's also a very specific story playing out I haven't seen anywhere else. Look at this man-cat." She pointed. "If you follow him you can catch it. He's in a processional with these other creatures. They're marching in a parade formation. It's a celebration, you can tell from the garlands around their heads." She gestured to another drawing. "You can recognize that same group of half-men, half-animals here. In this section it appears as if the man-cat is being chosen for something. Now if you follow him . . ." She walked a few feet down. "And look here, he's being bathed . . ." Another few feet. "Here he's being fed." She skipped over a group of other drawings done in slightly different style. It was getting easier to figure out which belonged to the specific sequence she was following. "He's here again. Walking into the cave, the same way we are. Leading us, taking us deeper and deeper inside."

Jac used her cell phone to take pictures. There was no reception here, but the flash on the camera worked perfectly. "Do you see these horned centaurs? They're the only ones not engaging with the man-cat or any of the people around him. They seem to be watching over the proceedings."

Jac noticed that the bottoms of the drawings weren't always finished. She stared at the feathery workmanship. It was an uneven line of demarcation on the walls, below which there were no paintings. And then she realized what it was.

Pointing it out to Theo, she asked, "Why would they have painted on the walls knowing the sea was going to wash the drawings away?"

"Maybe back then, when they were drawn, the cave didn't fill up with as much water. Or any. Serious erosion in the last two thousand years has changed all kinds of elevations."

They'd come to the end of the corridor and a small archway.

Theo went through first and Jac followed. The stones underfoot were uneven and slippery. Water clearly came this far into the cave at high tide.

It was icy cold and quiet here except for the sound of bones and shells crunching beneath their feet and water dripping, slowly, evenly, in the distance.

Theo's lamp revealed a room about ten feet square, with a low ceiling, barely six feet tall at its highest. Theo had to hunch over, but Jac was fine with more than half a foot of headroom.

There was only one drawing here of the man-cat: he knelt by a depression in the ground, and a larger creature, half-man, half-buck, poured water over him. "It looks like a cleansing bath," Jac said.

She turned and walked to the center of the room, where, in fact, there was a hollowed-out depression in the ground, lined with pale yellow, iridescent shells and bordered by flat oval stones, not unlike the stone circle that had brought Jac and Theo together at Blixer Rath. "It's the same ritual bath that's in the drawing," she said.

There was nothing else to inspect, so they

proceeded to the threshold of the next chamber. The sound of splashing water echoed more loudly now. As Jac stepped inside, she felt as if she were entering a cathedral. The ceilings were at least twenty feet tall, with stalactites. A double row of monolithic stones, each eight to ten feet tall, marched shoulder to shoulder down the center, creating an aisle leading to another circle of stones. In its middle was a stone slab resting on two square rocks. The configuration reminded Jac of Stonehenge and the ancient mystery that had never been solved.

A waterfall splashed down the back wall, its scent a combination of salt with a hint of sulfur. Were they walking in a circle? Coming to an exit? Or was the water coming from a source inside the rocks?

Theo's lantern cast light in the immediate vicinity, but the space was so deep it was impossible to illuminate all at once. The crevices and corners remained in unfathomable shadow.

Jac focused on what she could see well—more black, brown and ochre paintings on the right wall.

"The same figure is here too," she said. "Half-cat, half-man."

Theo looked over her shoulder. He stood so close she could smell his cologne over the damp scents of the tomb-like cave.

"It looks like he's being dried off here, then

clothed here, and here they are festooning him with beads and feathers."

Following the creature, they journeyed farther into the room, reading the story the paintings told. In the next section women were bringing him platters of food. In the next, feeding him.

They'd reached the back wall now, where the water fell from cracks in the high rocks, sluicing down and into a deep gorge in the floor. A fine mist coated Jac's face. She could taste the water. It wasn't seawater at all but lake or river water.

"Where is this coming from?"

"I don't know what's above us. I'm not sure how deep in we've gone," Theo said.

The water dripped down the rock wall into the rut that cut across the room and then, following a slight decline, disappeared into a second rut that surrounded the largest monolithic stone of those they'd already seen.

She knelt. The centuries of flowing water had worn down the gulley's sides and it was as smooth as a porcelain tub. Plunging her fingers into the pool, she had a sudden sense memory. Somewhere, some other time, she had done this. The flashback was distinct, but she couldn't place it. She felt instead as if someone had told her they had done this, and their description was so real it seemed as if it had happened to her.

While she had been inspecting that side of the stone, Theo had walked around to the other side.

"Jac . . . Come look, I think I found something." Theo's lamp illuminated a deep niche in the stone. Inside was a second stone, darker, blacker and about five feet tall. During high school, Jac had studied the meteorites in the Museum of Natural History. She couldn't be certain, but this resembled those melted rocks that had fallen from the asteroid belt between Mars and Jupiter.

The boulder was rounded and pitted and felt like glass. Its matte-black shiny rind curved around its depressions, or thumbprints, she remembered they were called. Some went so deep they created cubbyholes. And all those little alcoves appeared to be filled with small objects.

Theo reached in and extracted a small carving of one of the centaurs from the wall paintings. It was rustic and awkward. But also strange and beautiful.

The way Theo was holding the statuette and the lantern sent the light upward, and for a second Jac could see inside the now empty slot. "Wait. There's still something in there," Jac said as she reached deeper inside and pulled out a pale white object.

"It's a bone," she said. "Very old."

"A human bone, isn't it?"

She nodded. Jac was thinking too about the catacombs in Paris where the bones of more than six million people had been deposited and decorated the caves with macabre beauty. "Human . . . yes, I think so."

"Look. There are more of those figurines." He pointed his torch toward one niche after another. Then he gave her the lantern and pulled out more carvings. "Behind every one of these is another bone. What does it mean?"

"Each of these little gods or warriors is standing guard, I think," Jac said.

"Are all the bones from the same person?" Theo asked.

She looked down at what he'd pulled out. "No, these are all sacrum bones. It's at the base of the spine, where the autonomic nervous system ends. We each have only one and it's very special in ancient cultures. The Romans called it the *os sacrum*, which translates to the "holy bone." The Greek name for it was *hieron osteon*, which means the same thing. There are people who believe that enlightenment can be achieved by awakening the spiritual energy in the sacrum. Holy yogis say that awakening would be a resurrection."

"So it's tied to reincarnation?"

Jac almost didn't want to answer. The concept of being reborn, of soul migration, of a soul returning again and again to complete its karmic path seemed to be following her everywhere since she'd gone to Paris at the beginning of the summer.

"Yes. The sacrum is the last bone in the body to

rot, and ancients believed that it was the nucleus around which the whole body would be rebuilt in the afterlife."

"You've been on a lot of digs, haven't you?"

"Yes, why?"

"Have you ever seen anything like this?" he asked. "Anything to explain exactly what we're looking at?"

She shook her head. "Never . . ." She thought. "Well, one thing is slightly similar. In Egypt the dead were buried with small shabti sculptures about this size. Their job was to protect the deceased on their journey to the afterlife."

Theo had emptied eight niches. He reached into a ninth.

"This isn't a bone," he said as he extracted something else.

Jac shone the light on it. It was as slender as a bone but dark and polished. She touched it. "It's wood . . ."

"It's a pipe," Theo said. "Not as old as the rest of these things. Probably a hundred years or so. We have a few in the house that belonged to some ancestor or other."

Jac was still sniffing. She laughed. "It's hashish."

"Really?"

"I think they smoked hashish in the eighteen fifties. So this was someone's den of iniquity—"

"Jac, there's more here." His voice was tense with excitement.

Theo was holding a leather-bound book, somewhat worn. It smelled slightly of mold. A leather strip wrapped around its middle kept it closed. Embossed on the front were two gold letters, still shining.

V. H.

Theo was trying to untie the knot.

Jac stopped him with her hand. "Be careful. It could be fragile."

He gave it to her. "I'm too nervous. You do it."

Holding the book gingerly, she walked around the stone and placed the journal on the slab table.

Theo put the lantern next to it and peered down, watching as, very carefully, Jac unknotted the binding and opened the book.

There was no title on the first page, no salutation, just line after line of script, slanting heavily to the right, almost as if a wind were blowing them in that direction.

"The ink isn't at all faded. It's possible this hasn't been opened in years. Maybe even since it was placed here." Jac whispered as if paying homage to the book.

"It's in French," Theo said. "Can you read it?"

Jac read the first few lines out loud, translating as she went.

Every story begins with a tremble of anticipation. At the start we may have an idea of our point of arrival, but what lies before us and makes us shudder is the journey, for that is all discovery.

This strange and curious story begins for me at the sea.

She stopped and turned to Theo. "You found it! This is Hugo's story about what happened to him here on the island."

"I almost can't believe it's real."

For the first time since she'd come to Jersey she saw an actual expression of happiness on his face.

"It's real. Can you smell it?"

He bent over and sniffed. "Yes, what is it?"

"Mold, leather, the particular scent of paper decaying—it's like a combination of grassy notes with an acidic tang and a hint of vanilla."

But there was something else Jac smelled. A rich and spicy perfume that combined roses, ylang-ylang and oakmoss. Trapped in the pages for how many years, a fine French perfume was escaping. It was the kind of scent she had grown up with. Nothing like most modern mass-produced fragrances, but beautifully articulated and rounded. She sniffed at it. There was one note that she couldn't quite figure out, and that note was similar to the mysterious note in Ash's cologne. No, not similar, it was the same note. It was that curious amber she'd found in Fantine's studio.

Was this another of Fantine's scents? Was the amber note her signature? The way vanilla was Jean Guerlain's? The way tuberose was her grandfather's?

Theo was trying to read more of what was on the page. "I wish my French was better. You're going to have to read it to me. Do you mind?"

"Mind? It would be an honor to read this."

She started to translate the next line and realized she was talking over the sound of rushing water. "Do you hear that?" she asked.

"The water?"

"Yes, doesn't it seem louder than it did even a minute ago?"

"It does." Theo turned around. "Damn it," he said. "The waterfall's stream has swelled."

Jac inhaled and said, "The scent of the minerals is stronger too. I never thought of that before, but primitive men must have learned to smell certain dangers. Rising waters. Rain storms."

"We should go. The tide must be surging." As Theo reached for the journal, he knocked over one of the little creatures and it fell to the ground.

Jac reached down, found the totem and picked it up. It had landed on a wet patch of ground, and now the figurine was sticky and gave off a more pronounced sweet and earthy smell. It was the same note of amber from Fantine's studio. From Ash's cologne. From the perfume in the book. She didn't know of any resin that came alive when it was wet. She rubbed the effigy and its dirt and grime came off on her finger, revealing a semi-translucent golden creature. Glowing.

She thought about the beautifully carved amber

owl Malachai had shown her the night she'd found the letter from Theo. If this wasn't the same material, it was close. Malachai would note the synchronicity of that event and this. *Not a coincidence,* he'd argue, *but events coming full circle. The infinite possibilities of energy and spirit.* The more she rubbed, the stronger the aroma. Even without burning it, it had a scent? How was that possible? The small sculpture in Malachai's study didn't have an odor. This amber was different and it was familiar. From a long time ago. But that wasn't possible either. She'd been sure in Fantine's laboratory she'd never smelled it before coming to the island. So how could she be remembering it now?

Twenty-six

56 BCE
ISLE OF JERSEY

When Owain walked into the hut, Gwenore was standing by the hearth. She looked up, a welcoming smile on her lips. But beneath it he could see worry in her eyes. He'd been gone for four days. The longest he'd ever spent, and the retreat had been exhausting. He could see in his wife's reaction that his ordeal must be showing on his face.

"You look like you need to eat and to sleep," she said. "Which first?"

"I'm starving." He sat at the table, hoping she'd busy herself with making him food and not ask too many questions. Not yet. Not until he could talk to the elders. Perhaps the worst part of the retreat was the walk home, knowing she was going to want to know what path the gods had told him to take. What preparations the tribe needed to make.

Owain almost sobbed again as he thought of the revelation. Even though he'd already cried and beaten his fists on the ground for hours, his agony was still fresh and new. His anxiety as sharp as any knife's edge.

Gwenore poured her husband a mug of ale. While he drank a long draft and then another, she brought over a plate of wheat cakes, set it down and sat next to him. He took a cake and bit into it. She was a good cook, but it tasted like straw. Why had he thought he could eat? He felt as if he could barely breathe. She put her hand on his thigh as if she was making sure he was real and not an apparition. It was a quiet gesture, and he remembered that when they were first together and she was still shy with him, she had touched him this way too, often.

"So tell me about the mission. Was it very difficult? Why were you gone so long?"

How could he ever explain? What could he say? His fear made his voice gruff, his tone angry.

"I'm hungry, woman. Can't your questions wait?"

She rose, went to the hearth. From the pot hanging over the fire, she spooned stew into a wooden bowl. Once she placed it in front of him, he fell to eating it, forcing the food down. Anything to prevent the inquisition.

Gwenore poured him more ale. He stopped eating to take a draft, then went back to the stew. It was well cooked and spiced correctly, but like the cake, he wanted nothing to do with it. He filled his stomach only because it ached from being starved for so long, and eating gave him an excuse for not speaking.

"Did the visions come?" Gwenore asked.

"They did." He had spent his days in the cave, fasting, dreaming and then meditating on his dreams.

"Were you able to interpret them?"

"I believe so," he said, and then spooned more food into his mouth. Feeling as if he was going to choke on it.

"You stayed longer than I expected."

He nodded.

"Why?"

"The messages were complicated."

She frowned.

"What is it?" he asked her.

"You tell me."

"What do you mean, woman? Don't speak in witches' riddles."

"You're not reporting on what you learned. You always do. Right away. Usually you can't wait."

"Is that true?" He really wasn't aware that he was so quick to confide in her when he returned from a retreat.

"Yes, Owain. You do. As soon as you come home, you tell me what you learned. I've been with you for fourteen years. I've watched you go forth on quests four times during each of those years. Over fifty retreats. You always return after two nights, spent but refreshed. Now you stay away twice that amount of time and you come home exhausted and sickly. Worry lines are around your lips, on your brow. Trouble in your eyes."

"The visions were complicated, Gwenore. I'm not sure I understand what I saw, or what it means. I need to consult with the other priests tonight."

"Can't that wait till tomorrow?"

"Not really. No."

"It must. You can barely keep your eyes open."

He knew how tired he was. From the moment he had gleaned an interpretation from the vision, he had been unable to sleep. To rest. To do anything but worry. Was it possible that he'd misread the dreams? Might one of the other priests find a different interpretation? Oh, how he prayed they would. He was not a man who was often wrong, and he prided himself on that. But now? To be wrong would be a blessing.

"Come," she said, holding out her hand. "At least try to sleep. If you can't, you can go to see the others."

Usually he washed before going to sleep, but he'd washed just hours ago in the cave, using the spirit water that spilled down the rock. That icy cold water he always used to come awake from the visions.

Gwenore stayed with him as he stripped off his tunic. He wondered what else the witch sensed, but he didn't want to ask lest he invite more questions. Owain was afraid of what she could intuit. And he didn't want to have to explain. Could not bear it. Not yet. Not while there was still a small chance that he was wrong about what he'd seen in the cave. Not until he'd consulted with the elders and made certain his interpretation was the correct one.

He lay down on the mat. Yawned. He really was tired. The visions always wore him out. But this exhaustion went deeper. It struck his heart. It tore at his guts.

Gwenore lay next to him.

He shut his eyes and then asked the one question he did need the answer to. The one he'd been afraid to ask for fear of how his voice would sound saying his son's name out loud. "Where is Brice?"

"Wth a group of boys on a fishing excursion. I expect we won't see him until tomorrow or the day after. They planned on staying on the other side of the island at least for tonight."

A burst of relief was followed by one of panic. He wanted his son home. Wanted to see him. To look into his eyes. To discover that Brice wasn't the same boy he'd seen in his visions. That his son didn't look as Owain saw him in the trance. That the boy in the dreams was someone else's son.

Even as he wished it, Owain knew it had been Brice. Owain knew his own son. How could he not? How could he mistake him for anyone else? Unless the herb combination had been too strong. That was possible, wasn't it? Maybe the smoke from the sacred fire had too much magic in it. That was possible, wasn't it? Maybe the gods were playing tricks. Maybe . . .

"What is it?" Gwenore asked. "You are so restless."

He shook his head. "I don't know."

"Do you need a potion?"

"No, I'll be fine." He didn't want her ministering to him. Didn't want her kindness now. It would only make her fury that much worse when she found out the awful secret that had been revealed to him in the cave of the visions.

Still unable to accept what he'd seen, now he set to wondering if there was something wrong with his abilities. Maybe he was no longer capable of seeing the messages from the spirit world. Or maybe someone had invaded the sacred place where only priests were allowed, and altered it somehow. Corrupted the magic.

Was that possible?

The entrance to the cave was hard to find. In fact it had been chosen by the ancients because of how the grouping of rocks curved and obscured the access even when the tide was low. At high tide the entrance was hidden from sight and water flooded the front chambers. You could be trapped during storms. Just a dozen years ago, a priest who had been trying to escape had drowned.

No one but the elders knew the location of the cave. Each generation passed it down to the next. Only holy men could go there. And only holy men could be entombed there. Deep in the inner reaches, far back, Owain had buried five elders there, two of whom were his mentors. Those had been difficult days. Even though Owain believed that the men's souls would return, he'd been close to the men and their passing had been hard for him to accept. He'd missed both of them more these last few days than he had in years. In the cave, after the visions, he'd visited their tombs and tried to conjure and communicate with them. He'd prayed to them to help him understand the vision another way. To have it mean something else.

Why not me? Why don't the gods want me?

"What?" Gwenore asked, her green eyes staring into his. "You were crying out in your sleep."

He was amazed he'd actually fallen asleep. With

378

all he had on his mind, he hadn't thought he'd be able to.

"You were arguing with someone, Owain."

"What did I say?" Perhaps his dream conversation would be important and reveal some flaw in his interpretation of the message he'd received in the cave.

" 'Why not me?' That's what you said. Over and over again."

Owain nodded. Closed his eyes. No, it wasn't a new divination. It was the same thought he'd been having continuously since his terrible revelation.

Gwenore stroked his hair. Combed out his tangled curls with her fingertips. She smelled of the food she'd cooked, of earth and herbs, of the sweet flowers she brewed and the oils she used to concoct her remedies. His wife came from a long line of witches, herbalists and healers who passed down their elixir recipes. Their potions soothed the skin, relaxed the soul. Some, even, could draw out and expel evil powers.

The first time he'd lain with her he'd been so intoxicated by her aroma that he'd accused her of drugging him. She'd said no, there was nothing in the oils she wore except nature's perfumes. But he wasn't certain. Just as he wasn't positive that the beverage she made for him and Brice every morning wasn't a magical brew.

He'd watch her crush grasses, herbs and minerals, mix them with spring water and pray over them. He'd never seen her add anything suspicious. But still, how was it that he and Brice were the healthiest men on the island? That neither of them, or she for that matter, was ever sickly?

Gwenore's fingers massaged the base of his skull, moved down the back of his neck and to his shoulders. Kneaded out the terrible knots in his muscles. She was using one of the minted oils, and the menthol was seeping into his skin and relaxing him despite his resistance. Under her skilled fingertips he was letting go. Giving up his fear. Not trying to work out his problems anymore. With each downward and upward stroke he became less in his mind and more in his body. He was not on a sacred retreat now. Not on a quest. This was his home. This was his wife.

The smoke he'd burned in the cave put him in one kind of trance. All mind, no body. His wits danced with ideas, with images. He witnessed a play of scenes acted out on a stage in the air. A theater of the gods. He lay on his back on the raised stone slab where he was protected from the waters that rushed in when the moon rose too high, and he disappeared into the visions.

But this, what Gwenore did to him, was a different kind of trance. All body and no mind. He became the sensation of his skin beneath her fingers. He was his own rising and falling and quickening breath. He was the hardening of his cock and the pulsing in his veins.

Owain was amazed he could react at all. Amazed his body was able to dismiss what his thoughts had been fixated on. Could he give in? Did the gods need him to be aware of his physical self now?

Or was he was convincing himself of that? Maybe he just desperately wanted Gwenore to take him to the forgetful place between her legs.

She disrobed. The star-shaped mark on her breast looked redder to him tonight. He reached out and touched it and his fingertip burned.

Pushing him back, Gwenore mounted him. Kissed him. Kept massaging him. Her hair was spread out on his belly. Every strand like a lick of fire, teasing him. His blood was finally warming after four full days and nights of cold. He felt it quickening as the pressure inside him built. His head fell back. He closed his eyes. Concentrated only on the touch of her lips. The hot inside of her mouth. The motion of the tides, the ebb and flow of the waves on the sand were in her movements. He thought only about the naturalness of their being together. Of the wonder that one body could effect this in another. Gwenore had told him once this was the real magic they were all searching for. That they were wrong to search for it in caves. That this coaxing of a man's blood to the surface, this building up of pressure, this sweetness that came from a man and woman lying together was the secret.

He reached down and his fingers found the other cave, the one between his wife's legs. Where she was slick. Where she was ready. He traveled into her and she took him in, deeply, with a soft moan of pleasure. Owain wanted her to absorb him. Wanted the oblivion her lips and her legs were promising, but at the same time he was frightened of going to that sweet place. It would be a relief, yes, but what if it was such a relief, he didn't come back? What if the job ahead of him was so horrible to contemplate that he let himself disappear? He knew of others who had left their minds, never to return. As much as he didn't want to do what had to be done, he must. No one but him could make the sacrifice the gods were demanding in exchange for keeping the tribe safe from the Romans.

His movements became the rhythm of her breath. His breaths became the rhythm of her movements. There was nothing to tether him to reality anymore. Nothing to keep him from losing his mind.

Owain let go.

Twenty-seven

Theo knelt beside Jac. Her eyes were open but she wasn't seeing him. He said her name. Once. Twice. A third time. The panic rose in him.

"Jac!"

She remained unresponsive.

It was happening again. He flashed back to the time they'd spent together as teenagers at Blixer Rath. Those horrible, wonderful days. Something like this, or exactly this, had happened once before. On his last day there. She'd been present and aware one minute and then gone the next. Not asleep exactly. Not unconscious, but totally unresponsive. He'd lifted her out of the water and half-carried, half-dragged her back to the clinic where Malachai Samuels had thrown questions at him while listening to Jac's heartbeat, feeling her pulse, pulling down her eyelids.

Theo had watched in horror. He had never been more frightened. She was his friend. Fiery and stubborn. And of course, like him, damaged and vulnerable. The idea that he'd done something to her was more than he could bear.

Malachai had repeated her name several times. When she hadn't responded . . . what had Malachai done? Theo tried to remember, but his mind was a blank. What should he do? What could he do? He tried to go back to that day. To build the doctor's office in his mind. To see Jac on his couch.

Yes!

Ripping off his shirt, Theo dipped it in the water in the rut. As he did so he noticed for the first time that the floor around them was wet. Was the water from the rock splashing this far? He looked. No, the rising tide was doing more than swelling the waterfall, it was seeping into the cave.

He had to get Jac out of there. And it was going to be hard if she was still nonresponsive and half asleep like this. Theo needed her to be able to walk. As he wiped Jac's face, he talked to her. His hand was on her back, supporting her. He felt her bones through her shirt. Felt where her flesh stopped and her bra started. He was unnerved by the intimacy.

Theo rewet his shirt and pressed it to Jac's wrists, first the right and then the left, and then placed it on the back of her neck. He was fairly sure this was what the doctor had done. Chilled her blood and cooled her body temperature until she came to. But she wasn't responding. Maybe he hadn't kept it there long enough.

Again he wet the cloth and then wrapped it around Jac's left wrist. Counted to thirty. Then the right wrist. Counted again.

What should he do if he couldn't bring her out of this? How hard would it be to pull her through the narrow passages they had just traversed? And how much time did he have to wait before they'd be forced to leave?

The water level was rising quickly. His shoes were now soaked. Even if the inner chambers and tunnel didn't completely flood, and he knew they didn't from the water lines Jac had pointed out, it was possible the entrance might. He could probably wait it out, but what would happen to Jac if she stayed like this? How long was too long?

Pressing the shirt to the back of her neck again, he counted. Five seconds. Ten. Twenty. They couldn't swim for long in the sea this time of year. The temperature was too cold. Hypothermia was a threat to anyone who did cave explorations in Jersey. When he was a boy his mother had warned him and Ash about it all the time. No matter how warm it might be outside, freezing water could cause serious harm if they were submerged for too long.

Jac opened her eyes. Stared right at him. Frowned.

"Are you all right?" he asked.

She didn't answer. She was looking around the cave: at the lantern on the rock slab, at the walls, at the monolithic stones, then down at the amber totem she was still holding.

The last thing she'd done before going into her trance was take it out of the niche, drop it, then retrieve it.

"We need to get out of here. The cave is filling up with water," he said.

She didn't react at all. Theo wondered if she'd even heard him.

"Fast," he said urging her to focus.

"Brice?"

She was scrutinizing him as if she didn't know who he was, and worse, was afraid of him.

"What?"

She said something quickly. A string of words that he couldn't quite understand except for the repeated name, *Brice*.

"Jac, we've got to get out of here." He took the carved figure from her, put it back in one of the niches. Then rethought that, picked it back up and pocketed it. Putting one arm around Jac's waist, he tried to help her to stand. But she pushed him away.

The water level was creeping up. It was above his ankles now. It must be seeping in through multiple cracks and crevices. He felt his toes starting to go numb.

"You have to let me help you. We have to get out of here. The cave is flooding." He pointed.

She looked.

Theo saw her eyes go wide with fear.

When he put his arm around her again, she didn't push him off. As he helped her up, she faltered. It was as if she were drugged. She was disoriented but able to walk with his support, and that was all he cared about for now.

"Come on. This way." He led her out of the cavernous chamber, into the next and finally into the tunnel. Here the water was almost up to their knees. It was extremely difficult to trudge through with her on his arm like a dead weight. She was leaning into him, and the journal he'd put in his pocket was pushing uncomfortably into his ribs. He probably should have left it where it was and come back for it. What if he slipped and got it wet? If the ink ran, everything Hugo wrote would be gone. How stupid he'd been.

Finally they made it out of the cave. The enclosure was filled up with water that lapped above Theo's knees. How was he going to climb up and out of here with Jac?

Theo hadn't taken the line in Hugo's letter about the tides seriously enough—*the phase of the moon will keep our secrets.* The tide must have kept these caverns often inaccessible. Today he and Jac must have just caught the end of the hour when entering them was possible.

Suddenly Jac pulled away from him. She was wading to the wall. As if she had done it a dozen times, she put her hands on two protruding rocks Theo hadn't even noticed, and began the climb out of the chasm.

Theo followed her, wondering as he watched her scale the wall without hesitation or faltering, how she had found the hand- and toeholds.

When she reached the ground up above, she took off without looking back or waiting for him. Walking quickly, she headed in the opposite direction from where the car was, where they'd come from. He called out to her, but she didn't respond. He ran to catch up, reached her side, put his hand out to stop her.

"Jac, where are you going?" he asked. "My car is the other way."

She frowned at him, quizzically.

Did she really not understand what he was saying?

He took her hand. "This way."

As it had in the cave, as it had so many years ago, fear flooded her eyes. She tried to wrest free. He managed to hold on and pulled her toward the slipway and then to the parking area. When they reached his Jaguar, she gave his car the same uncomprehending look that she'd given him. He didn't know what to do except force her into the car. But she fought back. Lashing out at him, Jac managed to punch him in the side of his head. Her moves were that of an experienced fighter, but her strength didn't match her training. She hadn't hurt him, only surprised him long enough to take off.

For one stunned moment he watched her running away, astounded. *What was happening?* He took off after her, trying to catch up, but she was fast and the best he could do was keep her in his sight.

They were out of the clearing and in the woods now. The wind sang in his ears. Branches snapped across his face. He called out to Jac to stop, but she either didn't hear him or didn't care. Theo wasn't sure why, but he thought she wasn't so much running away from him as toward something.

But that was impossible. She'd only been on the island for three days. She couldn't know the way.

She was still running fifteen minutes later. And he was still lagging behind. He'd push himself to catch up, and then she'd find another reserve and sprint ahead. No matter how fast he ran, she ran faster. And then the unthinkable happened. He lost sight of her.

Dread mixed with adrenaline. What to do? Logic told him to just keep on, straight ahead. There was no way of knowing if she'd turned off. Another hundred meters and he saw the giant stones peeking through the trees. When he hit the clearing he didn't slow down, and just missed tripping over her.

Jac lay prostrate in front of an outcropping of ancient rocks.

This was the circle of stones he'd been alternately terrified by and fascinated by as child, and which he most often gravitated to as a teenager. Even though it sometimes frightened him to be here, this was where he came to be alone. To think. To weep. This was where he felt the most in touch with himself. Even if that self was in hell.

At the far end of the circle, a dirt tunnel led to a shallow hollowed-out cavern. When he was a kid, he almost thought he could hear voices in there sometimes, echoes of people speaking, even though he knew no one was there. No one could be. The rock temple was a famous landmark on the island but few people visited because it was difficult to get to. Deep in a forest, access to it passed through land owned privately. You had to trespass to get to it.

He and Jac technically would have broken the law to get here if they were anyone else. But the stone edifice dug deep into the earth was on the Wells in Wood land.

Jac had taken him on a five-kilometer run, right back to his own home.

He watched her now, lying on the ground, her back racked with sobs. Her cries haunting yet somehow beautiful. An operatic aria of grief. It was a song to the dead, he thought. Although he wasn't sure how he knew it, he was sure of it. She was honoring those long gone with a keening that bypassed his intellect and reached him purely emotionally. A song that rose to the heavens, implored the spirits, defied time.

It was here, hiding in these shadows, where he'd smoked pot while he cursed his father for being so strict and his brother for being so bloody perfect when he, Theo, was never even close to being good enough. It was here he came when he felt the most miserable and frustrated. Where he allowed himself to wallow in his depression. The one place in the world where he felt more alone and bereft yet complete than he did anywhere else.

How had she known this place was here? Why had she come? What did it mean to her?

Twenty-eight

Jac lay on the grass to the side of the Celtic ruin. Minerva leaned over her, taking her pulse. Theo hovered nearby, nervous, concerned, watching.

"When was the last time she said anything that made sense to you?" Minerva asked.

"I don't know."

"Try to remember," Minerva said.

He ran through the last hour. "In the cave, she picked up a totem and was talking about how similar it was to something the ancient Egyptians buried their dead with."

"And then?"

"She sort of disappeared. Not literally of course. But she was looking off into space and not responding to anything I said. And then the few things she said didn't make any sense or even sound like her talking."

"What did she say?"

"Gibberish. Nothing I could understand. No, that's not true. She said a word, maybe a name: she said *Brice* a few times. At least that's what I think it was."

Minerva was listening, nodding.

"Do you have any idea what's wrong with her?" he asked.

"Not really. She seems drugged, but you said

you didn't see her take anything. Did she drink the water in the cave?"

"Not that I saw. But even if she did, could water do this?"

"The water could be tainted with goodness knows what. Or there might even be fissures in the cave with hallucinogenic gases escaping that she inhaled. It's not unheard of at all on the island."

"But I'm okay."

"She could be more susceptible for any number of reasons."

"Can you help her?"

"I should be able to. None of her vital signs are worrisome. Move back a little and be quiet. I want to try to talk her out of it, but for it to work I need her to hear my voice without any distractions."

Reluctantly, Theo walked off and leaned against an oak tree, close enough to give his aunt room but still allowing him to see and hear what was going on.

"Jac, I want you to listen to me. It's Minerva. I want to help you." She was speaking softly, rhythmically, in an almost singsong voice. "I want to help you. I want to find you and help you back."

Jac remained unresponsive. Her eyes were open but she didn't seem to be focused on Minerva. She was still weeping, but silently and more gently now. A steady stream of tears like a late-afternoon rain.

"Jac, all you have to do is listen to my voice,"

Minerva chanted. Her cadence was soothing even to Theo. And she was swaying a little too, like a human metronome, he thought.

"I want you to know you are safe. I'm here and Theo is here. And we care about you and can take care of you, no matter what is wrong. We can help. You don't have to stay where you are. Even if you think you're trapped, you're not. I can bring you out. Just listen to my voice. Listen and let go of your fears. Listen and let me help. Listen and I will pull you out of where you are. Just listen to my voice. My voice is a powerful thread made of spun gold, twisted with copper, as strong as a tree trunk. Just listen to my voice and grab hold of it. Feel how strong it is? It's so strong that if you are holding it, I can pull you out of wherever you are. Just relax, and listen, and hold on, and I will pull you out. Just listen to my voice. I'm pulling you out. You can feel yourself being pulled back. Back to where we are. Where Theo is. Where I am. Keep holding on."

Theo thought he could see some change. Jac seemed to be leaning forward a bit. Swaying slightly to the rhythm of Minerva's chant.

What was his aunt doing? Hypnotizing her?

"You're going to be fine now, Jac. I have one end of the thread and you have the other, and I'm pulling you up. You're surfacing. Up. Up. Out of the dark place where you've been trapped and into the light. Theo is here and waiting for you, and we're going to go back to the house and have dinner and be together. You're going to be fine. And safe. Just listen to my voice. It's a strong, strong thread that is pulling you up, pulling you out of the dark. You're not to be scared anymore. Or sad. Or worried at all. You're going to be fine. Just hold on to the thread."

Twenty-nine

Something was breaking inside Jac. She didn't understand the feeling or where it came from, but she had never experienced anything like this before. This wasn't like coming out of the hallucinations she'd had as a girl in Paris or this past summer. Those were easy transitions. She would just step past the dream and be back to being herself, and remember it all clearly.

But not this time. She wasn't sure who she had been or even where she was. As the impression of leaves and trees and water and rock came into focus, all she could think about was how she wasn't ready to leave this place. Wasn't done mourning. Someone she loved had died here. And she couldn't go out in the world yet. Not without him.

No. That was wrong.

This was where someone she loved had lived.

"Jac, hold on to my voice."

The chanting interrupted her thoughts. Yes, her name was Jac, of course, but that was only half of her. She felt as if there was another self. Two of them warring with each other—one wanted to stay, the other wanted to go.

"Hold on to my voice. Let my voice pull you up. You're not to be scared anymore. Or sad. Or worried at all. You're going to be fine. Just hold on to the thread."

Jac didn't want to be scared anymore. Or sad. She pushed hard, as if she were shooting up from underwater. Breaking the surface, she took a great gulp of air. Focused her eyes in the direction of the voice.

A woman was sitting next to her, watching her. From the expression on the woman's face, Jac knew something was wrong.

"What happened?" she asked.

Jac recognized the woman as Theo's aunt.

"You're going to be fine," Minerva said.

Theo ran over, knelt down. "Are you all right?"

Jac remembered seeing his face like this once before. When? Why? Then she knew. At Blixer Rath. But under what circumstances?

"You both look so worried," Jac said to them.

"You know who I am?" Theo asked.

"Of course. Why wouldn't I?"

"And where you are?" Minerva asked.

"Not exactly this spot, no, but in Jersey, yes. Why are you asking me these questions?"

"You've been not quite with it for the last hour or so," Minerva said in that voice Jac knew. A therapist's voice. Giving only the most minimal information, making an effort not to influence the patient as she tried to calm her.

"How did we get here? I remember we were in the cave." She looked at Theo. "We found that strange rock and the little amber totems and . . ." She had to think. "Oh. You found the Victor Hugo journal." She searched his face. "You still have it?"

He nodded.

"You found it?" Minerva asked, astonished.

"We did," Theo said.

Jac was still trying to work her way out of her confusion. She could smell Minerva's perfume. It was of this time and place. Not of that darkness where she'd spent the last hour. A whole hour? Was that really what Theo had said?

"So how did we get from there to here?"

"Let's go home to Wells in Wood," Minerva said. "We can go over it once we're inside and have some tea and cake. You've been through quite a bit for one day."

Theo helped Jac up. She was still looking around, trying to get her bearings. "I thought we were down by the beach."

"We were. But we took a long walk—a run actually. You're a very fast runner, you know. I couldn't keep up at all."

"I don't run. I haven't in years. I swim but don't jog."

Theo had a strange expression on his face, as if he was hearing her but not believing a word she said.

"Let's wait to talk about all this till we are back at the house," Minerva said. "I'll get the car and pull it closer. Theo, bring Jac down to the road."

Theo took Jac's arm to help her. They took a few steps, and then she stopped and looked back at the stone ruin.

"You said I ran here?" she asked Theo.

"Yes. We were getting into the car, down by the beach, and you broke away from me and ran off."

"Did something scare me?"

"I don't know. You didn't say anything. Didn't explain. You just took off as if you knew where you were going and led me right here."

"This was his house. He lived here with his family." Jac had shocked herself. She didn't actually know who she was talking about, but there was knowledge about a man that she had now that she didn't have before. The knowing was just there in a niche in her mind. The way the totems had been sitting in the rock, protecting the bones, waiting all this time to be discovered. To reveal their treasures.

"Who? When did he live here?" Theo asked.

Jac shook her head.

"You were crying when you got here. Do you know why?"

"No. Wait. I do. Something had gone very wrong. As I started to come back, I was still holding on to a terrible loss. As if everything that had mattered to me, that would ever matter to me, was gone."

Theo nodded.

"You know the feeling?" Jac asked.

"I do. And I don't quite understand how to explain this, but whenever I come here, and I have been coming here since I was a boy, I've always felt a particular loneliness. A profound sadness. This place is part of the reason I wound up at Blixer Rath. I was spending so much time here, becoming more and more depressed, until I . . ."

He stopped, kicked a rock with the toe of his boot.

Jac looked at him. She empathized with this man. She understood him in a way that she understood no one else she'd ever met. As if she were inside his head somehow. It was a very real connection. One she didn't think she should ignore.

"Let's go. Minerva will be waiting with the car by now. Once we get back, we'll try to figure out what happened," he said.

Jac was still staring at the ruin. Stones surrounded by trees. Ancient stones and holy trees. "You know exactly where we are, right?"

"Yes, of course."

"So if I wanted to come back, you'd be able to bring me?"

He nodded. "But we're not going to come back." He said it as if he were trying to will it so.

"Before, you said when you were a teenager you'd come here all the time until—until what?"

"I tried to kill myself here."

Thirty

Jac was wrapped in a pale-rose cashmere shawl, sitting on the settee in front of the fireplace drinking a cup of tea laced with brandy. Just the way her own grandmother used to make it. The way her brother made it. The way she herself had made it the night when this excursion had really begun, in Connecticut, in Malachai's house, when Jac found Theo's letter.

Eva was in the kitchen making soup and sandwiches while Minerva and Theo kept Jac company. They were also sipping the fortified tea. Neither of them had asked her any more questions. At least not yet. But she kept running over the episode in her head. It was so confusing, and the answers that Theo had given her had only made everything more complicated, not less.

"Did you take the figurine?" Jac asked Theo.

"Yes." He reached into his pocket and pulled it

out. He placed it carefully on the coffee table. Jac looked at it but didn't reach for it. Not yet.

"What is that?" Minerva asked.

Jac had just started explaining when Eva came out with a tray of cheese and tomato sandwiches. As Jac smelled the toasted bread, she realized how hungry she was.

While Jac ate, Eva picked up the statuette and examined it.

"This is very curious," she said.

"Why?" Minerva asked.

"I think we have one of these somewhere in the house. I've seen something like it before." She put it back, and Jac reached for it. She lifted it up gingerly, as if it were burning hot, and turned it over in her hand.

"I think you should stay here tonight," Minerva told Jac, as she watched her.

"I'm fine to go back to the hotel."

"Yes, you are now. But something happened this afternoon, and speaking as a doctor, you would be best served staying over. I don't think you'll have any kind of relapse or reaction, but if you do, there should be people around."

"I appreciate it but—"

"My sister's right, Jac," Eva agreed. "We really can't let you go back to an empty hotel room."

"If I stay, then I want you to help me figure out what happened," Jac said to Minerva.

"There's time for that tomorrow. What you need

now is food and calming rest and a good night's sleep."

"And I'll get it once I understand what happened."

"I don't think—" Minerva started.

Jac interrupted. "Please? I feel a little crazy right now. I need to know."

"All right." Minerva's voice sounded soothing. But at the same time Jac heard some reluctance. Why would that be?

"Theo, help me clean up," Eva said. "We'll let you talk."

Together the two of them picked up the dishes and cups and took everything to the kitchen, and then Eva came back.

"I have something to give you," she said, and pulled a twisted length of silken red thread out of her pocket. "Give me your wrist."

Jac obediently held out her hand.

"This is your lifeline. My sister pulled you out of the state you were in by having you grab on to her voice as if it was a rope. I want you to have your own rope in case she's not around. You can use it if you feel yourself starting to float off."

The cord was dyed the most brilliant scarlet Jac had ever seen.

"Is this Wiccan?" Jac asked, as she watched Eva tie the ends of the thread. She'd been collecting bits of thread and ribbon all her life and felt an instant kinship with the bracelet. As if she'd been waiting for it, but that made no sense either.

Eva laughed. "No. It's a mystic kabbalist tradition. It's called a *roite bindele* and was said to ward off misfortune and the evil eye. A client of mine asked me to make one for her years ago and told me all about it. I've been weaving them ever since."

Jac touched the thread and ran her finger down its silken length. "The evil eye . . ." she repeated.

"The evil eye itself goes back over five thousand years to ancient Babylon—" She stopped. "Oh, you know all that part probably, don't you?"

Jac nodded. "I do. Every culture had its version. It's universal. One of the things that is most fascinating about studying mythology is how so many of the stories and symbols are the same through the centuries and cultures. Just renamed and slightly altered." She looked up from staring at the red thread into the woman's eyes. "Thank you for this."

Eva smiled. "Now I'll leave you to Minerva," she said, and ambled out of the room, favoring her right leg just a fraction.

"Why don't you move over to the chaise?" Minerva said. "It will be more relaxing for you."

Once Jac was settled, sitting up with her feet stretched out in front of her, she drew the cashmere shawl over the lower half of her body like a blanket. She was still chilly.

Minerva pulled up an armchair and sat.

Jac was aware that the furniture had been reconfigured to resemble a therapist's office.

"Okay, let's go to work. You might want to shut your eyes. It sometimes helps." Minerva smiled.

Jac did.

"Good girl. Let me lead you in a deep-breathing exercise to relax you."

Minerva talked Jac through a series of steps that were the same as the square breathing Malachai had taught her so long ago at Blixer Rath.

"Breathe in one, two, three, four . . . Hold for two, three, four . . . Now breathe out slowly for two, three, four. And now hold for two, three, four . . . and again . . ."

Jac felt her body giving up the last of the tension she was still holding in her neck . . . her shoulders . . . the backs of her knees. She was getting soft, letting go.

"Now, tell me, what is the last thing you remember before we found you at the ruin?" Minerva asked.

"Being in the cave. Theo finding the journal."

"All right. Very good. Let's stay in the cave for a while. Look around. Do you see Theo? Look down at your feet, your hands. What do you see?"

Jac described the cave and the strange meteor rock with the cubbyholes filled with totems and bones.

"Tell me about the totems."

"They were roughly carved figures, little, half-man, half-animal, like on the wall paintings. I found one that was a man-cat. It was wet and I was rubbing it, and it had this amazing odor."

"Can you remember that smell now?" Minerva asked softly.

Jac could smell the amber totem and it prompted a stream of images. She watched the movie going on inside her own head and recounted the action. It was a complicated story about a small family— a mother, father and son. And even though she didn't know them, Jac felt the emotions of these people. Every pang of angst, every explosion of anger, every touch of love.

These images, these people and their crisis were not at all familiar. She didn't sense the story had come from her deep memory. Instead it was foreign to her. It had come from someplace else.

Jac was overwhelmed by the pain of the man whose drama she was watching. "I'm in a cave. The gods are giving me some kind of vision, so I know what to do on behalf of my community. But the weight of this responsibility is too heavy. I would rather die than accept this mission. I must be wrong, must have misunderstood the message. This can't be right. Cannot be what is expected of me."

When Jac opened her eyes, Minerva was still in the chair, leaning forward, still listening. She didn't say anything at first. It was Theo, who must have come back into the room at some point, who spoke first.

"You saw all that?"

Jac nodded. "Yes."

Theo shook his head, incredulous. "I don't understand this," he said. "But I know that story."

"What do you mean?" Minerva asked.

"It sounds familiar to me. Everything Jac said, it was almost as if I was anticipating it."

"What is going on?" Jac asked. "How could I imagine a story that Theo would remember?"

Minerva looked from Jac to Theo. "This might have happened before."

"What has?" Jac asked.

"I need to make a phone call," Minerva said, standing.

"Now?" Theo asked. "What in the world—"

"I need some information first," Minerva said. She looked at Jac. "You've done a very good job. And I promise I will help. Let me just go and make this call, and then I'll explain. Don't worry. It's going to be all right." She left the room.

Theo looked at Jac, and she thought his eyes looked even paler, sadder. Sweat had broken out on his forehead. He kept clenching and unclenching his hands.

"Do you have any idea what is going on?" he asked.

She shook her head. "No. Theo, you did find the journal, didn't you? I didn't imagine that?"

The clouds in his eyes lifted. "Yes."

"Can I see it?"

Theo was back in a few seconds. Carefully he handed her the notebook.

Jac touched the worn leather. Opened it. In the dark cave she hadn't been able to see it well. Here in the bright light, it was far easier to examine the tight slanting script. She reread the first paragraph, then skipped ahead to the end. The pages were numbered up to twenty-five.

Jac was one of those people who always read the end of a book first. Not the whole last chapter, but the final five or six lines. She needed to know about the journey she was about to take. To know if it was going to end happily or sadly.

Her brother had once asked her why. After thinking for a minute, she told Robbie she wanted protection from surprises. She'd had too many of them in her life, and they'd brought too much grief.

The last three words on the last page, though, brought a different kind of surprise. She showed Theo.

"This isn't the only journal," she said. "Look."

Theo peered at the words. "Translation, please?"

"This story continues in the next volume," she said. "So there must be another notebook."

"I didn't see one."

Once you found this one, did you keep going through the rest of the cubbyholes?"

"No, the cave was flooding."

"We'll have to go back."

"*I'll* have to go back."

"I'm going with you."

"We can talk about that later. For now we can read and translate this one. Something to do while we're waiting for the sea to comply and—"

Minerva had come back into the room. She was holding a phone. "I just talked to Malachai. He'd like you to call him after we talk, Jac."

"What does this have to do with Malachai?" Jac asked.

Theo stood up to go.

"No, stay, Theo," Minerva said. "You should hear this too." She waited until he was seated and then took a long measured breath. "Maybe Eva should too." She left the room and got her sister.

When everyone was assembled, Minerva began. She addressed Jac and Theo. "At Blixer Rath, Malachai and the other therapists were proponents of Jungian therapy, and as such they believed in the collective unconscious."

"We know this already," said Theo.

Jac nodded. What she'd learned at the clinic had helped her. The theory that the unconscious incorporated memories, instincts and experiences that are common to all humans for all time was at first hard to grasp. But then she began to understand and see how knowledge was inherited and incorporated into her own dreams and actions.

That personal understanding of Jung's theory had been instrumental in her healing and had then cemented her fascination with mythology. It was the cornerstone of her decision to become a mythologist.

"Several of the therapists at Blixer believed, as Jung did, in reincarnation, and that many psychological problems that appear to have roots in someone's present life stem from past-life issues."

"No," Jac said involuntarily.

Minerva looked at her. "What is it?"

"This can't have anything to do with reincarnation."

"Why?"

"I don't believe in it."

Minerva was watching her. "I understand. I really do. But I'd like to finish explaining."

Jac sighed, shifted on the chaise and crossed her legs at her ankles.

Minerva continued. "When you were both at Blixer Rath, some curious things occurred. Jac, you remember the drawings you did that turned out to be the same rock circles Theo drew? Those rock circles are here, in Jersey. You saw them on your walk."

"Yes, of course."

"There were some other occurrences you might not remember. Malachai told me he hypnotized you so you wouldn't."

"Why would he do that?" Jac was confused. Then disgusted. "How could he do that?"

"Is that even professional?" Theo asked on top of her question.

"It's not fair of me to voice an opinion about that without knowing all the facts. I wasn't there. But Malachai is one of the best therapists I've ever known. He told me just now he did it because he believed that if he didn't, you would have a serious setback in your therapy, Jac, and he didn't want that to happen."

"What did he hypnotize me to forget?" Jac asked, her voice tense with anger.

"When you two became friends at Blixer Rath, Malachai was, at first, very pleased about it. And he encouraged it. He called and talked to me about it. Your mother, Theo, had asked Malachai to consult with me on your case. The summer was going so well for both of you. You were developing coping skills and learning to deal with your individual issues. The closer you became, the more rapid the progression. Until the day of the accident, the day that you fell, Jac. Do you remember that?"

"Of course. That was the same day Theo left."

"Malachai sent me home even though I had nothing to do with it." Theo's voice was hard with fresh anger. "No one would even let me say good-bye. Or give me a good reason why I couldn't. They said they were sending me home for breaking the rules, but I assumed they blamed me for the accident."

"They did send you home because you'd broken too many rules too many times. Smuggling in wine and marijuana, mushrooms . . . what were you thinking?" Eva said.

"But they also sent you home because of what was developing between you and Jac," Minerva said. "Friends were one thing, but Malachai believed you were trying to seduce Jac. And at that point in your therapy, both of your therapies, that could have been dangerous."

"A few kisses and some grass?" Jac looked at Theo. For one moment the current mystery took second place to the memory of those innocent embraces in the woods. But his face was twisted in anger and his eyes were clouded over. His torment was so much more complicated than Jac could understand.

"No," Minerva said. "There was something else. Something that he said even he hadn't seen very many times. He told me tonight that on that day, Jac, you had a past-life regression so deep he had been afraid he wasn't going to bring you out of it."

"I don't remember that, and even if I did, I still don't understand what that would have had to do with Theo," Jac said.

"You weren't having your own past-life memories, Jac. You were having Theo's. You were remembering someone else's reincarnations."

Thirty-One

"Are you saying that I was remembering Theo's past life? Not my own?"

"Yes. And that during the regression you became quite violent. That's how the accident happened."

"Have you ever heard of this before?" Jac asked Minerva.

"No. But Malachai thinks it's possible that it happened again today."

Theo got up from the chair and sat beside Jac on the settee. He put his arm around her shoulders, and only then did she realize she was shaking.

"What did you remember about who you were?" he asked.

"I was a priest. It must have been a pagan priest . . . a Druid . . . because he had a wife and a son. I kept thinking I should have been inside the woman's mind . . . in her thoughts . . . but I wasn't. It didn't make sense. I was seeing what the priest was seeing. His wife was an herbalist. A witch," Jac said. "Not a black witch. An important member of the tribe. I . . . he . . ." She faltered, unsure of how to talk about the person in the dream. "The priest," she finally said, "and his family lived in a stone hut in an

411

area that looked like the place where we were."

"The pile of stones I've been obsessed with my whole life," Theo said.

"My home," Jac said, not realizing she'd said the word *my*. She was picturing it in her mind now, not seeing the ruin deep in the forest, but a home fragrant with food cooking on the hearth, a man and his wife making love.

Jac started to shiver. She had come to Jersey to get away from Malachai's incessant talk of reincarnation. Ruefully, she thought of Oedipus and the futility of trying to escape your fate. *But she didn't believe in fate.* She looked at Minerva. Jac felt as if she was standing on the edge of sanity. Was there a whole episode of her life that she knew nothing about?

"Did Malachai believe that I had Theo's memories at Blixer and they somehow caused the accident? Is that why he wiped the incident from my memory like erasing chalk from a blackboard?"

"Yes. Malachai hypnotized you, but to protect you. He wanted to block you from having any more past-life regressions until he could understand better what had happened. He was afraid of how dangerous they were for you. He said that you were lost in memories, Jac. In Theo's memories. That he couldn't get you back. Like you were today. It scared him. He'd never seen anything quite like it. It's one thing to remember fragments of your own past life, but to remember someone else's . . ."

"And he told you all this tonight on the phone? Before he told me?"

"I'm a therapist. I'm here with you now, and something happened to you today that concerns me medically."

"But if he hypnotized me to stop me from having past life memories, why is he so convinced I was having them in Paris this summer?"

"You'll have to ask him. I don't know anything about this summer," Minerva said.

"But you think that what he described is what happened to me again today?"

"I do."

"You said Malachai has never heard of anyone having someone else's memories before. Have you?" It was Eva asking.

"No. But I'm not an expert," Minerva said. "I haven't studied reincarnation or regression the way Malachai has."

Jac stood up. She didn't know if her anger was greater than her fear. Or which made her stumble. She would have crashed into the glass coffee table if Theo hadn't grabbed her by the arm and steadied her. Only hours ago she had believed he'd been the one in trouble. The one who was damaged. The one who needed help. Now he was helping her.

"Where are you going?" he asked.

"I need to call Malachai."

• • •

"You were in danger," Malachai said on the other end of the phone. "You weren't yourself. You became belligerent. You pushed Theo away, he fell—and then you threw yourself off the cliff."

"How do you know this?"

Jac was sitting on a green couch in the library. The tweed weave was made up of more than just one color yarn. There were three or four shades of blue from cobalt to turquoise. And there were three shades of green: emerald, lime and pine. A turquoise thread had come loose, and Jac tried to tuck it back as she listened to Malachai explain his actions.

"In the days before the incident, I'd become concerned. Your attitude was changing. You were becoming rebellious in a way that didn't fit your progress or personality. I was fairly sure that Theo had drugs and was sharing them with you. And when you didn't come back from your walk on time that day, I went looking for you. When I finally found you, you were in a deep state of regression. I saw what happened. Saw you jump. Saw Theo go after you. When you came out, you weren't yourself. You were the person whose life you were remembering. And you remained in that state for a long time, and I couldn't bring you back."

"Why do you think I was remembering a past life that wasn't my own?"

414

"Because of the regressions I'd done with Theo. Because of the drawings you did."

"So who exactly was I?"

"I was never sure."

She heard a hesitation in his voice. "What aren't you saying?" He'd sounded almost flustered, and she'd never heard him like that before. Malachai was the master of control.

"I'm telling you what I know."

"Tell me more than you know. Tell me what you think." Jac had wanted to scream it. It was all she could do to keep her voice under control. "Why weren't you sure who I was channeling—"

"Regressions aren't channeling, that's—"

"I just found out you hypnotized me when I was fourteen years old and I never knew it. I'm not really interested in semantics right now, okay?"

"Jac, please—"

"Why weren't you sure who I was?" she interrupted.

"You weren't speaking English."

"So I reverted back to French. Why is that unusual?"

"No, Jac. You weren't talking French either. As far as I could tell, you were conversing in an ancient tongue. A mix of old Irish and Welsh. I wasn't able to follow what you were saying, but it was clear you were devastated and in despair and didn't want to live. You had jumped off the ridge trying to kill yourself."

Jac took a deep breath. Tried to remember that day. Going out for the walk. The kissing and touching that at fourteen were monumental and astonishing. How they'd made a stone circle and sat inside it and Theo had given her a piece of mushroom. Finally waking up in the infirmary with Malachai by her cot.

There was a large gap. A chunk of her life that was missing. She'd never thought about it before.

"Tell me about today, Jac. Tell me what it was like in comparison to the regression episodes you had in Paris this summer."

"I don't want to do this, I want to—"

He interrupted. "Listen to me. I know how resistant you are. I'm not sure why. But I can tell you this. I have never worked with anyone who could remember for other people. You can. And Theo isn't the only one whose past lives you've been able to access. From the work we did at Blixer, I realized you have a very unusual ability to remember for—"

"Is there more work we did that I don't remember? How much of my memory did you get rid of?"

"We got permission from your grandmother to do two more hypnosis sessions."

"And?"

"You were able to remember memories that corresponded to other students' regressions."

416

"This is impossible." Jac cradled the phone and crossed her arms over her chest.

"After those sessions your grandmother and I decided that until we could understand more about your ability, we needed to put it on hold. It wasn't a dangerous process. While you were under hypnosis, I suggested you stop having any more spontaneous past-life memories. I taught you to block them."

"But you think I was having regressions all summer. How can that be?"

"I think the memories were so strong they simply, finally, broke through." He let that sink in for a moment. "Jac, can you tell me what today's episode was like in comparison to the episodes you had earlier this summer?"

She was still angry, still wanted to fight. But even more, she wanted to understand. Because there was a difference, and it did fit what he was telling her. And now her fear was stronger than her rancor. So she answered him. "Before I came to Jersey, when I was in Paris, I felt as if the scenes I saw were my own dreams. That regardless of whether they were past-life regressions or hallucinations, they tapped into what you taught me. What Jung called my own mythical pasts."

"Quite right. Most people say regressions feel like memories. Something like rewatching a movie you've seen multiple times before."

"Today, it wasn't like that. What I saw didn't

come from me. Whether what happened earlier this summer was me remembering a past life or inventing one, it came out of my own psychic DNA. I can't explain it—"

"You are doing extremely well. Keep going."

"In Paris the stories made some kind of intuitive sense. What I saw today was totally foreign. It didn't come from my core."

"No, it didn't. That's right."

"How do you know?"

"I believe it's the same thing that happened to you when you were fourteen. An intense regression into someone else's memory bank."

"But how is that possible?" she whispered.

Once again she was faced with a dilemma. Believe in a psychic world that didn't fit with her rational worldview, or accept that she might be losing her mind and had deeper psychological problems than she could even guess.

"We don't know. As I said, it's rare. Through deep meditation and hypnosis, receptive people can revisit their past lives in order to find their karmic crises and repair them. Experience again what was left unfinished. Learn what needs to be done. That's not dangerous—that's progress. It's cathartic. Unusual but not unheard of. You know how many cultures revere those who are able to remember their pasts. But it's almost unheard of to be able to remember someone else's past life. We are not meant to take on other people's psychic debts and crimes. We are not equipped to feel the weight of our own souls' needs and theirs. I'm nervous, Jac. I didn't want you to go to Jersey. I think you should come home."

"What?"

"Come home, now. I told you before you left and I am telling you again, I think you might be in danger. Psychic danger. At Blixer Rath you remembered Theo's past life. You were trapped in his karmic grief and almost couldn't come out of it. You slipped back there today. What happens if you go there again and you really do get lost? What happens if you have a psychotic break? You can't take that chance."

"Did you throw him out when he needed help in order to protect me?" Jac remembered waking up in the clinic and finding out Theo was gone. How hurt she'd been that he hadn't said good-bye. How strange it was that no one could give her a real reason he'd left.

"One of you had to go, and he'd been breaking the rules. He would have been asked to leave anyway. He was stealing liquor and getting drugs sent to him. He didn't belong at Blixer Rath. And you don't belong with him in Jersey."

"But the real reason you had him sent home was to protect me." She felt terribly guilty. What if because of her, Theo had not gotten the treatment he needed and deserved? If because of her, Theo had not been able to complete what might have been his best hope for healing? How would she be able to reconcile herself to that?

"The two of you were toxic for each other," Malachai said. He was always so calm, so soft-spoken, and so erudite, but she thought his voice was straining now. If she could see his face, maybe she could read him better. Still, he was the king of enigmatic; if he didn't want her to know something, she wouldn't.

"One thing I don't understand"—she laughed sardonically—"of the million things I don't understand is that Minerva told me you hypnotized me to protect me from having any more past-life regressions."

"Yes."

"But you are convinced that my memories broke through and I had past-life regressions this summer in Paris."

"Yes."

"But why? Why in Paris? How do you explain that?"

"I think that the fragrance you found in your brother's laboratory in Paris had something to do with it. You are extremely olfactory-sensitive. I'd guess that you smelled something today that affected you again, and that's why you had a spontaneous regression.

"Jac, I want—"

"I don't care what you want. You screwed with my head and never told me. You were my doctor

420

and you kept secrets from me. You hypnotized me without my consent."

"Stop. Think. Remember. I could never have hypnotized you without your consent. Your subconscious won't allow it. We had hypnosis sessions all the time, didn't we?"

"Yes."

"Try to remember the one after the incident on the mountain. You went in and out of knowing who you were. You'd taken on Theo's broken soul. After the incident you had crippling headaches. Do you remember those?"

"Yes." And now she did. She had forgotten that.

"We worked on them in hypnosis, and I suggested to you that, because of the journey you'd taken, you not allow yourself to go into the past again. I wanted to give you the power to protect yourself."

"And you think I still need protecting because of something I did while I was stoned when I was fourteen? This is all crazy. I'm here to study Celtic myths and I'm staying. This island is a treasure trove of historical ruins. The ones we saw today look barely disturbed and appear to me as complete as they were thousands of years ago. I'm not ready to leave."

"What do you mean that they are as complete as they were thousands of years ago? How do you know that?"

Jac thought for a moment. It *had* been an odd thing to say.

"Tell me what you were doing today when you had the memory surge," Malachai asked with new insistence in his voice.

"I can't go through this again."

He sighed. "Jac, I am sorry. I have never done anything for any reason except to try to help you."

"You kept everything a secret."

"The plan was always to reveal it to you. Your grandmother and I talked about it at length and she planned to tell you after you left Blixer and were back home."

"She didn't."

"No. When you first returned from Blixer, she was so relieved at how well you had recovered and how healthy you had become, she wanted to give you some time. Then you chose to live in America, and she didn't want to tell you before you left in case it caused you some kind of stress. We talked, she and I, several times over the years. She always made me promise that if she died without telling you, and if you ever needed to know, I would tell you."

"And you never found a reason?"

"No, not till now, no."

Jac picked at the aqua thread again, rubbing it between her fingers, pulling at it now. A little, and a little more until she had drawn it out. She wrapped it around her forefinger, like a ring. Of everyone in her life who was still alive, Malachai and her brother Robbie were the only two people she truly trusted. They were both always there. Her constants. Her security. Now her confidence in Malachai was threatened. He'd kept something back from her. Something key and intrinsic to who she was.

"If you are totally determined not to come back, please, at least, indulge me for a few more minutes. If we can figure out what you did today to cause the regression, maybe we can figure out how to make sure it won't happen again. What were you doing when it started? Where were you?"

Jac had no desire to relive the memory of her afternoon or discuss it. But at the same time she didn't want to actually go through anything like that again. So she told Malachai about the cave and the monolith and the black stone hidden inside it. "It has small niches carved out of it. There were dozens of little totems, each in its own hollowed-out cubbyhole. You know those amber figurines you have?"

"Yes?"

"These are similar."

"Tell me."

"Each one is about three inches tall, crudely carved, but very expressive. All half men, half animal or half bird. They all have carbon residue on them. From being burned, I think. When I touched one, it was sticky. My hand was wet and—" She broke off.

"What is it?"

"I think I got it wet and that's when I smelled it. I remember thinking how unusual it was that a solid like that would emit the same odor as when it was burned."

"How do you know what it smells like when it's burned?"

She told him about finding the ritual fires the day before and how she'd had the first signs of an episode then. Finally she told him about the essence of amber in the Gaspard studio.

He was silent when she finished.

"Malachai?"

After a moment he spoke. "I think the smell had an effect on you."

"Because I'm susceptible to scent? You think the amber is another trigger."

"Yes, and that that hallucination you had was a past-life memory. It's quite common for some people to be able to enter past-life regressions without any aids at all. For others to get there with simple hypnosis. Some people only need to meditate on the sound of a bell. So yes, I certainly think that you could be responsive to olfactory triggers. Especially if the scent has any kind of hallucinogenic properties like the one you found in Paris. It's also possible you ingested some of the resin. You said your hand was wet and you touched the stone. Did you by any chance touch your face or your mouth?"

"I don't know."

"Do you have the amulet?"

She had still been holding it when she left the living room and it was sitting in front of her now, perched on the edge of the desk. She lied to Malachai without knowing why. "No." Jac leaned back, let her head rest on the couch cushion. She felt the beginning of a headache. She didn't want to be thinking about any of this. Or worrying about regressions. Or talking to Malachai about reincarnation. She had come to Jersey to immerse herself in work. To study Celtic ruins and caves and find the fountainhead of a myth. To get over the ache of losing Griffin and accept the emptiness in her life, a hollow hopelessness that she'd never felt this acutely before.

"Why can't I simply have had a hallucination? A drug-induced vision."

"Because you have regressions. You are very susceptible. You have been since you were a child."

"So I'm some kind of freak?"

"What you are experiencing is amazing. It's remarkable."

Jac heard the longing in Malachai's voice. He'd studied reincarnation his whole life but had told her once he'd never been able to access any of his own past-life memories.

"You have a precious gift. A dangerous one. Yes, that's why I am begging you to come home."

The headache had worsened. "Can you hypnotize me over the phone?"

"Why?"

"To make these visions stop."

"I don't know."

"Can you try?"

"Come home and I will. You know where the cave is now. You can go back on your own later."

"I'm not ready to leave. And having some kind of theater of the absurd act out in my head isn't enough to make me. There are stories here, Malachai, I can tell. Who knows what amazing myth might have started here? I need this. I'm staying. There's nothing for me at home."

Thirty-two

The second floor of the Gaspard house had two wings. Walking Jac to her bedroom, Minerva had pointed out where her own was.

"Just two doors down if you need me. Eva is on the opposite side of the staircase, and Theo is downstairs in a suite of rooms. It affords him more privacy."

"Did he live here with his wife?" Jac asked.

"No. They had their own house on the grounds. The old gamekeeper's cottage. He moved back here after she passed." She paused for a moment. "It was a car accident." Minerva shook her head. "She was a careful driver, but there are dangerous turns on these roads, and so much fog. Naomi was from London and used to streetlamps. She wasn't careful enough."

Or she was very unhappy, Jac thought.

They said good night. Then, for more than an hour, Jac lay sleepless in a four-poster bed in the powder-blue and white bedroom, listening to the sea crashing on the rocks and thinking about everything that had happened since she'd arrived. Finally giving up on falling asleep, she slipped out of bed, wrapped herself in the robe Minerva had given her, nestled into the window seat and looked out at the view. The horizon's line had vanished. Sea and sky melded into inky blackness. The waves' phosphorescent glow looked ghostly against the dark backdrop.

Somewhere to the left of the window, a sweep of car lights passed by. Had Theo gone out? Then she heard Tasha's bark. He must have taken the dog for a walk somewhere. A car door opened. Closed. Jac saw the dog bounding across the grass, illuminated for a brief second before she disappeared around the corner.

Feeling restless, Jac decided to go downstairs. Make some tea and find a book to read. As she left the bedroom, she remembered the last time she'd done this in someone else's house. Over a month ago, at Malachai's, the weekend she'd almost been hit by lightning. Found out she'd lost Griffin's baby. The night she discovered the letter from Theo that had brought her here.

There was so much to think about, to think through. What had happened to her today? Why had she been drawn to this island? Had she been hunting down a myth or chasing the fantasy of a boy she'd known when she was a teenager? Her first kiss, her first crush. The idea of exploring a relationship with Theo, which had seemed possible in theory, was now complicated by his brother. And as interesting as both these men were in different ways, Jac was still getting over losing Griffin. One day she would get used to the idea that he was really gone from her life. That was progress, wasn't it? To at least admit that she'd get past it eventually?

Pulling her robe tighter, she slipped her cell phone into the pocket and left her room. Jac trod the wide carpeted staircase, fingers sliding down the polished railing. What she really wanted to do was talk to Robbie. But her earlier call had gone to voice mail.

The two of them spoke in shorthand that made conversations so easy. Robbie could see inside her in a way that could make her angry but was always reassuring. Sometimes he was too sure of the advice he gave. *Count Toujours Droit*, she'd dubbed him in a mock knighting ceremony when they were little. *Count Always Right.* The times they spent working at the miniature perfumer's organ their father had built for them were the most perfect memories Jac had. That little desk with its rows of essences and absolutes had occupied them for hours. Their grandfather would always stop by at the end of the day and smell what they'd blended. Grade it. And when he gave high marks to a fragrance that Jac had concocted, Robbie was always careful to give her the credit. Even though she was older, he'd taken care of her.

In the kitchen she turned on the electric kettle. Opening first one cabinet and then another, she finally found some tea and was delighted to see it was the same brand Robbie favored, Mariage Frères. She scanned the black canisters. Earl Grey. Russian Star. Marco Polo. She chose Des Poètes Solitaires.

While she waited for the kettle to boil, Tasha came into the kitchen for a drink of water. The beautiful dog did look as if she hailed from another era, much like the house. Like the sisters. A lot of the past lived on here, sharing space with the present. What Jac didn't sense was the future.

Smelling the tea's flowery aromatic scent waft up around her as it brewed made her even more anxious to talk to Robbie. Tell him what happened. Hear what he thought.

Robbie, call me.

She pictured her brother sensing her, picking up

his head. Looking into the darkness. Of the two of them, Jac knew she was fine-looking, but it was Robbie who was beautiful. They had similar features, his slightly too refined for a man and hers slightly too coarse for a woman. Looking at him was like staring into a mysterious mirror and seeing another version of herself. Robbie and Jac. Jac and Robbie. They'd always been desperately connected, the way children of damaged parents and a shared tragedy can be.

It had affected them so differently, though. Robbie had turned to Buddhism and become spiritual and contemplative. Jac had become hard, cynical and suspicious. Robbie embraced people. Jac didn't connect to anyone easily. She worried too much about loving someone and then losing them. What if they disappeared? And as with Oedipus, her fears were realized no matter how hard she tried to avoid them.

The tea was brewed. She took a sip. Its familiarity offered a modicum of comfort. Just as with people, she wasn't that good with strange places. Even though she traveled so much for her job, she still got anxious easily and longed to be home, secluded and sequestered in the little apartment on Sutton Place overlooking New York's East River.

Mug in hand, Jac walked out of the kitchen and into the hallway, the marble cold on her bare feet. Without Eva's bustling about and chattering and

Minerva's searching eyes and endless questions, the house's melancholy was more pronounced. The quiet became a mysterious presence that knew so many secrets, the chill air seemed to hum with them.

As she walked toward the library she was pleased to hear the sound of a fire crackling and find Theo sitting beside the hearth. So engrossed in what he was reading, he didn't hear her come in.

"Hi," she said softly, trying not to startle him.

But she had, and he jumped.

"I'm sorry, I didn't mean to alarm you."

He had a faraway look in his eye. "No, of course, it's fine. It's all right." He gestured to the chair. "Come, sit. I'm so glad you've appeared. I wanted to wake you, actually, but figured you needed the rest."

She looked at the book he held in his hand, Hugo's small, brown leather journal they'd found in the sea cave. "I couldn't sleep. Too much to think about."

"Do you believe what Minerva told us? Did you talk to Malachai? Do you think you were remembering my past?"

"I'm not sure what I believe, but I talked to him and that's what he told me he believed."

"Could it be? What an odd connection we have."

She nodded.

"Jac, are you very frightened by all this?"

"I suppose so. Yes. Are you?"

"Not at all. But I'm not the one having the memories." He took her hand and held it as if he was warming it. It was a caring gesture, and she welcomed it.

"I don't know what to think," she said.

"Neither do I."

She nodded toward the journal. "And how are you doing with that?" She was relieved to talk about something else but what was in her own head.

"My French is terrible. I'm having quite a time of it."

"Isn't it astonishing that after all this time it was still there? How much have you read? What have you been able to figure out?"

"It's very odd. Stranger than I would have imagined. I think you should give it a try." He looked disturbed. "I might have gotten it all wrong. I almost hope I have."

"What do you mean?"

"Here," he said, and offered her the slim volume. She'd looked at it briefly in the cave, and then earlier that evening she'd just opened it when Minerva had interrupted. For the third time she held the journal in her hands.

Seven inches wide and nine inches tall, it was made of dark brown leather, still supple. Its twenty-five pages were all edged in gold, though some of that had worn off. She smelled the sea and mold and the strange and beautiful perfume.

She looked at the frontispiece. It was dated. December 1855. Nearly one hundred and sixty years old. She wondered if Fantine had ever gone down to the sea to look for it. Had she found it? Read it? Put it back? Or had no one but Hugo ever touched it again, till now?

Jac settled back. The armchair enveloped her, offering a false sense of security. When you sat in a chair like this, nothing was ever supposed to go wrong. You sat on your grandmother's lap in a chair like this. You lounged in this kind of chair while listening to soothing classical music. But as she scanned the first paragraph, Jac guessed that what she was about to learn wasn't going to be calming or soothing.

Jac began to read out loud, translating as she went.

> Every story begins with a tremble of anticipation. At the start we may have an idea of our point of arrival, but what lies before us and makes us shudder is the journey, for that is all discovery. This strange and curious story begins for me at the sea. Its sound and scent are my punctuation. Its movements are my verbs. As I write this, angry waves break upon the rocks, and when the water recedes, the

rocks seem to be weeping. As if nature is expressing what is in my soul. Expressing what I cannot speak of out loud but can only write, here, in secret, for you, Fantine.

Thirty-three

OCTOBER 19, 1855
JERSEY, CHANNEL ISLANDS, GREAT BRITAIN

What I fear the most about keeping a record of my experiences with the Shadow of the Sepulcher is that someone else will use this window to the world of spirits for nefarious purposes. But can I prevent that from happening? I didn't reach out to him. He arrived via the séances, and there is no secret to those. Once I asked him how to call upon him, and he spoke of obscure methods perfected by ancient Egyptian mystery schools and by alchemists in the sixteenth century. Would that I could commit them to paper, but I could hardly make sense of the magic of which he spoke.

Here is what I know. Or do I know anything? It could be madness. For still, I am not certain that I haven't indeed lost my mind. How can I, who abhor the superstition and illusion the Church perpetuates, be involved in this black relationship with a spirit? With a specter who offers to bring back the dead in exchange for having his name and reputation restored so that mankind will stop confusing him with the Devil. But are they not one and the same?

This is what I know about calling him forth:

It must be twilight or evening.

It must be either at the séance table or down by the sea. In the last two years he has appeared at seven séances and seven times either near or inside the cave with the fantastic paintings. I believe that is his dwelling place. Lucifer's Lair, I have taken to calling it.

And the sea is where the ephemeral creature feels most at home. He even visited me on board a sailboat.

That was the next to last time I ever saw him.

It was the second week of October, and Robert and Pauline St. Croix were visiting from Paris. The weather was fine, and our next-door neighbor, Monsieur Rose, had offered to take us out on his charming sloop. My wife had sent fruit, cheese and wines ahead. We were all in good spirits as we set out. Overhead the sky was without clouds and the slight breeze promised perfect sailing conditions.

Adele, my wife, seemed happy that day, which pleased me since she did not altogether enjoy Jersey. She called it provincial and never really stopped missing Paris. No political regime lasts forever, and I tell her soon we will be able to return to our beloved city. I do hope the government doesn't make me a liar for much longer.

The relationship between a man and his wife has its seasons. As the carriage approached the dock, I looked at Adele and thought about the young girl whom I'd fallen in love with, and who since had surprised me in so many ways. Some wonderful, others heartbreaking. I wondered: If she had not been the first of us to take a lover, had not strayed so far, how would I have fared? How different would everything be if she had not been the one who introduced infidelity into our lives? Would I have eventually been unfaithful regardless? We would never know.

I took her hand.

She turned to me and smiled. "I think we should stop the table tapping," she said in a kind, concerned voice.

It was the very last thing I had expected her to say.

"It's not Christian," she continued.

Robert, who was, like me, against the Church but not against God, asked, "Why is that?"

"It's unnatural. The concept of speaking to the dead was at first novel and seemed a game. It has turned into a macabre obsession. It has turned our house into a mausoleum."

"But we have been able to talk to Didine," I said.

Adele lost both her firstborn and her second born. She has been tested. That a mother can endure that and survive at all is a miracle. My wife is not a hard woman, but she has become practical in a way that can seem rigid at times.

"We have not talked to her, Victor. A wooden leg has bounced against a tabletop. That is not our daughter. What we are doing is prolonging our grief."

"How do you know that is not her?" I asked.

"Husband, you sound like a fool. What is it that you hope will happen? That the table will turn to flesh and blood?"

"Of course not!"

"You know what I am saying is right," Adele said softly, even kindly. "It will be best for all. Our live daughter, our precious Adele, is becoming ever more nervous by the day. All this talk of the dead and the departed is affecting her."

Perhaps Adele was right. We'd been at it for two years, and I'd conversed with so many spirits by now, I had to refer to my records to remember some of their names. Perhaps I was becoming obsessed in a way that wasn't healthy.

"Yes, yes, as you wish."

"But please, not until we leave?" Pauline asked. "I was hoping we could experience one of these séances. Just one more before you give them up?"

I looked from our guests to my wife, who nodded in acquiescence.

So we would have one more séance and then bring them to an end. I felt, if truth be told, some measure of relief. Perhaps if the séances stopped, my shadowy visitor would come no more.

The first half of the boat trip proved a pleasant excursion. The repast was delicious, the sea was calm, the company stimulating. As we came in sight of the Elizabeth Castle, our host told our friends the story of my heroic rescue of the fishmonger's daughter—the legends of which had grown to include me fighting off a pack of attack dogs. I was quick to correct him and his exaggerations.

"And that wasn't Monsieur Hugo's only rescue," Monsieur Rose continued, and proceeded to tell Pauline and Robert about the second child I had found, in Lucifer's Lair. He pointed toward the shore, making me aware for the first time how close that cave was to the castle where I'd found Lilly.

"Two children? That's suspect. Don't you think, Hugo?" Robert asked.

"Of course," I answered. "The authorities are concerned someone on the island is behind it and is somehow using his dog to lure the children. Every father with a daughter is afraid."

"How old were the girls?" Robert asked.

"Ten and twelve," I told him.

"Well, they are certainly old enough to explain what happened to them. What do they say?"

"They both tell the same story, but it makes little sense," Rose explained. One of the volunteer policemen, he imbued his recounting of the story with official gravitas. "They describe a large black dog, beautiful, with honey-colored eyes, that came to their window and barked and whined and seemed to be in distress. So much so, they went to tend to him. Once they were outside, he let them approach and then led them away. Neither child remembers many details after they went to their respective destinations: the castle in the first girl's case and the cave in the second. Where they should have memories, there simply are none."

"Well, they should try mesmerism," Pauline said. "Hugo, you know of it, don't you? In addition to health benefits and cures, don't they say that it allows your hidden and forgotten memories to come to the foreground?"

"Yes, and I've suggested it," I said. "I had good luck with it in Paris. But there's no one on the island who knows how to administer it."

Just then the weather began to change. Brutish dark clouds blew in from the west, hiding the sun and casting us in gloom. The winds picked up. The sea grew restless and rough. The boat was suddenly being tossed from side to side.

"I think we'd best head back to shore," Rose said. "These squalls can come and go quickly, but I'd rather not take a chance. This one looks exceptionally bad."

As he brought the boat about, the wind picked up yet more power, and he struggled with the jib.

"Do you need help?" I asked.

He welcomed the offer and suggested first I get everyone below and show them how to tie themselves to the bunks. "Men have drowned in better weather than this. You can be swept off a boat in seconds."

As soon as the words left his lips, I saw the horror flash in his eyes as he realized what he'd said.

I rushed to help safeguard my wife and friends and had just returned to the deck when the full force of the storm hit.

Looking back, trying to recount it, I cannot fully explain that next half hour any better than I can explain anything else that's happened in Jersey.

Even at my worst, after Didine had been taken from us, I did not ever seriously contemplate taking my own life. Nothing is as valuable to me as an individual's right to freedom. Death was not a possible solution for my grief. But from the moment I tied myself to the mast and set to helping Rose bring the boat to port, the sea called out to me with the insistence of a lover. Whispering soft entreaties, she beckoned me to let go, to give up on my struggles, to liberate myself from the sadness. With death would come peace, a final and complete cessation of questions. I would experience what my darling Didine had experienced. Be reunited with her. And would finally be freed from the temptations the Shadow was constantly placing in front of me.

Thank goodness for the ropes, or I would have willingly slid off the deck. That was the power of the hold the Shadow had over me by then. I would have considered giving up my own life to get out of his grip.

My wife was right. I resolved, after that night, there would be no more séances.

The storm blew away as quickly as it had come upon us. The wind died down. The rain ceased.

Adele and our guests returned to the deck. As we passed by the section of beach where Lucifer's Lair was, I could see, despite the dark, a large dog standing on the rocks above, staring out toward us. He howled, and the sound traveled over the water to reach us. Inside it somehow, I heard a familiar soft-spoken golden voice, whispering to me.

Bravo, Hugo. I was afraid there for a moment I'd lost you. And we have so much left to accomplish between us.

"Do you hear that?" I asked our host.

"The sea?"

"The dog."

He shook his head.

As Monsieur Rose had said, the menfolk had never stopped trying to track the creature.

441

Organizing search parties, they took shifts walking the section of island to which they'd been assigned. I knew their cause was hopeless. Other than the children and myself, no one had seen the dog. And no one would, not if they hunted day after night. The hound was an aberration. He would never reveal himself to them unless he had a reason. But there was no way I could tell them to call off their search. No way to make them believe me.

That evening, after dinner and postprandial brandy, as our guests had requested and my wife had agreed, we held our last séance. Adele was too considerate a hostess to do anything less. Both my sons and my daughter joined us.

We extinguished the kerosene lamps, lit the candles and set up the table. François-Victor was ready with his paper and pen and ink to record the number of taps.

I noticed that my daughter looked pale and the circles beneath her eyes exaggerated. I suggested that she go up to bed, but she shook her head.

"I have to be here in case she comes," Adele said, her voice tight and nervous.

Yes, my wife was right, we had to end this obsession. We all wanted our dear Didine back too much. Desired to talk to her with too great a longing. We were not past our grieving and more than a dozen years had passed. It was time. Perhaps ending these sessions would help.

"Who is here?" my wife asked, once we all had our fingers touching the round wooden stool.

The atmosphere in the room was pleasant. There were none of the odd odors or cool breezes that sometimes accompanied our less than desirable spirit guest. And there was no response from the table.

My wife tried again.

The table began to tap, and at the same time I heard the voice in my head.

"It's Shakespeare," I said. For once I wasn't disappointed that it wasn't Didine. I was just relieved that it wasn't the Shadow.

There were murmurs of surprise from Robert and Pauline, who then began to ask questions in earnest. For the next fifteen minutes, the tapping continued without dark incident. And then I felt the cold come in the room. Smelled the smoke and ash I had come to associate with the arrival of the Shadow.

Were there two spirits in the room? Had one left as the other arrived?

I glanced at the faces of those around the table. No one but me seemed to have noticed.

For a few more minutes the tapping continued. Shakespeare hadn't left and he was still communicating with us. And then suddenly the candles went out of their own accord. Darkness overwhelmed us.

Pauline exclaimed. "What has happened?" she asked with trepidation in her voice.

"Nothing at all," my wife said, as she began to rise to relight the tapers. "Just the wind. Let me—"

"No, do not break the circle," Robert said in an almost harsh tone. The request was so forceful, Adele remained seated, her fingers, like mine, still on the stool.

Beside me I felt my daughter tremble. "What is it?" I asked her.

She shook her head. "There's something not right."

"With what?" I asked.

She pointed to Robert, our guest.

How can I explain this?

There was enough moonlight coming through the windows for me to be able to gaze upon my friend and see his face clearly. His musculature had changed and he no longer looked quite like himself. Certainly his hair was still gray and his mustache still thick. The scar on his chin was still visible. But his mouth had hardened and narrowed. His flesh had tightened. His eyes were filled with someone else's soul, as if he'd been taken over from the inside.

"You have to follow," he said to the others. His voice was foreign.

Impossible! I tried to deny what I alone heard in his voice. *Whom* I heard in his voice.

"Robert?" his wife asked, her voice panicked. "What is wrong?"

He didn't turn to her, didn't respond.

I thought it must be some kind of trick of the acoustics of the room. The shadow could not be speaking through Robert!

"Follow whom, what?" I asked.

"The path you have started to walk."

"My political efforts? My novel?" I asked.

He laughed sarcastically. "She's waiting to come back. You can't disappoint her now."

"What does he mean, Victor?" my wife asked. She was always suspicious about my other relationships. I feared she assumed Robert was talking about another woman.

Pauline started to cry. "Why do you sound so strange? What is wrong? Robert?"

Her words were like the annoying buzz of a fly. I turned to her and told her to be quiet. "He's fine. Stop whimpering."

My wife glared at me, but I ignored her.

"What do you mean?" I asked the man who was talking to me through Robert. "Who is waiting?"

"You know the one of whom I speak. She doesn't have the strength to wait indefinitely. It takes great effort to hover between two worlds. You must do this, and do it now."

"What's going on, Robert?" It was Pauline again. I didn't even bother to tell her to shut up this time.

"How can I? The price is too high."

"How can you not?" the spirit asked.

Beside me, Pauline fainted. My wife jumped up to attend to her. The continuity of our fingers on the tapping device was broken. I still had questions to ask, but it didn't matter anymore. The entity had abandoned my old political ally's body. Robert looked like himself again and was utterly unaware that anything strange had occurred.

"Pauline, what is it?" he asked, bending over his wife, trying to revive her. His voice had returned to normal.

Regaining consciousness, she looked at her husband with fearful eyes.

"What is it, Pauline?" he asked.

"You were talking using someone else's voice. You were a stranger."

"Ridiculous," he said, and turned to me. "What is going on here, Hugo?"

My wife offered to take Pauline up to her bedroom to help her to bed, but Robert insisted that she stay. "We're going to get to the bottom of this so Pauline can see it was just a game. I won't have her afraid. Hugo, explain the trick to us so my wife can understand."

"It wasn't a game and there were no tricks," I said. "Do you remember anything of the last half hour?"

"Of course, I'm no fool. I sat down at the table and then some nonsense ensued. You told us

Shakespeare had arrived to talk to us. And our fingers somehow made the little stool go into a tapping fit. One of you"—he looked from me to my wife to my children—"must have manipulated it."

"You remember nothing about what you said?" I asked.

"I said nothing."

Just like the two girls, I thought, seduced by the large black dog. With no memories past a certain point.

"I want to know, now," he asked, his face reddening. "Hugo, what hocus-pocus are you playing with here? Have you abandoned politics and philosophy and become a spiritualist? Are you living out your fictions?" His voice was loud and reverberated through the parlor. "I don't appreciate being the object of your game."

"It was no game," I said.

"Robert," Pauline interjected. "You must remember what happened. You were talking in another voice, your face looked different. You even smelled different."

"How did he smell?" I asked.

"Like smoke. Like ashes left on the hearth."

"Hugo!" Robert shouted. "I want an explanation! My wife is frightened and talking nonsense. If this wasn't a game, what was it?"

"A spirit borrowed your body in order to communicate with me," I told him.

Robert threw up his hands in exasperation and then took several breaths so deep I imagined he was going to absorb all the air in the room. "This is preposterous."

"I saw it, Robert," Pauline said tearfully.

My wife tried to explain. "The fact is, none of us has understood what has been going on here these last years."

"Surely you are not saying you believe all this?"

Adele shrugged. "None of us knows what to believe."

Pauline now took my hand. "Can you help me talk to my brother? Can you help me talk to George?"

Robert put his hands on her shoulders. "He will do no such thing. Hugo can no more talk to the dead than I can make that cat speak to us in Italian. Let us go to bed, my dear. These are just spiritualists' games." He shot a look at me. "You'd be better off applying your imagination to novels and poetry. At least those can keep food on your table."

There was no point in arguing with him. No point to any of this anymore, really. My wife wanted us to stop. My daughter was becoming more nervous by the day. And I'd just lost a good friend, of that I was certain.

Yes, it was time to give up.

Everyone went upstairs to bed, but I remained in the parlor. Looking out at the sea from the large windows. Watching the moon send silver shivers over the water's surface. And somewhere out there in the night, I heard barking. A lone dog barking. Barking, it seemed, directly to me.

Thirty-four

Jac finished reading the last paragraph in Hugo's journal.

> Everyone went upstairs to bed, but I remained in the parlor. Looking out at the sea from the large windows. Watching the moon send silver shivers over the water's surface. And somewhere out there in the night, I heard barking. A lone dog barking. Barking, it seemed, directly to me.

She pointed to the bottom of the page and showed Theo the line that was written there. "And here it says, *the story continues in the next volume.*"

He took the book from her and stared where she'd pointed. Jac drank what was left of her third cup of tea. It was two thirty and she had been reading out loud since midnight. Twice they had put down the book to boil more water and once to make toast.

"We have to go back to that cave," she said. "Today."

"I will. But I can't take you with me. It's too dangerous."

"I didn't come all the way here to stay in a hotel room. If I don't touch the totems, nothing bad will happen. I need to see the cave again, to photograph it and the plinth. There's research to do on this find. This could be an important Celtic discovery. A myth's roots proven."

From the way Theo nodded, she knew he wanted to believe she'd be fine as much as she did. Even if she slipped into a fugue state again, Minerva now knew what to do. The thought chilled Jac and she tried to shrug it off.

"Are you sure it's as simple as not getting too close to the amber or touching it? What if it gives off fumes?"

"I was all right until I touched it," she reassured him. "Besides . . ." Jac played with the red thread that Eva had tied around her wrist. "I have my own life preserver now. I'm protected."

The next morning Jac woke at seven, suddenly and anxiously, the dream she'd been having still fresh and disturbing.

She'd been the Druid priest from her hallucination. Highly agitated, he was meeting with a group of men, telling them a story, asking them to interpret it. And he'd been wrapped in a cocoon of silken strands, bound and immobile.

As she dressed, still haunted by the priest's fears, Jac tried to remember what the story had been about. But all she could recall for certainty was the phrase he'd been repeating over and over.

There must be another meaning . . . There must be another meaning.

Jac met the others for breakfast at eight. Minerva was already at the table along with Theo, who looked as if he'd never gone back to sleep at all. Eva poured Jac a glass of cold orange juice and then got up to tend to what was cooking in the kitchen.

Minerva was concerned to hear that neither of them had slept much because they'd been up so late reading the journal. And then Theo told her there was a second volume and that they intended to find it.

"We all need to understand what is going on here. It's not as simple as going back into the cave and getting the next journal. Yesterday's incident was serious. Theo, I know how much this matters to you, but your actions could have serious ramifications for Jac, and maybe even for you."

Before either of them could argue, Eva came out of the kitchen with a platter of eggs and bacon. Just as she placed it on the sideboard, a male voice called out from the front hall.

"Are you all at breakfast?"

"Oh, it's Ash," Eva said.

Was the excitement in her voice pleasure or nervousness? Jac couldn't be sure. She glanced at Theo and noticed that Minerva had done the same.

If it was possible, Theo's face was now even more ravaged, his eyes filled with even more worry.

Ash kissed first Minerva and then Eva on the cheek, and then looked at Jac. "I'm surprised to find you here. Have you moved in, then?"

"No," she said, almost embarrassed for a moment. "Things got complicated yesterday and your aunt wanted me to stay over. For observation." She was caught off guard by her instinct to explain.

"Are you ill?"

She shook her head. "I'm fine." She stopped, not sure how to describe it in a succinct way.

"Why don't you sit down, Ash," Minerva said.

"Let me get you a cup of coffee," Eva added.

"Why are you here?" Theo asked his brother. He looked first at Eva, then Minerva. "Did you ask him to come? Don't you trust me with the journal?"

"Of course we do, Theo," Minerva said.

"What are you talking about? They didn't ask me to come. What journal?" Ash asked.

"They found Victor Hugo's journal in one of the caves," Eva blurted out.

"Really." Ash looked from Theo to Jac. "Are you sure that's what it is? You must be good at spotting fakes. Is it the real thing?"

"There's no way to know that yet. It has the look and feel of something that's the right age and in the right condition. But there are extensive tests, including handwriting analysis, that would have to be—"

"It's the real thing," Theo interrupted. His voice was thick with indignation. "What do you want, Ash?"

"I called you a half-dozen times yesterday. We have to resolve the issue with the Renoir pastel now. Today."

"I told you, the Gaspard receipt indicates a sale, and I'll get to it."

"No. You have to get to it now. It just can't wait."

"What is this about?" Minerva asked.

Ash filled her in, ending by explaining, "Timmonson claims her client's grandfather was acting under duress when he sold it in 1937."

Eva shook her head. "It's so disturbing to think of these poor people haunted by their memories of lost loved ones and lost family heirlooms."

"Ash, we've been over this. I have the letters to prove there was no duress," Theo said.

"So what are you waiting for? Get them to Timmonson. We got the preliminary injunction papers at the bank yesterday. This is going to go to court and cost a fortune to defend. I don't want to waste money on a suit."

"Davis sold us the Renoir and bought a Dürer," Theo insisted.

"Just take care of it, Theo. And we must hire someone to attend to the rest of the cache of artwork immediately. We can't afford to have this drag on and on because you aren't ready to deal with it." Instead of looking at his brother, Ash looked at Minerva. "It's urgent we move on."

There was a moment of quiet, which Eva interrupted by asking Ash if she could get him some eggs.

He looked at Theo, then at Jac. "Yes, please, Aunt Eva. I love your eggs, and I'd actually like to hear a bit more about Jac's opinion of the journal."

Theo got up, threw his napkin on his chair and walked out of the room.

In the long silence that followed, the only sounds were Theo's thunderous footsteps as he walked across the marble hall.

"You need to be more patient with your brother," Minerva said. "Less strident. Your tactic isn't working. It never has."

"I can't afford to be more patient. We're on the verge of calamity here. A lawsuit could ruin us. Can't you get him into therapy?"

"It isn't that simple," Minerva said. "I'm trying to work with him. It takes time."

"Time? It's taking forever. He was bad enough before Naomi died," Ash said. "He's become impossible now."

"Theo is haunted," Eva said.

Both Minerva and Ash looked at her with surprise. Jac guessed she'd never said anything like that before.

"Yes, he's having a hard time getting over Naomi's death, but—" Minerva began.

"No, it's more than that. He's haunted," Eva repeated.

"Whatever do you mean?" Minerva asked.

"I've watched these boys grow up. Seen the troubles between them their whole lives. I've listened to you explain it psychologically but it's never made sense to me. There's no solid psychological basis for their problems with each other. You keep trying to spin one out of thin air. Because I was neither a mother nor a therapist, I kept my own counsel. But since we took out the Ouija board the other night, things have seemed different to me. Falling into place in a way they didn't before—" Eva broke off.

Jac watched the older woman's face. Eva was weighing her words carefully. Where there had been confusion in her expression was deliberation and then finally resolve.

"The air here is poisoned," Eva said. "It is for us and was for our grandfather. And it's time for us to attend to it."

"What on earth are you talking about?" Ash asked.

Eva turned to face her sister. "What do you know about how our grandfather died?"

"It was late and not all the lights were on. You and Grandfather were coming down the steps and didn't see the cat. Grandfather tripped and in trying to regain his balance pushed you or pulled you, and you tripped too. Both of you fell. You broke your hip, he broke his neck."

Eva stared at her plate of eggs and toast as if for clues. "He had started to pursue you, Minerva. In the same way he'd been going after me. I recognized all of it. He'd get you all worked up and frightened with the Ouija board, and then he'd soothe you. Whisper and comfort you with soft touches, sweet words. Nothing too overt, nothing too traumatizing. Not at first. But he was leading up to more. Much more." She was still looking down. "It was wrong. Very wrong."

Jac was watching Eva's hand on her lap, clenching and unclenching. Then Eva opened it and kept it open. She lifted her face and looked at her sister.

"There was no cat on the steps."

"Why did I think there was?"

"That's what I told everyone."

"Then what caused the accident?"

"It wasn't an accident. I tripped him on purpose. Before he could do to you what he was doing to me." Eva pushed her plate aside with too much vigor. It jostled the juice glass, which tipped over. Bright orange liquid spread out over the linen tablecloth in a large irregular pattern. Eva put her napkin on top of the stain. She righted the glass and looked back at her sister.

"The more séances there were, the hungrier he became. I don't know what the psychological explanation for it is, or what his condition was called, but he believed this Shadow existed. Our grandfather was listening to this spirit. What do you call it? An associative disorder? A psychotic break? I'm not sure, but he created a monster so he could take orders from him and become a monster himself. He had become a sexual predator, and I couldn't stand by and watch him hurt you too. I didn't think he was going to die. I don't know what I thought. I was just so angry and so scared. First I set up the Ouija board in the library, then I went to Grandfather's room and woke him up. I told him the spirit was in the library and using the board without us. I said it was spelling out a message. That the spirit wanted to rest, and that we had to stop forcing him out, and if we didn't he was going to punish us. I told Grandfather I was scared and wanted him to see it. When he started down the stairs . . . I tripped him . . ."

She stopped talking. A lone tear escaped and made its path down Eva's cheek.

"To protect me?" Minerva asked, stunned. "And all this time you never said anything?"

"It went so wrong." Eva's voice cracked.

Minerva stood and walked around to her sister. She pulled Theo's chair over and sat down. Minerva wrapped her arms around the weeping woman.

"What a terrible burden to carry for so long. I wish you had told me. I wish you had."

The two sisters sat like that for a few moments, then Eva pulled away, straightened up and collected herself.

"What's important now is Theo. All this talk about the Shadow and Theo thinking it's possible to communicate with him. Was what happened to us when we were children actually real? I always was sure Grandfather made the Shadow up, but I'm not so sure anymore. Is our house being revisited? Something's wrong here. With us. With all of us. We have to address it."

Eva reached out and with a shaking hand picked up her coffee cup. Lifting it to her lips, she took a sip of what was by now lukewarm. "You can live with a painting on your wall your whole life, and then you wake up one morning and the light is shining on it in a different way, and it's as if you'd never seen it before. Theo is troubled. He always has been. He was born troubled. Therapy hasn't helped. Nothing has. And now he's getting worse. I can see it in his eyes. I see it now in a different way than I have before. He's haunted, and he needs more powerful help than we've given him so far." Eva looked at Ash. Then at Minerva. And then finally at Jac. "He needs some kind of magic."

Thirty-five

Ash left for the bank. Minerva went to her office. Eva stayed, sitting at the table, alone, nursing a second cup of coffee.

Jac found Theo in the library studying the tide tables.

He said that because of the tides they couldn't try to visit the cave for another hour or so. But there was one other monument he wanted to show her, and he led her out to the car.

The ten-minute drive that took them through picturesque countryside ended when Theo parked the car by the side of an inauspicious road. There was nothing around to indicate they'd arrived at a destination.

"We have to go the rest of the way on foot," Theo explained. "This place is called *La Pouquelaye de Faldouet.*"

"*Faldouet* means fast-running stream, doesn't it, but what's *pouquelaye*?"

"Some think the first part of the name comes from Shakespeare's Puck in *Midsummer Night's*

Dream, who was one of the 'little people' or dare I say 'fairies,' and *laye* can be deciphered as 'place.' So we get 'fairy place of the fast-running stream.'"

Turning a corner, they came upon a group of towering stones.

"This is astonishing!" Jac said. More than a dozen monoliths formed a pathway that led to a large circular chamber, beyond which was a second chamber with a gigantic capstone.

"That stone is over twenty-four tons," Theo said. "It comes from an area half a kilometer away from here. How did they move it? And why did they move it?"

"Like Stonehenge, there are only guesses about what these sites were. So many of them are burial grounds," she said.

Jac's work continually exposed her to reminders of loss, secrets gone, history covered over and forgotten. People who would never speak again. Their souls like fragrances that linger in the air for a few moments and then disappear forever.

And all these gravesites . . . this site . . . brought Jac's own losses to the forefront. Always they had made her think of her mother, and now in addition there was the loss of her lover, and the pregnancy . . .

For a moment the idea of a baby—of her and Griffin's baby—was so real that she lost a step. She put her hand out and touched the wall. Stood still. Trying to get her bearings. The grief was like fog.

"This area has been excavated several times," Theo was saying. "Starting in the mid-eighteen hundreds. They've found the bones of two children and three or more adults here."

Jac shivered. She had seen so many excavations, she could picture the scene they had come upon.

"One skeleton was in a seated position in one of the side chambers," Theo continued. "They also found utensils and household items. Some bowls, stone axes, greenstone pendants, tools made of flint. I've read that the household goods weren't buried ceremoniously but instead seemed to be positioned as if they were in use. No one is quite sure if the site was a graveyard, a temple or a dwelling."

"This place is aligned with the solar equinox, isn't it?" Jac asked as she tried to focus. *Be present,* as Robbie would say.

Theo nodded. "Yes. Most of the sites on the island are. Is that common?"

"Yes, Neolithic-period temples and burial sites often are aligned on ley lines. Have you heard anything else out of the ordinary about this one?"

"About thirty years ago, some strange occurrences were noticed in many houses west of here. Objects seemed to be moving around. A chair was no longer next to the fireplace but halfway across a room. A plate from a coffee table was found on a shelf. A painting no longer hung on the wall but leaned against a door. Because the local black-magic circle used this place as a sacred site to hold meetings, the rector of the Anglican church was called in to help. He worked here for three days, exorcising the spirits from the dolmens. After that none of the residents reported any more polter-geists, but I've heard from some of the guides that they still find remnants of witch covens here. Stubs of burnt-out candles left on standing stones. Grass wreaths studded with flowers on the floor. There's even gossip that, around the time of the equinoxes, there's been evidence of blood sacrifices being carried out. According to people who study paranormal activity, through ceremonies and chanting, the area's ley lines might have been reenergized or overenergized."

Jac heard the intensity in Theo's voice that she'd come to recognize when he talked about the ancient sites. Did his passion border on obsession? Was Ash right? Was Theo preoccupied with the past to the point of distraction? Was there something wrong with how fixated he was on these ancient monuments? Was he, as Eva had suggested, haunted?

Jac walked around the dolmen. "Look at it from this angle. See the way the dirt is mounded?" She pointed. "There's a theory that these kinds of sites represent the pregnant stomach of Mother Earth." She felt a butterfly in her own stomach. Why had she brought this up? *Keep talking,* she thought. *Work through this. Get past it.* "The main chamber represents the womb, and the entrance and the passageway represent the birth canal. The ancients believed all life came from the Earth Mother, so this formation could be recreating the scene for a birth in reverse. If at your death you were buried in a symbolic womb, it might facilitate your rebirth into the next life."

"That's fascinating," Theo said. "I've never heard that before."

"There's something else, though." She was walking the length of the ruin. "I don't think that's the key reason this monument was built this way."

"How do you know?"

She shrugged. "No idea. But I can feel it. Almost as if this place is alive. As if it's trying to talk to me."

"I believe that. No matter where we go, there's a past on the island that is just waiting to come alive again," Theo said. "I can feel it too. I always have. I think Hugo felt it also. I think that the island rekindled his fascination with reincarnation. Jersey is rich with past-life mythology."

"If Malachai were here now, he would remind us that it's no coincidence."

Theo frowned. "I wish you wouldn't bring him up so much. You see him as some kind of hero, but he's manipulative too, Jac. He has his own agenda."

463

Theo's anger at Malachai was pronounced. "You rely on him too much," Theo continued.

"I don't think I do."

"You need to dissociate yourself from him."

"Why?"

"I know he didn't want you to come here. He doesn't think you should be with me. Isn't that true?"

Thinking of her recent phone call with Malachai and his concerns, Jac felt a shiver of apprehension.

"Yes, but I didn't listen to him, did I?"

Theo stepped toward her, and before she realized what he was doing, he leaned forward and kissed her hard and long. This was not a goodnight kiss. His lips were cold on hers. His arm went around her back and pulled her with too much force. This didn't feel right.

She pulled away. Stumbled backward.

"It's been a long time for me since I've kissed anyone," he said, embarrassed. "I hope I remembered how to do it."

She laughed but it sounded artificial.

"We belong together, Jac."

"No, not in that way, Theo. I don't think so." A wave of sadness coursed through her. Did she *belong* with anyone but Griffin?

"Are you sure? Can't you give it a chance?"

The sun was shining in her eyes. He was backlit and she couldn't see his face clearly. In the shadows, he became threatening. Something about how he smelled alerted her that there was potential danger here. Then with horror she saw the air around her waver the same way it had so many times in her life—the visual precursor to an episode, or what Malachai liked to call a memory lurch. An intense burst of scent assaulted her. She smelled sage, hazel, juniper, frankincense and that odd amber from Fantine's workshop.

Jac felt herself starting to stumble. She was seeing the same scene but there were other people there. Ghostlike at first, but then becoming flesh. Having substance. And sound.

A throng of people were lined up and waiting to come into the dolmen. All of them were dressed in natural-colored robes—white, cream or brown linens. Both the men and the women were chanting. Many were holding wooden plates of vegetables, fruits and flat round disks of bread. The air was perfumed with roses and cloves. Sweet and spicy. Fresh and pungent.

The woman called Gwenore was with her son, Brice. Looking at the boy, Jac felt pride, deep and complete.

If you feel yourself starting to float off, pull yourself back . . . you have a lifeline to the present now . . .

Jac fingered the scarlet thread. Concentrated on the silk next to her skin. It was working. The scene was dissipating.

"Are you all right?"

She was sitting on the ground. She'd fallen, a physical parallel to her psychic mishap.

Theo was beside her. Staring at her. Watching her.

But she wasn't just seeing Theo. She was seeing Owain, too. The man whose thoughts she'd just been thinking. She had been seeing Gwenore and Brice through Owain's eyes. Looking at the tall, gangly boy, Jac's heart had swelled as she felt a kind of love she'd never before felt. She'd been feeling what Owain felt for his son. A love that was pure in a way that romantic love can never be, without the pain of passion but fraught with something much more absorbing.

Suddenly Jac understood. Theo was the reincarnation of Owain. Jac had, as Malachai had explained, truly been reliving a past that belonged to someone else. A past that belonged to Theo. She had been remembering for him.

The thread wound around her wrist. She followed its route with her fingertips as if it were a road she was traveling. She closed her eyes. Just concentrated on the silk. What was happening to her? She should be afraid, and part of her was. But there was something else too. Jac felt energized by what had happened.

The double image of the two men superimposed on each other burned into her retina.

"Are you all right?"

Opening her eyes, she was relieved to see only Theo.

"Jac?"

"I'm all right. I had—I don't know—a flash, I suppose. Not what happened yesterday, but just a glimmer."

He ran his hand through his hair. "Are you safe? I can't bear the thought of anything happening to you."

His concern was comforting. She didn't make friends easily. Not because she didn't want to or because people weren't attracted to her, but because she wasn't very good at the kind of sharing that bonds people.

Her hallucinatory episodes in childhood, losing her mother to suicide, the year she'd spent visiting doctors to try to find a cause for her problems, the twelve months at Blixer Rath, then meeting Griffin and losing him too—you don't discuss those things at casual dinner parties. As she became close with people, intimacy was so hard fought and so hard won, she shied away from attempting it most of the time.

It was difficult for her to relate to most people and for most people to relate to her. But Theo was different. He'd been at Blixer. He shared her history. They both had suffered from debilitating psychological trauma and survived. She didn't have to worry about his not understanding her demons. He had them too. She didn't have to be afraid of telling him that sometimes she thought she was crazy. He thought the same about himself. He'd known her at her most vulnerable, as she had known him at his.

"We were very young at the clinic," she said.

He nodded. "And troubled. That was a bleak time. You know you were the first person I'd ever met who seemed to understand. You were a miracle."

"For me too."

"You were the first person I met who made me feel like myself," Theo said. "As if we were the same somehow, and you would accept me for who I was. It was a very important discovery."

What he was saying was important, Jac thought. It was key to what was going on with her, but she didn't quite understand it yet.

"What did you discover?" she asked.

"That I could like myself. Or at least I liked the person I was with you."

"What about yourself did you like?" She didn't know why, but she was sure this was a critical question—a clue to a puzzle she hadn't even known existed.

"Other people would have asked me why I didn't like myself, not what I liked. But you're not like other people. You never were. I'm relieved you still aren't."

"You still haven't told me." She needed to know.

"You were the first person I'd met whom I

wanted to help. You were in so much pain. I wanted to take care of you."

"Because if you could take care of me and lessen my pain, it would lessen your own?"

"Yes. How did you know that?"

She shrugged. "I'm not sure." She looked away from Theo. At the stones. She reached out and touched one. It was warm from the sun. "I think I've had dreams about a place that looks like this," she said quietly. Almost not wanting it to be true. "I always call them my stone dreams."

"Maybe because of my drawings that you saw at Blixer Rath? I drew this place all the time too. I drew all these monuments."

"We all dream in mythology," she said, echoing something Malachai had told her so many times. "I've never been able to attach a myth to my stone dreams the way I have to other dreams."

They'd started walking, and Theo had led her away over a stream and beyond it to another ruin—an archway built of stone. Ivy climbed the walls.

"What have you dreamed about since you've been here?" he asked.

"The last few nights I've dreamed about threads. I saw someone from the episode I had, tied up in threads. And another dream of Moira, the goddess of fate with her beautiful silks in shimmering colors—gold, silver, aqua, cobalt, purple, rose. All of them thin—too thin to be so strong. She sat cutting the threads, weeping, singing. I even remember the words to her song. *We are the keeper of the threads*."

"And what do you think it means?"

"I think I was thrown by the incident in the cave. All I want is to have control over what I see. Over my hallucinations. That and being influenced by your aunt's loom."

He nodded.

"Tell me about your dreams?" Jac asked.

"I used to have dreams about being sacrificed to the Minotaur when I was at Blixer Rath. I was one of the teenagers brought into the labyrinth to feed him." Theo actually shuddered, and it made the hair on the back of Jac's neck tingle. "I stopped having them," he continued, "and then . . . when my wife died they came back. More lurid and frightening than ever."

For a few moments neither of them said anything.

"Are you still having them?"

He nodded. "I never sleep a night through."

She touched his hand. Felt how cold his skin was.

"It's because I feel guilty. I'm responsible for what happened to her," he said.

"What do you mean?"

He took a deep breath. "I killed her."

Thirty-six

Ash sat in the library of the house where he grew up and opened the journal that his brother had found in a cave by the sea. It still seemed impossible that this fragile document had survived all these years despite the damp, but here it was.

> Every story begins with a tremble of anticipation. At the start we may have an idea of our point of arrival, but what lies before us and makes us shudder is the journey, for that is all discovery. This strange and curious story begins for me at the sea. Its sound and scent are my punctuation. Its movements are my verbs. As I write this, angry waves break upon the rocks, and when the water recedes, the rocks seem to be weeping. As if nature is expressing what is in my soul. Expressing what I cannot speak of out loud but can only write, here, in secret . . .

His French was rusty and a few times he had to stop and look up a word, but the story carried him from its somber beginning to the place where it ended without conclusion, telling of a second volume.

Ash found his aunts in the great room of the house, Minerva editing an article she'd written for a psychiatric journal, Eva weaving.

"Have you both read this?"

"Not yet, no," Minerva answered. "I asked Theo for it. Where did you find it?"

"In the vault. I suppose it didn't occur to Theo that I'd go looking for it, or he might have found a better hiding place."

"He's too preoccupied," Eva said.

"What do you make of it?" Minerva had gotten up and walked over to Ash so she could get a better look at the book.

In broad strokes, Ash described what he'd read. It took the better part of fifty minutes, and both his aunts remained riveted to the end.

"I don't know what to think," Ash said. "Victor Hugo really believed he was talking to ghosts of long-dead men and spirits from another realm. I've read about Hugo. He was one of the most respected authors of the nineteenth century and a proponent of reason. How could he have written this?"

"He was also a massive narcissist and a hashish smoker. He had an imagination as big as all of France. I think he believed what he wrote, but that doesn't make it true. We all know how easy it is on windy, dark nights to believe in ghosts." Minerva glanced over at Eva for a moment and then back at her nephew. "Perhaps it's a novel written in the form of a journal. An experiment."

"Just because we can't explain it doesn't mean it didn't happen. That it's not real," Eva said. "I'm worried about Theo," she said. "And what he thinks it means."

"And what the second half of the journal says," Ash added. "There's a powerful synchronicity between what Hugo was going through when he wrote it and what Theo is suffering."

"You're talking about the power of suggestion," said Minerva.

"This journal was written by a man who had endured the greatest loss of his life and who met a devil who offered to bring his daughter back from the dead," Ash said. "Theo has lost his wife."

"It's a very dangerous connection," Eva said. "Your brother is in the grip of something that's greater than he is. And he's susceptible."

Minerva looked at her sister as if she was going to argue. Instead she shook her head. "I've tried to help him. Have found him dozens of doctors over the years. I've exhausted every avenue. I don't know anymore. Maybe Eva is right."

Ash was surprised. "I've never heard you admitting defeat. Never thought I would."

Eva came to her sister's side and took her hand. She patted it the way one would a child's. For the first time in his life, Ash watched the two of them switch roles, Minerva clinging to her sister, Eva taking charge.

"I know you want to understand everything and

find a way to process it that makes sense to you. But there are mysteries that defy even you, Minerva. Even you."

"Oh, the things you aren't saying!" Minerva's laugh was self-deprecating.

"They don't need to be said." Eva kept her arm around her sister but turned to Ash. "We need to find Theo before he finds the next part of that book. There's no telling what he might do. What kind of crazy plan he might try to follow."

"How are we going to do that? We don't even know where the cave is," Minerva said. "He didn't tell us."

"He didn't have to," Eva said. She pointed to the picture. "Jac noticed it in that photograph."

"But those rocks could be anywhere."

"They could, but they aren't. I know where the cave is."

Minerva looked at her sister incredulously. "You? How?"

"Our grandfather took me there once." Eva bit her bottom lip. "He told me that the Shadow showed him the way."

"You were inside?" Ash asked.

"I wouldn't go inside. I ran off. I was scared."

"I don't believe this—" Minerva started and then stopped herself. "It doesn't matter what I believe, does it? Eva, can you tell Ash where it is?"

"I can't climb down there with these old bones, but I can show him the way."

Thirty-seven

As Jac and Theo journeyed away from the monument, he explained that before her death, his wife had been seeing a therapist and talking about a separation. "It was my fault our marriage was in bad shape. She said I was jealous and overly protective. She hated living in Jersey. Said it was like being in a fishbowl. She wanted to go back to London. I should have just said yes. Moved there. Taken her back to London. Anything to get her away from Ash."

"Ash? What did your brother have to do with it?"

"My brother was pursuing her. Trying to seduce her. He was in love with her, Jac. He was attempting to steal her from me. He was making all kinds of promises to her. He even was helping her get a flat in London—"

Theo broke off and looked down at his watch.

"We can go to the beach. It should be low tide by now," he said.

She wanted to know more, but he certainly had changed the subject.

Jac and Theo walked down the slipway and reached the shore.

"We must have been lucky yesterday to get here

when we did," Jac said. "The sea must completely hide the entrance during high tide."

"Which had to be why Hugo chose it and how the journals remained undiscovered for so long. But I'm surprised he didn't just destroy it. It would have been so much easier."

"He was already a famous writer and so well aware of his own celebrity. I don't think it would have been easy for him to do that." Jac peered over the edge of the rocks. She felt the familiar jolt of fear from being on a ledge but fought it.

They made their way down to the entrance. There was still an inch of water on the ground from the recent flooding. They sloshed through the first tunnel to the innermost cave where they'd found the stone hiding place. The floor here was dry.

Together she and Theo removed the amber totems from the front of each cubbyhole and searched each niche.

"There's nothing else here. Just these little statues and bones," he said, his voice dejected. "Maybe Hugo didn't leave the other volume in the same place after all." Theo shone the strong lantern around the cave, swinging it almost wildly. "Where else could he have put it? This place is filled with cracks and crevices. It could be anywhere." He sounded panicked.

Jac was systematically going through the cubbyholes again, reaching deeper into each one.

It didn't make sense that Hugo would have hid the two volumes separately.

And sure enough, in the fourth from the top on the left, her fingers felt something. She pulled out an identical package to the one they had already found and unwrapped. It was another journal. The same material and type as the one they had found yesterday.

"Theo, look. I found it."

Jac opened it. Breathed in the centuries-old fragrance of ink and mold and Fantine's perfume and began to read.

Thirty-eight

OCTOBER 26, 1855
JERSEY, CHANNEL ISLANDS, GREAT BRITAIN

A week had passed since the incident with Robert and Pauline, and true to my word to my wife, we had not engaged in another séance. Already my daughter seemed less nervous and said she was sleeping better. Neither of my sons complained that our nighttime activities had been abandoned. Charles was still obsessed with the new art of photography and François-Victor with translating Shakespeare's entire oeuvre into French. They had no trouble keeping themselves busy. Only I felt lost.

There was unfinished business with me and the spirits. To distract myself I took it upon myself to try and help you, Fantine.

I met on Monday and then again on Wednesday and Thursday with the town's most accomplished jeweler, Pierre Gaspard, from whom I'd purchased several lovely gifts since moving to Jersey. He was much taken with the idea of creating fine silver and gold perfume bottles and jeweled chatelaines. And equally taken by your fragrances, which I'd borrowed from Juliette's vanity. He even escorted me out to his studio to show me where you might have a laboratory to concoct your elixirs. Gaspard was like a man on fire and had dozens of ideas for how the two of you might collaborate, and he asked me if I would bring you round to meet him.

I didn't tell him that I hadn't yet even broached the subject to you, but after seeing his enthusiasm and his interest in meeting you, on Thursday night I went down to the beach to find you so I could tell you.

When I came upon you, you were looking out to sea, hands pressed together, fingers pointing toward the heavens. The aura of sadness around you was so palpable it was almost visible. By then I'd come to see us as partners in grief, and I think I believed that if I could rescue you from your misery, I would finally find relief as well.

"Were you praying?" I asked.

You nodded, and I was surprised. I had not thought you religious.

"For what do you pray?"

"Deliverance."

"From?"

"From the pain of my grief. I pray for the courage to walk into that water and just keep walking so I might join my child's soul. Maybe if Antoine had not deserted me . . . perhaps if he had come as he had promised and we'd married, then together we could have faced this loss. But I can't do it alone. I've been humiliated and betrayed, first by my uncle, then by my lover, then by my own body. To love and then have it gone . . . to feel life and then feel only emptiness . . . to have this part of me die and yet the rest of me live . . . What kind of game are the fates playing with me? How much longer can I stand to mourn? I watch for his ship every night, knowing it will not come, and yet I keep walking the beach. I have had enough."

To hear you wish for the end of your life was an affront to everything I believed, and yet how I understood it. I knew the level of your pain and the intensity of your desire to die.

"You don't have to give your heart away again, but you can find someone to marry. You can have more children. It would honor the child you lost to have another."

You turned now, finally faced me for the first

time. I saw the tracks of tears on your cheeks. "Does having three other children lessen your pain over the one who is lost?"

"Not lessen the pain, no. But it keeps me wanting to draw breath. It keeps me alive. In nurturing and caring for another child, you can love the child you lost. You are still young, Fantine. You can raise strong sons and daughters in the other's memory."

"And in your novel, Monsieur Hugo, who marries this ruined servant girl?"

"In my novel, the question is who marries the perfumer."

"I am not a perfumer."

"Ah, but you are. And I have a proposition for you. I've spoken to the jeweler Gaspard, who is very interested in showcasing your perfumes and selling them in his establishment. He's even come up with ideas for special flacons for them."

"He wants to sell perfume?"

"Your perfume."

"How does he know about my perfume?"

"I am quite an accomplished thief. I took the ones you created for Madame Juliette."

"You've been quite busy." You were clearly flustered.

"I've just had a meeting or two."

"There's a lot of effort involved in doing what you suggest. To set up a full working laboratory is not a simple task."

"I'm sure it will take some effort, but think of the results."

"More than effort, it will take desire, and you forget, I have none."

"Not now, you don't. Or you believe you don't," I said. "But once you get started you will."

"Except I am not interested in cultivating desire. Why are you meddling in my life like this? I didn't ask you for help. I don't want to talk to people and sell perfume and be reminded of my father and my life in Paris and Antoine and our—"

I interrupted, unwilling to be deterred. "But the life you have built for yourself has no future."

The look you gave me said more than a hundred words could have. And I read them all without exertion. I had seen the haunted eyes you turned on me in my own mirror.

"Come, let's walk," I said, taking your arm. Even though we were on sand, I heard pebbles shifting and looked down for an explanation. There were not even shells on this part of the beach. What was that sound?

"Will you consider the offer? Even if you can't imagine wanting this for yourself, will you allow that I know it could be a good life for you?"

You didn't answer at first. It seemed to me that the night grew quieter. The waves stilled, almost as if even the sea was waiting for your response.

"I appreciate what you are trying to do, but I

would ask you to stop. I don't want you to try and save me. Can you honor that request?"

"No. My daughter lost her life, but she had no choice in the matter. You do have a choice. I cannot bear to see you squander it. And for what? A system that is prejudiced? A man whose family would not accept you because you were of the working class and he of the aristocracy? An uncle who was able to throw you out of a family business because you were a female? There has been no fairness shown to you, and I want to right those wrongs." I had begun to weep openly, but I didn't care. I was fighting for something important.

"You cannot. Don't you understand that? I don't want your help. Please leave me be."

I was disappointed and angry. I threw up my hands. Maybe there was nothing I could do for you.

"As you wish," I said, and then I turned and stomped away. I'd gone twenty or thirty steps when I felt a sudden need to look back. Not more than two minutes could have passed, but already you were gone.

"Fantine?" No answer. "Fantine?" I shouted louder. You didn't respond.

I ran back to the shore and saw what I had not been able to see from where I'd been standing. You had walked into the sea. Were walking still, your clothes billowing out around you. I didn't have to stop and think. I knew exactly what you were planning. You wanted to drown yourself. I understood the sounds I'd heard when you'd moved earlier—not pebbles underfoot but stones you'd sewn into your dress.

And so the battle began. The water was freezing. You were heavy because of all those rocks in your pockets and in your hem. And you fought me with a ferocity I wouldn't have expected. I'd never known anyone who wanted more to die than you did that night. But something in me could no sooner let you drown than I could have let Didine drown.

A wave crashed over us, and for a moment I lost you. I swallowed too much water. Came up coughing. I wondered if I was going to be the one to drown. Would you watch as I lost my life in that cold, salty water? Or would you come to my rescue? Then I caught my breath, found my footing and grabbed hold of you.

You fought and hit and scratched and pulled at my hair. Another wave came and we both lost balance. I managed to keep hold of you and together we were thrown toward the shore, then pulled out toward the sea again. When the water receded, you were still in my arms and you'd stopped fighting. You were limp. In the breakers' turmoil, as I later found out, you'd hit your head and now were unconscious and even heavier than before. I ripped at your dress and pulled off the

483

skirt that was full of rocks. With that weight gone, I was able to fight the current and drag your body up onto the beach.

Your breathing was shallow and your eyes were closed and you were unresponsive. I didn't know what to do. Or how to get help. To do that I'd have to leave you, and that seemed the most dangerous path to take. It was cold out, the water had been freezing and we both were soaked through. I knew that if you were going to survive, if I was going to survive, we needed to warm up.

Lucifer's Lair was just behind us. I'd seen kindling there and flints. If I could carry you to the cave, perhaps there was a chance. Perhaps.

Thirty-nine

We were lucky that the tide was low enough that I was able to carry you to the rocks, lower you down to the entranceway to the cave and pull you inside. I dragged you to the innermost chamber, where I worked for what seemed like hours but was in fact mere minutes, rubbing the flints together to get a spark and finally light a fire. I noticed that pieces of ancient carved amber were mixed in with the kindling, and on any other occasion I would have stopped to take them out, but there was no time. Some of the hashish from my pipe was close to the fire too and in my haste fell onto the flames. As a result the smell of the fire was sweetened by the combination of the drug and the resin mixed with the wood. The cave took on the odor of a forest burning down, of endings, of disasters, of the world not caring what it takes, destroys and chews up. You lay there as proof of its ambivalence. So pale you were almost incandescent.

"Fantine! Fantine!"

You didn't respond.

In the firelight I could see blood on your neck. I needed to attend to that, but first I pulled off your outer clothes and mine. It wouldn't matter if I stanched your wound if you froze to death first.

Laying you as close to the fire as I could, feeling its heat in my own bones, I searched for and found the gouge where you'd hit your head. Then I grabbed a piece of my own wet clothing and held that to your wound.

I've seen men fight for their lives and others who beg to die when the pain is too great. Watching over you, tending to you, I recognized you as one of the latter. There was nothing holding you on earth. I felt your willingness to let go.

"Fight, Fantine," I whispered over and over. And finally I heard an answer. But it wasn't coming from you.

Let her go, Hugo. Don't fight for her. She's moments away. I'll take her and give you your daughter back.

I turned. The Shadow of the Sepulcher was making his way toward me. Not quite walking and not quite floating either. It was an otherworldly movement. In his presence I felt as I always did, as if every breath I took came from a deeper part of my chest. I could see with more clarity, hear with more acuity. I was more alive in the presence of death than at any other time in my life.

"Why are you torturing me?" I asked. "I already told you no, I will not help you."

I need you, Hugo. I need you to resurrect my stature. I need you if I am to be redeemed. What I ask is so little, what I offer in return is so great.

"It is impossible!"

Not impossible.

"Impossible and so very wrong. It's evil to take one soul in exchange for another." I glanced down at your sleeping form, naked in the firelight. Your beautiful spirit, broken. You only wanted to escape your disconsolate condition. And I only wanted to save you. Why? Why did you matter to me so much?

It was as if the Shadow could hear my thoughts.

You showed me with the first two girls the mistake I was making. They were full of life and the future. You could never have let them go. But this one wants to go, Hugo. She yearns to join her baby and hold the infant in her arms. Even as a spirit it would be more gratifying to her than this

*world of flesh and blood. Why do you resist? That
woman has already given up.*

"What you are suggesting is horrible. No man
should be offered such authority or power over
another."

*I can see in your eyes how much you want to
say yes. Yes, say it. Yes! Yes! Say yes and your
Leopoldine will wake up in your arms.*

The Shadow was watching me. The firelight
played in his hair and illuminated the topaz eyes,
giving them their own burning glow.

*This sacred site has been a place of sacrifice for
the greater good for centuries. Here ancient,
sometimes brutal rituals have been enacted out of
a desire to protect the tribe. In older times men did
not question the spirit world as they do now. They
killed if that was what was asked of them.*

There was a forlorn lilt to his words, a sense of
longing for that past.

*Magic was revered. Worship was meaningful.
The spirit world was honored and obeyed. Your
séances reanimated a spirit long gone silent on
the island. We are always available to visit when
we are invited. I sensed in you an intellectual
equal. How could I resist a chance to discuss
grand philosophical topics with someone who
comprehended them as you do? I thought I had
found a believer, a man of great mental acuity who
would lend me his voice.*

"I cannot accept what you offer," I said again,

but my voice didn't have the strength it had had. I was worn down, exhausted and more afraid than I had been on any of the other nights I'd passed in this creature's company.

The Shadow was watching me so carefully, I felt as if he was seeing my mind working.

In the meantime, you had not stirred. You'd lost so much blood, and though I'd stanched your wound, your color was now unearthly pale. Or was that a trick of the brightly colored fire? How much longer could you last?

Suddenly, I felt as if someone had poured lead into my body. Moving even a finger was a great effort.

"What have you done to me?" I asked the Shadow.

It takes enormous concentration for you to hear and understand me for such a length of time. That's what is making you so lethargic.

"If Fantine woke up now, would she hear you?"

No. My voice is inaudible to all but you. It's inside your mind.

"But your mouth is moving. I hear the fire under your words."

The imagination is a powerful tool.

"Can I call you forth at will?"

He laughed.

Ah, what a terrible, beautiful sound it was. As if he'd created his laugh from nightingales' songs, from bells. The sound was glorious, and when I

488

heard it, I felt anointed. I think I've written about what a handsome man he was. But I'm sure I've failed to really convey his appearance. His skin was shimmering. His eyes were deeper than infinite space, and looking at him was like looking up at the heavens and letting their full wonder overwhelm me. His limbs were long and moved with a fluidity that mortals cannot manage. And he exuded a scent—a lush smoky scent that was both ancient and modern, filled with sweetness.

No, this isn't magic. You can't say a spell and have me show up like a genie from a lamp. I have come for a purpose. Once I leave I will be gone. Lucifer will not be available to you for mere conversation.

I knew I needed to break free of his words, but I couldn't make myself stop listening to that mellifluous voice.

I only want to give you what you desire more than anything else on earth.

My eyes started to smart. The cave was filling with thick smoke. I lost sight of the walls, the floor. It seemed to be coming from the Shadow himself. And in the smoke, I saw Didine. Her clothes were in tatters. There was mud and debris woven in her hair. She lifted her arms. Her fingers reached for mine.

"Didine?"

The smoke swirled. She was disappearing. I grabbed for her. Clutched air.

"Didine?" I was losing her all over again.

I chose a woman who wants to die, Hugo. It is in your power to give her that gift. Fantine will have her relief, and your daughter will be returned to you. Are you capable of denying Didine—of denying yourself?

My daughter wanted to come back to me. It was in my power to bring her back. But how could I make this choice? One life for another? If only I could lie down next to you and sleep your sleep and escape this apparition and his beguiling offer.

All Fantine wants is to go to her child—a child she has never seen take a breath. And you are preventing her.

"If Didine comes back in Fantine's body, will she even know me? Will she know her mother?"

He shook his head, and his curls danced in the firelight.

Not at first. She won't remember the details of her life before for weeks. But her love for you, for her mother, that will be instantaneous. The soul can recall what the mind forgets. She will love you as her father from the first moment she opens her eyes. The bond between the two of you will be restored.

"But what price will I pay?" I cried.

For liberating one soul and rescuing another? Why should you pay any price?

I watched the flames and tried to grasp what he was saying. Could this be?

490

Beside me, you moaned in your semiconscious sleep. It was the first sound you had made since I'd pulled you out of the sea. It was one of the saddest sounds I think I have ever heard, filled as it was with a mourning parent's pathos. I too had felt it, I understood. It made me want to weep.

Do you hear how unhappy she is?

His voice was compassionate.

Fantine has lost so much in such a short time. Two years, is it? Parents, lover, child, home, livelihood.

"Why? Why has she lost so much? Is it just the way of the world?"

Yes.

"To what end?"

You will have to live your way into those answers. But of all the men I have met, you, Hugo, are capable of finding those answers and sharing them.

"How can you be so sure?"

I have known you for millennia. We have walked these paths, you and I, before. Many times, my friend, dating back to all beginnings.

I had so many questions. And I had a true and real sense that this was my last chance to learn from him. Or from any of them. No matter what happened, after tonight this chapter of my life would come to an end.

The ancients had instincts and abilities that are lost to civilization today. Magic was real. It lived inside the shamans. Inside the priests. They passed it on from generation to generation. You have the dregs of that power in you. It is not the strength that it was, but you can access it. But to do so you must be willing to travel deep into your own darkness and be open to risk. To pull from the earth's energy.

I shook my head. "Utter nonsense. I have heard enough. You need to release me. I need to get up, to carry Fantine out of here, and get her help."

No, Victor, it's not nonsense. It is not. You asked me about the ancient truth and I have given it to you in good faith. Now let us finish what we have begun. Free this child and regain yours.

It was the first time he'd used my Christian name, and he'd said it so tenderly and with so much compassion, I felt like a young boy again at my mother's knee. My father was off fighting and she called me to her and told me she'd had very bad news she needed to share with me.

Had Papa been hurt? Captured?

I must have been only four or five and began to cry. She scooped me up and gathered me on her lap, putting her arms around me. She soothed me and solved half the world's problems with that sour and sweet, lemon and sugar embrace. I remember holding Didine like that and comforting her when she was small. And now, here in this ancient ritual cave, the Shadow was offering me that same solace. His words were my mother's arms. He was conjuring the scents and filling the cave with them: sweet and sour, lemon and sugar.

Oh, Fantine, I do not know if you believe what you are reading. If you heard through your dreams that night, if you today remember any of what came next. I can understand if you are thinking I was mad . . . intoxicated by fumes of the hashish and of the bits of amber that burned in the fire. But I do not believe outside influences were affecting me. I was not imagining the incident; the episode was as real as the paper in this book.

I am writing to you now, explaining what happened, as part desperate apology and part plea. I hope that you will forgive me, but even more that you will keep our secret, because no one must ever raise the Shadow of the Sepulcher again.

What he offers is too tempting for mortal men. It was in the end too tempting for me.

Victor?

The Shadow whispered my name. He stroked my cheek. I had never lain with a man. Never wanted to, but this was not sexual lust. This was beyond passionate physical yearning. This was beyond man, woman, skin, lips, tongue, fingers, breasts, loins. He was neither man nor woman but was all: parent, lover, wife, child, husband. All that can be between any two people, he was. Whispering promises, he put his lips to my forehead and sealed those pledges forever. His hair was soft against my skin. His touch intoxicating.

I wanted to give everything and anything to please him. I wanted to fulfill his request so he would fulfill mine.

I was pressing up against flesh. Pleasure and pain and yielding flesh. Not his flesh, though. Not anymore. It was you I was holding. You I was touching.

Somehow, I cannot explain how, he had merged with you. It was as if he had walked into your sleeping form and become you. He was speaking again, but now his words were coming from your lips, even as you continued sleeping and while I made some kind of desperate love to you.

Take me, Victor. Put your hands around my throat. I want you to so very much. I am waiting for you to liberate me. Your daughter is waiting for you to liberate me, waiting for you to bring her back.

I was high up inside you. My fingers were wet with your blood and around your throat. As I felt your faint pulse, I felt your womb throb around me.

Take me.

I would never have imagined it would be as easy as it was to squeeze the life out of someone.

I will not suffer.

He left your body then and entered me. His

fingers were inside mine, and he was squeezing your throat. I fought but was losing my battle with his strength.

Put pressure here on her throat. She will feel nothing. Will not suffer. Let her go, Victor. Give her what she wants. Let her go, and as her soul departs her body, Leopoldine's will enter. Fantine's body. Your daughter's self. Put pressure here. And here.

I looked down at you as if from a great distance. Half asleep, half dead. Halfway to where you wanted to go. And then you gasped. It was a small noise. A cat might not make one any louder. Not a sound of defeat but of resistance. Was it an automatic response or an emotional one? I had no idea, but it was the sound of a living being fighting for breath. It shuddered through me and shook me. I spilled myself inside you with a great huge shiver. You were not my child. She had stopped breathing. You had not. You were the future.

I found the strength to loosen my grasp, horrified by what I had done. Shocked. And then I knew something the Shadow didn't. I knew it in that instant. You had life in you. If I took you and that life too, the devil would own me forever.

It wouldn't matter if I had Didine back. I would not have my self, my sanity, and I would not have my soul. What good would I be to my daughter, or to anyone, then?

You are a coward, the Shadow said, but his voice was weaker, harder to hear.

Fantine, you were breathing deep breaths by then. Your color was returning. You were moving, returning to us.

Yes, coward, the Shadow cursed me.

"All this was about you wanting to own me, wasn't it? To add me to your list of men who have fallen under your spell. You wanted to seduce me into becoming yours. What you've done to me—almost made me do—was monstrous."

The Shadow said my name twice, first as a prayer and then as a curse.

Victor. Victor.

And then your voice joined his.

"Victor." Both voices harmonized.

You opened your eyes and looked up at me. I saw fear there. And pain. Both tore at me.

"Victor . . ." His voice had disappeared. Only you were speaking. "Victor, why are you crying?"

Victor Hugo
October 30, 1855
Jersey, Great Britain
For Fantine and the child who will be mine.

Forty

Ash had found the cave with Eva's help and climbed down. In the first tunnel he smelled sweet smoke and carefully continued further inside. Jac's voice grew louder the closer he got to the innermost chamber.

He stopped on the threshold and stood, captivated by the words she was reading. The story that was unfolding. A mesmerizing tale.

As Ash stood there breathing in the scented air and listening to her hypnotic voice, he felt as if he were falling into a dream. Something was making him dizzy.

He had to hold on to the wall to keep himself upright.

Lucifer's words were so enticing. What an astounding idea to trade one soul for another. Especially with one who didn't have any desire to live. Was it possible? Had Hugo done it?

Ash thought of Naomi while he listened to Jac reading. He pictured his brother's beautiful, sad wife, who'd hated this island. Who'd wanted only to go back to London. Who needed his help. Needed Ash to help her make her escape.

How Ash hated Theo for not taking care of what he was so lucky to have. For causing her such distress. Theo didn't deserve her. Couldn't be trusted with someone as special as Naomi. Hadn't done the right thing.

And now she was gone. And it was all Theo's fault. Always his fault. Always.

Forty-one

While Jac had been reading, Theo had kept the fire burning, and fragrant and sweet smoke had filled the cave. Was she getting drunk on the smell? More than once she'd felt reality waving away and had managed to keep in the moment only by touching the scarlet-threaded bracelet on her left wrist, letting go just to turn a page. Now, without the book to concentrate on, she rolled the silk against her skin and tried to focus on what Theo had just said.

"I'm sorry, what?" she asked.

He'd been leaning over her shoulder, looking at the pages. Now he was standing, his body shaking, swaying slightly. The fire flared just then, and in the light, Theo's eyes burned brighter. Had she ever seen a face so twisted with pain and desire at the same time?

"Is it . . . is it possible? What Hugo wrote?" he asked, speaking slowly.

"You mean was the Shadow real? Victor Hugo thought he was."

"Would you be able to resist that offer, Jac? If

you had the chance to bring someone you loved back from the dead?"

The book was still open in her lap. She couldn't close it, not yet: she was too moved and confused to know how to react. In the shadows of the cave, farther back than they had yet explored, she could sense, no, she could see shapes moving, circling around another fire. She could hear far-off keening, and chanting. A woman crying. A man shouting.

Jac pushed the thread up an inch on her skin and then down.

"Imagine if it was possible," Theo was saying, "to bring someone back from the dead. If the Shadow really talked to my ancestor . . . if he really talked to Hugo . . . if the Shadow is real . . . just imagine!"

The smoke grew heavier. The scent sickly sweet now. Jac coughed. It was hard to breathe.

"The Shadow is real," a different voice said from farther away.

Jac recognized Ash's voice. How had he gotten here?

"And he's here. The Shadow is here."

Ash was coming closer to where she and Theo were sitting.

"Can't you smell him? He's real." Now Ash was so close to Jac, his breath was warm on her skin.

Why was she shivering? It was so warm in the

cavern, how could she be cold? Ash's breath was warm. The fire was warm.

There was a moment of quiet. And then Jac felt the slightest breeze as Ash reached out for her. She thought he was going to embrace her. Wasn't sure why here or why now in front of Theo, but his hands were coming closer, his fingers outstretched.

"The Shadow is going to bring Naomi back from the dead," he said, and then Ash's fingers went around her throat, not to pull her, not to kiss her, but, she was sure, to kill her.

The fire blazed. The scene was waving and she felt herself slipping into a hallucination of smoke just like this smoke. Of a cave just like this cave. But not in the present. She was going into the past.

Behind her, Theo was shouting, "Stop! Stop!" She heard it doubled. Was it two men shouting the same words? Or were the words echoing through the cave? Despite the pressure on her neck, Jac held on to the red thread and kept herself where the pain was, where it was hard to breathe, in the present. She knew that if she didn't, she would be lost. Finally and completely lost.

And then the hands lifted. No fingers were gripping her neck. She touched the place where it burned, where he'd been twisting her skin, and gulped for air and started to cough.

"What the hell were you trying to do, you idiot?" Theo was screaming at his brother.

Jac turned around.

Theo had pulled Ash off her and had him pinned up against the wall.

"Are you crazy? Trying to reenact a drugged man's ramblings? Hugo was mad when he wrote that journal!" Theo screamed.

"Don't interfere. Don't you dare. Not again," Ash shouted, and he pushed back at his brother and threw him off. "Naomi wouldn't be dead if you hadn't been so pitiful. If she didn't feel so sorry for you, she would have left you sooner and she'd be alive now. Alive and living with me. Happy. I don't destroy people, Theo."

He punched Theo in the face. Theo threw the next punch, but Ash got out of the way and then reached out and grabbed Theo. Locked in an angry embrace, the two of them wrestled, pulling and pushing at each other. On the walls of the cave, their shadows fought as well. Leaping and springing forward and back.

Jac was trying to understand. Had Ash been lying all this time? Had he actually been in love with Theo's wife, not just helping her? Had he been having an affair with her?

For all Theo's psychological issues, had he been right in his suspicions? Had Ash seduced Naomi? Had Naomi betrayed Theo?

The brothers were an even match. And each time one of them got the advantage, the other managed to turn it around.

Ash grabbed Theo, spun him around and threw him against the wall again. Theo pushed him off with so much force Ash stumbled backward and fell.

Theo jumped on top of Ash and kept him pinned to the ground.

Ash's head just missed the pyre. The fire was raised off the floor but only by six inches.

Ash broke free and rolled to get away but moved dangerously closer to the flames. Ash's hair caught fire. Feeling the heat, his energy surged. He rolled in the other direction, batting at his head, extinguishing the charring, and then, getting to his feet, he threw a punch. This one caught Theo by surprise, and he stumbled.

The two of them struggled for the next few minutes, neither gaining an advantage, first one in control, then the other. Then Ash pushed Theo far enough away to take off, running farther into the cave, into the unexplored next chamber where Jac had thought she'd seen people in robes. Where she thought she'd seen a woman standing, crying over a burning bier.

Theo followed Ash.

Jac ran after both brothers, into that innermost, deepest chamber.

The enclosure was smaller than any of the other rooms. The ceiling was barely six feet high. The walls curved inward and were smoothed to a polished finish. Every surface was decorated with paintings. The processions that had begun in the outermost entranceway to the cave with the half-man half-cat culminated in this room.

The two brothers tumbled over one another.

Jac hovered by the door, wanting to go in, to break them up. Not knowing how she could.

Ash was on top of his brother now, his hands pinning him down. Bucking, Theo threw Ash off, then jumped on him, pinning him with a firm grip. Finally subduing him.

Theo was out of breath, gasping for air. So was Ash.

"You stupid fool," Theo said. "You're insane! Do you know that?"

With his arms restrained, it seemed the fight was going out of Ash. He stopped resisting. Lay still. Theo took a breath.

And then with a burst of sudden energy, Ash jackknifed and threw Theo off, smashing him into the wall. Jac heard the impact. She gasped.

Now Ash held Theo to the wall, the two of them exhausted, out of breath and energy. But the brothers' anger was fierce. In such close quarters, if they started fighting again, one shove could result in a fatal head wound.

She had to stop them. But how?

Jac's right hand was clasped around her wrist, covering the bracelet up as if protecting it from the destructive energy in the cave. There was something beyond what was here and now. In the shadows of this room were the answers she needed in order to understand what had happened to her since she'd arrived, and maybe even longer than that. Jac knew that something more important than her work had brought her to Jersey. That she'd needed to come here to help Theo. Destiny or fate or magic or alchemy or the collective unconscious or a mystical secret, whatever Theo's grandaunts or Malachai wanted to call it, had brought her here.

What if our souls are connected to each other and flow together in and out of time like a giant woven tapestry? What if it was that simple and that real? The laws of physics state that energy cannot be destroyed, and we are made of energy. When each of us dies, that energy reenters the atmosphere. What if it does become part of the collective blanket of souls? Threads of energy that connect us each to the other. What if it is our obligation to follow them, despite the knots and tangles, through to the end?

Jac was certain that as long as she had the red thread Eva had tied around her wrist, she could venture out and search for the answers she sensed were waiting and work her way back.

Maybe if she took this psychic journey she could discover who she was to these two men and who they were to each other.

When she was younger, Theo had saved her life when he pulled her out of the lake. Tonight he had saved her life again when he pulled his brother's fingers from around her throat.

Owing him for both, she also owed herself whatever knowledge there was to be gathered. Maybe it was time to learn why she was so afraid of this ability she'd had since childhood. Instead of running away from this gift or this curse, the moment had come to understand who she was and what it was.

Jac closed her eyes. Inhaled the fragrant air, identified the sweet notes of the amber resin that wasn't supposed to have a scent. Inhaled again. Took the drug into her lungs. Felt the dizziness. Saw the room wave around her. Saw the shapes begin to change. Began to think another's thoughts . . .

Forty-two

56 BCE
ISLE OF JERSEY

Owain knelt before Brice and bowed his head. The ceremony was under way—father and son engaged in the honored tradition of passing the priesthood on to the next generation. Brice was clothed in the white robe befitting a novitiate. He wore a crown of leaves Gwenore had woven for him, sewing six small talismans into the halo, six being the holy number. They were bits of stone and shell that she had inherited from her mother, who had inherited them from her mother before that.

Owain had watched his wife these last few days with a heart that grew so heavy he didn't think he would be able to keep it from breaking. Gwenore had not slept but had stayed up burning candles, sewing the robe and the crown, preparing for this honor.

And weeping.

Owain had wept too but secretly. When he was around his wife he tried to keep his emotions in check.

For the last two weeks she had tried to hold on to some hope that there would be a reprieve from the gods. Every morning she'd brewed herbal potions for Owain to drink so that he could engage with the spirits and find an alternative sacrifice, another way to interpret the visions.

Every night he prayed to the Sky Father, to Sucellos, to Lugh, to send other dreams. And every morning he took their meager offerings to the elders whose job was to divine the wishes of the spirits. But the senior *vates* saw no other solution.

The Roman soldiers were on a rampage and would reach Jersey soon. There were not enough men or boys on the island to fight the onslaught. The only hope was divine intervention. A storm bad enough to capsize the Roman ships. A plague.

But in order to engage the spirits, a sacrifice was required. And the gods had told Owain in dream visions that the sacrifice they required was Brice, the only son of the highest priest in all the land. To be offered on the solstice and no later. Given up willingly and with honor.

And now that day was here.

The Druids and the witches and the *vates* and princes had gathered for the anointing feast. They drank mead and ate toasted bread cakes. Owain painted his son's feet with the herbal dyes that Gwenore had prepared, and they were now stained a royal purple from the thistle and violets and sage that grew wild on the island. Owain remembered when those feet fit in his hands. When Brice was a baby and he used to let the boy stand on his palms and dance with him in the tall grass behind the house. Those small baby feet now supported his son as he faced his mortal end.

Owain felt the tears coursing down his face.

Brice, who had been schooled in the ceremony that would initiate him, put his hand on his father's head and said as he had learned, "I accept the responsibilities of being a priest, thank you, Father. I will be true to our people and try to be worthy of their trust."

Owain stood. He put both hands on his son's shoulders and turned Brice around so the boy faced the east wall of the temple, where the sun entered and cut across the structure and illuminated a series of runes carved into the rocks on the floor.

Together father and son, now priest and priest, walked the dozen steps to the opening. This was called the holy walk, symbolizing the path a priest takes in his life, toward the light, toward knowledge, toward the mystical secrets that are revealed only to him.

They reached the ritual bath fed by a sacred spring. The last act of every novitiate was to be submerged in the water, to be cleansed, then to emerge unsullied and ready to interact with the spirits and gods.

The pool also had another use, one Brice didn't know about. It was the last step in what was known as the Threefold Sacrifice.

Owain leaned forward and pressed his lips to his son's forehead.

"This is a great honor you do your people." Owain's voice broke. He couldn't continue. Couldn't say the words that he had said at every other ceremony like this that he'd presided over. He grabbed his son, held him close. He whispered to the boy, "I wish I could give myself instead of you."

Brice looked up at his father. He didn't understand.

Owain didn't explain. He put his hand gently on the boy's head and pushed so Brice's head was again bowed. Owain would not, could not let his son see what was coming. At least the boy would not know what horrible thing was to befall him.

It was time. Owain tried to bring his hand up for the blow. The first of the death efforts. For one second Owain looked away from Brice, out at Gwenore. Desperately he wished she could somehow stop him.

He brought up his hand.

Whether it was because she understood what his eyes implored her or she was acting out of a mother's great and abiding passion, he didn't know. But Gwenore ran forward and threw herself at Brice, pushing him out of the way, so that it was her head that Owain's stone came down on.

She fell, blood streaming from the wound. Her eyes were wide, looking up at her husband. "Me instead, please."

Owain bent down to her, this woman of his soul. She lay at his feet, perhaps mortally wounded. After all these days of thinking it would happen, his heart was finally shattering. How could he do what had to be done? How could he do his job, knowing what it would do to her? To him?

One of the elders came forth and put his hand on Owain's shoulder. "You have an anointed task to perform," he said. "The entire tribe is depending on you."

Owain had been trained his whole life to obey. He didn't know any other way.

Brice was kneeling by his mother. Holding her in his arms and cradling her. Her blood staining his white robes. As grown up as he had seemed during the ceremony, he was now a boy again, crying on his mother's shoulder.

Owain became enraged. Even though a moment before he'd silently begged her to, now he was angry at Gwenore for interfering when she knew better. At Brice for not being man enough to hold his emotions in check. At himself for the agony he would bring upon the only two people he loved in the world.

This torture was taking too long. Owain inspected Gwenore's wound and saw it was superficial; scalp wounds bled more than seemed possible. He pulled her up by the arms and pushed her to the side of the temple. Then he grabbed his son and quickly, without giving mother or son a chance to speak to each other one last time, brought the stone down hard on his son's head.

The young man dropped first to his knees and then fell forward so that he lay prostrate at Owain's feet. All he could see was the top of the boy's head and the back of his neck. The soft skin where the downy hair stopped growing. The very spot where, when Brice was a baby, Owain would put his face and smell the infant's innocence.

No, he could not think of these things.

No, he could think of nothing else. He was doing the most horrible thing imaginable, even if it was for a higher purpose. He must feel the sacrifice. Let it destroy him too. He didn't care. He couldn't really live after this. He would do his duty but his life . . . his life would be worthless.

Owain pulled the garrote out of the pocket of his robe and wound it around his son's neck. *This I do for the spirits.* Pull, tighten. *This I do to honor the gods.* Pull, tighten. *This I do for the good of our tribe, for the sustenance of our people, for the future of us all.* Pull, tighten.

Whose blood was on the stones now? Mother's? Son's? Only Owain's had not yet been shed. The river of blood flowed toward his feet, was dyeing his toes red, was slippery, was warm. He could not allow himself to think that this was his son. This was instead his gift to the gods.

With all the strength he possessed, Owain lifted Brice, dragged him to the pool and pushed him into the ritual bath. Within seconds the water darkened with the boy's blood. Brice was not moving, not fighting or struggling for breath. But still Owain held him under the water. Longer and longer. The ritual had prescribed steps. A threefold death had to happen in sequence and with haste. A clean death. An honorable death. That was the least he could give his son.

He did not hear Gwenore crawling toward him. Did not sense her approaching until suddenly he felt her leap upon him like a wild animal, beating on his back, spitting on him. Cursing at him.

Owain didn't loosen his grip on Brice. Even as Gwenore bit and kicked him, Owain kept Brice submerged. He couldn't break the sacred act now. He had to do this thing. Had to bring it to its end.

The elders came and dragged Gwenore off and Owain was left to his death watch.

When he was certain that all his son's life force was spent, Owain lifted the boy in his arms, and whispering his name over and over, carried him out of the temple and down to the cave on the beach to his final resting place, the most sacred on the island, where only priests were buried, where one day Owain would join his son.

It was a journey meant to be undertaken by the head priest alone. But Owain no longer felt like a priest. The burden he carried was too heavy.

Owain laid his son at the entrance to the cave and lit the first candle. Using that to guide his way, he walked inside, lighting other candles along the way and then setting fire to the pyres he had organized the day before. Each was part of the ritual burial. Six fires made from dried hazel twigs, sage, mistletoe and bits of the golden rocks the tribe treasured.

Once all the fires were burning, cleansing and scenting the air, preparing the cavern for the acceptance of the sacrifice, Owain carried his son deeper inside.

In the innermost chamber, Owain laid Brice on the sacred hearth. Then he dipped his bunch of dried wheat into the candle's flame and touched it to the hazel kindling.

The fire sizzled. More of the scent of burning wood, sage, mistletoe and the sweetness from the golden rocks filled the air.

And then, there, alone in the cell that seemed like a prison to him now, he lifted his son's body one last time and set him up on the flames. And when the first orange tongue licked at the boy's skin, Owain began to scream.

Owain was not required to stay, but he chose to. It was the ultimate honor. And so he stood guard, engulfed by the heat and sweet, terrible scent. Watching as the beautiful boy was consumed by the brutal god of fire.

For the second time that day, Owain did not hear Gwenore coming. Not expecting her or anyone, he was caught by surprise and had no time to react when she crept into the chamber and, without saying a word or even acknowledging that he was there, as if she were wading into the sea on a pleasant day, Gwenore walked into the fire that was consuming her son and took her baby in her arms.

Her hair, her beautiful hair, caught fire first, and the halo around her head burned brightly in the dark.

Owain buried his head in his hands, but now he could not weep. He tried to tell himself that this was only one end. They all believed that their souls would live on, be reborn, find each other again one day, and the echo of them would pay in the next life for the mistakes they had made in this one.

The elders came for him the next day but he would not go with them. Owain remained there for the next twenty days, sitting vigil, slowly, slowly, slowly starving to death, mourning his wife and his son, his past and his present, and fearing for his future soul. And theirs.

Forty-three

Theo was the first one in the chamber. He had blood streaming down his face from a cut above his eyebrow. Ash followed, limping badly and holding his side. He was in serious pain. His nose was swollen and bleeding. Both brothers were filthy. Their clothes were ripped. Out of breath, hurting, they had exhausted each other.

"Are you all right?" Theo asked Jac.

"What's wrong with her?" Ash shouted.

"Jac?" Theo called. And when she didn't respond, said it again.

Owain knew that Jac wasn't his name, but that it was the name of the body he was trapped in.

At the same time, Jac understood she was still reliving the life of the priest named Owain who had once lain here, in the innermost cave, his arms reaching out, his hands immersed in ashes, his fingers grasping bones.

Thoughts crashed into each other. Two consciousnesses struggled to make sense of the present and the past.

Theo and Ash stood watching.

Owain knew the brothers were in the future he'd dreamed of as he lay dying. The one carried Owain's own soul. The other carried his son's soul. And these two men were living out his and Brice's karmic struggle. Still.

Jac tried to push off the waves of memory. Tried to find her voice. Her mind was still half in the priest's body, half in her own. She was both Owain and herself simultaneously. She tried to form a word, any word.
 "Brice," she heard herself say.

Owain was looking at the stranger who contained his son's soul. He could feel Brice's aura. Sense his presence. He said his son's name. "Brice."

Theo was leaning over her. "You said that before too, Jac. Who is Brice?"
 Jac wasn't sure she was supposed to come back

yet. Was there still more to learn? Should she remain with the priest who had starved himself to atone for his sin of doing what had been asked of him instead of what he knew was right?

"Jac, you have to listen to me. You need to come back."

Yes, he was right. Theo was right.

The story she had to tell Theo and his brother about Owain and Brice and Gwenore would explain. The father and son were still working out their struggles lifetimes later. The father's sense of failure was so overwhelming, it poisoned all his future lives. The son's sense of betrayal, and the guilt of having his mother kill herself rather than live without him, informed every incarnation he'd inhabited.

Jac had to come back. If she didn't, these two men, Theo and Ash, would stay enemies forever. It was in her power to change that.

She was trying so hard to break through, her whole body ached. Her head throbbed and her ears rang in pain. She couldn't do it. Not yet.

There was still something she had to understand about what had happened to Owain.

In what was left of the fire, Owain's fingers touched a bit of metal. He felt the outline of a star. Its edges were rough. They cut his skin. The pain sent shivers up and down his arms. It was the star that Owain had made for Brice, forging it in the

516

fire and hanging it over his crib. The star that represented the blemish that his wife and son shared on their skin and that marked them as special. Gwenore must have sewn it into the crown she had made for their son, that she had stayed up all those nights weaving with sacred herbs and amulets.

With a great effort, Owain pulled it out of the fire. He looked down at it in his hand. At the blood. He wondered how it had made a perfect circle around his wrist.

Jac realized she was staring not at blood but at the red thread that Eva had wrapped around her wrist and said would protect her. She had entered into this past holding on to the thread. Now it was time to use it to return to the present. She took a deep breath. It was like climbing.

Another breath. The burning sensation was lessening.

Jac took another breath. She tried to speak, but nothing came out.

Theo took her hands. Held on to them tightly. Too tightly. Something was pressing into her skin.

She pulled back and opened her right hand. Inside was a piece of roughly cut metal in the shape of a star. Theo was staring down at it. So was Ash.

Theo reached out and touched it. "Like the

birthmark on Naomi's neck," he whispered. "The same strange seven-sided star."

Jac had to tell Theo and Ash about the woman in her vision. She'd had a seven-sided star birthmark too, on her chest.

"Naomi. Gwenore. Two thousand years apart. Both branded by the same star. Souls connected. Both of you connected to both of them. To each other."

"What are you talking about?" Theo asked.

"The star. Owain had made it for his son when Gwenore was pregnant."

"Who is Owain? Who is Gwenore?" asked Ash.

"The three of them loved each other," Jac was trying to explain. But there was so much to tell them. Where to start? Tell them they had been a family. But Owain had been forced to obey his gods. He couldn't defy them and put his whole village at risk. And so he did what they asked him to do. He sacrificed his son.

They were both waiting for her to continue. She wasn't sure if they'd understood anything she'd said. She was so tired but she had to tell them. They needed to know, so they could heal. But then she heard the loud scream of a police siren.

Forty-four

When Jac opened her eyes, she saw Robbie sitting by her bedside. *Her brother Robbie was here.* Her beautiful, kind and stubborn brother was here and watching her and smiling. The curtains in the pretty blue room were drawn, but golden shafts of light filtered through the slim space where they met. A big vase of dark red roses on the table perfumed the air with their sweet, voluptuous spice.

"Whew," Robbie said. "I've been worried. We all have been. You've been sleeping for a very long time."

"How long?" Her voice sounded hoarse.

"Two days, Jac. Two whole days."

He leaned forward and pressed his lips to her forehead and kissed her. He smelled of so many wonderful scents: sandalwood and vetiver, ambergris and oakmoss and smoke. Robbie's smell. Robbie's smell that was comforting for its familiarity despite its mystery.

"What time is it?" she asked.

"It's six o'clock."

"In the morning?"

"At night."

"How did you get here?" Everything seemed a wonder to her.

"When Theo and Ash brought you back, Minerva called Malachai, who called me. He wanted to be the one to come, but I was closer and could get here faster. Last time I talked to him he was threatening to come if you didn't wake up by tomorrow morning."

She thought about that for a second. Why would anyone have to come? Then she started to remember. At first slowly and then in great gulps. Finding the second journal. Reading it. Ash's being affected by the drug and his strange attack on her. The brothers' fight. Her going deep into the past to find the memories of who they had been to each other. Finding the clues she needed to unravel their tragic past that informed their conflicted present. The human bones in the funeral pyre. And the strange-shaped star. The same shape as Gwenore's birthmark. And the same shape as Naomi's, Theo had said.

"I need to tell you what happened. And tell Theo and Ash who they are and what—"

"You can do all that," Robbie said. "But first you need to have something to eat and get some of your strength back. You haven't had anything in forty-eight hours."

Eva brought Jac tea and toast with strawberry jam that Jac thought tasted better than anything she'd ever eaten. The sweet fruit studded the bread like little jewels and burst in her mouth. The fragrant tea was hot and bracing and she could smell the jasmine and green leaves as if she were standing in a field of them. All her senses were exaggerated. The sheets were silky against her feet and the pillows embracing. She could hear deep, luscious music coming from beyond the bedroom, full of inspiration and magnificence.

"I don't feel the same," Jac said.

"What do you mean?" Robbie asked.

"I'm not sure."

"Is it better or worse?"

She thought for a moment. "Better."

He smiled.

Once she'd finished eating, Jac took a long hot shower, dressed and then went downstairs to find everyone.

Eva, Minerva, Theo and Robbie were in the great room waiting for her. Eva had made coffee and put out a platter of biscuits. There was a fire in the hearth and the room glowed with the firelight and soft lamplight and smelled of the burning wood.

Minerva looked concerned but glad to see her. Theo seemed very worried and nervous. Jac knew he was blaming himself for what had happened to her. But nothing really had happened to her, had it? She thought she'd remembered most of the experience by now. Were there gaps?

"Where's Ash?" Jac asked as she sat.

521

"In the hospital." Theo said, his voice riddled with disgust. "He broke a few ribs. He's under custody."

"Under custody. Why?" she asked.

"Why? You really don't remember? He attacked you."

"It wasn't his fault."

"Of course it was," Theo said.

More and more of the scene was coming back to her. "No, it wasn't," Jac argued.

"Jac, he could have killed you," Theo insisted.

"He was drugged. The same way I was. He must have been standing there listening to us read the journal for a long time. He was seduced by the Shadow's offer the same way Hugo had been. Ash thought he could bring Naomi back. Or maybe it was Gwenore he thought he could bring back."

"Gwenore?" Eva asked.

Jac nodded. "She was his mother . . . Brice's mother. I'll explain it all when Ash is here." She looked from Theo to Eva and then to Minerva. "When can he come home?"

"They're ready to release him to us," Minerva said. "They just need to be sure you don't want to press charges—"

Jac interrupted. "No, goodness, no. I don't want to press charges. It was the scent. I know it was."

An hour and a half later everyone was together. Robbie sat next to Jac on the couch. Minerva was opposite them, and Ash and Theo had taken chairs on either side of the fireplace.

Ash was paler and more bruised than Theo. He moved stiffly because of his ribs. He couldn't bring himself to look at Jac.

Eva busied herself offering everyone refreshments. "Do you want some coffee, dear?" Eva asked when she got to Jac. "Or wine?"

Jac asked for wine. Eva handed her a long-stemmed crystal glass filled with a fine, dry vintage. Jac inhaled its bouquet and thought about how she was going to start explaining and what she was going to say.

Eva took a seat next to her sister. Everyone was waiting, looking at Jac expectantly. All except Ash. He still couldn't face her.

Jac cleared her throat. Would they believe her story? Would they think she was insane? She'd spent her whole life worrying about that, hadn't she? And where had it gotten her? She cleared her throat once more. The time for caring what people thought was past. She had a chance to heal the rift between these two men and avert further disaster and she was going to take it.

Jac shuddered, then looked at Theo. "I think in a past life you were a Celtic priest named Owain." She turned to Ash. "You were Brice, his son. I think Naomi was Owain's wife, Brice's mother. Her name was Gwenore. If it works the way Malachai says, the way Hindus and Buddhists believe, we all come back in the same soul circles and get a second chance to get it right. Life after life, over and over until we finally manage it. You two are acting out a tragedy that happened thousands of years ago."

Jac stopped. The most difficult part was coming up. How was she going to tell Theo that once he'd been a priest who'd sacrificed his only son? Or suggest to Ash that in this life he was punishing Theo for how Owain's heinous sacrifice had destroyed Brice's mother? How to explain to these men that the soul of the long-dead Gwenore—beloved wife and mother—had lived again in Naomi? And that the brothers, still stuck in their awful destructive pattern, had harmed her again?

They had been burdened with guilt through the millennia, but now, finally, they could learn from their past and make amends. It was their moment, their karma.

But what was hers?

As Jac reached for the glass of wine, the red thread still tied around her arm slid down her wrist. She stared at the insubstantial woven braid that had protected her.

"Eva?"

"Yes, dear."

"It was your bracelet that saved me. I held on to it and it kept me tethered to the present. Thank you."

"You're welcome, dear." Eva's smile was beautiful.

Jac could see in the older woman's eyes that she wasn't haunted by the past anymore. Since telling them all about the part she'd played in her grandfather's death, she'd faced her demons and begun to move on.

That was what they all had to do.

For a moment Jac felt an overwhelming sadness. For all she'd lost, and for knowing she was going to have to finally deal with all that loss if she ever wanted to heal and move on. She touched the scarlet thread. As she fingered the silk and rubbed it against her skin, she realized part of what her karma was. It had been there all along, she just hadn't seen it. Her job was to deliver these messages. Malachai had hinted at it on the phone, but she hadn't understood what he had been saying.

Jac knew *she* was what Malachai had always been searching for. *She* was one of his long-lost memory tools. A *living* memory tool. That was why his instincts were to safeguard her. Why he hadn't wanted her to come here. Jac was the embodiment of the objects he had devoted his life to finding.

Now that she knew, she would have to decide if she wanted to accept what that meant or walk away. But either way, she would confront the opportunity, tackle the challenge and decide. She'd spent too much of her life avoiding things.

Her mother's death. Her disappointment in her lover. Even the pregnancy that she hadn't acknowledged until after she'd miscarried.

She took a breath and began to tell their story.

Forty-five

Jac and Robbie had decided to remain in Jersey for a few days until she had all her strength back. And Eva and Minerva had insisted they stay at the house.

In the morning, after breakfast, Jac made a phone call and then asked Robbie if he'd take a walk with her. She had something she wanted to show him.

As they strolled on the path that led away from the main house into the woods, Jac asked her brother how he thought Theo and Ash were going to fare. The night before, after she'd told everyone the story she'd pieced together from all her different hallucinations, there'd been dead silence in the room.

First Minerva and then Eva asked her some questions. But neither brother said a word. Finally, Theo had left, mumbling good night to no one in particular. Ash, who hadn't made eye contact with Jac since he'd come back from the hospital, had gone a few minutes later, limping as he walked out.

Neither brother had been at breakfast.

"The two of them need time to digest what you told them," Robbie said.

"Do you think they believe it?"

"I think Theo does. At least a little. Ash will, in time. He's too distraught now about how close he came to harming you. But the metal star you found, telling them about Gwenore's birthmark, the same as Naomi's—even a cynic would have a hard time claiming those were all coincidences."

The path twisted through a grove of blue-green pines. Jac took deep breaths of the sharp evergreen scent. "I hope they're going to be all right."

"So do I." Robbie paused. "I know you will be," he said, and put his arm around her shoulder.

They walked on together like that until, a few minutes later, Jac told Robbie they'd arrived.

"Here?" Robbie looked around. He didn't see anything at first and seemed confused. Then he noticed the Victorian building partially hidden by the curtain of ancient ilex, elm and hazel trees. "What is this place?" he asked.

Jac looked at the graceful ivy climbing up the brick walls, covering several windows. She wondered if Fantine had planted the ivy, if she'd planted the wisteria vine too. Had it wound its way around the porch railing during her lifetime, had she seen it begin to reach for the roof?

"Come, I'll show you," she said.

When she'd phoned Ash after breakfast, he'd said he was going to see the doctor at ten, but of course she could bring Robbie by. He'd be sure to leave the door open. Maybe it had been an excuse so Ash wouldn't have to see her too soon. If it was, Jac thought, that was fine. He was going to need time to accept what had happened.

Jac walked up the stone steps to the front door. "Pierre Gaspard built this to be his showroom," she told Robbie. "He was a jeweler who worked in glass too. Then when he married, his wife, Fantine, worked here too." As Jac touched the knob and felt the cool metal under her skin, she had the strange sensation of coming home.

"Fantine, the woman in Hugo's journals?" Robbie asked.

Jac nodded. He'd told her he'd read the journals over the two days while she'd slept.

As she led Robbie into the house, Jac told him the story Ash had told her. How it had been abandoned for decades until he renovated it ten years before and found all the contents intact.

Even though she'd only seen these rooms once before, she knew her way without hesitating. She almost felt as if the house had been waiting for her and now was content. The dining room's Moroccan blue glass fireplace sparkled like the sea. The stained-glass standing lamps in the living room shone in welcome.

At last they reached the hallway illuminated with green glass wall sconces. As she stood outside the dark mahogany door, elaborately carved with garlands of flowers, Jac could smell a hint of what awaited them.

"This was where Fantine worked," she said, and opened the door.

The odor reached out and pulled her in.

Ash had left the light on for her. The hundreds of small bottles glinted in the lamplight. The sun coming through the windows sent shimmering liquid reflections on the ceiling and walls.

"Ash told me Fantine made perfume here for almost seventy years," Jac said, "until she died in 1924 when she was ninety-four."

"It's so similar to our laboratory at home," he said.

"Strange, I thought so too."

Robbie walked over to the perfumer's organ and sat down at the bench. Jac joined him.

"This is fancier than ours at home, though," he said touching the desk's carvings.

"I'd imagine Fantine's husband had a hand in the design. It fits the style of the rest of the house."

Robbie was sniffing the air just as she had the first time she'd come here. Today the scent of faded vanilla and rose, lemon and verbena seemed even more pronounced than it had before.

"It's lovely," he said.

"Yes, a beautiful signature." She nodded. "It's haunting. Like she is. I asked the Gaspards about her. What her maiden name was. Who the family of perfumers were who threw her out. None of them know."

Robbie was inspecting the rows of small brown bottles of oils and absolutes. Each had a rectangular paper label, yellowed and faded, with the name of the essence written on it in once black ink in a feminine hand.

"Amazing so many of the labels are still intact," he said. "After so long."

"She must have sat right here to compose her fragrances." Jac reached out for one of the bottles, twisted off the top and bowed her head to inhale.

"Ash has all Fantine's notebooks." She put down the bottle, opened one of the desk drawers and withdrew a green suede-covered journal with the initials FG stamped in gold on the front. She handed it to Robbie.

"Her formulas are wonderful. I mixed one. It's so rounded and rich. Ash said he would back us if we wanted to work on them."

"Us?"

"I want to go home, to Paris, with you," she said. "I'd like to bring Fantine's strange amber essence with me, the one that causes the hallucinations, and her formulas. The ones for *Morning Pearls Alone* and *Emerald Evening Shivers*. All of them."

Robbie was smiling.

"I want to rebuild these long-forgotten scents, and I want to do it with you."

And maybe, she thought, while she worked on the perfume, she could figure out what it meant that she could enter someone else's past and relive it for them.

Malachai was right when he said coming here might be dangerous. But in that danger she'd also found a gift. Minerva had called it that, hadn't she? And Eva had honored it with her finest silk. Jac knew she was going to need Robbie to help her learn how to use it properly, respect it, and most of all, not fear it.

Absentmindedly she noticed that the bottle she'd picked up to smell didn't have a label. Hadn't there been some blank ones in the drawer where she'd found the ribbons the first time she'd been here? Jac opened it and looked. Yes, there they were along with a pot of glue, a fountain pen and a bottle of ink. Everything she needed.

Robbie was still examining the book of formulas. "You're right, these are fantastic," he said.

Jac dipped the pen in the nib and wrote out the name of the essence she'd been smelling. She unscrewed the glue pot and found it too was fresh enough to use. Was that possible? No. At some point Ash must have replenished these items. Over the years surely he'd reattached some of the labels.

"I love the names she's given her scents," Robbie said.

"I know."

Jac brushed the glue on the back of the parchment and affixed the label to the bottle. She kept her fingertips pressed to its edges to give it a chance to dry.

"Jac, did you see this?" Robbie was holding the notebook open to the back inside cover.

Still holding the label down, Jac looked to where he was pointing.

It was signed and dated in faded black ink.

Fantine Gaspard, May 16, 1886.

And underneath her name was a small drawing. An insignia of an *L* and an *E* inside a crescent moon. It was the family crest of the House of L'Etoile. The same emblem that was on every bottle of perfume that Jac's family had made since before the French Revolution. They both looked at each other with astonishment.

The glue was dry. Jac put the bottle down. Robbie pointed to its label. "Jac, did you just write that?"

She nodded. "Yes, of course. Why?"

"It's amazing."

It was just the one word. *Jacinthe.* The French word for what she'd smelled in the bottle— essence of hyacinth.

"You mean the coincidence that it's my name?"

Jac thought of her wonderful grandfather, who'd

brought his daughter-in-law a bunch of deep-purple *jacinthes* the day his first grandchild was born. And how Audrey had so loved their sent she'd named her daughter after the flowers.

"No, not so much that it's your name. That could be a coincidence. Every perfumer uses flower essences."

"What then?"

He pointed to the label again. "Look at your handwriting."

She did.

"Now look at the handwriting on the other bottles." He pointed to one small brown bottle. And then a second and then a third.

Jac scanned the row of them. There was nothing unusual about them except that they were very old. "What is it?" she asked.

"Your handwriting, Jac. It's the same as hers. Exactly."

And it was.

In the curls of the letters, Jac could finally imagine Fantine. In the ascenders and descenders could suddenly see her. An earlier L'Etoile sitting at this organ mixing perfume.

Making scent was in Jac's blood. More than her heritage, it was her inheritance. What she was meant to do. What Fantine L'Etoile Gaspard had been meant to do.

Feeling she had nothing to live for, Fantine had almost died in the sea. But she'd come back from that precipice to create all these glorious scents.

As Jac traced the L'Etoile insignia in the notebook with her fingertip, she thought of the words of the man who had led her here. Who had, like her, and like Fantine, lost something so precious, he wasn't sure he could survive. But who had, in the end, chosen life.

Every story begins with a tremble of anticipation. At the start we may have an idea of our point of arrival, but what lies before us and makes us shudder is the journey, for that is all discovery.

Acknowledgments

To Sarah Durand: I am so lucky to have you as my editor. You are amazing and smart and know how to push me onward without ever making me feel like I'm being pushed. Thank you for your help and confidence and enthusiasm.

To the wonderful marketing and PR group, especially Hillary Tisman, Lisa Sciambra, Cristina Suarez and Paul Olsewski.

With heartfelt appreciation to Judith Curr for her vision and guidance and Carolyn Reidy for her wisdom and support.

And to everyone else at Atria Books—from the art department (who does such beautiful covers) to the sales folks who get my books in stores— this novel is so much a team effort and I'm so lucky to have you all on my dream team.

To Dan Conaway for being my agent/knight-in-shining-armor. You have never let me down and always know just how to shore me up. To Simon Lipskar, Amy Berkow, Maja Nikolic, Steven Barr, Katie Zanecchia and the rest of Writers House— simply the best agency in the world.

To Douglas Clegg, Lisa Tucker and Steve Berry for always being there when I think I've forgotten everything I ever knew about writing—to remind me that it's always this hard! Randy Susan Meyers, Jenn Risko and Linda Francis Lee—my non-girly girlfriends who are not only fun but wise, wonderful and generous almost to a fault.

To Amy Bruno, Emily Faust, Sunil Kumar and Vicki VanValkenburgh who help so much and so creatively with so many things that go on—some behind the scenes—some in front. To Megan Mitzel and everyone at Blogads who are kind supporters and all the bloggers who help so much. To all the wonderful people on Facebook and Twitter and Goodreads and Pinterest who spread the word—it makes a difference, it matters and it does not go unnoticed.

To my family of course: my father and Ellie (my special cheerleader), the Kulicks, Mara Gleckle (even if there aren't blood ties, you are family) and to Doug Scofield who makes every day worthwhile.

And to every single bookseller and every single librarian and every single reader for stocking, selling and buying my books and making it possible for me to travel the exciting road of being an author.

Author's Note

Pablo Picasso said, "Art is the lie that tells the truth." Whenever possible in this novel, I've told the truth in order to tell my lie.

I am indebted to the truths I learned in Graham Robb's *Victor Hugo: A Biography* as well as *Conversations with Eternity: The Forgotten Masterpiece of Victor Hugo* by Victor Hugo, John Chambers, and Martin Ebon.

So much about Victor Hugo's life is as it appears in this book. His beloved daughter did drown, and he did discover the news of her death as I've described. He belonged to a hashish club with Dumas and Baudelaire. He exiled himself to the Isle of Jersey and lived at Marine Terrace. Descriptions of his daily regimes, his wife, his mistress, how he wrote, his family life, his pets, his beliefs in reincarnation and his engagement in more than one hundred séances are all based on his letters and conversations he himself transcribed. The séances began because he desperately wanted to know his daughter was at peace. They continued because, as he said, he became obsessed with the spirit world.

Victor Hugo claimed to have "spoken" with all the entities I mention in the book—including Jesus,

Napoleon, Dante, Shakespeare and especially the spirit he called the Shadow of the Sepulcher. Hugo maintained that the Shadow asked him to write a poem to restore his reputation as an enlightened creature instead of an evil force, and indeed in 1859, Hugo wrote "La Fin de Satan" (The End of Satan).

And that's where the facts end and my fiction picks up. The particular bargain that my Shadow offered Hugo is not recorded anywhere. Fantine Gaspard is also my invention. Hugo's mistress was indeed installed in a house within walking distance of his family home, and Juliette did have servants, but who they were is unknown.

"The Body Electric" by Anne Downey does appear online, and she and her group were hit by lightning in the manner described.

Jersey itself is rendered as close as possible through the help of my amazing guide and wonderful photographer, Peter Webb. If you find yourself traveling to the Channel Islands, hire him and have him show you the mysterious caves and sights of the lovely and haunting island I've hardly done justice to in this book.

The Celts inhabited Jersey centuries ago; visual proof of it is everywhere you look. The dolmens and menhirs and passage graves I describe are for the most part the ones that actually exist. These Neolithic monuments have been dated as far back as 4800 BCE. Sadly human sacrifice was practiced by these spiritual people in a time very different from ours.

What we discover in Hugo's cave is invented. But the photograph that gives Jac her clue about where that cave might be is real—Hugo's son took that picture of his father, and it remains one of the most evocative portraits of the great writer, poet and statesman. Hugo was a genius—one of the most creative and important writers of his time, perhaps of all time, and he's not only been a very gracious host for the last few years, but a very, very great inspiration.

Afterword

I love challenges, but to tell the story of Victor Hugo's experiments with séances in his own voice? What kind of crazy idea had I come up with? Surely it was lunacy to even attempt it.

I don't have literary illusions. I had just fallen in love with Hugo's story and wanted to tell it. What fascinated me was how much had been written about his life as a statesman, poet and author of *The Hunchback of Notre-Dame* and *Les Misérables*, but how little had been written about a certain part of his personal life: his dabbling with hashish, his preoccupation with reincarnation and the more than one hundred séances he'd conducted during a two-year period while he lived on the Isle of Jersey.

During my research, I hadn't once stopped to think that in order to tell the story of Hugo's seduction by the spirit world, I would have to find his voice.

But there I was. Finally ready to write, sitting at a computer in a very twenty-first-century world trying to conjure a mid-nineteenth-century genius. For weeks I was stumped.

Then I had a revelation. I didn't need to invoke the genius, just the man. I had read Hugo's letters.

I knew that the eloquence and brilliance of his poetry and prose didn't always exhibit itself when he was writing to people close to him. Sometimes he was an extraordinary man saying ordinary things to his family.

That was the Hugo I needed to try to find. The one who was relating a tale to an intimate. Not writing for the ages. Not trying to be brilliant—just attempting to reason out an unreasonable time in his life that had disturbed him.

But I still couldn't do it. The cold keyboard, the sound of the mechanical clicking, the icons at the top of the page, the spell-check. All of it was a gulf between me and the man I needed to channel. I decided it was hubris to even attempt to write this novel. Absurd to try. And yet, I couldn't give up.

Carl Jung said that often coincidences aren't coincidences at all.

One day in a fit of frustration I got up from my desk in a huff and managed to tip over a jar of pens. One was an old fountain pen. It rolled and fell on the computer. I stared at it for a moment. What if. . . .

I found a bottle of ink. Filled the pen. Then pulled out a simple notebook and started to write. Not the way *I* write, on a computer, but the way Victor Hugo would have written more than one hundred and fifty years ago. Pen on paper. I began. And as the ink flowed . . . the words flowed.

I don't remember writing this book. Each day when I sat down and uncapped my pen, I disappeared into the world of the novel. Three notebooks and 122,833 words later, I finished *Seduction*.

Seduction is the first novel I've written by hand. Perhaps the last. Definitely one of the most fascinating journeys I've ever taken.

I do very much hope it proves fascinating for you as well.

Victor Hugo on the Rock of the Exiles, Isle of Jersey, between 1852 and 1855.

Center Point Large Print
600 Brooks Road / PO Box 1
Thorndike ME 04986-0001 USA

(207) 568-3717

US & Canada:
1 800 929-9108
www.centerpointlargeprint.com